Praise for Tina Wainscott

I'll Be Watching You

"A nail-biting roller coaster of lies, betrayals and deadly secrets . . . chilling narrative and intense character interaction add to the dramatic feel of this highly entertaining novel . . . a gripping novel of sheer suspense that will keep the reader turning pages . . . Tina Wainscott is definitely an author to watch; with her unique talent for creating suspense that is as unexpected as it is chilling, she's definitely on my auto-buy list!"

—*Romance Reviews Today*

"Romantic suspense that never slows down until the climax. The story line is action-packed and keeps readers guessing . . . The cast is a delight that brings a small isolated Everglades community to life, alligators and all, so that the audience receives the usual entertaining thriller from one of the best writers today at keeping the tension high."

—*Midwest Book Review*

MORE . . .

Now You See Me

"Incredible! I could not put this book down. It caught me from page one and REFUSED to let me go until the very end. Author Tina Wainscott has the shining talent of being able to combine the genre of 'thriller' with the genre of 'romance' and somehow make it work! Once again Tina Wainscott delivers a heart-stopping story that will make many readers stay awake reading long into the night."

—*Huntress Reviews*

"Ms. Wainscott does a great job. Lots of tension and you're not sure who the killer is."

—*Old Book Barn Gazette*

"WOW! Ms. Wainscott is a suspense reader's dream author. The plot twist that develops halfway through threw me for a loop and I loved every minute of it. More twists and turns kept me turning the pages, cursing myself for not being able to read faster. Not only is the suspense at a fever pitch, but also the chemistry between Max and Olivia. . . . I'm on my way out to get more. I can't think of a higher recommendation than that."

—*Rendezvous*

Unforgivable

"*Unforgivable* is unforgettable, a rich, dark tapestry of good and evil—and the threads that bind them together. Excellent suspense; it literally kept me up all night reading."

—Kay Hooper, author of *Touching Evil*

"*Unforgivable* is a truly great read! Wainscott creates finely honed tension in a first-rate thriller where no one is who they seem and everyone is someone to fear. Don't miss it!"

—Lisa Gardner, *New York Times* bestselling author of *The Third Victim*

"Tina Wainscott kicks off her foray into the suspense genre in a very big way. *Unforgivable* is gripping, gritty, and quite terrifying."

—*Romantic Times* (Top Pick)

"How Mary Higgins Clark used to write . . . I will be keeping a sharp eye on this author!"

—Detra Fitch, *Huntress Reviews*

"Tina Wainscott delivers hard-hitting suspense with a touch of romance. With each turn of the page, the plot moves in surprising directions. The characters are finely crafted and complexly layered—nothing is as it seems. Be warned, this is not a story for the faint of heart; Wainscott's writing is often brutally direct and forthright. *Unforgivable* is unforgettable, romantic suspense of chilling intensity. Readers who appreciate well-written thrillers will enjoy this book."

—Megan Kopp, *Romance Reviews Today*

"Ms. Wainscott shows another side of her true talent as a writer . . . [The] suspense . . . grabs the reader from the very beginning and keeps the reader hooked until the very last page . . . I look forward to Ms. Wainscott's next mystery."

—*Interludes Reviews*

BACK IN BABY'S ARMS

"Ms. Wainscott sure knows how to add depth to her characters . . . The whiff-of-paranormal aspects, the passion, and the assorted conflicts within *Back in Baby's Arms* are what make Ms. Wainscott a favorite with both contemporary and paranormal fans."

—*Rendezvous*

"*Back in Baby's Arms* is a story of rebirth and renewal. . . . It is a tightly woven, very readable story . . . The suspense . . . makes this book a real page-turner."

—*HeartRate*

A TRICK OF THE LIGHT

"Tina Wainscott is back and in a big way. *A Trick of the Light* is suspenseful, poignant, and gripping. A great read."

—*Romantic Times*

"Wainscott delivers an unusual and satisfying romance with a supernatural twist."

—*Publishers Weekly*

"A five-star reading experience to savor . . . unforgettable!"

—*The Belles and Beaux of Romance*

"Ms. Wainscott has done a great job and has written one for your keeper shelf."

—*Old Book Barn Gazette*

"Fans of paranormal romances will feel they are on the way to heaven reading Tina Wainscott's latest winner . . . Wainscott makes the unbelievable feel real and right in such an exciting manner that her audience will want her next novel to be published tomorrow."

—*Affaire de Coeur*

"Quintessential romantic suspense. Wainscott, an award-winning author, knows how to keep her story moving and the sexual tension flowing . . . a book that will speak to both the primary fear of all parents and the hearts of all readers."

—*Once a Warrior Review*

"Remarkable . . . one of the most touching love stories I've read in a while . . . this is truly a 5-star!"

—*ADC's Five Star Reads*

In a Heartbeat

"Contemporary romance with an intriguing twist. A pleasure for fans of romantic suspense."

—Deb Smith, *New York Times* bestselling author

"Wainscott . . . makes the impossible possible."

—Harriet Klausner

"Tina Wainscott has her finger firmly on the pulse of the romance genre, and with *In a Heartbeat* she catapults to the top of her peers . . . run, don't walk, to the nearest bookstore to buy this novel, which could possibly be the best contemporary of the year."

—*Under the Covers*

Second Time Around

"Ms. Wainscott has a talent for making unusual situations believable . . . bravo!"

—*Rendezvous*

"A fabulous romantic suspense drama that melts readers' hearts . . . *Second Time Around* is worth reading the first time around, the second time around, and the nth time around."

—*Affaire de Coeur*

"A must-read . . . a well-written, romantic, feel-good story."

—*Gothic Journal*

ST. MARTIN'S PAPERBACKS TITLES BY TINA WAINSCOTT

I'll Be Watching You

Now You See Me

Unforgivable

Back in Baby's Arms

Trick of the Light

In a Heartbeat

Second Time Around

Dreams of You

Shades of Heaven

On the Way to Heaven

What She Doesn't Know

TINA WAINSCOTT

St. Martin's Paperbacks

WHAT SHE DOESN'T KNOW

ISBN: 0-312-98424-3
EAN: 80312-98424-3

Printed in the United States of America

St. Martin's Paperbacks edition / October 2004

St. Martin's Paperbacks are published by St. Martin's Press, 175 Fifth Avenue, New York, NY 10010.

10 9 8 7 6 5 4 3 2 1

Dedicated to my mom, Christine Ritter; my friend Pam Kraft; and my intrepid critique partner, Marty Ambrose, for never giving up!

My everlasting appreciation goes out to Vicki Hinze for being my literary angel, and to Joan Johnston, Julie Ortolon, Kay Hooper, Lisa Gardner, and Heather Graham for your kindnesses.

And last but not least, this book is dedicated to a writing angel in heaven who fought a valiant battle like a true heroine—Susan MacGillivray.

Acknowledgments

My gratitude goes out to many people who assisted me in the research aspects of this book. Whether it was just a quick call or a lengthy conversation, that they took time out of their busy schedules to help always touches me. Of course, any errors are due to my misinterpretation of the facts.

Michael Geraghty, Ph.D., who graciously spent lunch answering my many questions.

Joe Agresti for assisting on matters of police procedure.

Sherrilyn Kenyon, who helped me sort out the computer end of gaming.

Andy Kraft for computer geek help.

What She Doesn't Know

Prologue

JANUARY 1

Something wasn't right. The moment Brian LaPorte walked inside his home he sensed it, tired as he was from managing a French Quarter hotel full of New Year's guests. He stripped off his tie as he tried to figure out what it was. Dark quiet permeated the house as it always did in the evenings. Shadows clung to the corners and hung in doorways. The scent of pine cleanser hung in the listless air. He looked to the top of the curving staircase to his bedroom. Light crept beneath the door, and he heard a faint tapping sound.

As soon as he opened the door, the person sitting at his computer turned around. The gold- and black-feathered mask startled him as much as the person's presence. The mask ended below the nose and revealed lips painted dark burgundy. Emerald-green eyes blinked in surprise through the eye slots, but surprise morphed to a mixture of hurt and determination.

"Who the hell are you?" he asked, taking in the black bodysuit and long, black hair as she stood. Purple shoes with spike heels made her look taller than she was.

"Don't you recognize me, baby?" Her body was thin, muscular, but the suit sculpted small, firm breasts. There was something familiar about her, but before he could pinpoint it, she said, "It's Sira."

A cold chill washed over him. Sira, here. No, that wasn't right. How had she found him? It was a violation of the rules, a breach of trust. "What are you doing in my house? On my computer?"

"You used me, and now you want to replace me."

His anger turned to apprehension. She'd gone so far as to track him down and then hack into his computer. "You're not supposed to know who the players are. That's one of the rules."

Her smile looked eerie beneath the mask. "I'm playing by half the rules. You still don't know who I am."

The teasing words prickled at the edge of his senses. "You have to leave. Now."

She did leave. Only she went out the French doors leading to the gallery. There was no exit from there.

He followed her out into the crisp, late December air and grabbed her arm. "If you don't leave, I'll call the police."

She pulled free and walked to the end of the gallery where the staircase spiraled up to the rooftop deck. Seductively, she slid her fingers along the curving banister. "You'd be violating your own rules. You'd have to tell them where we met . . . and how you betrayed me."

Dammit, she was right. No, he couldn't tell them the truth. They'd think he was a freak who deserved a drop-in by another freak. But he had to get rid of her. She climbed the steps to the deck. His fingers gripped the cold metal railing as he followed her. She stood with her arms crossed in front of her, looking as though she wouldn't leave until she got what she wanted. He'd better find out what that was.

"I've watched you up here," she said, "leaning against this railing. I hoped you were thinking of me."

She'd been watching him? The thought chilled him even more. "What do you want?" he asked through gritted teeth.

She trailed a finger down his chest. "I want you. I want to be your queen. I deserve that after all I've done for Xanadu."

Foreboding pressed against his chest. "What have you done?"

"Protected it. Cherished it. Loved it. That's all I want for myself, to be protected . . . cherished . . . loved. I've been a part of Xanadu from the beginning. I helped build it. And I am your perfect other half. That woman won't be a player. She'd never have the guts to do what needs to be done."

He didn't like that last phrase. "What needs to be done?"

"Rita Brooks is a shrink! She might tell you we're all crazy. She might convince you to close us down. She needs to be banished."

Anger and fear churned inside him. He especially didn't like that she knew who Rita was. "She's not playing yet. She doesn't even know about Xanadu."

"Banished, before it's too late," Sira said, ignoring him again. "You need a powerful queen. You need me."

She started to move toward him, but he pushed her back. His anger overrode his fear. "I don't need you. I don't want you. You broke the rules."

"No, I—"

"I'm going to banish you."

"No!" Fear gripped her features, and she lunged forward and grabbed his sleeve. One of his cufflinks skittered across the deck.

The threat backfired. Her reaction was pure panic, her movements frenzied as they struggled.

"You will never banish me. Never!" she said in jerky breaths.

He needed to overpower her and try to talk sense into her. She was smaller than he was, and he tried not to fight too hard. He didn't want to hurt her, only to get rid of her.

That turned out to be another mistake. Her strength surprised him as she hit him on the side of his head. He punched her in the face, but he'd still been holding back. She shoved him so hard he was thrown against the short railing. His head spun from the blow, but even through the floating spots in his vision he could clearly see the look of pure madness in her eyes. He held out his hand as he tried to gain his breath. "Sira. . . ."

She rushed forward and pushed him. His stomach took the brunt of the force. He lost his footing—and went over the railing. As his arms and legs flailed, images from his life flashed before him: the swordfight with his brother, his father's funeral where he'd said hurtful things he couldn't take back. But his final thought was of Rita. He had to warn her. . . .

1

JANUARY 2

Dr. Rita Brooks was thinking about falling in love. Considering it, the way one would consider buying a car or a house: the pros and cons, risks, comfort levels. It had been a long time since she'd let herself entertain such a thought. That the man in question lived fifteen hundred miles away in New Orleans actually made things easier. That they'd never met wasn't important.

As a hobby, she scrounged through flea markets and resale shops for things she could sell at online auctions. Brian LaPorte had e-mailed her about a dagger, and soon they were writing back and forth. They had proceeded right past easy camaraderie and flirting and moved to a deeper relationship.

She ran through the cold rain to her car, her Chinese takeout in a brown paper bag. For a second, the air froze in her throat. A shadow shifted behind her car. She blinked, and it was gone. She glanced in the back seat, just to make sure, before sliding into her Volvo S40. She locked the doors, turned the engine, and pulled out of the parking lot. A car two spots away did the same and fell into place behind her. That was probably the shadow she'd seen: someone else getting into their car.

Heat slowly emerged from the vents. Her cheeks

stung from the cold, and she aimed one of the vents at her face. The dark, blotchy sky dumped down slushy rain that glowed in the streetlights. The Montreal Express was in full tilt, the northern wind crushing Boston in its winter grip.

She'd been putting off Brian's request for a photo exchange with excuses about finding the right picture. Truthfully, she had this fantasy of him based on the poetic way he spoke and didn't want to spoil it. It was time, though. She'd gone through boxes of photos last night and found a decent shot where her light blue eyes weren't washed out and her wavy hair wasn't a brown cloud. Tonight she'd scan it and surprise him.

The next step would be a face-to-face encounter. What harm could come from that? A safe, public meeting of course, in case she'd misjudged him. But she doubted it. She was trained in judging people, after all. They'd take it slow. And maybe, just maybe, this would go somewhere. Her heart spun with possibilities.

She couldn't help but remember how her last burgeoning relationship had ended a year ago, with her running out of his apartment and Bill calling after her. *Rita, what's wrong with you?*

The car that had followed her out of the parking lot was still behind her as she navigated the icy highway. *Right* behind her. Its headlights blinded her in the rearview mirror. She pushed down on the gas but lifted her foot again. "I'm not going any faster, jerk. You want to kill yourself on these roads, go around me. Just don't take anyone else with you."

The car did start to pass her. She glanced over, expecting to see it full of teenagers who considered themselves immortal. Her heart jumped at the sight of an inhuman face. Before she could make any sense of it, the car slammed into her.

The wheel pulled out of her hands. She grabbed it as her car swerved toward a concrete barrier. She had no time to scream or pray. Only to realize that in her haste, she hadn't put on her seat belt.

JANUARY 6

Rita, what's wrong with you?

First the words resounded through her mind in her mother's voice, a rail-thin woman glaring at the sloppy job a nine-year-old Rita had done making macaroni and cheese.

Rita, what's wrong with you?

Then it was her father Charlie's voice chastising her for daring to intrude into his sacred office to bother him over a broken pinky finger.

Rita, what's wrong with you?

Bill's voice now, as she made the passage from one place to another, all in the dark recesses of her mind. When the voices and sounds from the outside world faded, when her friend Marty's voice wasn't commanding her to "Wake up from that damned coma! You know how I hate hospitals!", when Rita didn't feel the prick of a needle or anything else to remind her she was still alive, that's when she made the journey.

At first she felt herself swimming beneath the sea, the surface becoming a muted reflection of the life that went on around her. Everything was dark and liquid, and she became liquid with it as she tried to swim free. The thickening liquid held her arms and legs immobile. She imagined herself a piece of fruit suspended in a dark blue ring of Jell-O.

That's when the voices would come, snatches of words and memories. She didn't know what was real anymore. Was she a little girl again, wishing her mother would come home from the bar she tended . . . dreading it at the same time? Was she a teenager, wearing an outlandish outfit in hopes that her father might notice her? It seemed odd that she should see the scenes, hear the words, and not feel the pain. Maybe this was the place between life and the hereafter, where one came to terms with one's grief, shortcomings, and fears.

She never had enough time to contemplate it thoroughly, for soon she would pass into the gray place. It seemed to go on forever, shimmering waves of gray. When she'd first come, she thought it must be where your sins were called up, where you watched every mean, selfish thing you ever did and begged for forgiveness.

There were others in this place. No one spoke or smiled or even looked at her. The gauzy texture of the air made it hard to make eye contact. This was where she went when no one pulled her back to reality. The strangest part, she thought, was that it didn't seem strange at all. She and everyone else were supposed to be there, together, yet locked in their own worlds. A sense of waiting permeated her whenever she came here. Waiting to go back; waiting to go on.

On this journey into the gray, she felt a throbbing pain in her head, an overwhelming fatigue in a body she had not felt at all for so long. She wasn't supposed to feel pain here in the gray place. It had followed her, as did some of the other sounds from the world: blips and humming noises, voices. The others were there, as always, though they seemed gauzier than usual.

Except for the man. He moved through the people, his journey purposeful somehow when everyone else moved lethargically. He came to a stop in front of her. He was handsome, with blond hair and blue eyes filled with urgency and clarity. His presence infused her with warmth. Had he come to lead her onward?

She wasn't afraid. But when he set his hands on her shoulders, violence shattered the peace. A barrage of images flashed through her mind, so fast she couldn't hold on to any of them. She could feel them, though, shock and pain and fear, especially fear at the end. Then she was falling, her arms flailing, a scream caught in her throat. A scream that was her name. Before she hit the ground, she felt a gust of air rush through her body.

After she came to, she hardly had a chance to register shock that she'd been in a coma for four days. And that her mother, whom she hadn't seen in three years, had played doting mom for the first time in Rita's life. She could hardly register the humiliation of being an inconvenience to everyone. She could vaguely remember the place of bad memories. There was something else, too. Something important. But she couldn't quite remember.

"How are you doin', honey?"

Angela Brooks stood beside Rita's bed two days later, wringing the black knit hat with the Jersey Devils emblem on it like a washcloth. None of the hospital staff saw Rita's mother sitting vigil as the anomaly it was. Angela had only been a mother for Rita's first ten years of life, and barely that.

"I'm okay, Angela. Tired, achy. But okay." Rita's attention kept drawing back to the green Jell-O on the plate in front of her.

Angela's face pinched, deepening her wrinkles. "You don't have to call me by my name. I know your dad made you call him Charlie, the bonehead, but I'm your mama."

Mama. The word wanted to roll out, but Rita held it in. It burned like one of those cinnamon jawbreakers.

Angela awkwardly took Rita's hand, overly cautious of the IV still imbedded in her wrist. That motion seemed as odd as the woman's presence, but Rita didn't pull away. Instead, she studied the wiry woman who looked so much older than her fifty years.

"You know what they call this place?" Angela asked conspiratorially. "Massive Genital. That's what they told me down at the diner by my motel. That doesn't sound too reassuring, a big private part. Maybe we should move you somewhere else."

"It's just a joke. Mass General is a good hospital."

"If you're sure. How's your doctor? He okay? I can get you another one."

"I'm fine, really."

Angela looked around, as though searching for something else she could find at fault and fix to prove her good intentions. When she could find nothing, she went back to mangling her hat. "Honey, I know I wasn't the best mother." She laughed harshly. "Or even a good mother. Lord knows I made mistakes. Let me be your mama now. Let me take care of you, cook for you, make sure you're okay. They said you have to take it real easy after you're released."

Rita ignored the way something inside her ached. "No." As Angela's hopeful—desperately hopeful—face crumpled, Rita felt obliged to add, "I don't need help. I couldn't. . . ." Her words drifted off, because she couldn't say them. The truth was, she thought she'd worked through her mother issues during her psychology training in college. That's why she'd found Angela five years ago. But she was having trouble connecting to her and a part of Rita couldn't bear getting used to having her around before she left again. She'd lost her mother once, when the social worker had taken Rita away to live with her father. And again when she realized Angela wasn't even trying to get her back. "I don't want to inconvenience you." She'd once believed that if she didn't bother her mother, or Charlie, or his mother, Maura, that maybe they'd love her. Needs, wants, boo-boos, and colds all fell under that category, so she'd learned to handle them herself. "I've been on my own for a long time now. I've taken care of myself—"

"I know, since you was a little girl. I dumped a lot on you." Angela looked away in shame. "At least Charlie gave you food, clothes, a home."

Rita swallowed the truth. "I had what I needed." The essentials, but never a home.

"You had to know I was only thinking of your welfare when I let them take you. Even with child support, I just couldn't make it. I was stressing myself out trying. I'd become an awful person."

Rita swallowed back more words, wondering how long she could do that before they all exploded out of her. She and Angela had been here before, when Angela had apologized a thousand times for the neglect and bouts of rage that consumed her when the burden of merely surviving became too much to bear.

Rita looked up to see Marty in the doorway about to turn away at the sight of mother–daughter conversation. "Come in!"

Angela moved out of the way and watched the two women hug. Rita wished she could include her, but she didn't know how. Wasn't sure she wanted to start something. Allowed her to back away with the excuse of needing a smoke.

"I wasn't interrupting, was I?" Marty asked, perching on the side of the bed, more comfortable with Rita than her own mother had been.

"No, not at all."

Rita and Marty had met in college during graduate school. They had both done internships at the Warner Center for Mental Health and had stayed on where their friendship had deepened. Rita tried to ignore the fact that

Marty was a tall, blond beauty. They were opposite in both looks and personalities—Marty's effervescence to Rita's no-nonsense. It was Marty's phobias that fueled Rita's interest in phobic patients. Marty had shared the aspects of her childhood that led her to phobias, like being locked in the bathroom for punishment and having to use the same towel all month. Only she hadn't told Marty the truth about a lot of her life.

"She was here every day," Marty said.

"How did she even know?"

"I called her. I thought she should know, in case. . . ."

"I died." Rita had been knocked around the car hard enough to put her in a coma, but aside from a mild head injury and massive bruising, she'd had no other serious injuries. *Thank you, God,* she mentally added. "I could hear you talking to me."

"Could you? The doctor said you might, but I wasn't sure. You looked like you were far away. It was scary."

"Thanks. For talking to me and for being here."

"You couldn't keep me away." Marty returned the squeeze of her hand.

"Have you gotten over your hospital phobia, then?"

"Yes, you cured me by extreme-exposure therapy. It wasn't easy. I'd close my eyes in the elevator and then race out as soon as the door opened. I couldn't just keep sitting outside in my car thinking that was enough, you know."

They shared a smile. It felt good to latch on to something familiar.

Marty's expression grew more solemn. "The officer who investigated your accident is down the hall. He was talking to your doctor about asking you some questions."

"I don't remember much." The doctor had told her it was normal not to remember a lot about the accident.

A handsome man with silver hair and blue eyes

knocked at her open door. "Rita Brooks?" he asked, walking in. "I'm Officer Michael Potter. I was on the scene of your accident. You up for some questions?"

Rita shifted in bed, sitting up straighter. "I have some of my own, actually. I'm afraid I don't remember much about that night." She introduced Marty and invited the officer to sit in the vacant chair while Marty settled on the bed.

"Your doctor said that might be the case. I was hoping you'd remember something, anything, about the driver. The car that hit you was stolen. We've had a rash of teens taking cars for joyrides, though this is the first time there has been injury to others. We caught three kids pulling off a theft a week ago and we're trying to tie them to some of the other thefts. Particularly yours. The car that hit yours was wiped clean of prints." He handed her three arrest photos. "Do you recognize any of these kids from that night?"

Rita tried hard to pull up something. Sometimes she'd get a flash, a sliver of memory. After a minute, she shook her head and handed the pictures back. "Sorry, I wish I could help. These kids . . . how old are they?"

"Two are fifteen; one's seventeen."

Rita grimaced. They *were* kids.

"A witness saw the accident from a distance, but unfortunately he can't ID the occupants. He wasn't even sure there was anyone but the driver. The other vehicle came up beside you as though he were going to pass but then slammed into the side of your car."

"You don't think they intentionally ran me off the road, do you?"

"Hard to determine. Drugs or alcohol or plain inexperience could be factors." He put the pictures away. "How are you feeling?"

The car came up beside her . . . something niggled at

that, but she couldn't draw it close enough. "Good, thanks. It looks like I'll survive."

He nodded at both her and Marty. "If you remember anything, please call me." He handed her a card and left.

"They . . . ran their car into me. Why?" Rita asked Marty.

"You can't look at it as something personal. When you're feeling better, we'll discuss rage, helplessness, and the whims of fate."

Rita nodded. But why did she feel this was no whim of fate?

2

FEBRUARY 10

Rita's mind drifted through foggy images.

The man coming toward her. His hands on her shoulders, his blue eyes urgently staring into hers. Frames of a life flashing through her mind.

A dark-haired boy wielding a sword. A long, silver blade flashing in the light. Blood. Rage.

A funeral on a bleak day. Sadness. Harsh words, "The prodigal son returns. Too bad no one wants you here." Regret.

A black-clad figure rushing forward, green eyes glittering with anger. A gold mask concealing identity, a spray of black feathers. A falling sensation. Fear. Rita!

"Brian!"

"Rita?"

The nudge of her arm was definitely not in the dream, and her mind picked through the swampy darkness of half-sleep. Since her coma, waking was harder than she would admit to anyone. It was a slow process, dragging herself through the layers until she could put her surroundings together.

Marty smiled as Rita's mind and vision came into full focus. "Oh, my gosh, I fell asleep at work," she muttered, glancing at the clock. An hour had passed since she'd closed her eyes and pondered Anna's persistent obsessive-compulsive disorder. They'd been able to vanquish her germ phobia that had her washing her hands more than eighty times a day. Her other compulsion was proving much harder to control. Rita glanced at her clock. It was after five.

"I told you it was too soon to go back to work," Marty said in a mother-knows-best tone.

"I would have gone crazy if I'd stayed home another week. Besides, I have a light load. I've only taken back three of my clients."

Or was she already crazy? That slideshow of images had plagued her sleep for the five weeks since she awoke from her coma. The mystery of it had been a distraction from the aches and the sight of her battered body at least. But now her body had healed, and the images were becoming more persistent.

"It's this weather," Rita said, gesturing to the window. Bleak skies expelled wet snow that made everything glisten under a coating of deadly ice. "It makes me sleepy."

"Who's Brian?" Marty asked, stretching out on the leather chaise longue.

"Brian? I, uh . . . Why do you ask?"

"You said his name in your sleep."

Rita had said his name. She just hadn't realized she'd said it aloud. Why had she said *his* name? Probably because she hovered between worrying and being mad at him. She hadn't heard from him since her accident. She had e-mailed him twice from the Internet café at the hospital, unable to remember his phone number. He'd never called. By the time she'd gone home, she'd been too put off to call him. Then she discovered that her PC had crashed and swallowed everything. Giving him the benefit of the doubt, she'd sent another e-mail last week. Still no answer. She'd told herself to forget about him, but she couldn't. Maybe she'd gather her courage and call him tonight. She wasn't ready to give up on him—or on herself.

She reached for the file on her desk. "I'm not sure why I said that name." She hadn't told anyone, not even Marty, about her relationship with Brian. "Let's talk about phobias. No repercussions on the exposure therapy of the hospital phobia?"

"I've had a few of my hospital dreams where I go in for an appendectomy and come out an old, Oriental man. What I don't have a problem with is avoiding answering questions."

"How are you coming along in your napkin therapy?"

Marty's father had made each member of the family use one napkin per week. Now Marty couldn't bear to even look at a used napkin.

She rolled her eyes at Rita's stubbornness, no doubt. "Last Friday I tried really hard not to get freaked when someone at lunch put her napkin on the table next to me. It was wrinkled, with a smudge of ketchup, and I started getting queasy just looking at it." She shuddered. "I lasted two minutes, fifteen seconds; twenty seconds longer than last week. Then I had to ask her to put it on her lap. Okay, enough about me. You do look a little like hell, Rita."

She rested her chin on her hand. "I'm just not sleeping well, that's all." The problem wasn't lack of sleep; it was too much dreaming.

"You know how I know you're not ready to be back at work yet?"

Rita gave her a patronizing smile. "How is that?"

"Because your pencils and pens are all mixed together. And your stack of folders isn't precisely lined up. See, there's an edge sticking out."

Rita eyed the stack. "Are you trying to tell me I'm obsessively neat?"

"Of course not. You're neurotically neat. I've been in

your closet, remember? You are the only person I know who color-codes her clothes and shoes. My diagnosis is you need to get a life. But I've been saying that for years and you haven't listened. You're a therapist's nightmare."

Rita wrinkled her nose. She'd been close to getting a life. "I really do appreciate your taking care of things for me while I was in the hospital." She subtly straightened her folders.

"And I know an evasive tactic when I see one."

"Coffee? I could use a cup."

"Textbook!"

The two women walked down to the break room.

Marty asked, "Heard from your mother?"

Rita poured her fourth cup of coffee, ignoring her jittery hands. "Once. We've left things on neutral ground for now." She took a doughnut from the box on the counter, trying to forget that she'd already had one. "I don't know who keeps bringing in these doughnuts, but they've got to stop." She sighed as a billion grams of sugar dissolved in her mouth on the first bite. "I think there's a fat person inside me screaming to get out."

"Bill called while you were in the hospital. He'd heard about your accident. He told me he's tried to get back with you over the last year, but you keep putting him off."

"He's not my type."

"He's exactly your type, that sweet Bill Pullman kind of guy who calls to check on a woman who ditched him a year ago. Is he the reason you're eating these sugar-coated deep-fried rings of dough with absolutely no nutritional value whatsoever?"

"Not hardly."

Marty lowered her voice. "He told me about your nosebleed when he tried to kiss you."

Rita took in the break room, noting that no one had walked in. "So I got a nosebleed. Big deal."

"If it's no big deal, why are you pulverizing that doughnut?"

"Shh!" Rita tossed the mashed doughnut in the garbage.

Marty followed Rita back to her office, whispering, "It's all right for those schooled in the mind to ask for help. Heck, I think most therapists need counseling even after their early training. This has something to do with the fact that you haven't had a real boyfriend since I've known you, doesn't it?"

Rita closed her office door behind them. "Let's just talk about you, okay?"

"That's the problem; I can't focus on my problems because I'm too worried about you."

Rita walked to her desk, wanting to feel in control again. "It's just a little problem relating to men. Nothing for you to worry about." Marty wanted to understand . . . to know her deepest, darkest place where she hid the girl whose father had only one lesson to teach her: men were removed and aloof, mysterious and alien.

"I think you have a phobia about people worrying about you," Marty said, crossing her arms. "Why is that?"

"Because—"

Barbara, the receptionist, tapped on the door and poked her head in. "Oh, excuse me, I didn't know you were busy."

"We're done," Rita said with a big smile.

"Done!" Marty said, throwing her hands up. "She's hardly opened up at all."

Rita kept smiling at Barbara, wishing she could kick Marty under the desk.

"There's a gentleman here to see you, Rita. Christopher LaPorte." She raised her eyebrows and waited for a reaction.

"I don't have anyone else scheduled for today."

"Oh, I thought you knew him." Barb's brown eyes twinkled. "Thought maybe he was your new guy. I was going to applaud your outstanding taste. He said he didn't have an appointment, but he acted like it was pretty important that he speak with you."

"Barb, can you tell him that I only counsel female patients?" How could Rita help men figure out their problems when she had problems figuring out men?

A few minutes later, Barb was back. "He's not leaving until he speaks with you. He says it's personal."

"Personal," Rita repeated, pulling herself to her feet. How could she have personal business with someone she'd never heard of?

"Wish he had personal business with me," Barb muttered, backing out of the door and heading to the ladies' room.

Rita's heartbeat jumped. *Wait a minute. LaPorte? Is that what Barb had said his last name was? Brian's last name. But not Brian. A mispronunciation, then? Coincidence?*

He was standing with his back to the hallway, reading the positive messages hanging on the walls about self-esteem, love, and friendship. His dark, short hair looked wet from the snow. He had a backside that belonged in one of those Chippendales calendars and a well-built chest encased in a black sweater. A wrinkled winter coat was slung over his shoulder. Not Brian, who said he had blond hair and was only five ten.

"Can I help you?"

As he turned around, he may as well have punched her in the stomach.

It was *him*, the man she'd seen in the gray place. The intense dark blue eyes and that mouth with the built-in pout. She felt her knees go soft.

"You're Rita Brooks?" he asked in a voice flavored with a hint of Southern Comfort, like Brian's voice.

Her mouth opened, but she couldn't utter a sound. She just kept staring at his eyes.

"Yes, she is." Marty stepped in at last to save her. "What can we do for you?"

He acknowledged Marty's protective stance but trained his eyes on Rita as he took a step closer. With him came the aroma of grapes mixed with the subtle spice of deodorant. His face was dry and red, as though he'd hastily shaved in a gas station restroom on his way here. He had the handsome, angular kind of face she'd seen in advertisements for shaving cream.

"Do you know my brother, Brian? Brian LaPorte?"

Brian, he was Brian's brother, and he was here, which meant something was wrong with Brian, and that's why she hadn't heard from him. As her mind clamped around those facts, Christopher's similarity to the man she'd seen during her coma still confused her. "Excuse us for a moment," she mouthed to Marty as she led Christopher to the front corner of the lobby. "What's wrong with Brian?"

"You do know him."

"Yes, we're . . . friends. We met online about two months ago. Please tell me what's going on. Is he all right?"

He seemed to gauge her, though she wasn't sure what he was looking for. Maybe he saw the tension on her face, because he finally answered. "Brian had an accident. Well, not really an accident. He jumped off the rooftop deck of his house. He's in a coma."

Her mind spun. Jumped? Coma? "Oh, my God. Since when?"

"January first. I'm trying to. . . ."

His words faded beneath the buzz in her head. January first. She'd gone into a coma January second. That meant they were in a coma at the same time, for four overlapping days. Christopher looked like the man she'd seen, the man who had urgently sought her out. He probably looked like his brother, though Brian had blond hair. So did the man. *It was Brian.* Her analytical side wanted to deny it, but she knew it in the deepest recess of her soul. Brian had come to her.

Christopher was still talking, and finally his words penetrated the buzz. "If you broke his heart, and he tried to take his life . . . Well, I just need to know."

"Wait a minute. You're saying he tried to kill himself."

"Yes, he did."

She blinked, realizing that he was trying to find out if she had anything to do with Brian's fall. By the hard look in his eyes, he had already made that assumption. That and the fact that he'd tracked her down . . .

"How did you find me?" she asked, trying to ground herself in concrete facts.

"From your e-mail to him."

"I didn't put my full name and address in that e-mail. I didn't put my work address in it." She was starting to feel suspicious, too. She slid a glance to Marty, who was surreptitiously hanging around Barb's desk.

"That's not important. What's important is finding out what drove a man who had everything to live for to try to kill himself. I think you know why."

Important. There was something important. Brian found you. Why? He tried to kill himself? No, it couldn't be. She put her hand over her mouth, sorting through the improbability of it all, and yet she could see the man clearly, holding on to her shoulders, staring into her eyes as though willing her to do something—

Christopher's hand on her shoulder jarred her out of

those thoughts. "Tell me what was going on between you two."

Conflicting emotions bombarded her, and to her horror, she felt the tingling that preceded her nosebleeds. *This cannot be happening.*

He moved closer. He knew he was intimidating her, and the jerk was using it against her. "What is it that you're hiding?"

She felt the first trickle of blood and pressed her finger against the side of her nose. Something was very wrong. "I can't believe he tried to take his own life. Are you sure it wasn't an accident?" Her voice hardly sounded convincing, all nasally like Fran Drescher in *The Nanny.*

Christopher looked at her like a tiger moving in on something that's caught its eye—with interest and suspicion. "I'm sure." Besides, he'd probably read their e-mails. The anger at that thought evened out the strange sense of panic for a moment.

Rita inched toward the receptionist's desk just as Barb returned. He watched her, the muscles in his jaw working as he chewed what must be grape gum. Rita found the Kleenex and covered her nose with a wad of it. "I'm fine," she assured Marty, who clearly didn't believe her. Before she could ask any questions, Rita walked back to Christopher. *Control, control.* "Do the doctors think he'll come out of the coma?"

"I'll answer your questions when you answer mine."

"I did answer yours."

"Look, Rita Brooks, I know you're hiding something. I can see it in your eyes, in your body language. Spill it."

She *was* hiding something, but she couldn't tell him that she believed Brian had come to her during her coma. She needed time to sort it out. The revelation had totally knocked her off balance, and Christopher's presence wasn't helping. "I can't help you. If I knew something,

I'd tell you. I can tell you I had nothing to do with any suicide attempt. I can't even believe it."

"What's wrong with your nose?"

"I have a cold," she said, pitifully aware of how it sounded.

Marty, however, had to be more helpful. "Rita, you're bleeding!" She stalked over and turned an outraged glare to Christopher. "Did you *hit* her? Barb, call security."

He looked calm, despite his obvious impatience. "I didn't hit her. I only—"

"He didn't hit me. I can handle this," Rita interjected, wanting no more to be said.

"Well, you're not handling it." Marty turned to Christopher. "Look, you're upsetting her. Why don't you leave?"

Yes, he should leave, Rita thought. She pulled the Kleenex away from her nose and saw the spot of bright red blood. Why was this happening? Her nose only bled in one situation. "I really don't know anything, and if you won't answer my questions about Brian's condition, you should leave." Dammit, she wouldn't be able to find out on her own, though.

He stood there chewing his gum as though contemplating throwing her over his shoulder and hauling her off for further interrogation. Despite her nosebleed, that thought sparked something primal inside her. She squelched it and turned away.

"Rita."

The way his voice wrapped around her name made her shiver. She didn't want to turn and face him again, but she did anyway. He handed her a business card.

"I'll be at the address and phone number on the back. In New Orleans." He paused, his narrowed eyes telling her he knew she was holding something back. "If you decide you want to talk, call me." His voice softened, thick as honey. "You're the key to this mystery, Rita Brooks. I feel it in my gut. And I will find out the truth."

He seemed to weigh whether to say more, but her friends must have swayed him. He left, without a scuffle, without Barb having to call security as she was poised to do. But his words, soft though they were, pounded through Rita's system louder than her heartbeat.

"What was that all about?" Barb asked.

"Just a misunderstanding," Rita said, waving it off as she walked to her office on wobbly legs.

Marty wouldn't be so easy to deal with. "Disclosure," she said as soon as Rita closed the door to her office. "And don't tell me it's just a coincidence that the name of his brother is the same as the one you called out in your sleep. I saw the look on your face when you saw Christopher LaPorte. You were spooked—enough to get a nosebleed."

Rita slumped in her chair, still trying to get a handle on it all. Marty was waiting, and by the way she tapped her fingers against her crossed arms, she wasn't going to wait patiently.

So she disclosed. She told Marty about meeting Brian through her eBay auction and their developing relationship. "It was nothing kinky. In fact, it was rather romantic. He talks like a hero from a historical romance novel. He lives in New Orleans and manages a hotel. Marty, he made me feel so good. About myself, life, my future. I told him things I haven't told anyone else. The fact that we were talking on the phone helped a lot. It was part of the appeal, I'm sure. But it was him, too. We were friends with a touch of something else. I was so sure he was going to change my life. I could feel it." She could see Marty's expression fall with each word. "I didn't tell you because I knew you'd either warn me about all the crazies out there or think I was desperate. For the first time I was being adventurous, and I liked it. I didn't want you to talk sense into me."

"You *were* desperate. And I would have warned you. There are a lot of crazies out there. Why would you have a relationship with someone on the Internet?"

"It was Brian. And it was the Internet itself. The physical distance made it easier somehow." Easier to get past her fear of intimacy barriers. "For the first time in my twenty-eight years, I felt ready to embark on an actual romantic relationship. Brian was the only man who has ever given me a sensual charge and made me feel safe at the same time. He bolstered my confidence and made me wonder if I could get over my little problem." She dabbed at her nose and was relieved to see no blood on the tissue this time. "I was totally ready to fall in love with him before my accident. A little scared, but ready."

"And you never told me, you little bugger. I share all my idiosyncrasies with you, and you hold back something like this. We're supposed to be best friends, equally sharing our dreams, pain, and secrets."

"I know." It wasn't fair, she knew that.

"Did you ever meet him?"

Rita felt that ache she'd been feeling whenever she thought of Brian lately, only now it was twofold. "He wanted to meet. Even invited me to New Orleans or offered to come here. I kept putting him off, but I was about to invite him here. When I didn't hear from him, I thought maybe he'd changed his mind or found someone else. Then Christopher LaPorte shows up. Yeah, I was spooked. He looks so much like Brian. It was just a shock, that and the news about Brian's suicide attempt. It was too much to handle at once." *That must be why I had the nosebleed.* "I can't believe he tried to kill himself. I mean, I really can't believe it. It doesn't feel right. We'd spoken on the phone on New Year's Eve. He called me from the hotel. He sounded great."

Marty seemed to accept everything. That was only because Rita had left out the important parts: the man she'd seen in the gray place . . . and the fact that she'd never seen Brian LaPorte.

3

Plain out, the woman was holding something back. Christopher slid into his winter coat as he walked to his car. Her reaction to Brian's name screamed guilt, and when he dropped the news about the coma, her concern went deeper than a casual, perfunctory interest.

She hardly looked like a heartbreaker, though. A professional woman with initials after her name. Soft and flighty as a hummingbird. Not Brian's type, at least the type he used to go after. Brian only went for the prettiest, best-connected girls, the kind Daddy would approve of. This Rita would not send a man into the abyss of despair. It had nothing to do with her plain-pretty looks, or the soft curves he detected beneath her business attire. In those light blue eyes of hers, he saw vulnerability. The way her face paled when she saw him, the way her body stiffened. He'd been sure she knew something, but he didn't like the way he'd used her trepidation against her.

You are used to intimidating people, after all. And you're good at it, a voice reminded him. Normally, it didn't bother him.

He thought about trying to talk to Rita again, maybe wait at her apartment until she got home. He knew the information highway better than any virtual road. More to the point, he knew the illegal byways that allowed him access to the private life of Rita Brooks. He glanced at the address he'd scrawled on a piece of paper. She'd likely call the police, and they would likely frown on the way he'd obtained her home and work addresses.

Her e-mail had come into Brian's in-box last week. Just a few words: *"Brian, haven't heard from you in a while. I was in the hospital but am home now. If you want to break things off, please at least let me know so I won't worry."* And simply signed, *"Rita."* The weird thing was, there were no other e-mails from her in his in-box. Old phone bills were gone, too. Christopher had tried to obtain copies, but he wasn't authorized.

He'd let her go for now. He'd been away from Brian for too long. It was time to go the airport, back home to New Orleans.

No, not home. Not in thirteen years. Just a place now, a city torn between old-line social traditions and political correctness; between crime and past glory.

Maybe this whole Rita thing had been a waste of time. When that e-mail had come in, he had wanted it to mean something, wanted this Rita person to give him the reason Brian had tried to throw his life away. Maybe Christopher had just wanted a reason to get away from that hospital and the lifeless form of his brother. Away from the realization that the man he'd hated his whole life might die . . . and that he was the wrong person to be standing vigil by his bedside.

By the time he landed in New Orleans it was late Wednesday night. The City that Care Forgot was gearing up for Mardi Gras. Natives had mixed feelings about the festivities that held New Orleans in its grip for the weeks between the Twelfth Night of Christmas and Shrove Tuesday, better known as Fat Tuesday. Those who stood to profit from it, of course, loved it. The krewes—the social clubs that went back decades—were getting ready to put on their parades, the culmination of an entire year's worth of preparation, planning, and pageantry. The police dreaded it, the same way Christopher did, but for different reasons. He'd never been able to shake off the annual family ritual that had forever tainted the holiday. Or the bloodshed on his last New Orleans Mardi Gras.

The flow of traffic was already thickening like gravy. He fought impatience as he headed to the hospital. Classic Aerosmith pounded from the stereo. He hadn't seen Brian in a week, the time it had taken to track down Rita Brooks and to stop in Atlanta and cram in three business meetings for his Web site design business.

Sasha, the respiratory therapist, had Brian on his side and was tapping his back. To promote the movement of secretions in the lungs, Christopher remembered. She was talking softly to him, so softly he couldn't hear what she was saying. He knew more about bodily functions and the risks of long-term unconsciousness than he ever wanted.

He walked up behind her and caught the words "come out of this—" before she turned and jumped. "You startled me!" She was a trim woman in her thirties with blue eyes that held an almost too-bright shine. He thought she looked familiar, like someone from school maybe, but he didn't care enough to ask. She laughed a bit nervously. "I was talking to him, just making conversation. How was your trip?"

"Fine. Anything changed?"

She shook her head, repositioning Brian so that he lay prone. "Brain injuries are the most frustrating. We don't know how long he'll be under or what he'll be like when he comes out." She patted Brian's arm. "But you'll be fine, won't you? And you'll tell us what was going on in that pretty head of yours before this happened." She jotted down some information on Brian's chart and hung it up. "Talk to him." She patted Christopher's arm in the same way she'd done Brian's as she walked past him. "He likes to hear your voice."

"How can you tell?"

"Just watch that monitor. The transducer measures his heart rate and blood pressure. Sometimes I see a change when I'm talking to him." She started to leave, then paused at the door. "Did you . . . find what you were looking for?"

He shook his head, and she left the room.

He felt that familiar tightness in his chest every time he walked close to Brian. He opened his mouth, closed it again. Looked at the monitor. He wasn't sure what he should feel. The golden boy was as pale as the sheets and blankets that covered his body. He looked like a robot, with all the tubes and wires and monitors. His eyes were taped over so they wouldn't dry out. An endotracheal tube ran through his vocal cords and down his throat to assist his breathing. His white teeth weren't showing in the cocky grin Christopher remembered. What did he say to a man he hadn't spoken with in years? This man who wasn't anything like the brother he had known?

On the surface, he had seemed to be a man who had it all: handsome, polite and friendly, well off. But something had happened, slowly, according to those who knew him best. He had retreated from the society he had once thrived in.

Christopher wanted to know why. And he wanted to know where Rita Brooks fit into it.

She watched Christopher LaPorte standing by Brian's bedside. He'd gone to Boston. He'd probably talked to Rita Brooks. Damn. If only that last e-mail had been intercepted like the rest . . . if Rita had died in the accident. So many ifs. Christopher seemed to accept the attempted-suicide theory. For his sake, she hoped nothing changed.

She'd been considering whether to return to Boston and finish Rita off but hadn't wanted to leave Brian in case he started to come around. So far Rita wasn't a threat. If she came here . . . if she came, well, then everything would change. And Rita would have to die.

Rita forsook her comforting evening routine of immersing herself in *Buffy the Vampire Slayer* reruns, *Angel*, and the latest *un*reality show, as she called them. Her reality was much more bizarre. First she searched the Internet for a news story about Brian's fall. Though she found the New Orleans papers online, the articles weren't accessible. Then she'd done a search on comas and spent four hours reading documented stories of recovered coma patients with memories of a different plane of existence. These people weren't nuts. They were respected professionals who had experienced something incredible and strange.

No matter how *un*real it all seemed, she couldn't ignore the facts. And those facts screamed that Brian had tried to find her for a reason. Maybe people's souls went somewhere while they were in a coma. The gray place. Maybe all those people she'd seen were also in comas. But while no one else was making any contact, he had sought her out. It was important, she knew that. She closed her eyes and remembered how he'd squeezed her shoulders and stared into her eyes.

What did you tell me, Brian?

She sank into the moment, reliving the sensation in the gray place. He found her. Put his hands on her shoulders. And . . . her body seized as a barrage of images flooded her mind: the flash of a long knife blade, blood, everything coming so fast she couldn't pick out much more. Each image seemed attached to an emotion: regret, forgiveness, sorrow . . . fear. But this time she was able to cling to the last image. Fear pounded through her and made her hands clammy. She tried to call back the image. A dark night. A gold mask with black feathers highlighting green eyes. A struggle. Then the sensation of falling.

She slapped her hand to her chest, her eyes wide. If this connection was real, if it was Brian LaPorte, if she could believe any of it. . . .

"He didn't jump. Someone pushed him. That's why he found me."

Brian knew that everyone thought he'd jumped, probably because his loved ones held his hand and asked him why. Their voices pulled him from the gray place just as Marty's voice had pulled her. So he'd found her and showed her these images.

Something kept niggling at her. She recalled the images again, trying to hold on to them frame by frame. They were as slippery as mercury. What was it that bothered her even more than the figure pushing Brian off the roof?

The mask.

She felt chilled as she pictured it. Gold mask, black feathers, green eyes. She'd seen it before, she was sure of it.

She closed her eyes, willing her brain to remember. The mask, the mask. Where had she seen it?

Her brain wouldn't supply the answer. She leaned forward and rubbed her forehead. Brian had sought her out in another plane of existence. Did she believe that?

"Yes. Maybe. I don't know."

That's why she needed to go to New Orleans and see Brian. If he was the man she'd seen while in a coma, then she would go to the police and convince them to investigate his fall.

Her heart was hammering now at the prospect, but she had no choice. Because if Brian was pushed, that meant someone had tried to kill him. Which also meant that someone might try to finish the job.

4

Rita had two nights in New Orleans. After that, every hotel room in or near town was booked as Mardi Gras celebration kicked into full gear. Joyce, her travel agent, suggested she wait until after Mardi Gras, but Rita couldn't take the chance. Since making up her mind two nights ago, she felt an urgency she couldn't describe. Joyce had pulled some strings and a chunk of Rita's bank account and had gotten her the last seat on a Thursday-afternoon flight.

Sandwiched between a young woman and a middle-aged man on the Atlanta–New Orleans leg of the flight, Rita spent her time sketching the mask. It still bothered her, but she couldn't figure out why. Finally, she put away the pad and closed her eyes. The hum of the engines lulled her into a half-sleep state where images of the last few weeks scrolled across the movie screen of her mind.

She saw scenes from purgatory, the gray place, and her mother sitting next to her at the hospital. Officer Potter's voice echoed in her mind: *The other vehicle came up beside you as though he were going to pass but then slammed into the side of your car.* The scene sprang into her mind. She saw a black SUV pulling beside her on wet roads. An idiot in a big hurry to pass her. But no, he didn't want to pass. He careened into her car. She fought the wheel. Why was he doing this? She looked his way for a second. And in that second, she saw light reflecting off the gold of a mask and a spray of feathers.

"No, it can't be. Can't. . . ."

Even as she spoke, she rummaged through her purse for the business card given to her by the officer she had spoken with at the hospital. She swiped her credit card for the airplane phone and dialed his number. The woman to her left was listening, though the man, a business traveler, was asleep.

Once she had Potter on the line, she introduced herself. "Any news on the case?" The last she knew, the police hadn't been able to connect the teens to her accident. When he gave her the expected negative answer, she said, "I may have remembered something from the accident. Was the vehicle that hit me a black SUV?"

"Yes, I believe a black Ford Explorer, but I'd have to check."

"I think there was only one person in the car. He did try to run me off the road. It was definitely intentional. And there's something else. He was wearing a mask."

"A mask? Like a Ronald Reagan mask?"

"No, this one was gold and had black feathers." The masks were blurring in her mind now. She wasn't sure if the one she pictured was from the accident or the one she'd seen while in a coma.

"Like a Mardi Gras mask, you mean?"

"Yes." Mardi Gras. New Orleans. "That's exactly the kind. Did you find anything in the SUV?"

"I'd have to look at the full report, though I know offhand we found nothing useful. The owner of the vehicle has three children, so we found a lot of hairs, threads, toys . . . you name it, it was in there."

"How about a feather? A black one?"

"I'll have to check on that."

She gave him her cell number.

"Is there anything else?" he asked, probably sensing the hesitation in her voice.

"Uhhh . . . no. Nothing I'm sure about. I'll let you know if I come up with anything solid."

Such as this same person had killed a friend of hers in New Orleans. Then she realized something else: that person had tried to kill her, too. She could hardly choke out the word *goodbye*. It took her five minutes to catch her breath. She rubbed her sweaty palms over the soft fabric of her pants. Her matching blue shoes peeked out from beneath her cuffs. *Keep it together. Brian needs you. That's why he came to you.*

The revelers had been revving up on the plane, wearing their shiny beads and throwing back shots with smuggled liquor. They hooted when the plane touched down and made imaginary toasts to each other at the baggage claim, strangers united in the spirit of celebration. Why did it have to be Mardi Gras, where fantasy and reality twisted together, where good became evil, and evil dressed up as good?

Evil. She was already searching the people around her, thinking of the evil that had brought her here. She didn't even know if the person behind the mask was man or woman, how old, or more importantly, the reason behind two attempted murders. She had been a target hundreds of miles away in Boston. The distance hadn't been enough to keep her out of harm's way. Now she was here, where surely the evil originated. Where she could trust no one.

The buzzer jarred her out of her fearful misery, signaling the arrival of their bags. After grabbing her luggage, she registered for her rental car and walked outside to the curb where a bus took her and thirty others to their waiting cars. Dusk cloaked everything in a blanket of darkening gray. Even the city's lights didn't lift the ominous sense of bleakness. The chill in the air didn't have the bite that Boston's had, and there weren't clumps of dirty snow pushed to the corners of parking lots. Still, it felt colder, chilling her through her heavy wool coat.

While the car warmed up, she unfolded the map and tried to find her location in the dim interior light. She hated maps and she was sure they hated her, too. She considered that she was simply inept at reading them but preferred the hate/hate scenario. A few minutes later, she navigated through traffic and hoped she'd read the darn thing right.

She found herself turning on the radio, something she rarely did. She usually went over the day's patient list during her commute. The deejay warned listeners about parking in parade zones and certain areas of the French Quarter. Don't grab doubloons, he warned, lest the grabber get his or her fingers crushed beneath someone's shoe. Don't carry a lot of cash. "It's going to get crazier, folks. The madness has only just begun."

During the drive to the hospital, she encountered signs of the celebration: windows decorated in gold, green, and purple flagging, beads hanging from rearview mirrors. Some of the buildings looked like old matrons trying desperately to hold on to their former beauty with patched-up cracks and colorful banners draped over their doorways.

The hospital's façade had a Gothic air about it, with old, elaborate cornerstones and eroding statues braced against the wind. Probably gargoyles, though she didn't take the time to find out. The woman at the reception desk breathlessly told her where to find Brian LaPorte's room. Rita had been doing fine until she reached the seventh floor, until she took those first steps off the elevator. Even though everything looked as she'd expected, she felt further removed from reality with every step she took.

She paused outside the room and took a deep breath, noticing for the first time the smells of urine and disinfectant and the underlying mustiness that went along with old buildings. Would Brian look like the man she'd seen? If he didn't, then the similarities between Christopher and that man were only a coincidence. Then perhaps she could convince herself that the mask, both at her accident and in the image of Brian being pushed, were just her imagination. Then this trip would simply be a visit to a friend. She hoped that was the case. The other scenario was scaring the hell out of her.

She stepped through the open doorway but halted. Christopher stood by the hospital bed, his back to her. She knew she should announce her presence, but she was rooted to the spot by the memory of facing him. He had unsettled her in her own environment; here, she felt totally disconcerted. Still, she couldn't back away, especially when he spoke. His voice was deep and so soft she had to strain to hear it.

"The last time I saw you in a hospital I put you here. Seems like all of the people in my life end up in the hospital . . . or worse." A few long seconds passed as he stared at one of the monitors. "How does Rita Brooks fit into your life? Every time I say her name, your heart rate jumps."

Hearing her name felt as though a thousand-pound weight had slammed into her. *Move, move,* her inner voice urged. *Before he turns around and catches you there.*

"I know she was holding something back. I'm going to find out what she knows."

Those words finally broke the spell that kept her frozen to the spot. She took one step back, then another. Her legs felt shaky. Her hands were clammy where her palms were pressed together. She was nearly outside the room now. Three more steps. . . .

He started to turn. She pivoted, letting her thick hair swing around to hide her face as she walked back down the corridor. She heard his footsteps following her and ducked into the restroom—and right into a nurse fixing her hair in front of the mirror.

"Sorry," Rita said, slipping into a bathroom stall and waiting until the nurse left. Then she waited fifteen more minutes. She was pretty sure Christopher hadn't seen enough of her face to recognize her, but her cagey movements could have piqued his interest.

She sat on the commode and dropped her face into her hands. He had put Brian in the hospital before. He knew she was holding back. Well, of course he did. She hadn't been very good at it. *I'm going to find out what she knows.* Even she didn't know how she fit into all this. She sure didn't like his assertion that he was going to find out.

She stepped out of her stall. The woman staring back from the mirror looked pale. Her hands trembled as she washed them under the cold stream of water and splashed her face. She pulled on her cashmere hat, making sure her shoulder-length waves hid as much of her face as possible. A few minutes later, she pushed the door open.

Apparently, Christopher hadn't given up so easily. He stood in front of the elevator, watching the brass dial depict the car's progress. The doors slid open, and he walked inside just as she stepped back inside the restroom. She waited another few minutes before opening the door again. This time he was gone.

As she walked into Brian's room, she felt cold inside, cold and alone. She approached the bed, taking in a soft breath at the sight of all the wires and tubes connecting him to machines that probably kept him alive.

A respirator made a *whump* sound in a steady rhythm. A tube disappeared into his mouth. She swallowed, forcing her gaze to the man's face. Or what she could see of it. His eyes were taped shut, the white patches blending into his pale face. Round monitors were taped to his chest, checking his heart rate. Other tubes snaked out from beneath the blankets, either draining fluids or supplying them. One tube came out of his head; a large swath of hair had recently been shaved. They had probably done surgery to eliminate the swelling of his brain.

Her eyes watered. She swallowed, focusing not on the equipment but the person. There were no similarities to the man she'd seen in the gray place. She wanted to leave it at that. *Maybe this is better. Maybe the whole gray place was a concoction of my mind.* She may have been able to convince herself of that if she hadn't noticed the display on a small table. On the white cloth covering the table were an array of cards, an unlit candle with what she thought was one of the Catholic saints embedded in the white wax and pictures. A blond man laughed at something, his blue eyes sparkling. In another he was about fourteen, wearing a costume and wielding a sword. Her legs went weak, and she had to grab on to the corner of the table. It was him. Oh, yes, it was him.

She turned back to the hospital bed. Somehow she hadn't expected him to look like this . . . so helpless and pale, no expression on his face. Had she looked this way when she was under? Had she looked so . . . lost?

No, she hadn't been on life support. And she hadn't been in a coma for long. Brian had been in his coma for six weeks.

"Brian." Her voice was a coarse whisper. "Brian, it's me. Rita."

The numbers on one of the monitors jumped higher. Christopher had said that every time he mentioned her name, Brian's heart rate increased. He knew she was there. "I just found out you were here. I'm so sorry." She looked behind her to make sure no one was listening before turning back to him. "You . . . you came to me. You really did come to find me. But I don't remember much of what you showed me. Just the person in the mask. I know he pushed you off the roof. He came to Boston and ran me off the road. That's why I was in a coma, too. I'm going to the police. I'm going to get you protection."

If only she knew more. Why had this person tried to kill him? And more importantly, why had he or she also tried to kill her? Was it a jealous lover? Someone out for revenge? If she had some idea of the motive, she could begin to figure this out.

"I need to know more. Some of what you showed me, well, it was too fast for me to see. Blood and a knife and a funeral. A young man with dark hair." She looked at the picture of young Brian. The boy was Christopher, she realized, a darker version of Brian. How was he involved in all this? Too many questions and hardly any answers.

She wondered if touching him would reestablish their connection. She reached for his hand.

"Who are you?"

The sharp, feminine voice startled Rita, who whirled around with her hand on her stampeding heart. "You scared me!"

The woman didn't return Rita's flustered smile. She walked in with authority, yet she wore no uniform. Unless hospital policy loosened during Mardi Gras to include black pants, an orange blouse that accented angular shoulders, and a green beret. The woman was in her early thirties, Rita guessed, with a smooth complexion and regular features. Her short, black hair sported strands gelled to her cheeks, spikes pointing forward.

"Who are you?" she asked again, dark lipstick making her lips look harsh and small.

"I'm—my name is Rita. Rita Brooks from Boston," she felt inclined to add, as though that would lessen the suspicion in the other woman's eyes. Good American city and all that. "And you are?"

"Tammy Rieux." She sat on those words for a moment, sizing up Rita with gray-green eyes thickly rimmed in black liner.

"Wait, wait, wait a minute," Tammy said, moving between Brian's bed and Rita. "I've heard of you. Christopher LaPorte was asking around at the hotel to see if anyone had heard of you." Her voice lowered, and her eyebrow arched. "We hadn't. How do you know Brian?"

Christopher had been asking about her. Of course, after he'd intercepted her e-mail, he would have asked around. The hotel she referred to was probably the one Brian managed.

"He bought some merchandise from me on eBay."

Tammy eyed Brian, as though he could refute Rita's tale. Rita noticed how shiny the woman's hair was. A wig? Tammy's fingers stroked the long strand of pearl beads hanging around her neck, making the plastic click together. One side of her mouth twitched. "Was it some kind of lurid online thing?"

"No." Rita found herself laughing at the comparison between something tawdry and what they had shared. "Nothing like that. We were just friends." That was the story she was sticking to. It was simpler and required less qualifying.

Rita wondered if Tammy was a lover in past or present terms. Brian had claimed not to be seeing anyone, but men did lie sometimes. They had talked about their towns, about the house she'd been saving to buy, about her hobby wheeling and dealing. She knew he was old-fashioned about life and love. He cried during sad movies. He was a *Buffy the Vampire Slayer* fan, but he liked *Angel* better. But she didn't know everything about him; only the parts he wanted her to know.

"How did you know he was here?" Tammy asked.

"Christopher found me. He wondered if I knew anything about Brian's state of mind before his . . . fall. I came to see if there was anything I could do. Are you his girlfriend?"

"He's my boss." A non-answer, though Rita could hardly press. "I suppose Christopher brought you here," Tammy continued. "I passed him in the lobby."

And Tammy wasn't all that happy about it, Rita could see. "No, he didn't bring me. He . . . doesn't even know I'm in town."

That clearly piqued Tammy's interest. "Why not?"

"He . . . I just didn't tell him, that's all."

Tammy's expression relaxed, though Rita got the impression it was calculated. "He does have a way about him, doesn't he? Brian ever mention him?" A test question, Rita realized.

"He didn't talk much about his family, or his past. Are they close?"

She uttered a humorless laugh. "Not by a long, long, long shot."

"Was there bad blood between them, then?"

"You could say that."

This wasn't getting her anywhere. Maybe a blunt tactic would work. "Could Christopher have pushed Brian off the roof?"

Tammy made a sound of disbelief. "For one thing, Brian and Christopher haven't even seen or, as far as I know, talked to each other in years. Secondly, he wasn't even in town when Brian . . . fell. And third, Brian wasn't pushed. He had no enemies. It wasn't a break-in. Nothing else makes sense." Her eyes narrowed. "Why are you here, anyway?"

Rita saw the numbers on one of the monitors change. Brian was there. "I'm a psychologist. He's a friend. I want to understand what happened."

"You were friends." She pressed her knuckles against her mouth. "What did you talk about?"

"TV shows. Knives. Internet auctions. The meaning of life when we were feeling philosophical. Not once did he talk about death and what an escape it would be. Do you really believe he tried to kill himself?"

Tammy remained silent for so long, Rita would have thought she was being insolent except that her eyes were filled with pain as they focused on Brian. "You probably knew him better than I did. Do you realize how unfair that is when I saw him almost every day for the past sixteen years?" Her expression softened. "We both started at the LaPorte right out of high school."

"The LaPorte?"

"Yeah, the family hotel in the French Quarter. You must not have known Brian well if you didn't even know that." She seemed relieved, so Rita didn't bother to say she knew he managed a hotel. She just hadn't realized he owned it. Tammy said, "Brian's father opened it back in the seventies. My dad and Mr. L—that's what I always called Mr. LaPorte—went back years. Brian and I went to school together. We were best buds. His mother was so mad when he didn't want to go to some fancy college. He took business courses at Tulane and worked at the hotel. He loves that place, just like I do. When his father died, we became a team to make it work. We were only twenty-two, but we did it. I'm his right hand, that's what he always said."

Her mouth stretched into a frown as she stepped away from the bed. "At one time I could have said I knew him better than anyone. We laughed together, went to management seminars, and invented inspirational sayings." Her eyes darkened. "Then over the last year, he started slowly withdrawing. At first he was just distracted a lot, but it got worse. He was still here, still basically working. But not here, either. He'd say hello but be a million miles away. I asked him what was wrong, tried, tried, tried to reach him, but the more I tried, the more he retreated. Do I believe he tried to take his life? Not the Brian I used to know. But nobody knew him anymore."

"Was he seeing anyone?"

Her eyes flashed. "You."

"I mean physically."

She seemed to weigh her answer. "Not that I know of," she said at last.

Rita couldn't help but think she knew something, but accusing her of that would get her nowhere.

"What happened between Christopher and Brian?"

Tammy walked back over to him, as though he were a magnet whose force she could not resist. She took Brian's hand, rubbing each finger. "You were supposed to be king that year." She said this to Brian, and Rita wasn't sure if it was an answer to her question.

"King?"

"Yeah, you know. Each krewe selects a king and queen to preside over Mardi Gras." At Rita's blank expression, she added, "The krewes are the social clubs that put on the parades."

"Oh, right. The people who throw stuff from the floats. Bacchus, Rex." She recalled only that much from hearing others talk about it.

"It's more than that. It's a huge honor to those lucky enough to be asked. Once the king has been chosen, the pageantry goes on all year long. The king sponsors a ball. It was all Brian talked about. That's when it happened."

"What?" Rita asked after a moment.

"You'll have to ask either Brian or Christopher. They're the only ones who know. The day before the parade, Brian had some kind of accident. That's what they said, anyway: *accident*. The next time I saw Brian, a few days later, his shoulder was bandaged, but he wouldn't talk about it. And after that, Christopher became the pariah. Not that he'd ever been the favorite son anyway, you could always tell that. He was the one who got into trouble, sneaking into blues bars, hanging out with the wrong crowd. But after the accident, he was on the S-list for sure. He left town when he graduated a few months after that. I didn't see him again until a year later, at Mr. L's funeral. I overheard Brian telling him that he didn't belong there. He didn't come back for Mrs. LaPorte's funeral three years later, and hasn't until now." She squeezed his hand. "Brian was always the worthy son."

The prodigal son returns. Too bad no one wants you here. Rita remembered that from the images Brian showed her. And then the regret.

Tammy had been talking to Brian's hand the whole time. She obviously had feelings for him. Rita couldn't help wondering how deep those feelings went, and how resentful she would be if she'd known that he'd withdrawn from her and connected with an unknown woman in Boston.

"Where are you staying?" Tammy asked, shaking Rita out of her harrowing thoughts. "Sorry, it's a habit, habit, habit."

It took a moment for Rita to refocus her thoughts. "Habit, ha—?" She stopped herself from copying Tammy's tendency to repeat words.

"Of working at the LaPorte. Whenever I meet someone from out of town, I always want to know where they're staying."

"I'm staying at the Ashbury. It was the only hotel my travel agent could find."

Tammy's cell phone went off, a pleasant chiming sound. She eyed the display. "Can't these people handle anything on their own? No, I must remember what Brian always says: in the middle of difficulty lies opportunity."

"Actually it was Albert Einstein who said that."

Tammy waved away the notion. "But you know how Brian was, always quoting expressions like that. Don't you?"

Rita shook her head. She couldn't remember him quoting even one.

Tammy answered the phone with, "I'm on my way back," and hung up. She planted a kiss on Brian's cheek. "Winners never quit. Quitters never win." She looked at Rita. "Whatever happened . . . it's really not your business. If you weren't involved with him, that is."

Oh, but she was involved. "I have a professional interest. And he was a friend. I want to know why a man who had everything to live for would throw himself off his roof," she said, using Christopher's earlier words.

"Maybe it was an accident. That makes the most sense." She wasn't smiling when she said, "Have a safe trip home."

Rita tried to sort through her thoughts after Tammy left. Whoever pushed Brian must have had a personal reason to do so, considering they'd also gone after Rita. Whoever it was had access to Brian's e-mail.

"Like a hacker," she said, thinking of Christopher. Or an ex-girlfriend. It could even be shady business dealings that Brian became involved in. In one of their last conversations, he'd hinted at something exciting he was involved in, something he wanted to share with her. He'd asked her if she liked video games. When she'd admitted she was terrible at them, he said he knew one she'd be good at, though he hadn't expanded on it. She thought maybe he was investing in a game company.

If only he could tell her, the way he'd shown her that he'd been pushed. She reached out to touch him, hoping he could show her more.

A young nurse with vivid red hair pushed a cart into the room, saying in a singsong voice, "Excuse me. Time to give our boy a bath." Her skin was smooth, eyes a brilliant, artificial green as they surveyed Rita. Her smile and even her voice sounded phony, all thick and whispery. "Did I hear you say you met this gentleman online?"

"Were you listening to our conversation?" Rita asked, noting the woman's nametag: Aris Smith.

Aris laughed breezily. "Honey, y'all weren't saying anything *that* interesting." She let out a long sigh, tilting her head as she looked at Brian. "I think it's a wonderful place to meet a loved one. Shame you met your man in person too late."

"It's not too late." Rita's voice sounded as defensive as she felt.

Aris shrugged shoulders that looked padded. "Well, of course not. Forgive me. I'm a floater, you see, just did a few months on the AIDS floor. That's where they treat the patients in the final stages of the disease. When they get there, there isn't much hope. If you'll excuse me, I have to get to work."

For a reason she could not name, Rita felt reluctant to go. Aris pulled a wet sponge from a basin and squeezed it. Her nails were painted green, gold, and purple, the colors of Mardi Gras. Tammy's were painted those colors too, but Rita couldn't remember the design. Probably a lot of women who went in for acrylic nails had them painted up for Mardi Gras.

Aris stopped mid-movement. "Are you just going to stand there and gawk?"

"Er, no. No." Rita walked out of the room, feeling her face flush. She was still caught up in this surreal world of New Orleans, and of the realization that two nights weren't going to be enough to find out what had happened to Brian.

Aris glanced out of the doorway at Rita Brooks who was waiting by the elevator. She'd only been coming by to do her usual check on Brian's condition, to see if there were any signs of him coming out. Rita had stopped her dead cold. Rita, here in New Orleans. Rita, asking questions about who might have pushed Brian.

Aris had altered her appearance and gotten into uniform to shoo Rita out of the room. She ran the sponge down the length of Brian's skinny leg. "There you go, sweetheart. Doesn't that feel good, good, good?" She chuckled at the use of the three-word repeat, but her smile didn't last long. She lowered her voice to a whisper. "What's she doing here? I knew I shoulda made sure she was gone dead. She was asking way too many questions. You said she didn't know about Xanadu. Well, we'll just see about that."

The numbers on his monitor increased with each word she spoke. He was afraid, and helpless to do a thing about it. She at least got some satisfaction from that. She glanced out at the elevators again. The doors had just closed.

With her singsong voice, she said, "I won't let anyone threaten our special place. Someone's got to protect it. It's the only place I ever felt like I belonged. Like . . . I was wanted. 'A savage place, as holy and enchanted as e'er beneath a waning moon was haunted, by woman wailing for her demon-lover!' When Coleridge wrote that, he dreamed of me. Just like I know you dreamed of me once." The numbers kept increasing. "It's your fault. You brought her in. Now she's going to have to go and die."

Aris walked to the stairwell. The elevators were slow; she had time to sprint downstairs to the lobby, changing clothing and hair as she went. By the time she emerged from the stairwell, she was unrecognizable as the nurse. Rita was walking out the automatic doors, and Aris followed her to a bland rental car. Bland was good. Bland could change contacts and hair and be someone else.

In her own car, she caught up with Rita at the light exiting the lot. She expected her to head to a hotel. Instead, she turned into the police station.

Aris cruised by, her foot lax on the gas pedal as she watched Rita walk inside.

"Don't panic," she whispered. "No way can she know who you are. No way can she know anything about Brian's fall." But she knew something.

"I'll just have to kill her. Yeah, baby. Nothing to it."

5

Rita waited twenty minutes to talk to Detective Alex Connard. He was one of the detectives who had been called to the scene at Brian's house several weeks earlier. The thought of trying to explain all this twisted her insides like a tornado.

"I understand you have information?" he asked once he'd led her to his desk. He was a slight man, not what she'd expect a detective to look like. He was in his forties, with fine, pretty features and a shaved head.

She took the chair he'd indicated. "I hope you'll keep an open mind."

He didn't commit either way as he looked over the report. "Is Mr. LaPorte still in a coma?"

"Yes."

"What is your relationship to him?"

"We had an online friendship. I live in Boston. We'd never met or seen pictures of each other. We'd talked on the phone several times."

He leaned back in his chair. "Romantic?"

"Leading to." When he waited for her to continue, she said, "I have reason to believe someone pushed him from the roof in an attempt to kill him."

Connard sat up straight again, his interest level higher. "Why is that?"

Okay, here we go. "Six weeks ago someone ran me off the road."

"In Boston?"

"Yes. The person behind the wheel was wearing a Mardi Gras mask, gold with black feathers. That same person pushed Brian off the roof."

"You were a witness?"

"This is where the open mind part comes in. I want you to know that I'm a professional in the mental health field. Nothing like this has ever happened to me before." His expression was annoyingly neutral as she told him everything. Hearing it made her realize how far out it sounded. "I did some checking on the Internet. This kind of thing does happen." She handed him copies of the Web pages she'd printed out. "You can call the officer who investigated my hit-and-run. He's checking to see if a feather was found in the car that hit me."

She couldn't tell what he thought so she forged on. "Did you check Christopher LaPorte's alibi at the time of Brian's fall? He's Brian's brother."

"You think he may have been the one wearing the mask? Says here he lives in Atlanta, that the two weren't close. He arrived the day after Brian's fall. We didn't check his alibi because there was no indication of foul play at the scene. No signs of a struggle, as you described, nor of an intruder. The only thing out of the ordinary was a cufflink on the deck floor. That in itself wasn't strong enough to suggest anything sinister. Had Brian mentioned trouble with his brother?"

"He never mentioned his brother at all. From what I understand, there's bad blood between them. When I arrived this evening, I overheard Christopher at the hospital. He said he had to find out what I knew. He said he'd put Brian in the hospital before and something about everyone close to him ending up in the hospital . . . or worse."

That got Connard's interest. "When did he say this?"

"Just a little while ago. Apparently he's staying in New Orleans."

He had her repeat what Christopher had said and wrote it down. "We'll check into this. But the rest"—he picked up the sheets she'd handed him—"I have to tell you, it sounds pretty crazy."

"At least promise you'll check into it."

"I'll call Officer Potter in Boston, ask about your accident. And I'll check out Christopher LaPorte. If I find something that even begins to corroborate your story, I'll look further."

If. Well, she was grateful for that, and for his hearing her out. "Thank you. I know you can only do so much without evidence. But what about keeping Brian safe? If this person wanted him dead—"

"They would have already done it. I can't post an officer at the hospital based on"—he gestured to his notes—"this. We're already shorthanded going into Mardi Gras."

She would call the hospital and ask them to keep an eye on Brian. Connard was right; the masked person had plenty of opportunity. He or she was likely waiting to see if Brian survived. He would only be a threat if he regained consciousness. She got to her feet and gave him her business card. "Thank you for whatever you can do."

She walked out into the chilly night air. By the time she reached her car, her hands were numb. But the cold wasn't the reason she shivered. She scanned the well-lit parking lot. She should be perfectly safe here. Why did she feel the eyes of evil watching her?

He watched Rita get into her car and drive away. What had she told the police? He followed her through the streets of the French Quarter where she took a long, convoluted route to her hotel. He would have suspected she was making sure she wasn't being followed except that she kept stopping to look at street signs.

The Ashbury was a small, elegant hotel at the edge of the Quarter. Rita parked in the small lot adjacent and carried one bag into the lobby. He walked in a few minutes later, lingering behind her as she checked in. She had glanced back at him when the door had opened, but had only given him a cursory look before returning to her check-in. There was only one desk and one clerk. He was exceedingly patient.

"You're staying with us for two nights," the young woman behind the desk confirmed and then frowned. "You're leaving before all the fun."

"It's all I could get a room for. Unless you've had a cancellation?"

The woman shook her head. "Afraid not. We're booked from tomorrow on through Mardi Gras."

Two nights. How much trouble could she cause in just two nights?

Enough.

"All right, Miss Brooks, you're in room 315. Go out that door and you'll see stairs to the right and the elevator to the left. Your room is on the third floor and faces north into the courtyard."

The woman directed her attention to him.

"I'm looking for a room for a friend of mine. She'll be coming in for a month this summer. I told her I'd check out hotels for her. Can you show me a room like the one you just gave that woman?"

He watched Rita gather her bag and head out the door. She didn't even look back. The clerk tapped on her keyboard. "Yes, I have one available. Come this way." She grabbed a key off the rack behind her. "Wait until you see our beautiful courtyard."

He followed the woman up two flights of stairs to the room just below Rita's, according to the numbers. All the rooms surrounded a splendid courtyard with strategically lit plants and a small pool. The lights provided plenty of shadows. The fence around the courtyard was climbable, and he spotted a shadowy corner perfect for slipping over.

"It is lovely," he said, leaning over the railing and spotting the lighted window next to door 315. He noted the room layout, and more importantly, the flimsy locks. "It's perfect."

"Your friend will love it here," she said.

"Oh, she certainly will."

Christopher answered the door, wondering who would be dropping by this late in the evening. He was surprised how few people called to inquire about Brian's health. Tammy Rieux was probably the most interested; a little too interested, he thought.

"Christopher LaPorte? I'm Detective Alex Connard with the New Orleans Police Department. I'd like to ask you some follow-up questions with regard to your brother's fall."

"Follow-up questions? Why now, after all this time?" Despite his puzzlement he backed up to admit the detective and gestured toward the living room.

The detective shook his head. "This won't take long. We have some new information we need to check on. A woman who had a relationship with your brother believes—"

"What woman?"

"Hear me out, please. She believes someone may have

pushed Brian off the roof. Do you have any reason to believe your brother was pushed?"

"Pushed? As in murder?" When Connard didn't comment, Christopher leaned against the foyer wall. "No. He lived like a hermit. I can't believe he put enough into his life to make an enemy."

"Was he involved in anything illegal?"

"I don't know. I hadn't spoken with him in years. But no, I don't think he'd be involved in anything like that. Brian could do no wrong. As far as I know, he never even smoked pot."

"What about you?"

"Have I smoked pot?"

"No, what about your relationship with your brother? We understand there was animosity between you."

Where was he getting this information? Tammy? No, why would she bring this all up now? "We weren't close, never had been. We had a blowup thirteen years ago. I left town soon after that and I've only been back once."

He checked his notepad. "Where were you the night your brother fell off the roof?"

Christopher could do nothing but blink in surprise at the question. "Am I under suspicion?" he asked at last, unable to believe what he was hearing. Before the detective could answer, he said, "I was at my cabin in northern Georgia. I live in Atlanta, but I bought an old place on a lake. I go there on the weekends, and no, I can't prove it. I suppose someone in town could have seen me buying supplies, but I have no phone there and rarely even use my cell phone." He pushed away from the wall. "Do you really believe someone might have tried to kill him?"

"That's what we're trying to determine. You made a threatening statement at the hospital today. Care to tell me about it?"

"Threatening?" This conversation was getting stranger and stranger. "I have no idea what you're talking about. I only spoke to my brother and maybe said hello to a nurse or two."

Detective Connard checked his notes again. "Something about putting your brother in the hospital before and that everyone you're close to ends up in the hospital or worse."

Someone had been listening to his conversation. Someone who had been standing in the room. "That was a childhood accident." He wasn't going to spill his guts to this guy. "Who reported this?"

"You also said something about finding out what a Rita Brooks knows."

"Oh, wait a minute. Rita Brooks is here, isn't she? She's the one who told you all this." The detective didn't deny or confirm it. "Let me tell you about Miss Brooks. She was having online hanky-panky with my brother. I found her in Boston and asked if she knew anything about my brother's state of mind. She denied knowing anything about it, but I could tell she was holding something back." And now she was here trying to implicate him. As payback maybe? "She's a piece of work, that one. She got kind of freaky and then her nose started bleeding."

The man's brows furrowed. "How could you tell she was holding something back?"

"Same way you know when someone's lying. She clammed up, but her mind was going over the possibilities, you know, like she was figuring out what she could safely tell me. And now she's here, what, telling you that I had something to do with Brian's fall?" He ran his fingers through his hair. "This is just great. Where is she staying? Maybe I can straighten all this out."

"I can't disclose that, sir."

Christopher nodded. "I know what's going on. I may have insinuated that she was responsible for Brian's state of mind. I figured she broke things off, and he didn't take it well. She's giving me grief back. If there's anything you want to know about my brother, ask. Have a look around here if you'd like. I want to know what the hell was going on with him as much as anyone else."

Connard slid his notepad into his pocket. He'd been nodding in agreement, but Christopher wasn't sure if it was over the revenge of Rita Brooks or his cooperation.

"Thank you for your time, sir. Do let me know if you find anything."

Christopher closed the door and thought about Rita. She was in town. And he was damn well going to find her and get to the bottom of this.

By the time Alex Connard returned to the station, the officer from Boston had returned his call. He didn't know what to make of Rita Brooks and her allegations, not to mention her bizarre story about coma connections. His father, a seasoned veteran, had taught him to listen to everything without reacting. Now that he'd had the time to take it in, he still wasn't sure what to think. He was pretty sure the brother had nothing to do with Brian's fall, and that Rita had probably misunderstood what she'd overheard at the hospital. Maybe she was trying to cause trouble.

He called the Boston officer in hopes of clearing things up.

"She hit her head pretty hard in the accident," Officer Potter said once Connard explained his side. "I understand it can take a long time for the brain to get back to normal, if it ever does. She never mentioned the coma-connection thing to me, only that the person in the car that hit hers was wearing a feather mask. That in itself seemed pretty strange. She asked me to check, but I haven't had time. I think she's having a problem coming to terms with the accident, being in a coma, and whatever's going on in her personal life."

"That's what I figured. Luckily, she's going back to Boston day after tomorrow. We're heading into Mardi Gras. Not only will there be lots of feather masks around, but we're going to have our share of nut cases. We certainly don't need one more. Thanks for your time."

Even so, Connard flipped through Brian LaPorte's file once more. The attempted suicide made sense in light of his withdrawal from friends. The bruising on his face made sense in light of his fall. The only strange thing about the case was Rita Brooks.

And speaking of her . . . he pulled out the number she'd given him and called.

"Miss Brooks, this is Detective Connard. I checked into Brian LaPorte's case and I can't find anything that indicates foul play."

"Did you speak with his brother?"

"Yes, but again, nothing suspicious. I think you just misunderstood what he said. I suggest you say your goodbyes to your friend and go home. Oh, and be aware that Christopher LaPorte knows you're in town, and he didn't seem too happy about it. You might want to steer clear of him. Have a safe trip home."

He returned the file and headed home.

She waited until after midnight before paying a visit to Rita Brooks. She slipped over the fence and landed in a clump of bushes. Though she'd made minimal noise, she remained still for three minutes just to make sure no one had heard her. Luckily, it was too cool for couples to sit amid the shadowy beauty of the courtyard and share quiet whispers.

Satisfied that no one was around, she emerged from her hiding place and proceeded up the stairs. The doors of the rooms were dark green, and she had worn a similar color to blend in. She stopped in front of 315. It was a good thing she was strong enough to do whatever it took to protect what was hers. And there was, after all, a certain power in it. That pleasure couldn't be denied.

She picked the lock and disappeared into the dark room. It took only a few moments for her eyes to adjust. The rest she filled in from memory. Table and chairs by the front window, double beds toward the back.

Raspy breathing led her to the second bed. There the interloper lay. By the contrast of shadows Rita appeared to be lying on top of the bedspread on her back. This was almost too easy. She slid out of her thick jersey jacket and bundled it in her hands. It had to be half over before Rita knew what was happening.

Rita let out a low moan and started to shift. Or perhaps awaken. No more time to ponder. She slid atop her and pushed the bundle of material over her face in one movement. Rita awoke slowly and started to struggle.

"It's just a bad dream, baby," she whispered. "You go on back to sleep."

Rita thrashed but, in the end, didn't give much of a fight. Just to be sure, she checked her pulse before removing the jacket. She knew some people played possum to save their lives. No way could Rita live. No pulse, no blood moving through her veins.

She put her jacket back on and looked out the window. Quiet as death, she thought with a smile. As quietly as she'd come, she slipped back out into the night.

6

Rita became aware of the noise first, an uneven thumping sound from above. There was a high-pitched keening sound, too. She pulled the blanket up over her head and tried to drift back to sleep. When her mind identified the noise as crying, she climbed slowly to full consciousness. The room was shadowy, even though shards of light crept around the edge of the insulated curtains.

She rubbed her eyes as she pulled herself out of bed. Sleep had eluded her for hours, filling her mind with Brian, the masked figure, and the images Brian had shown her. As tired as she'd been the night before, as soon as she'd unpacked with the sole intent of falling right into bed, she'd discovered a leak in her bathroom. She'd called down to the desk and had been moved to 215. By the time she'd repacked and moved, she'd been awake again.

She peered between the curtains and saw people on the other side of the courtyard looking at something above her room. Over the fence she saw an ambulance parked by the curb. She dressed and walked out to the balcony. A man was coming down the stairs at the end. She guessed he was another guest.

"What's going on?" she asked him.

"Apparently the maintenance woman fell asleep in the room upstairs after she fixed a leak. She died in her sleep. She's the owner's aunt, so she's pretty broken up about it. I guess she was having health problems, so it's not a big surprise."

She remembered the plump, tough bird who had shown up with a toolbox just as Rita was vacating the room. She'd looked pale and her breath rattled. Rita had probably been the last person to see her alive. The thought filled her with an eerie sadness. She wished she'd said more than, "Sorry you have to deal with this so late." She said a prayer for the woman's family and went back inside.

Once she was dressed, she headed to the hospital. She needed a chance to touch Brian, to see if the connection could be reestablished. She needed answers and proof. It was clear that the detective had done only a cursory check and chalked her story up to madness or hormones or whatever he felt comfortable with. Not that she could blame him. If she wanted anyone to take her seriously, she needed something concrete. And that wasn't going to be easy.

He watched Rita leave the hotel, unable to believe his eyes. *She* had failed. He had driven by the hotel to see if Rita's body had been discovered. The sight of the ambulance had buoyed his spirits, until he spotted Rita emerging from the parking lot. Who had she smothered, then?

He didn't have time to ponder it. He followed Rita to the hospital, where she was undoubtedly going to visit Brian. Why wouldn't she die? It would have been so simple if she'd died in Boston. Unease tightened his chest. What had she found out that sent her to the police? What did she know?

He watched her go inside. He'd have time to figure out

what his next step was. He scanned the parking lot and the distant spot she'd had to take. Yeah, he had a plan.

I'm the boy. I'll take care of it this time.

Rita made the long, cold trek into the hospital, getting that spooky watched feeling the whole way. She glanced around casually but saw nothing out of the ordinary. Maybe it was the dreary weather, overcast skies, and the fine mist floating through the air. *Or maybe it's knowing someone tried to kill you, and they probably know you're here.* She shivered.

This time she checked before walking into Brian's room. No Christopher. She really didn't want to see him now that she'd sent the police to question him. Even worse, he would know she'd eavesdropped on his conversation.

She watched Brian for a few minutes, finding the rhythmic sound of the respirator comforting. He was alive, at least. Would he ever come out from the coma? What would he be like? *Brian, talk to me. I miss you. I feel kind of hopeless about the future, yours and mine. Besides, I need your help.* She felt a wave of sadness that the man who would come out of this coma might not be the same man she'd been ready to open her heart to.

She reached out and took his hand in hers. His skin was cool and dry. She hadn't realized she'd closed her eyes as she waited for the jolt of those images. Nothing came. No images, no revelations, not even a nuance. The connection didn't extend beyond the gray place.

"What the hell are you doing?"

She spun at the voice behind her and came face to face with Christopher LaPorte. And he wasn't very happy. He advanced on her until he was way too close.

"I asked you what you're doing. I'm not sure whether to think you're just a little nuts or firmly on the psycho side of things. Back in Boston you withhold information, and now you're here telling the cops I'm threatening you because you eavesdropped on a private conversation. Inferring that I had something to do with his condition. What kind of game are you playing?"

She let go of Brian's hand and gestured toward the door. "Let's talk over there, where he can't hear us."

Perhaps he knew that coma patients could sometimes hear what was said around them, because he followed her without argument.

It also bought her a few seconds to figure out how she was going to handle him. Not long enough, unfortunately. He spun her around to face him, his jaw rigid and his eyes an angry blue. "I want answers, Rita Brooks."

She didn't know how much to tell him and she certainly didn't trust him.

"I just asked the police to check into all the possibilities."

"Why do you think someone tried to kill him?" he asked. "Was he involved in something? You're involved in it, too, aren't you?"

"I don't have to answer your questions," she said, walking out of the room. The truth was, she had no logical answers. She didn't want to wait for the eternally slow elevators, so she looked for the fire exit. He was right behind her as she pushed through the doorway and took the stairs at a sprint.

"You'd better damn well tell me what you know," he said behind her.

She needed to get away from him. He'd pin her down and force her to tell him everything, and then she'd really come off as more than a little nuts. Since he hadn't mentioned the coma connection, she assumed the detective hadn't told Christopher about it. She needed time to think this through, to figure out what her next step was and who she could trust.

She pushed through the ground floor doors and headed straight for the entrance. He grabbed her shoulder and spun her around. "Leave me alone," she said in a strained voice.

"Or what, you'll call security?"

Of course she couldn't call security. He hadn't done anything wrong. The cold air embraced her. She headed to her car where she could lock him out. If he tried to follow her, she'd drive to the police station.

"Dammit, woman, if you know something, I'm the one to tell."

She spotted her car in the near distance. She was pretty sure he wouldn't accost her in the parking lot, not with people in the vicinity. She dared a sideways glance back and saw that he was a few feet behind her. He was probably deciding how far he'd go to get answers.

Her car was close now. Impending relief was only an illusion, as she found out. She heard tires squealing on the pavement first and then spotted the car flying around the corner. Someone tackled her from behind at the same moment the car veered toward her. She screamed as the strong arms that were clamped around her pulled her off balance. They went rolling beneath the back of a truck. She had only a moment to realize it was Christopher wrapped around her, rolling her on top of him as they hit the wet asphalt. The car screeched past them.

"You all right?" he asked as he disentangled from her.

She could only nod before he crawled out and jumped to his feet. She scrambled out behind him, feeling dazed. He was searching for the car, the muscles in his jaw and neck rigid with concentration. She looked, too, but the car was gone.

"Bastard," he muttered to the absent driver and turned his attention to her. He reached out and rubbed asphalt crumbles from her cheek while surveying her for injuries.

He knelt down, grabbed her cashmere hat and handed it to her, doing another scan of the lot.

She played the scene through her mind. What little she'd seen, anyway. She was shivering as she stared at where the car had been. It seemed unreal to her. But something *was* very real.

She turned to him. "You knew he was going to hit me, didn't you?"

"I didn't grab you for the fun of it." He rubbed the back of his neck and grimaced. "Did you happen to see the license plate?"

"No, but it was a beige sedan, late eighties, I'd guess. Did you see anything else?"

He took the hat she was scrunching in her hands and placed it on her head. "I was too busy trying to figure out where we were going to land. Come on, let's go inside and call the police. That guy needs to be taken off the road. And you should have someone look you over, make sure you're okay."

He guided her toward the entrance with his hand on her back. She fought the urge to move away, considering he'd likely saved her life. "How did you know he was coming at me? When I looked up, he was going fast but straight."

His expression darkened. "Call it a sixth sense."

Once they got to the lobby, Rita instructed one of the women behind the desk to call the police and ask for Detective Connard. Then Christopher insisted she be checked out by one of the emergency room doctors.

"You should be examined, too. You took a harder fall than I did." He'd pulled her on top of him so he'd taken the brunt of the fall. She needed to thank him, as soon as she got her bearings.

A doctor checked both of them over, though Rita had to insist Christopher remain for his examination. Her elbow was sore, and she suspected she'd have a nice bruise before long. He had a scrape on the back of his hand and fingers. His jacket and jeans had taken most of the scrapes. He let them clean the wound and put salve on it but not a bandage. By the time they were finished, Connard was waiting for them in the lobby. He was clearly surprised to see the two of them together, but she didn't give him a chance to ask.

She walked over to him. "Now you've *got* to investigate Brian's fall. Someone tried to run me down—again. I didn't see the driver, but it has to be the same person who came to Boston. Christopher was there, he can tell you what happened."

Connard's normally neutral expression was tainted with skepticism, but he turned to Christopher.

"I don't think it was intentional. The driver was probably stoned."

Rita's mouth dropped open. "What? How can you say that? You were there!"

He held up his hand as though to ward her off. "What I saw was a car veering toward you. I heard squealing tires as he took the corner too fast. I don't think he had control of the car."

"He drove right at me! Oh, this is ridiculous." She waved him away and faced Connard. "It was intentional, the same way the car hitting me in Boston was intentional."

"A car hit you in Boston?" Christopher asked.

She ignored him, which was much better than grabbing his coat and shaking sense into him. "Can't you see there's a pattern here?"

Connard said, "The officer I spoke with in Boston said he thought the driver was a teen who had stolen the vehicle for a joyride."

"Why would a joyrider purposely try to hit another car?" she asked.

"Why do joyriders shoot paint guns at pedestrians? Why do they run up on curbs and lay out people on the sidewalk? Drugs can make people do crazy things." He glanced at Christopher, and then pulled Rita a short distance away and spoke in a low, calming voice. "Brain injuries can make people do crazy things, too. Being in a coma could make a person paranoid, I bet. Maybe think that people are trying to kill her."

She had to rein in her anger. "I'm not crazy, and this has nothing to do with my being in a coma. Well, it does, but not because I'm brain damaged."

His hands were still on her shoulders. "Here's what I suggest: you get on your flight tomorrow and forget about New Orleans. Forget about that guy in the coma. Be safe."

She pulled out of his grasp. "Am I being paranoid when someone has tried to run me down twice in a six-week period of time?"

"I think you're just unlucky. We're talking two different states and two different types of accidents."

"Using a car as a weapon both times. I know you have to look at things objectively. That's your job. But you"—she turned to Christopher—"you were there, you saw what happened. Why can't you acknowledge that it was intentional?"

"I stopped seeing demons in every shadow a long time ago," he said, one of those shadows in his eyes.

Rita wanted to scream in her frustration. Since that would only contribute to Connard's view of her, and Christopher's as well, she simply stalked away. This time she kept a careful eye on what was going on around her as she made her way to her car. Once inside, she warmed up the engine and let the adrenaline and frustration drain from her body.

Was Christopher's denial a way of protecting someone? She had to admit, as much as she wanted to see him as a bad guy, that he had saved her life. She grimaced when she reached to put the car into gear. Her elbow ached.

"Breakfast," she said, heading out of the parking lot. She spotted a beige sedan in a spot near the exit that looked like the car that had tried to run her down. "It was on purpose," she said. She was sure that the driver wouldn't have left the car in the lot even if he had stolen it, so she continued on, keeping an eye on her rearview mirror . . . looking for evil in every shadow.

7

After breakfast, Rita felt the emotional effects of nearly dying and the physical effects of being tackled. She went back to her hotel room, promptly heaved up the three pancakes she'd managed to eat, and fell into a fitful, achy sleep for two hours. The images Brian had showed her saturated her sleep with feelings of fear. Finally, she dragged herself to full wakefulness, wrapped her wool coat around her, and found a cozy table down in the courtyard. The air was warming up some, and it helped to clear her head.

She had brought her cell phone and she called Officer Potter in Boston. When he got on the line, she asked him about the feather.

He paused, as though he wasn't sure he should tell her. Finally he said, "Yes, we found a black feather. And a red feather. And two painted macaroni noodles. Detective Connard told me what you're thinking, and I have to tell you, this feather doesn't mean anything. Not unless you can produce the mask it came from, prove who owns the mask, and that the person was in Boston at the time of your accident . . . you get the drift?"

Yeah, she got it. She thanked him for nothing and hung up. She might not have tangible proof, but that black feather was proof enough for her. She tucked her legs beneath her in the wrought-iron chair and tried to figure out what to do.

She kneaded her forehead, fighting off a headache. Her gaze drifted to room 315 where the woman had died in her sleep. Was that why she'd felt unsettled in the serenity of the beautiful courtyard?

It was everything, she decided. She wanted to call Marty and ask her advice. The problem was, she hadn't exactly told Marty she'd come here. She'd said she was taking a couple of days off and not taking her cell phone. She hadn't mentioned the trip at all to her mother, who was making a habit of calling once a week to check on her. She felt a prick of guilt that she hadn't initiated even one call and pushed those thoughts away.

"Tomorrow I go home. And I know nothing more than when I came, other than I'm not crazy. Brian did come to me and he didn't try to kill himself." How could she leave without getting someone to believe her, to check into it? To protect him?

She couldn't.

Turning away from conflict was her weakness. She had justified it all her life. The roots went back to her childhood, and any therapist worth his or her salt would advise her to face those issues first and then begin to face a big crisis. Had she taken her own advice, she'd be better prepared for this situation. But there wasn't time to backtrack now. Wasn't time to shore up her foundation.

She pulled the coat tighter and leaned her head back against the cushion, ignoring the throbbing ache in her elbow and the dull ache in the rest of her body. She needed more time, and she needed access to Brian's life. There was more to the man than what was on the surface.

That was true of Christopher, too. She couldn't trust him, but she was pretty sure he had nothing to do with the attempts on her life. Unfortunately, he was her only way into Brian's home. All she needed to do was get him to believe her.

She'd start by thanking him for saving her life.

Rita stared at the business card. The printed side hailed Christopher as owner of Web-Tekk, an Atlanta-based company that created and maintained Web sites . . . and did specialty information retrieval. Like tracking her down. And finding out where she worked. "Hmph."

She started the car, glanced at her map once more, and headed out. The address scrawled in his bold handwriting on the back was in the Garden District. Once she reached the area, she envisioned herself on a stage set of grand scale: plantation-style homes, cottages trimmed in latticework, a dull green streetcar moving between the two lanes of traffic, ornate iron fences, and . . . rooftops.

She took St. Charles Street east, wishing the serenity of the stately old homes would chase away her growing anxiety. *Run the other way!* the little girl inside her screamed. But her peace of mind wasn't at stake now. No, so much more rode on her being able to face this—and to face Christopher.

After two wrong turns, she stared at the pale yellow house with the deep porch along the entire front, the iron fence topped with uninviting spikes. Ornate columns supported the expanse of roof, and the porch itself was bordered with a low-spindled railing.

"Be brave like Amanda in *Buffy*." Of course, Buffy had special powers.

She stepped out of the car, hearing the crunch of cheap gold beads beneath her sensible pumps. The parades hadn't even started yet, but she'd already seen people wearing beads. A spicy scent wafted through the cool late-afternoon air, tweaking her trembling stomach.

A Mitsubishi Eclipse convertible was parked in front of the open gate, and the Georgia license plate further churned her stomach. He was there. Hard to picture him in this ornate home; she assumed it belonged to Brian. The white door was framed with sidelights and a fanlight, all shrouded in white curtains. She smoothed her hair, her pants, made sure her collar was turned down.

Gentle chimes resonated from inside, an incongruous prelude to the event of Christopher opening the door. She wondered if there'd ever been an *Unsolved Mysteries* episode like this, but didn't have time to ponder it as the door opened.

He filled the opening, not looking nearly as out of place as she'd imagined. She tried awfully hard not to notice the expanse of bare chest and the way it tapered down to narrow hips encased in a pair of white sweatpants. Or the six-inch fine scar that ran from his shoulder to his nipple. He didn't seem surprised to see her there, and that threw her off.

Instead, he merely stepped aside to let her pass. *Come into my parlor, said the spider to the fly.* The spicy scent she'd detected outside filled the house with a mouth-watering aroma. He closed the door behind her, but she avoided meeting those dark eyes for a moment. The walls were painted a cinnamon color, giving the room a cozy feel despite the tall ceilings. Not so cozy were the two gold swords with dragons' heads for handles on the wall to the left of the staircase. Their blades were crossed at the middle. Toward the back a winding staircase led up to a balcony and hallway. Next to the stairs an arched doorway led to other rooms.

"Coffee?"

"Thank you."

So he was going to play the polite host. It didn't fit, but neither did the faint rumblings inside that had nothing to do with her stomach and everything to do with the way his eyes assessed her. Nothing, of course, to do with the sway of his gait as he walked through the arched doorway. She focused on the room instead, because she didn't care for guys with bodies like that, or for guys who were so settled in their own skin, they didn't even think about it.

The furniture was antique in style, upscale, and too dainty for a man's abode. Too worn for museum quality, but beautiful nonetheless. Silver frames adorned a mantel, and she was about to inspect the photos when he returned with two mugs of coffee. He did have the decency to throw on a sweatshirt. Not that his bare flesh bothered her.

She accepted the large black mug with a polite smile and took his lead by sitting on the gold velvet couch. It didn't take a lot of deep self-analysis to understand why men like Christopher put her on edge. He had a moat around him, a "No Trespassing" aura stamped across his sharp, clean features. Even his short hair, spiky from a recent shower, said "Do Not Touch." Years ago she'd been too young, too desperate for affection, to see those signs, too naïve to think her own father would exhibit them. Now she recognized them clearly.

He sat across from her in a dainty gilt-edged chair, one bare foot on the cushion, leg bent up by his chest where he rested his arm. "You have my attention."

She could see that, thank you very much. If there was such a thing as lazy intensity, his eyes had it. He wasn't even trying, dammit, but he still intimidated her.

"I wanted to thank you for saving me today. And apologize for being so annoyed with you. You saw only what you saw. As you said, you were too busy looking for a good place to land." It was a subtle way of saying he'd just missed the obvious.

"And you were too busy seeing something that wasn't

there. Still, it was traumatic, so I can understand how you'd be confused."

Her fingers tightened on her mug as she held back her temper. "Regardless, I owe you a thank-you."

"Instead of that, why don't you tell me your story, Rita Brooks?"

Her story. What she'd come here for. She was so focused on what she was going to say, she didn't realize she'd slipped off her shoes and tucked her feet beneath her. "Brian and I have never physically met. I buy and sell things on eBay. I bought an unusual knife at a flea market and found out it was quite valuable. It was a Gil Hibben knife. Silent Shadow, a signed first production. I put it up for auction and Brian asked me some questions about it. We kinda clicked. I suppose you've read our e-mails."

"There were no e-mails other than the one you just sent him."

"They were erased?"

"Maybe he isn't a sentimental kind of guy."

She lifted the weight of her hair from her damp neck. "Oddly enough, all of Brian's e-mails to me are gone from my computer, too. When I got home from the hospital, my hard drive had crashed." She took a sip of coffee, moistening her throat, blinking at the strong, bitter flavor. He obviously wasn't used to being a host; he hadn't even offered her cream or sugar. She decided to make do, beginning with her accident and ending with, "I believe Brian found me to tell me someone tried to kill him. And that same person tried to kill me, too. For all I know, he or she will keep trying until they get it right. I'm not sure what Brian was involved in, but now *I'm* involved. And I figure I'd better damn well find out what it is."

He chewed his thumb and contemplated it the way Fox Mulder of *The X-Files* mulled over an unlikely clue. She should know; she'd worn out the first two seasons' DVDs. "And you thought I pushed him."

"I didn't know. I just asked the detective to check into it."

"But today you don't think I'm involved. Why?"

She decided not to mention how she had no one else to turn to. "Because you saved my life." When he continued to study her, she added, "I need your help. I can't leave New Orleans until I know what happened."

His foot dropped to the wood floor with a thud as he repositioned himself, leaning toward her. "Okay, now tell me the real story."

She let out an exasperated sigh, realizing she'd been on the edge of her seat. "What other motive could I possibly have to come here telling you what I just told you?"

He leaned back in the chair again, body lax, tapping his thumb against his lower lip. "I haven't figured that out yet. Look, fess up. You and Brian had something going on, you broke it off. He got mad, maybe you fought. He was devastated. You may not even have known just how broken up he was."

"Brian had no intention of taking his life. We had plans. Plans for the future."

"Maybe you and he had different plans."

"Fine." She stood, grabbing for her purse and realizing she'd left it in the car. "Fine," she repeated, covering her futile search. "I'll just continue looking on my own. Maybe you have secrets you don't want me to find."

He came to his feet, his mouth set.

My, but her mouth was getting her into trouble, and with Christopher blocking the way to the front door, too. Her heart stumbled as the facts mounted. She hadn't yet told anyone she was here. Joyce, her travel agent, didn't know why she'd come to New Orleans.

If she disappeared, no one would know.

And now he was advancing on her, his expression shadowed. She backed into the couch and then moved sideways knowing it didn't matter because there was no escape. Her calves cleared the couch, and she took two awkward, unbalanced steps back until she bumped against a wall. He stood in front of her, probably two hundred pounds of testosterone all bent out of shape because she was a loose-lipped idiot.

"I didn't—"

"Shut up."

She hated this power play, and this meek person she thought she'd whipped out of herself long ago. But here she was, brought fully to life by this muscular man who wasn't afraid to sit in a dainty chair and who was staring at her mouth as though ready to pounce on any word she dared speak.

"I don't want you to say anything unless it makes sense. The truth. No more of this crazy coma-connection nonsense."

He wasn't quite touching her, but if he inhaled deeply, his chest would press against hers. "Fine, I'll leave, then." She pushed him back and tried to step around him.

"Uh-uh."

Her mouth dropped open at his response, but he hardly gave her time to ponder it. He led her by the arm through the arched doorway where he'd gone to get the coffee, past a formal dining room, and into the kitchen. He sat her down in a chair at a small wooden table that overlooked a private courtyard. "You're not leaving until you tell me the truth."

"You can't keep me here. That's kidnapping."

"You came here, remember?"

She watched lamely as he ladled a cupful of soup from a large pot on the old-fashioned stove and set it in front of her, along with a spoon and a chunk of bread. He lifted the lid on a pot of white rice and put a dollop on top of the soup. The scrape on the back of his hand was still an angry red.

"What's this?" she asked.

"Gumbo. If I'm going to keep you here, I figure I'd better feed you."

She would have been more worried if he wasn't offering to take care of her at the same time as kidnapping her. He handed her the spoon. "Eat and talk."

This was crazy. She shifted her gaze to the autumn-gold fridge, salmon walls, floor tiles the color of mushrooms. His bare feet. Nice feet, for a guy.

He took the seat across from her and watched her. She looked down at the wide cup. Her stomach rumbled, not in the least concerned with her personal safety. Not bothered by the tiny red claw poking out of the thick, brown broth like a drowning . . .

"What is that?"

"Crawfish."

She realized he was enjoying her discomfort. He wore a snarky grin, more insidious than a smirk, not as friendly as a smile. She dipped her spoon, capturing several unidentifiable lumps, and gathering her bravado, put it in her mouth. It seemed to be a test, and she felt a strange sense of victory.

Until the fire in her mouth ignited. Her eyes watered, and she started fanning her open mouth and sucking in air. He had poisoned the gumbo! He got up and walked over to the refrigerator, while she stuffed a piece of bread in her mouth and gasped, "Water! Tonic!"

He furrowed his brows. "What's *watah*?" he asked, imitating her Boston accent. "And tonic? The stuff you put in your hair?"

"Wat*er*, for heaven's sake!"

He returned, dropping into the chair and pushing a bottle of Dixie Jazz Beer across the table toward her. "Don't have any cold watah."

"What did you put in here? Arsenic? Cyanide?"

"Cayenne."

As she gulped down the beer, her mind frantically went down the list of known poisons looking for a match to—"As in . . . pepper?"

"It's the lesser known of the popular methods of poisonin'."

He was so calm, so cocky, so damned sexy—she caught that thought before it could develop into anything more damaging. "You are an evil man."

He tilted his head. "That's what they say."

She reached for a napkin in the silver holder and blew her nose. Okay, she was fine. In control.

"It's not all that hot," he said with a shrug.

"No, not at all." Her voice sounded scratchy, thick.

He leaned back in his chair, arms crossed over his chest. "So, Rita Brooks, tell me why you're here."

She took another sip of beer and tried to downplay the scorching heat in her throat. "I told you. You don't believe me. We've come to an impasse." She started to cross her arms in front of her but stopped when her elbow protested. "Why do you think Brian jumped from the roof?" just as she'd tried to ask Tammy.

"That's what I'd come to you to find out." He got up and retrieved a Dixie Jazz for himself, returning to the chair across from her. He popped the cap and ran his thumb along the top edge. Finally, he looked up at her. "I lost touch with my older brother a long time ago. When I left, he was a man stuck on himself. He'd just turned twenty-one, had taken over the accounting department at the LaPorte, our family's hotel, drove a fancy sports car, dressed like a swinger, dated all the right girls, and plenty of them. He played the society game, schmoozed the prominent families. His biggest ambition at the time was to get invited into the krewe my father had founded."

She didn't want to hear this about Brian but she held her protest.

"Anyway, that's the Brian I knew, the Brian I'd always known. He was as see-through as chicken broth."

"I suppose you're gumbo, then," she found herself saying.

His voice grew as thick and Southern as that spicy broth when he said, "I'd rather be dark as a swamp and spicy as cayenne pepper than be chicken broth any old time."

"Okay, so Brian was chicken broth. There's nothing wrong with chicken broth, is there?"

He took on that snarky grin again. "If tha's what you like, *chérie*." She hated that grin. Even if it was kind of sexy. And she didn't like the way he was assessing her with those dark blue eyes, so casually, yet so thoroughly.

She averted her gaze, finding herself studying the gumbo in her mug. "Let's go back to the chicken broth." What she really wanted to do was explore the gumbo, find out why the gumbo left New Orleans behind, why he was the troublemaker, what he had done to Brian thirteen years ago.

"Brian's assistant Tammy called me in Atlanta and told me what had happened. The last time I was the dutiful son, I got stepped on. Guess I must be a glutton for punishment, 'cause here I am again. When I arrived and started asking around, I was baffled. You want to know why?" She nodded, too eagerly perhaps. "Because Mister Chicken Broth had turned into the murkiest gumbo I ever did see. Now, on the surface, he was still the broth. He dressed nice, went to work every day, was polite, everything you'd expect a proper Southern gentleman to be. But he stopped going to society functions. Stopped dating, or at least besides Tammy and the mysterious Rita Brooks, not one woman came out of the woodwork to visit or inquire about him. Nor did any man."

For a moment, she got caught up in the "mysterious Rita Brooks" comment. She took another sip of beer and refocused on Christopher's words.

"In fact," he said in a deliberate way that sounded like a TV-show detective, "Brian didn't have any friends at all. He didn't lunch with anyone, didn't call and chat. Didn't dine out, didn't dine at anyone's home, and didn't have anyone in here. Then one day out of the clear chicken broth, he threw himself off that deck up there."

Rita followed his nod, seeing a balcony along the upper floor, and above that, something like a large widow's walk on the roof.

"Not a high distance, to be sure, but combined with the deck below. . . ." He shook his head. "He seemed to have no enemies. There was no sign of a break-in, and the doors were locked. Because of his closed nature, the police deemed it an attempted suicide. Faced with this puzzle that my brother's life had become, I had only one clue." He pointed. "You."

"I want to know what happened, too. I care a great deal about Brian."

He lifted an eyebrow. "A great deal?"

"Yes."

"Any proclamations of love?"

I've grown quite fond of you, dear lady. Please allow me to send you a ticket so you may visit my lovely city. And so I may get to know you better. I think we have something special here. She pushed Brian's words from her mind. She wasn't able to tell Christopher how close she was to letting herself love him. "We were still getting to know each other."

"Phone sex? Lusty instant messages?"

"No, though it's none of your business."

"Sure it is. I'm trying to find out the truth."

"So am I. I know this sounds . . . unbelievable. I've tried to convince myself the gray place and the man who came up to me was in my imagination. But I'd never seen Brian. When you showed up, you looked like the man in the gray place. That's why I reacted so strongly. Seeing you meant this was real, that Brian had approached me and showed me scenes from his life, particularly the last thing he saw. You think I want this? I'm a therapist, for God's sake. I'm supposed to be in control of these things."

She went on, hoping he hadn't made much of that last part. "Your brother was pushed from that roof. I believe that with all of my heart. I saw it." She stood, trying to ignore the headiness accosting her. She'd only had one or three sips . . . she looked at the puddle of liquid so very near the bottom of the bottle. *Beer on an empty stomach. Great, Rita. Just great.*

He stood, too. Was he standing so close because he caught the slight sway in her stance?

"So you're sticking to that story?" he said.

She took a step away from him, trying to draw her focus from the broad expanse of sweatshirt. "Yes, I am. Now, are you with me on this or not?"

He scrubbed his fingers through his hair, making it stick out in the back. "You're plain out crazy, you know that?"

She met his gaze, and her stomach flip-flopped. She hadn't noticed that he'd taken another step closer, and she could smell, mixed in with the gumbo, his shampoo, or maybe it was his deodorant or, she didn't know, maybe she was crazy. "I suppose it would be easier for you to believe that. It would be for me, too. But I don't have a choice."

"Where you going?" he asked as she headed toward the front door.

"I'm going to see if I can find a place to stay for a few more nights. I have a room at the Ashbury for tonight and that's it."

"It's a week before Fat Tuesday."

"So?"

"Do you even have a clue about the significance of Carnival? Of the thousands of people who come here?"

"I'm sure I can find something. Maybe there's a cancellation. People get sick, change their minds. It happens."

"Sure it does. And the next person on the waiting list gets the room. Believe me, I know how it works."

"That's right; your family owns a hotel. Can't you get me a room?"

His laugh sounded dark and cynical. "I'd like to see you call them up and inform them that Christopher LaPorte insists they find you accommodations."

She remembered Tammy's opinion of Christopher and squashed that idea. So much for family pull. Then again, she understood too well how having family didn't guarantee you anything in life. She could get in touch with Tammy and give her some story about having to stay longer. Maybe she would take pity and find her a closet somewhere.

"Forget whatever it is you're thinking," he said, making her realize he'd been studying her. "Say you do find a place to stay. What exactly are you going to do?"

She saw the skepticism in his face. All right, she couldn't blame him. She needed to find something concrete to show him and the detective. "I'm going back to the hospital and talk to the staff, find out who visits Brian. Whoever did this is going to keep a close eye on him to make sure he doesn't wake up." She already knew Christopher wasn't going to be able to help much, since he'd been so out of touch with his brother. "If you think of anything, or anyone, who doesn't seem quite right, let me know. And I don't mean me!"

The corner of his mouth twitched. "Sure thing."

She handed him her business card. "My cell phone number is on there. Oh, there's something else you should know. Brian regretted telling you that no one wanted you at the funeral."

Her last words sank slowly into his mind. Brian wouldn't have told her about that. But he must have. Before he could ask, she opened the front door and walked to her car.

The lady was delusional. Maybe she'd fallen big-time for Brian and was having a hard time accepting that she hadn't seen his suicidal tendencies. After all, she was trained at reading people. She'd rather believe it was something else altogether. So let her sniff around and find nothing. Let her try to find a room, accept defeat, and fly home as scheduled.

He closed the door, but caught himself looking out the window as she headed out. As soon as she did, a black car pulled away from the curb and headed in the same direction. It was an old Buick with purple tinting that was peeling away. A thread of unease vibrated through his body, a reminder from long ago. Great, now she was infecting him with her paranoia. He closed the curtains and went back to work.

Once Rita found a close parking spot at the hospital, she sat in the car for thirty minutes talking to her travel agent. Every time Joyce thought she'd found something, it was either snapped up before she could book it or the wrong date.

"Sorry, Rita, but when you want last-minute Mardi

Gras reservations, you can't expect miracles. The closest I can get you is a room in Jackson, two hours away."

"Keep looking. That's too far."

"All right," Joyce said, sounding more than skeptical. "The other problem is your rental car. I'm having no better luck extending that or finding you another one."

"I'll see what I can do on my end. Thanks, Joyce. I know you're doing your best and I'm being totally unreasonable."

"Totally. But I appreciate your vote of confidence."

Rita rang off and opened her door—right into the black car that had pulled in soon after she had. She hadn't noticed how close the driver had parked. She slid out sideways and walked toward the front doors, keeping a careful eye on cars around her. Since it was busy, she doubted the masked one would try another stunt like yesterday's.

When she reached Brian's room, she was surprised to find a man sitting next to the bed talking to him—and holding his hand.

"We're fully booked, like always," he was saying. "Of course, it's harder than usual without you. Some of the regulars are starting to check in, and they're asking about you. We've decided on the party line that you simply had an accident." His soft voice lowered. "No need to tell them what really happened, isn't that right?"

What really happened. Did he mean the apparent attempted suicide or something else?

She ducked back out of the room and found a nurse. Luckily, not the strange one from her first visit, but an attractive woman named Sasha who was pinning her hair back as she exited the restroom. "Excuse me, hi, I'm a friend of Brian LaPorte's. Someone's in there with him now, so I thought I'd check with you to see how he's doing."

"Is Christopher here?" she asked, heading to Brian's doorway and peering in. She turned back to Rita. "I just came on duty, but I'm assuming he's still in stable condition."

"Do a lot of people visit him? I've met Tammy from the hotel, and of course, Christopher." She nodded toward the room. "I've never seen that guy before."

"I've never seen you here before, either," she stated instead of answering Rita's sly question.

"I live in Boston. I wasn't able to get here until now. It's good to know he has visitors," Rita tried again.

"He has a few regulars, and he's a favorite of the nurses, too. We're all rooting for him."

A few regulars. A favorite of the nurses. Could their enemy be a nurse or someone else working here at the hospital? The thought gave her a shiver. She took a closer look at Sasha, who had slipped away. Her blue eye color looked real, though there was no telling for sure. Strange that she hadn't asked Rita what her relationship was with Brian.

She spent a few minutes with the nurse in charge, checking on her earlier request that Brian be watched carefully. Unfortunately, without any proof, without police intervention, all she could obtain was a cursory assurance that all their patients were monitored.

That didn't completely assure her. After all, she'd been a stranger and no one had stopped her from visiting him. If she pressed that concern, they might question her now.

She returned to Brian's room and waited for the young man to say something either helpful or incriminating. He seemed content with just holding Brian's hand now, so she cleared her throat as she approached.

"How's he doing?" she asked congenially.

The man dropped Brian's hand as though it had suddenly burned him. His face flushed and he came to his feet. "Fine, I guess. Who are you?"

She gave him the abbreviated online-friendship story as she surveyed Brian. His blood pressure and heart rate were level, meaning that either he wasn't threatened by this person or he was in the gray place. She glanced at the man's hands, which were clasped and clenching nervously. "It's good that he has his friends to keep him company."

He was tall and lean, with blond hair that fell over the side of his face. A gold hoop glinted from both of his long, angular ears. He looked at Brian. "Yes. Well, I'm sort of a friend. I work with him at the hotel. I'm accounts payable."

She gave him a disarming smile. "That's a strange name."

He laughed, albeit a bit nervously, when he realized what she meant. "I'm Trent Kowalski."

She walked up to Brian and took his hand. "Hi, Brian. It's Rita. You there?" She glanced at the monitor, but everything remained the same. She turned to Trent, ready to push a bit. "It's good to hold his hand. I believe he can feel it, and we all need human contact."

Trent had tucked one hand between his elbow and his waist, obviously embarrassed at having been caught holding Brian's hand. "Yeah, that's what I heard."

She had a feeling it went a little deeper than that. Did Brian go both ways? That meant a spurned lover could include both men and women. Yikes. Instead of narrowing down suspects, she was increasing them. No, she couldn't believe her Brian was a bisexual.

You didn't really know him, Rita.

"Brian's absence must be making it very hard at this time of the year," she said.

"It's been crazy. He's a real hands-on manager. He's our inspiration."

How inspirational? she wanted to ask. "I'm sure he'd be proud of you, handling everything without him."

Instead of accepting the compliment, he said, "I'd better get back to the hotel." He didn't meet her eyes, only nodded as he left.

She settled into the chair he had vacated and contemplated Trent. He'd been nervous, embarrassed at being caught showing affection toward his boss. Brian obviously inspired feelings in his two employees. If she could get a room at the LaPorte, she might be able to talk further with Tammy and Trent, observe them. A shadow in the doorway caught her eye, and she spotted Sasha peering in. She turned and continued down the hallway, not looking entirely happy about Rita's presence. Rita was glad the hospital didn't limit visitors to immediate family. Probably because he had only one close relative.

It was Sasha who asked her to leave an hour later, citing that she needed to work on Brian's respiratory system. Rita used the restroom and glanced once more into Brian's room on the way to the elevator. Sasha wasn't in there. When Rita passed through the lobby, she saw Tammy lurking near a pay phone. At least she was pretty sure it was Tammy. The woman was wearing a dark red wig today, and she either didn't see Rita or was pretending not to.

"Tammy?" Rita asked.

She spun around, looking somewhat annoyed at being caught there. "Oh, you're still here."

"I almost didn't recognize you with"—she gestured at the wig—"the new hairstyle."

Tammy patted her hair self-consciously. "I felt in a red mood today. I have thinning hair," she seemed compelled to say. "So I make the best of it with different looks."

"Great way to deal with it," Rita said. "I had a patient who was undergoing chemotherapy. She cheered herself up by trying different looks, too."

"That's right, you're a shrink. Still poking around in Brian's psyche?"

"Actually, I've decided to stay a little longer. I don't suppose you would have a room avail—"

"Not a chance in hell, hell, hell," Tammy said, looking happy to supply the information. "You won't find anything for miles. A lot of the area communities have their own Mardi Gras celebrations. People book their rooms a year in advance, sometimes when they leave. If I were you, I'd give up that idea and head on home. Check on Brian from Boston. He has lots of people here to keep him company."

Rita ignored the advice to leave. "Yes, I met Trent Kowalski a while ago."

"Most of the long-term employees have been visiting Brian. The doctor told us to stimulate his brain."

"I understand even the nurses like him. Sasha seems protective of him."

"Too protective," Tammy said under her breath. "People love Brian. They always have." She glanced at her watch. "Speaking of, I only have a half hour to visit so I'd better go."

"Sasha's working with him. She just asked me to leave." Or maybe she was simply trying to get rid of Rita.

"I'll just go on up anyway, take a peek."

By the time Rita put on her coat and glanced back at the elevators, Tammy was gone. The elevators had never been that fast for her. She decided to get a cup of coffee from the cafeteria, and she checked her voice mail while waiting in line. Marty was looking for her. She knew her friend wouldn't understand her trip to New Orleans. Of course, she'd be concerned. Rita left a message for her and promised to check in again soon. She wasn't looking forward to fessing up, but it was time someone knew where she was.

Another message was from Tessa, one of her more interesting patients. Tessa had woken one morning convinced that her husband and two daughters were imposters. Though her problem was neurological in nature, and unfixable, Rita was helping her and her family try to reconnect. Rita found a quiet table and talked Tessa out of leaving her family because of her overwhelming guilt that she felt nothing for them emotionally. She wasn't going to give up on them yet.

Ten minutes later, she stepped into the cool late afternoon and, checking all around her, headed to her car. The black car was still parked next to hers. She peered through the crackled tinting on the windows to see if anyone was at the wheel. It was empty. She ended up sliding in sideways again, muttering the whole time. She headed into the Quarter to grab an early dinner. Then she'd spend the evening making calls to every hotel in the city.

It was nearly midnight when Christopher went out to buy a six-pack of Dixie Jazz beer. He wasn't out of beer; he had two more in the fridge. He hadn't even finished the one he'd opened an hour earlier. He told himself that since he planned on staying up most of the night working on a client's Web site he might want three beers. Except he never drank when he worked.

What he really couldn't understand was why he'd ended up in the Quarter, and why, particularly, he'd ended up driving past the Ashbury. He had no intention of stopping. She was probably asleep.

He had a better idea what had brought him there when he saw the black car with the bad tint job parked along the side street: that sixth sense he'd honed to an edge under the worst circumstances. Sure, it could be a different car than the one he'd seen outside Brian's house, but he didn't believe in coincidences. He pulled up behind the car. The license plate was missing, another sign of trouble. As soon as he opened his door, the black car's engine started, and it pulled away.

By the time he started his car and began to pursue, the car had disappeared. That uncomfortable feeling in his gut increased as he returned to the hotel. He woke the clerk and asked her to ring Rita's room.

A few minutes later, a sleepy-looking Rita shuffled into the lobby through a side door. Puzzlement creased her brow. Her brown, wavy hair was tousled, and a pillow crease marred her cheek. She had a little-girl quality that reached out and grabbed at him.

"Has something happened to Brian?" she asked before saying anything else.

He shook his head. "Can we talk somewhere?"

That obviously took her aback, as she blinked and scrubbed her fingers through her hair. "I, uh, well, I guess we could go out to the courtyard. What's this about?"

He merely nodded toward the door she'd come in through, and she preceded him out to the courtyard. She walked purposefully toward a grouping of chairs in a corner. She was wearing dark blue pajamas, he noticed, and her black wool coat over them. She'd thrown on loafers but not socks. She curled into one of the high-backed chairs and pulled her legs up so she could wrap her arms around them. The air was cold, but not biting.

"Did you find a room for after tonight?" he asked.

She raised her eyebrows. "Don't tell me you woke me up to ask me that . . . unless you've found something."

"Not a chance of that."

"No, I haven't found a room. What's going on, anyway?"

"Does that mean you're going home tomorrow as scheduled?"

That stubborn look returned to her face. "No. Why are you asking me all this in the middle of the night?"

"When you left Brian's house, a black Buick, an older model, pulled out right behind you. I don't know why I noticed it, but I did. Tonight I happened to be driving through this part of town. I thought I saw the same car parked across the street from this hotel. When I got out of my car, intending to see who the driver was, he took off. It was strange, and I never discount strange, even around here."

Her arms tightened around her legs. "Are you sure it was the same car?"

"Not sure, no. The one I saw had purple tinting, the kind that peels off after a while. I couldn't tell with the car I just saw, other than it did have tinted windows. Seen any cars like that?"

"I haven't really noticed . . . well, there was the one at the hospital that parked too close, but I can't imagine anyone would do that if they were. . . ." She dropped her arms and set her feet on the ground. "You think this car is following me?"

"Don't know."

"See, I'm unnerving whoever pushed Brian. Does this mean you're willing to consider I'm not crazy?"

He tried not to look too skeptical. "No. But with all your nosing around, you may have gotten the attention of someone who really is crazy. Maybe you ought to just take that flight on home before you get into trouble."

Her eyes narrowed. "Are you sure you're not fabricating this black car to scare me into leaving?"

He pinched the bridge of his nose. He should have expected this. "Positive."

She leaned forward now. "If someone is following me,

it means I'm getting close to them. They're keeping an eye on me." Her expression grew serious. "He or she wants me out of here. But if I leave now, Brian's would-be killer will go free. And he may just finish the job if Brian ever comes out of his coma. I can't take that chance. Can you?"

She wasn't going to go away. He had been afraid of that. She already thought someone had tried to kill her twice. Even warning her about the car wasn't going to scare her off. He got to his feet, his self-preservation instincts pushing him to get the hell out of there. "So what are you going to do if you can't find a room, which is likely?"

She shrugged. "I can sleep in the car."

She was even more stubborn than he'd given her credit for. "Yeah, that'd be safe, for sure. Just don't park in a parade zone, or they'll tow you away. Lock your doors real tight, too. A lot of people come here for Mardi Gras and don't have money for accommodations. They look for cars to sleep in. And be real sure that whoever it is you've got the attention of doesn't know where you're parked."

She shivered at those words, a sense of fear sinking into her expression. "Well, the car thing might not work out anyway. But I can't leave. Maybe my travel agent will produce a miracle. It could happen," she added at his skeptical look.

He got to his feet, irritated at her stubbornness. He'd wish her good luck and leave. He'd turn around, warn her to be careful, head out. Then forget about her. She wasn't his problem. He hadn't invited her here.

His feet wouldn't move, though. His mouth wouldn't form the word *adios*. He was going to regret this, he just knew it. But the words came out anyway. "If you don't think I'll snuff you in your sleep, you can stay at Brian's place."

For a moment she didn't answer. The surprise at his offer was evident. Then she pushed out the words, "I don't want to inconvenience you."

"You'll inconvenience me more if I'm thinking you're out there sleeping in your car."

"You don't strike me as the worrying type." She got to her feet, too, and jammed her hands into her coat pockets. "All right. Thank you, I'll stay. If I need to," she added.

"Call me if you don't get your miracle."

"If I need to," she said again, as though staying with him were the last resort. It was, of course. "But I'm not interested in your gumbo, got that?"

Rita was also painfully aware that she wasn't being entirely truthful. Something inside her did want some of that gumbo.

And she wasn't talking about the damned soup.

After he warned her to be careful, he watched her walk up the stairs and unlock her door. He waited until she was safely inside. She knew this because she peeked out the crack in the curtains and saw him leave only then. She was wide awake now. What was his motive for inviting her to stay with him? Clearly, he'd prefer that she leave town. She couldn't trust him. She couldn't forget that he'd driven by her hotel at midnight. And she doubted he'd just happened by.

8

Rita showed up on his doorstep late the next afternoon, a grateful, if sheepish, smile on her face. "Thanks. My travel agent is going to keep working to find me something, so hopefully I won't put you out for long."

Christopher wanted to snort at the idea of both her finding a room and not inconveniencing him. He contained it and stepped back so she could walk inside the house. He was sure she'd tried all day to find something, anything, else before calling him. He had hoped she'd come to her senses and decide to take her original flight home. Neither had gotten their wish. Her determination said something; he just wasn't sure what it was.

He realized he wasn't being a good host and took her bag. "Upstairs," he said, leading the way. "Did you visit Brian today?"

"Yes. No change. What do you think of the respiratory nurse, Sasha?"

He opened the door to the bedroom and set her bag on the bed. "She seems competent."

"But not very friendly."

"Maybe it's just you." When she looked at him in surprise at his bluntness, he added, "Maybe she doesn't like you nosing around asking a lot of questions."

She looked as though she were going to say something, but clamped her mouth shut instead. "I'd love a shower."

He opened the door that led to the bathroom and pulled a couple of towels out of the linen closet. "All yours."

He returned to the kitchen, the one place in this house that brought him familiar comfort. How many Saturday afternoons had he watched Rosie, their cook, make her famous Sunday gumbo? He was the only one in the family who had talked with her and not at her, and who was rewarded with her tales of her Creole childhood. And with her gumbo recipe.

He listened to the sound of the shower running and tried not to put a picture to it. The woman seemed to bring out the worst in him. Not that the worst was hard to find. He must be crazy for letting her stay. No, for outright insisting that she stay.

He caught himself smiling at the memory of her face when the heat from the gumbo lit her mouth on fire yesterday. His smile faded when he remembered pinning her against the wall in the parlor, wanting to light her mouth on fire himself. What was the deal with that, anyway?

Oh, yeah, to keep her off balance. Except that she was keeping him off balance. Was she involved in Brian's death? Obsessed with him? He'd been willing to write her off as crazy, but her determination had him wondering. He couldn't figure her out. But he would. If he couldn't charm it out of her, he'd resort to whatever tactics it took to get the truth.

Rita dried off and changed into a pair of casual pants and a long-sleeved shirt. Her room, like the rest of the house, had high ceilings and ornate scrollwork around the doors. The color of the walls reminded her of Dijon mustard. She hated Dijon mustard.

The old-fashioned furnishings reminded her of her college roommate's grandmother's house. Rita had tried to teach her father a lesson by making plans to spend Christmas with a friend. Good lesson. Her father had merely wished her well and sent the annual department-store gift certificate early. It was at her friend's home that Rita tasted real family life. How they laughed and lovingly nagged. The grandmother had hugged Rita as she prepared to leave. She'd never been hugged like that, a warm hug filled with affection. Unsolicited affection stunned her. Before she could stop herself, Rita had clung to the woman, fighting tears.

Her own grandmother was not plump and soft and draped in matronly clothing dotted with flour. Maura was sleek and seductive, like Lauren Bacall. The only affection she ever handed out was reserved exclusively for her son.

Rita packed her toiletries back into their assigned slots in her organizer and folded her clothes just so. *See, everything under control, as always.* She stared at her reflection in the large mirror over her dresser, wondering what Christopher saw when he looked at her.

She grimaced. Chicken broth.

French doors opened onto the balcony she'd seen from the kitchen, but she hadn't bothered to push aside the filmy fabric to peer out to the courtyard. Okay, *bothered* wasn't the right word. She didn't want to think about Brian splayed out on the concrete deck.

She swallowed hard, turning to her cell phone on the bed. She'd been putting off the call, but it was in her own interest to let someone know where she was. Just in case. Unfortunately, she had only one bar's worth of charge left. When she'd made her calls to the hotels, she'd discovered she hadn't brought her charger.

Marty answered the phone and without preamble asked, "Where have you been? You leave this vague message about needing some time alone, and *that's* not supposed to worry me?"

Rita couldn't help smiling at the motherly tone in Marty's voice, though she hated worrying her. "Guess where I am." It was in that same singsong voice that weird nurse had used.

"At Bill's?"

Rita grimaced. "Totally wrong. I'm in New Orleans."

"What?"

"Staying at Brian LaPorte's home."

"What?"

"With Christopher LaPorte."

"That's it! I want to see you in my office first thing."

"It's too late to talk me out of it. I'm here, it's done. I can't explain it, not even to myself. But I . . . I didn't tell you everything." Rita took a deep breath and described the gray place and the man who had approached her. "Now I know that the man I saw while I was in my coma is the Brian here at Mercy Hospital. I need to find something concrete so that these people will believe me. I swear, once I do that, I'll leave it to the police and come home."

"Rita, why are you doing all this for a man you never even met? Not only is this uncharacteristic of you, it could be dangerous."

"Because I'm the only one who *can* do this. Everyone else thinks I'm crazy."

"Ya think?"

"I'm not crazy. In fact, I feel more alive now than I have in years. This is something I need to do, for Brian and for myself. I can't walk away, not this time. You're the one who keeps telling me I need to face things and be more adventurous."

Marty let out a long exhale. "I can see there's no convincing you to come home now, this minute, on the next flight. I'm not sure I understand it, but I do understand your need to do this. Just be careful of him, you hear?"

"Christopher?" As if she had to ask. "I'll be on my guard." *Like you were when he backed you against the wall?* She shook away her conscience. "I'll be fine. I'll call you later."

She went down to the kitchen. On the table was a note, in that bold handwriting she recognized from Christopher's business card, saying that he'd gone out to get them something for dinner.

She wandered around the parlor taking in the objects that spoke of a long devotion to this party called Mardi Gras. A glass case was neatly arranged with origami invitations to masquerade balls, tiny jewel boxes, pins, purple and gold coins engraved with different years and insignias. In one enlarged photo a man sat high in his perch, wearing robes and a mask. A brass frame announced him as the king of Xanadu, 1972. That mask was sealed in the glass case. A gold coin set apart from the rest was engraved with a woman's face and beneath it, "Iris Deveraux, Queen of Rex, 1960." A glittering pair of gold shoes perched on a stand.

Atop the marble mantelpiece sat several family portraits. It didn't take an expert in psychology to see that Brian was the favored son, always standing closer to his parents than Christopher, who stood apart. Their parents usually had a hand on Brian's shoulder. Christopher usually looked either sad or indifferent.

So many women she had worked with over the years still dealt with the ravages of their parents' abuse and neglect. She felt the familiar anger engulf her, anger at the power parents wielded over their children's sense of self and value. In college her thesis had been a feasibility study of requiring parents to take a course in parenting. Not just on how to take care of babies, but how to love and nurture their children throughout their lives. She had published articles on the subject, as well.

"How much do you know about Brian's past?"

Christopher's voice startled her, making her whirl around and rushing the blood to her face. Was this being careful, letting him sneak up on her like this?

She caught her breath and tried to act calm. "He didn't say much about his childhood or his family. Only that his parents had passed on and sometimes he seemed worried that he was letting them down somehow. Come to think of it, whenever I asked if he had siblings he changed the subject." She looked back at the pictures, not able to meet Christopher's probing eyes.

"You said he regretted telling me no one wanted me at the funeral. How do you figure that?"

"I told you that when he touched me, I saw images of his life, like maybe what we see when our life flashes in front of our eyes. It's like a slideshow on hyperspeed. I was able to hold on to a couple of the images, and those images came with his feelings—what he was feeling at the time. I saw a funeral, heard words about the prodigal son returning. And I felt his regret."

He absorbed that for a moment. "What else did you see?"

Blood. A flash of a blade. Where did that fit in? "Someone wearing a mask rushing up to him at the end." Her voice dropped. "And he was afraid."

He seemed caught up in those last words for a moment. She could see in his eyes that he didn't believe—or didn't want to believe. "Dinner's ready." He walked to the kitchen and unwrapped two enormous round sandwiches.

Two Dixie Jazz beers thumped on the table as he set them down, and she wondered if he had anything else to drink besides beer. Tonic. Hmph. He could make fun of her accent with his?

She investigated her sandwich. "What is this thing, anyway?"

He took a big bite, talking around his food. "Looking for traces of cyanide?"

"Or cayenne."

His laugh was restrained. "It's a muffaletta." His accent thickened, as it did occasionally. "That's a big, round sandwich to you an' me." He leaned forward, and she tried to ignore the brush of his knees against hers beneath the table. "I'd stay away from those cherry-looking things. Hot stuff."

Hot stuff, indeed. She wanted to eat one of the peppers just to show him—no, to show herself. But she wasn't about to let him taunt her. He'd already gotten her with the gumbo.

She was getting hot just thinking about it.

So hot, in fact, that as soon as they finished dinner, she stepped through the door to the courtyard before thinking about Brian and the concrete deck. *Don't look there, don't picture it.* Still, her gaze went to the roof. The railing was only about three feet high, certainly not tall enough for current building codes. Not tall enough to keep Brian from going over. She forced her gaze back to ground level. Flowers bloomed here and there, though she could only identify the pansies. It seemed odd that New Orleans had an ordinary flower like that, as though it were some magical place different from any other.

The house was L-shaped, and the courtyard filled out the square. The air outside was cool, but the breeze didn't reach down into the courtyard. It rustled the tops of the tall trees that bordered the back of the property. The deck, made up of two-foot squares of concrete, was gray with dirt. Between those squares moss protruded like green grout.

"Get any vibes out here?"

She closed her eyes to his sarcastic voice for a second before turning to him. The dying afternoon light enhanced the angles of his face, making him look harsher.

"I don't get *vibes.* You think I'm some psychic melodramatic?"

Somehow she'd invited his scrutiny, because he took a long moment to assess her. "Don't know what you are."

But he knew who she was. "How did you find out where I worked?"

"You'd be surprised at what information is out there, for those who know how to find it."

To keep her gaze from straying to the roof deck, she wandered to the other side of the courtyard. She leaned against one of the sculpted white columns that supported the second-floor balcony. "You didn't answer my question."

"I know your driver's license number, your Social Security number, that you have two bank accounts at Boston National, that you just bought a 2003 Volvo S40 . . ." As he'd spoken, he'd walked closer to her. He stopped a foot away, and his voice lowered. "Don't look so shocked. I don't know all your secrets."

"What are you, some kind of hacker?"

"If I need to be." He moved closer still, and she wondered if he could hear the thumping of her heartbeat.

"What else do you know about me?" She felt the grooves of the column pressing into her back. Felt the heat emanating from his body, only inches from hers.

"I know you're afraid."

She met his eyes, could not look away from them.

Why couldn't he be fair and lighter, like Brian? Why did he have to look like . . . Christopher?

"I'm not afraid."

"But I don't know what you're afraid of," he continued as though she'd never contradicted him. "Losing Brian? The person you think tried to run you down? Me?"

She tried one of her old tricks: imagining him looking vulnerable in his underwear. Unfortunately, he didn't look vulnerable. He looked . . . sexy, sexy, sexy, she thought with Tammy's emphasis. It was better to imagine the boy in the pictures. Standing apart, always apart, his own island. She felt his hands slide up her arms, felt his fingers tighten on her skin.

"Are you afraid I might find out who you really are inside?"

No, he would never find that insecure girl who lurked inside her, the one who ached to know why she wasn't worthy of her parents' love. The woman who was still trying to patch up the holes in her self-esteem.

"I'm not afraid," she said.

"I don't believe you."

He had pinned her arms against the column, his body barely touching hers. Was he still that boy deep inside? He wasn't a hurting boy, he was a man. A large, muscular man who was arguing with her in a low, sensual voice that drugged her instincts.

"Tell me the truth, Rita."

The truth was, she needed to put some distance between them, tell him that she didn't appreciate his using this sexual intimidation. She did not like gumbo, she liked chicken broth. Her body, evidently, liked gumbo. Heat snaked up from where his hands touched her arms and swirled up to her neck and face.

"I told you everything."

Except that she'd never felt this hot, spicy heat that made her eyes heavy and her tongue tingle.

"I think you're holding something back."

What was he asking her? She'd forgotten what they were even talking about. Was he asking for her deepest secrets? Should she tell him about those dreams, how she woke in a hot sweat, her body throbbing and toes curled?

He opened his mouth to say something, but leaned forward and covered her mouth instead. The tip of his tongue against her lips electrified her, making her body stiffen, filling her chest with air. Her breasts pressed against the hardness of his chest, and he moved closer yet, so that their bodies touched more intimately. Her fingers stretched out but made no attempt to form fists to push him away. His mouth softened, and hers opened in some instinctual response she didn't know she even had. He deepened the kiss, and every stroke of his tongue sent warmth deeper into her body.

He'd drugged her. That had to be why she was kissing this man—and enjoying it, dammit. She even thought she heard music and could feel every stroke of the piano's keys. Were the words about fever?

Images sprang into her mind. Not a sensual feast, but an image of a younger, leaner Christopher brandishing a sword, aiming the tip at her, thrusting, parrying. Not his words, but Brian's taunting, biting voice . . . *Come on, is that all you got? You're getting pretty good for the loser . . . but you can never win, Christopher.*

She was seeing the scene through Brian's eyes. He danced in front of Christopher, feinting left and right. Every word stabbed Christopher, stiffening his body, reddening his face, until he lunged forward. Brian lost his footing and, instead of swinging to the right, stumbled to the left. Christopher's sword struck him. Brian screamed. *Blood. Rage.* The sword hit the ground with a thud.

"What the hell? You're bleeding."

Rita jerked out of the scene to discover Christopher had said those last words and was now staring at her with a mixture of concern and horror. She'd missed the tingling. He leaned forward and ran his thumb across her upper lip. She closed her eyes, not wanting to see the blood on his thumb, not wanting to think about what they'd been doing.

She pinched her nose as she ran into the house. How many times had she made this cowardly run?

She reached the bathroom that linked her room and the one at the end of the hall, leaning over the sink and washing away the blood. Catching her breath, she wiped her face with tissues and met the familiar, humiliated reflection facing her. But that expression was more than humbled; it was shocked.

What had she been *doing*? Her mind obligingly recalled the kiss, throwing in details such as the way his chest had felt against her breasts, soft against hard, how his hands had felt trailing over her body . . .

She shook her head. What was she *doing*? Had she gone mad for a few moments? And that scene with the swords and the blood. She sat down on the toilet. That hadn't been her imagination. It was one of the images Brian had shown her in the gray place.

After a few minutes, she dared to stand and look at her reflection. The bleeding had stopped, as it usually did once she removed herself from the threatening situation. Her lips looked fuller than usual. She ran her fingers through her mussed hair, pinched color into her cheeks, then told herself it didn't matter what she looked like. The reflection she saw in the mirror wasn't beautiful even when she tried.

Then why did he kiss you?

He was just trying to intimidate me, she told herself.

Exactly what kind of information do you think he intended to obtain with your mouth otherwise occupied?

With a sigh of exasperation, she flipped off the light and walked out.

Christopher sat at the wrought-iron table in the courtyard, his leg moving to the lounge music that drifted through the trees. He hated these situations, where he didn't know what to do. All right, kissing her was unexpected, and he shouldn't have done it. He hadn't meant to. After all, she was a woman his brother had feelings for. She'd looked into his eyes as though she were warring with herself, wanting him and hating him at the same time. He wanted to wipe out the hate part. He'd probably only strengthened it.

The nosebleed thing, that was weird. Just like at her office. Maybe she had anemia or some other medical condition. He'd followed her into the house, but let her go on. What was he supposed to do? He could remember from his younger days, guys would sometimes hold a girl's hair out of the way if she'd had too much to drink and started puking. Then she'd get all embarrassed because he'd seen her in that most unfeminine position. So what did a man do about a woman with a nosebleed?

Let her go, that's what, even if he had inadvertently caused it to happen. He'd turned on the courtyard lights, grabbed a Dixie Jazz, and settled back into the haze of soft lights and dancing shadows outside.

He liked evenings the best—here, Atlanta, anywhere—when the sun had just faded and trees cast their shadows across the lawn. He always took a few minutes to sit out on the porch of the fixer-upper he was crazy enough to buy in one of the suburban neighborhoods surrounding Atlanta. There was something satisfying about working with his hands.

He took a long swallow of beer. He'd forgotten Dixie Jazz. The music. And courtyards. He'd forgotten a lot about New Orleans. How quickly it all rushed back to engulf him. So did other memories. In his mind, he saw the bulky stone table and benches his mother had been so fond of. How the bloodstain wouldn't come out no matter how hard she'd tried to bleach it. And the look of hatred when she'd had to sell it, along with several other valuable pieces of furniture. Hatred aimed at him.

His mental gears shifted when he heard Rita walk out the kitchen door. He was facing away from the house, his foot anchored on the edge of the table. He felt awkwardness seize him as he wondered what he was supposed to do. Apologize? He hadn't meant to kiss her, but she sure as heck wasn't an unwilling participant.

She took a seat across the table from him, a safe distance away. Hell, he wasn't going to attack her. He wasn't even going to kiss her again. She had a hesitant look about her, her arms wrapped around her waist, staring at her feet propped on a lower rung of the table.

"I thought I was imagining the music," she said.

He nodded toward the corner of the property, the house next to the one behind Brian's. "Miss Velda Caprice plays it every night 'bout this time."

She glanced over at the trees that separated the two properties at the corner. "She must be nostalgic for the old days."

Dean Martin started singing, " 'Ain't that a kick in the head.' "

He realized she was picturing a sweet old lady. "For sure. Velda was one of the hottest strippers back in the nineteen-sixties. She moved in when I was a kid. Caused a bit of a stir with her reputation. She stripped well into her fifties. But she has to be in her eighties now. If that's even her. I'm just assuming because of the music." He shot her a sly grin. "Used to spy on her when I was a kid. She threw some outrageous parties."

Rita's mouth dropped open. "You're kidding. Aren't you?"

He took a swig of beer and chuckled. "Don't you know that New Orleans is the town of decadence, of sin and debauchery, of every sensual pleasure a man—or woman—can think of?"

He wondered what sensual pleasures she was thinking of when she glanced away. She ran her fingers through her chocolate-brown waves and tucked a bit behind her ear. He wondered how many men had done the same thing, mussed up her hair and made those light blue eyes go hazy.

"But the decadence only happens during Mardi Gras," she said.

"No, it just becomes mandatory during Mardi Gras. Amazing that it started out as a religious ceremony, isn't it?"

At her surprised look, he continued with safe talk. "I heard it was a spring festival to purify the soul. A goat was sacrificed and its skin was cut into strips. Those who wanted remission of their sins ran naked through the streets chased by painted priests who whipped them with the strips. The problem was, there were far more sinners than priests, so sinners were given the strips to whip one another with. You can probably imagine how the ceremony lost its religious aspects from there. The Romans had even more fun with it, dressing up as the opposite sex, hosting orgies." He was enjoying her appalled fascination. "Makes you long for the good old days, doesn't it?"

Her skin flushed pink across her wide cheekbones. "Er, no."

"Ever been to an orgy?"

"I played strip poker at a college party once, but we got busted halfway through." She fiddled with the edge of the table. "Have you?"

"Been to parties where clothes came off." He let his gaze drop to the full breasts she kept well hidden. "Dancing naked is one of the finer pleasures in life, for sure."

Her slender hand went to her throat. "Can we talk about something else?"

"Uncomfortable?"

"A bit."

He had to admire her honesty. "You pick the subject then."

"Okay. Did you ever stab Brian?"

That wasn't the question he was expecting. How dare he kiss her, what game was he playing, something like that. His tensed muscles probably gave him away, though he kept his face expressionless. "Why would you ask that?"

"It was one of those scenes I saw when Brian touched me, one of the scenes from his life. And it just picked . . . that moment to come out. When we were . . ." She could only wave toward the column where that soft body of hers had come alive against his. "You were fencing with him, a long time ago. He was taunting you, saying you could never win. You got mad, lunged forward, and stabbed him. That's when . . . my nose started bleeding." After a moment of silence, she asked, "Did it happen?"

He pinched his chin with his fingers, trying to figure out how she could have known. No one else had been at the practice session. Brian must have told her. "Yeah, it happened. It was an accident. I was mad, but it was an accident. The tip of the sword went into his shoulder. He spent a few days doped up on painkillers. Dad made sure no one found out about it. Wouldn't want to scandalize the family." He subconsciously brushed his fingers across his own scar.

She waited, perhaps for more explanation. "Why was he saying those things to you?"

"That's how we got riled up, how we got into the tableau." But why would Brian tell her about that? Especially since he hadn't told her he'd had a brother.

"What tableau?"

"Forget it. It was an accident, that's all." He pushed his chair onto its two rear legs and tilted back.

"It wasn't an accident," she said.

"Are you saying I did it on purpose?"

She waved away the tension she obviously saw in his face. "It was Brian's fault."

"What?"

"He lost his balance and stumbled in the wrong direction. I was thrusting too hard to pull back."

He had to reach for the table to keep from falling backward. No way could she know that. Brian wouldn't have told anyone that part. He had way too much pride to admit anyone had gotten the best of him, particularly his younger brother. If Brian didn't tell her . . . could her crazy story be true? No, he refused to believe it. Brian must have slipped and told her. "It was still my fault. I lost control."

She thought for a moment, tilting her square chin. Then she focused those eyes on him, light blue eyes full of understanding. "That's what drove you away, isn't it? And why Brian couldn't be king of the krewe, because he was injured."

"I suppose he told you about the king thing?"

"No, Tammy did. I met her at the hospital. She said no one knew why Brian couldn't be king, but that you left town afterward." Her voice went soft as marshmallows on a summer day. "If you want to talk about it . . ."

"If I need counseling, Doc, I'll give you a call."

She flinched at the hard tone of his voice. "Fine." After

finding the rounded tips of her nails interesting for a few minutes, she asked, "You lived here, in this house, when you were young?"

"Till I was seventeen."

She looked at him as though she knew some deep part of him. He didn't want anyone under his skin, especially not this crackpot who knew way too much.

Heavy gray clouds lumbered across the sky, obliterating the stars. Several minutes went by to the backdrop of Lou Rawls, then Nelson Riddle and his orchestra. The CD would start over again, just as it did every night he'd been out here. Three times Velda listened to it, doing what, he didn't want to speculate.

Her voice sliced through the night. "Why did you kiss me?"

She didn't look confrontational, merely curious. While she waited for an answer, Peggy Lee's "Fever" came on. The one they'd kissed through.

"Why does your nose bleed spontaneously?" he asked.

She narrowed her eyes at him, fully aware of his evasion tactics. He noticed how curly her eyelashes were, how thick her tapered eyebrows were. Great eyes, much too expressive. Then she looked toward the trees. He didn't know why he'd kissed her. She'd just plain out looked at him, met his eyes and hadn't backed down. She looked intriguing, washed in the shadows and light of the courtyard, set against the seductive beat of "Fever." He knew the heat of that particular kind of fever, and it ached in his belly. Just like a computer virus, it ate through his operating system, chewed up his logic processors.

He stood and stretched toward the muddy sky. "I'm going to have another bowl of gumbo." He rubbed his stomach, enjoying the disconcerted look on her face when he said, "I'm still hungry."

• • •

When Rita woke the next morning, it took her several disorienting moments to figure out where she was. For balance, she immersed herself in her morning routine and put everything back into its place in her bag. She was pleased to see the sun playing hide-and-seek through a thin layer of clouds. It amazed her what a little bit of sunshine could do to one's spirit. She drew it inside and readied herself to go downstairs.

Christopher wore blue jeans and an eggplant-colored polo shirt and was pouring himself a cup of that strong coffee. He merely lifted the pot toward her in offer, and she nodded in acceptance.

"What's different about this coffee? It's peppery, and bitter, like—"

"Poison. People sometimes think they're being poisoned." He lifted an eyebrow.

"Paranoid people maybe. But it's not poison," she clarified, just in case.

"It's got chicory in it, which comes from the root of the endive plant. There's no other coffee like it. I have a pound shipped to my place in Atlanta every month." He downed his cup and then set it in the sink. "I don't have much here in terms of breakfast food. We could get some beignets at a coffeehouse around the corner."

All he had to do was explain that beignets were New Orleans's version of a doughnut, and she was sold. She could always go for sugar-coated deep-fried dough with absolutely no nutritional value.

She'd been able to keep her rental car for another night, but the agency wanted her to bring it in that day. Then they would determine if she could keep it longer.

A slight older man was kneeling down among the multicolored flowers that flanked the stairs out front. His yellow cap covered straggly silver hair, which floated in the cool morning breeze as he nodded at her and Christopher.

"Hey, Henri," Christopher greeted the man, pronouncing it the French way, "Awn-ray."

Henri seemed overly curious about her, appraising her from behind sunglasses. When she looked his way just before she got into her car, he was still watching her. He didn't even glance away, only gave her a flat smile while he lopped off a blossom with his shears.

"The gardener, I presume," she said to Christopher, who had walked her to her car. Not a very good gardener apparently.

"I guess. He comes by for a couple of hours every Sunday, says he's been working for Brian for a few months. Didn't even want any money until Brian got out of the hospital." Christopher shrugged. "And here I thought old-fashioned generosity was dead."

She looked at him, at the hard lines of his face, and wondered if anyone had ever shown Christopher LaPorte generosity. When he realized she was studying him, he patted the roof of her car. "Follow me."

He waited until both cars had turned the corner and then chopped off another blossom, thinking of Rita Brooks. It didn't look like she was leaving anytime soon. In fact, it looked as though she had allied herself with Christopher LaPorte.

Allies, allies, always left out of the circle. . . .

The brother had been snooping around and asking questions from the beginning. He'd even asked Henri if Brian had shown any signs of distress. Distress. The sound of his laughter curled around his insides. Like Brian's terror when he fell to the concrete deck? He could only imagine the look on Brian's face. He wished he'd been there to see it. He hated Brian, hated all that he represented. All that he himself didn't possess.

Now that Christopher and Rita were allied, things were going to be trickier. He'd already made the mistake of hot-wiring a car and trying to run her down in Christopher's presence. Dumb desperation. He'd sure heard about that.

And Christopher had walked right up to his car last night, making him run like a coward.

I'm not a sissy! I'm the boy!

Christopher had gone to Rita's hotel room. After he'd left, she'd kept the light on all night. Now she was staying here in Brian's house. Again, where she didn't belong.

Anger boiled inside him. *No, no, breathe. Stay calm.* He would report all this to *her*. She would take care of everything. She always did.

9

Rita and Christopher settled at a tiny wrought-iron table at the coffeehouse. Watery morning sunlight washed across the Formica tabletop. The place was small, twelve tables in all.

The waitress brought them each a cup of the strong coffee with the peppery flavor. Rita found she was actually developing a taste for the stuff. Especially with cream and sugar mixed in.

She licked her spoon and caught him watching her. She had the sudden urge to run the tip of her tongue around the edge of the spoon. While giving him a sultry look, if that were possible. She put the spoon down beside her coffee. *Get real.* She'd probably seen it in a movie.

He picked up an abandoned newspaper and glanced through it. She allowed herself a breath of relief, an imaginary pat on her back. She'd done it, gone halfway across the country, faced the dark Christopher LaPorte with her crazy story . . . and survived. All right, she hadn't been brave the whole time, but she'd done a pretty good job overall. Here in this quaint coffeehouse in the company of a handful of strangers, she could feel like the lion at the end of *The Wizard of Oz.*

Amid the occasional clink of spoon against coffee mug

and a comment about a parade spoken between the people around them, she realized how normal she and Christopher must look. A couple having coffee together before starting their day. An odd sensation drifted through her at the thought.

She caught his gaze as she piled the empty packs of raw sugar on top of each other and swept the stray crystals onto her saucer. She also caught the slightest hint of amusement, though she couldn't figure out why. So she was neat. Perhaps a tad obsessively neat. Was that *amusing*?

The waitress brought a plate of beignets, and Rita shook off some of the powdered sugar on one before attempting a bite. It was hot and smelled like sweet flour and fresh oil. Heaven. She closed her eyes, savoring the way the dough melted in her mouth. She finished it and then licked the clumps of sugar off her fingers. He was watching her again, his mouth slightly parted. *He* had no trouble effecting that sultry look.

He reached over and ran his thumb across her mouth, making her jump. He showed her the white sugar on his thumb and then absently licked it off. Before she could react, he snapped the newspaper open. "The madness begins. First parade down our way starts tonight."

Madness was that move he'd just made on her. She took a deep breath and shook off the effects. "I never went to many parades."

"You get your fill of them here. Fifteen in downtown alone, plus all the truck krewes that finish up after Rex has done their thing. Twelve parades go near the house, creating a logjam of people and cars."

She was almost too busy imagining how nice it would be to have twelve parades at her doorstep every year to catch his lack of enthusiasm. "Come on, I'll bet you loved it when you were a kid."

"I was too busy getting ready for Xanadu's parade and the tableau."

"What was this tableau?" She remembered Brian's taunting voice: *You're getting pretty good for the loser . . . but you can never win, Christopher.*

He sat back in the chair and stretched out his legs. "Just a play."

From the shadow that moved across his face, that wasn't exactly true. "You and Brian were the main players, then? With your swords?"

"Yeah. Good against evil. Always the same theme, just different ways to present it. The parade would end up in one of the city's auditoriums, and those lucky enough to be invited watched the performance and then partied the night away." He took a long drink of coffee, and when she thought he was going to offer her more information, he asked instead, "When is your car due back?"

End of that discussion. "I've got a couple of hours," she mumbled around her second beignet. She wiped powdered sugar from her mouth before he could pull that mind-numbing, blood-slowing, thumb-across-her-mouth thing again. "I want to check on Brian first."

"Maybe you can resume whatever it was you two started online if he comes out." He stood and threw a few bills on the table. "It's on me. Ready?"

She swallowed the last of her coffee. "Yep. Uh, thanks."

"Follow me. I'll show you the fastest way to the hospital."

She grabbed up the last beignet and a napkin and followed him out. Did she want to continue what they'd started? A lot depended on Brian and who he'd be when he got out. Brian had been her only hope for a real relationship. Her heart ached at the possibility that she'd lost her one opportunity.

Fifteen minutes later, they walked into Brian's room. Christopher stared down at his brother without any expression. She couldn't help wondering about this enigma of a man standing next to her who obviously harbored years-deep layers of resentment toward his older brother, yet had come home to watch over him. Had flown to Boston looking for the reason behind his supposed suicide attempt. For all his bluster and hardness, deep inside he harbored a core of honor. And he wasn't exactly happy about it.

When she realized he still hadn't said anything to his brother, she stepped forward and whispered, "Hi, Brian. It's Rita. And Christopher." She settled against the bed and reached out to take his hand. It slowly began to warm beneath hers. "Look." She nodded toward the monitor. "He can hear us."

Christopher was staring at the change in the numbers. "That's what the nurse said."

"It's important to visit him often, keep talking to him, and never say anything negative around him. When I was in my coma . . . well, it meant a lot when someone spoke to me. It's the best way to bring him back." She smoothed Brian's hair, repeating, "It's going to be all right."

His hair was lighter than Christopher's, and longer. If—no, when—Brian recovered, would he tell her why he'd shut out everyone in his life? Everyone but her, it seemed. Would he tell her about the tableau he and Christopher acted out, the one in which Christopher always lost? She wondered how she'd feel about him. She had almost fallen in love with this man. She had hoped for a future with him.

She glanced up and found Christopher watching her hand pushing Brian's limp hair back from his face. He was so caught up in that action that he didn't even realize she was looking at him. And for a moment, she saw something in his eyes, something raw and tender, before he blinked and focused on the monitor again.

"I'll talk to him," was all he would commit to.

Was it jealousy she'd seen for that one moment? She realized her position now, a woman caught between two rival brothers. Wasn't that ironic when that woman was afraid of intimacy? She was drawn to them both, one by her experience in the coma, and the other . . . she didn't want to explore what drew her to a man who rattled her, who intimidated her, who had a darkness she could never penetrate. Probably a deeply veiled masochistic vein in her nature.

Sasha walked in. "Hi, Christopher."

"Sasha's his respiratory therapist," Christopher explained to Rita. "Sasha, this is Rita."

"We've met," Sasha said, a flat expression on her face.

"Do you need us to leave?" he asked her.

"You can stay. I've already done the suctioning part. I'm just giving him a little extra massage to loosen his chest." She bent Brian forward and tapped his back. She had strong-looking hands with knobby knuckles.

"Any changes?" he asked.

She looked at the monitor near the bed. "Nothing good and nothing bad. Blood pressure, intracranial pressure, and heart rate all look good and steady. Don't you want to wake up in time for Mardi Gras, Mr. LaPorte? Gonna be a good one, not too cold this year."

Rita asked, "There was another nurse here Thursday. She gave him a sponge bath. Her name was Aris Smith."

She continued to work on Brian. "I haven't heard of any Aris Smith. Could be one of the new girls."

"She had bright red hair. She was transferred from the AIDS floor, said she was a floater."

"We don't have an AIDS floor. We have a separate facility where all AIDS patients are treated."

Had she lied? "Can you check the roster for her?"

She looked at Christopher and then shrugged. "Sure."

When Sasha left, Rita glanced at Brian's monitor. The numbers were increasing. "What's wrong, Brian?" she asked. "Is it Aris? Or Sasha?" The numbers kept jumping. "He's afraid."

Christopher was studying them, too. "He's just responding to our voices."

Rita wasn't so sure.

Sasha returned a few minutes later. "Maybe you got the name wrong. There isn't any Aris Smith."

Dread curled through Rita's body. "How easy would it be for someone to put on a nurse's uniform and pretend to work here?"

"Usually not easy at all." The nurse furrowed her brow. "We've had a recent influx of new employees, and we've got extra help for Mardi Gras. Could be this Aris hasn't been added to the roster yet."

"But she lied about where she'd been working."

"Maybe you just heard her wrong," Sasha said. "Why are you so worried about her?"

He answered, "She thinks Brian's afraid of her. The monitor numbers jumped when her name was mentioned."

"It's probably just your voices."

"Can we get a guard posted at his door?" Rita asked as the nurse headed out of the room.

Sasha looked at Christopher. "Why? I thought he was a jumper."

"In case he didn't jump," Rita answered.

"You would have to arrange that with the police. And this time of year, I doubt you'd get much help, unless you have proof that he's in danger."

"Or we could hire our own, couldn't we?"

"You'd have to talk to our administrator, but I'm sure

it's possible. You can arrange to speak with him through the nurse's station. Excuse me."

Rita turned to Christopher. "There's no Aris Smith here."

Unfortunately, he looked as skeptical as he had when she'd told him her story. He tapped a finger against her temple. "Aris Smith sounds like something out of your imagination."

"Or someone else's imagination."

He crossed his arms over his chest. "You probably just misread her tag."

"I felt unsettled about the woman, and I didn't want to leave Brian alone with her. At the time, I thought it was overreaction. Not anymore." But that was hardly evidence enough to convince him that Brian was in danger. Not enough to convince anyone but herself.

"If she was dangerous, why didn't she do something when she had the chance?"

"Maybe she's hoping"—she glanced at Brian and lowered her voice—"that nature will take its course. I'll hire a guard." Even if it did dip into her dream-house fund. Brian's life was worth it. She found a payphone near the elevators and wrestled with the phone book. She located an agency with a large, impressive ad: Ironclad Security. After she dialed the number, Christopher took the phone from her.

"I'll handle this. He's my broth— Hello, I want to talk to someone about hiring a security guard."

He gave the specifics and got the agency's address to arrange payment in person. Even if he didn't believe her suspicions, she felt a mountain of relief. Brian would be safe.

"Tell them that the guards have to talk to Brian," she whispered as he wrapped up the call. When he gave her a questioning look, she took the phone. "Hi, I'm Brian's psychologist. There are a couple of things the guards need to know. Just because Brian is in a coma doesn't mean he can't hear what's going on around him. It's essential that the guard on duty talk to Brian as much as possible. It doesn't matter what he says. It can be about his family, his job, what's on television, anything. But it can't be negative, especially about his being a vegetable or other derogatory remarks. Got that?" She didn't hang up until she was sure the woman had a handle on the situation. Then she turned to Christopher. "If we're going to bring him back, we've got to stimulate him—I mean intellectually," she added at the surprised expression on his face. "That includes you, too."

"You're going to stimulate me?"

She choked. "No! You're going to stimulate your brother. Tell him what's going on in your life, in the city, anything. Can you clear the guard with the hospital? I doubt they'll listen to me. I'll wait with Brian until the guard arrives. Then I've got to go to the airport and try to sweet-talk them into letting me keep the car for another few days."

"Good luck," he said on a laugh. "Why don't you try licking your fingers? If it's a guy, you might have a chance."

She watched him walk to the nurses' station, her mouth hanging open. She turned to Brian. "Your brother . . ." She shook her head. "Was he always this impossible?" She let out a sigh and rubbed Brian's hand. "I want to understand you, and understand what happened between you two. When you come out, we've got a lot of talking to do." Would she tell him about the kiss? No, that was a fluke. She discovered she was running the tips of her fingers across her mouth. Guilt picked at her like a hungry buzzard. "We've hired a guard. I feel better knowing someone's keeping an eye on you. He or she will keep you company, too." She settled into the chair beside his bed. "He's supposed to be here in twenty minutes, and then I've got to go. But I'll be back. And so will Christopher."

Thirty minutes later Orville Dumas had reported in and been given the rundown on his duties. Rita wasn't sure she'd convinced him that Brian could hear what was going on around him, but the man had promised to talk. He was an older black man with five grandchildren and lots of experience telling stories. She felt safe leaving Brian in his case.

The airport was even more crowded with people dressed in Mardi Gras colors. One man with dreadlocks looped a set of purple beads over her head as she waited in line at the car rental counter.

"Happy Mardi Gras!" Then he added, "You looked like you needed some beads, *chérie*. Smile."

"Thank you." She fingered them as she continued to wait. The people working the counter were decked out in Mardi Gras finery too. She hoped they were in a festive mood, and therefore generous.

She asked for the shift manager and handed her the rental contract. "Hi, I'm supposed to be returning my car, but I'm extending my stay. The woman I spoke with said I had to turn in my car, but that I might be able to get another one. Is there a chance, a remote possibility—"

"So remote you have a better chance of catching the next shuttle to Mars." At Rita's crestfallen look, the young woman looked at the contract, punched in some keys at the terminal, and studied the screen. "The people who have your car next are already here. Sorry."

"Can't you just tell them you made a mistake? Things like that do happen, you know."

"I'm sorry, but I can't. I'll need your keys."

Rita didn't want to give up her independence. She held out the key tag, but her fingers tightened when the woman grabbed for it. They tugged for a few seconds, until Rita realized how ridiculous it was. She imagined beefy security men wrestling her to the floor, cuffing her . . . She let go.

"There are plenty of taxis around," the woman said, visibly relieved the mini-struggle was over.

Rita fought the crowds at the curb, finding people five deep waiting for a taxi. They all looked in a big hurry to get somewhere. Then she glanced across the lanes and saw him. Her heart leapt involuntarily at the sight of Christopher leaning against the green Eclipse, his arms crossed over his chest in a casual pose as he looked at her. At first she wondered what other business he might have there. She was the reason, had to be.

He didn't move until she came to a stop in front of him. "No luck?"

"Not a smidgen." She took a quick breath. "You came . . . for me?"

"Call me crazy."

He opened the door for her. She slipped inside without responding. She wanted to ask why but didn't press her luck. He got in and started the car, maneuvering into the flow of traffic as a Rolling Stones song blared from the radio.

"Thank you," she yelled over the music.

"What?"

She turned down the volume. "Thank you."

"No problem, *chérie*."

She watched the way he handled the sports car, the smooth way he shifted gears. She liked the way he drove, with casual dexterity, without showing a bit of agitation when someone cut him off. She was not that patient.

"What does that mean? *Chérie?* Some guy called me that at the airport."

"Who did?"

She was surprised by the sharpness of his voice. "Just a guy. He gave me these beads."

"Be careful about talking to anyone around here."

"Like I struck up a friendly conversation and invited him to dinner."

He shot her a look to make sure she wasn't serious. If she didn't know better, she'd think he was being protective. She probably didn't know better.

"So, what does it mean?" she asked. "You called me that, too."

"Something like *dawlin'*. It's a casual endearment, doesn't mean anything." He focused on the traffic again. "I thought I'd gotten rid of all that New Orleans slang. Soon as I came back, so did it."

He looked slightly annoyed at that, and she found herself wanting to tell him that she liked the Southern honey in his voice. Luckily, she got hold of herself.

"New Orleans seems like another world with all its customs, parades and costumes."

"It is another world. After growing up here, I thought Atlanta seemed like a foreign place. People in suits and sneakers all hurrying, all the high-tech companies looking toward the future. Here in New Orleans, people like to stay in the past. Some of the old-line krewes have been around for over a hundred years."

"Sounds nice, all that tradition, history."

"Only if you're one of the few, the proud, the secretive."

"Secretive?"

"The most prestigious old-line krewes, like Proteus and Comus, keep their members secret. It can be a big secret society, and if you're not born into the right family, you can't join. In fact, you can't join unless they decide to invite you in. It's their way of keeping aristocracy alive and kicking. Or at least that's the way they used to be. We knew families who were in a Mardi Gras state of mind all year long; it's all they lived for."

It did sound like another world. Although he kept his words neutral, she detected an underlying current.

"And you think it's all so much hogwash," she said.

"Yep."

She waited a moment before saying, "Ah, I see. You're only willing to talk if it's not about you personally."

"Why do you want to know about me?"

He had her there. "I want to know your opinion, that's all."

"My opinion," he said after he'd reached the highway, "is that it's all a bunch of hogwash."

"What a surprise. But your family was involved in a krewe. Your dad was president, or captain, if I recall correctly. You grew up in all that hogwash."

"Not by choice."

"So it shouldn't bother you to tell me why you think it's hogwash."

He shot her an antagonized look. "I just didn't get into all the pomp and circumstance. My mother was old-line New Orleans. She was born into one of the right families, and she went from being the flower girl to the maid and finally the queen of Rex, the highest honor a woman can achieve."

"Oh, yeah, I saw the medallions. And the shoes. She obviously thought a lot of her mementos."

"That was the most important event in her life. When you're king or queen of Rex, you're the royalty of Carnival itself. She talked about it till the day she died. My father, he was nouveau riche, which didn't count among the old-line krewes. He hated that he couldn't join Rex or Comus, even married to a former queen. He was gauche enough to ask to join Rex. They'll blackball you for that alone. And they, along with my mother's family, did.

They didn't want anything to do with their embarrassing relatives.

"So Dad formed his own krewe—the krewe of Xanadu. Then he decided who could play and who couldn't." He glanced over at her. "Is it starting to sound a little like kindergarten to you yet?"

"Obviously Brian was into the whole thing," she said. "Tammy made it seem like it was some tragedy that he couldn't be king."

He shook his head. "Armageddon."

"And they were mad at you," she said, trying to steer it back to him.

"It wasn't the worst thing I'd done." He pulled up to Brian's house.

She inhaled softly. "And what was that?"

"Why are we talking about me again? I thought you were here to help Brian."

"What did you do that was worse?" After all, stabbing a man, even accidentally, wasn't on the list of kindergarten assaults. "Tell me."

"I was born." He got out of the car and walked to the house and left her to ponder that.

The house was quiet when she walked in a few minutes later. There was no sign of him. She felt like apologizing, but how would she word it? *Sorry for making you bare some part of your soul*?

He'd opened his family home to her, even picked her up at the airport, and she'd poked at old wounds. For all his bluster, though, he was a man who needed some understanding. She wished she could give it to him, but his walls were too high. She found herself absently rubbing her nose. As if she, of all people, should even be *thinking* about it.

She walked up to her room and called Joyce. Still no hotel room to be found. She looked at the battery symbol on the phone. The last bar was fading. Outside her room, she heard Christopher's voice coming from the room down the hall from hers. He was discussing bandwidth with someone.

She stopped at the top of the stairs and looked over at what must be Brian's bedroom doors. Surely he wouldn't mind if she checked it out. Maybe she'd find some clue, something concrete to convince Christopher his brother was in danger.

The room was long, with French doors leading out to the same balcony outside her room. When she flipped on the light, she was surprised to find it a mess. Sheets and blankets were piled on the bed. Books and papers cluttered the desk, spilling onto the black carpet. *Black carpet?* Between the carpet, dim lighting, and curtains over the French doors, the room reminded her of a lounge.

She shook her head as she inched farther in. The walls were salmon-colored with dark yellow trim. The border around the ceiling looked hand-painted, a cityscape perhaps. Dragons and other mysterious creatures peered from paperbacks crammed on the bookshelf. She fingered the boxed set of the *Chronicles of Narnia*, remembering the tales from childhood. She vaguely recalled Thomas More's *Utopia* from her college reading days. She straightened the books and put order to the chaos of paper.

On the wall hung a sword, gleaming in the dull light, with an intricate gold hilt. Surrounding that in box frames were several knives that looked straight out of *Star Trek*, most made by Gil Hibben. The one that wasn't a Hibben was just as strange, a primitive, wavy-bladed knife labeled "West African Exorcism Dagger." She spotted the Silent Shadow in a place of honor, at the top of the arrangement. The knife had two rings for fingers and a rope pattern on the handle. A brass plaque proclaimed its name and maker. Strange that a knife had brought them together and then brought her here.

He had his own shrine to Mardi Gras, including pictures from a masquerade ball—"Brian LaPorte, King of Xanadu," a section from the society page read beneath a photo. King of Xanadu. . . .

She'd seen the swordfight. Maybe there were other scenes that would help. Maybe she could see the final scene better. She called up the slideshow again and let it flow through her mind. The sword, the blood, the funeral. She braced herself for the final scene, the sense of overwhelming fear. This time she heard something else, a sound, a word. She held on to it. *Sira.* It swamped her with the force of a flash fire. Who or what was Sira?

She searched the pictures and invitations on the wall around his desk. A conspicuous blank area caught her attention. Two pieces of tape were affixed to the paint, and she could see where something made of paper had once been attached. She searched everywhere, even the garbage can, but found nothing to match the shards of sketch paper still attached to the tape.

Her search gained momentum. Sira was her first clue. There had to be something here to tell her what it meant. She found a pocket calendar in the top drawer and flipped through the pages. Okay, maybe she'd hoped for a notation of a meeting with someone named Sira. That happened on detective shows, that vital clue that led to another and then another.

No such clue hinted at revelation. Every month he had an appointment at Hair and Now, even for the Saturday after he'd fallen. He'd made note of an upcoming auction the following week, a deceased New Orleans collector. And he'd made note of all the parades, or at least that's what she guessed *Pegasus, Tucks, Thoth, Zulu,* and *Rex* were.

One thing was undeniable: This was not the appointment book of a man who'd planned to take his life.

She found three science fiction magazines in the bottom drawer with colorful illustrations on the covers and short stories inside. In each one a story by Brian Caspian was flagged. She set those aside and pulled out a scrapbook, another testimony to Brian's dedication to Mardi Gras and Xanadu. She looked for something about Sira, but found all kinds of mythical and Egyptian names instead. Was Sira a krewe? If so, it wasn't a well-known one.

One picture showed both LaPorte boys, about eight years old, dressed in tuxedos and flanking the current king of Xanadu. Brian beamed; Christopher scowled. She found more pages from newspapers over the years, giving details about the Xanadu parade and subsequent party. Most of their themes did seem to be about good and evil.

She lowered herself to the chair as she read about the tableaux Xanadu put on. Each year it kept the theme of the parade, going all the way back to when the brothers were boys. Each year Brian and Christopher had the leading roles, dressing up in costumes and brandishing swords or other kinds of weapons. And each year, Christopher was the bad prince.

What had he done to deserve that repeated role? *I was born.* The memory of those words made her shiver. She put the book away and continued her search, but came up empty. With a sigh, she took the appointment book down the hall to the last bedroom on the right.

The door was partially open, and she could hear Christopher's fingers moving over the keys of his laptop computer. She meant to knock, really she did. But like that moment in the hospital when she could not make herself heed the rules of protocol, she pushed open the door and stepped inside. His room was a vivid blue, like the sky on a bright summer day. And the bed . . . wow. Even unmade, it was spectacular. A four-poster with a spindle on top of each post, the foot- and headboards looking like the ornate iron gate out front. Except it wasn't uninviting.

His back was to her. She felt an overwhelming urge to come up behind him, put her arms around those broad shoulders and tell him that she understood, that she had been the outcast child, too.

Her goal was to show him the appointment book, make him believe that Brian had no intention of killing himself. But she found herself standing right behind him, breathing in the faint scent of aftershave and grape gum, wanting to touch the place where his dark hair tapered to his neck. She forced herself to look away to the computer screen where he was writing an e-mail to someone. The subject read: "I'll Be Watching You . . ." Christopher's ID was "The Highwayman."

He heard the breath she sucked in and turned to find her standing there with uncertainty in her eyes. She backed away, holding out the appointment book like a shield.

"What are you doing, sneaking around?" He sent the transmission he'd been working on, disconnected, and closed the laptop. "Don't they teach you manners in Bah-ston?"

She moved closer to the door. Maybe she didn't understand him all that well. Maybe his role *had* turned him into the bad prince. "I . . . I wanted to show you this. It's his appointment book. Proof that Brian had no intention of taking his life. Look." She opened it to the appointments and the parade schedules. "Why would he make a hair appointment if he'd planned to kill himself? Why would he care about parade schedules? And I told you, we were talking about meeting. He was looking into the future, planning his life—not his death."

He didn't look at the entries. "Maybe he didn't plan on

doing himself. Some people probably just up and decide, or maybe something upset him and he couldn't take it anymore."

"Brian was a planner. He would have planned out the details, taken care of loose ends. And men use methods that ensure their deaths, like a gun. Jumping from a roof isn't a man's way to commit suicide, particularly one that close to the ground. It doesn't make sense. What if someone did push him off that deck? You're not willing to accept that because then you'd have to reexamine your roles. You'd have to accept that maybe Brian wasn't the good prince after all, which might mean you're not the bad prince, either. Isn't that right?"

His expression hardened. "How did you know about that?"

"He has a scrapbook in his office with articles about the tableaux."

He took a step closer. "You don't know me. You don't know Brian, either. If you want to investigate this presumed attempted murder based on something my brother told you while you were in a coma together, then go ahead. Don't expect me to buy your story. And butt your little therapist nose out of my business."

He walked past her and downstairs. She couldn't move for a moment. She glanced at the laptop, now closed. He was right. She didn't know him. Maybe she had been fooling herself. Maybe she didn't want to understand him, and at the moment, she definitely did not want to touch him.

And maybe she should be a little afraid of him. Just in case.

10

Rita stayed in her room studying Brian's appointment book and photo albums. She heard Christopher go into the bathroom they both shared and start the shower. Her gaze kept wandering to the white door that separated her from a roomful of steam and male, and "Fever" drifted through her mind.

Dammit, why couldn't the guy have been ugly? And short. Twig-thin, potbellied, whatever. She rested her chin on the top edge of the photo album, closed her eyes, and lost herself in the image of the steam curling under the door and floating across the floor like long, sensuous fingers. Those fingers climbed over the edge of the bed and across the tufted bedspread. She could almost feel the weight of the steam as it formed into a sleek, muscular body poised above her, pressing her down into the soft mattress. She let herself sink deeper into the fantasy, feeling his mouth on hers, his hands on her . . .

She looked at his face and saw Christopher.

"Oh, geez!" She jerked upright to see evanescent steam creeping from beneath the bathroom door. The water made a slurping sound as it drained. The light flicked off. She sat and listened to the faint noises in his room and then his footsteps in the hall. She stiffened in anticipation of his knock on her door and chided herself as his footfalls led down the stairs.

"Get a grip," she muttered, ignoring the rumble in her tummy. Damn. She hated being human.

She shoved herself off the bed, tugged a brush through her hair, and stared at her reflection. She wished she were prettier. She was okay, at midpoint on that stupid scale of one to ten. Nice skin. Thick hair. She aligned the brush next to her bottle of moisturizer and walked out.

The parlor was dim and deserted as she came down the stairs, the dying sunlight barely penetrating the sheer curtains. The smell of shrimp and spices filled the house, just as it had the day before.

His voice floated from the kitchen, as warm and spicy as whatever he was making. "I appreciate your checking on my place. No, I doubt anyone would think of breaking in; it looks like a renovation project. Do me a favor, though, and pick up a bag of cat food and fill the container. Make sure the water dishes are full. Have you seen them? Yeah?" He chuckled, and the sound tickled right to the bottom of her stomach.

She caught herself smiling and rolled her eyes. She was once again eavesdropping on him. Instead of lingering this time, she walked into the kitchen. The room was warm, both in temperature and light. He balanced a corded phone between his ear and shoulder, stirring something in a Dutch oven and looking way too good in a pair of black jeans and a deep red shirt.

"All five of them still there?" Another chuckle as the person on the other end perhaps related a funny story. "That's why I call the little stinker Megabyte. He likes to bite ankles. Sure you don't want one, Scott?" His smile disappeared when he saw her. "All right, thanks for checking on things. I owe you, buddy. See you later."

The bad prince was taking care of kittens? She tried to look casual as she walked up to where he was stirring a liquid concoction, but her arms didn't feel right no matter how she positioned them. She peered into the pot and said, "You have kittens?"

He followed her gaze. "Kittens are too bony."

"Christopher! I didn't mean kittens in whatever it is you're making! Augh!"

He had the tip of one hand stuffed in a front pocket as he leaned against the stove and stirred with the other.

"You don't really cook cats, do you?" she asked when he didn't clarify. "I know New Orleans is a different kind of place, and they practice voodoo, but—"

"Don't worry, dawlin'. Shrimp are the only creatures in my jambalaya."

She wrinkled her nose and recrossed her arms in front of her. "That sounds appetizing." Ugh.

"You can always order a pizza. But in case you're tempted, I didn't put a lot of hot spices in it. Try it." He held out a wooden spoon filled with a mixture of rice, a sliver of green pepper, and a chunk of chicken in a thick gravy; the warm tip pressed against her lips. She made the mistake of looking into his eyes and then forgot to open her mouth so he could slide the spoon in.

"You can swallow now."

She obeyed, feeling even more awkward. What were they doing here? He'd just told her to butt out of his business and now he was spoon-feeding her. She was getting lost in the murky gumbo of him, tantalized by his spices and the way he made her hungry, fearful of what she might find in the depths of his soul. She was here for Brian, because he was the man who would open her heart. Christopher was just trouble, plain and simple.

She smacked her lips together, evaluating the aftertaste. "Not bad. Do you cook like this at home?"

He chuckled. "I'm a Swanson gourmet, for sure. Being back here put me in the mood for New Orleans staples."

"You live alone?" She didn't want to know if he lived with a woman. Really, it didn't matter.

"Yep. Bought a place in Virginia Highlands, an old house I'm renovating. No one else would want to live there."

There was her warning, if she cared to notice. She focused on something safer. "You have kittens?"

"They're not mine. They just showed up one day and made my front porch their home."

She didn't want to imagine him sitting on an old-fashioned porch with kittens climbing all over him, but she did anyway. She didn't want to imagine there was some soft part of him that cared about a litter of homeless kittens. "Don't you know that if you feed strays they never leave?" she added with a grin.

"Is that so?" He nodded to the jambalaya and then looked at her.

"I'm not a stray, and I only plan to stay a short time. Have you named the kittens?"

"Only to tell them apart. Megabyte, CPU, SCSI, Gigabyte, and Dongle. I'm trying to find homes for them, but I hadn't gotten around to putting an ad in the paper before I got the call from Tammy. So, up for the challenge or is it going to be pizza?"

She was a coward in too many areas of her life. "Feed me."

After dinner, Christopher walked out to the courtyard. He needed some cool, fresh air. Rita Brooks had a way about her, a way that brought out his worst and best sides.

He hadn't invited her to join him. That kind of pleasantry didn't come naturally to him; he was used to being by himself. Mostly, he didn't want a repeat performance of the night before. Didn't want to hear her say his name again, the way her accent lifted at the end—*Christaphah.* Or notice her mouth as she did so. Didn't want to kiss his brother's girl.

Velda's music was nearly drowned out by the Pegasus parade. He'd forgotten the sounds of the marching bands and the crowd begging for beads.

Rita ventured out on her own, her head tilted up as she too heard the noise. "The parade." Her mouth curved into a soft smile. "It would be neat to live so near the parade route."

He took a sip of his beer. "Yeah, real . . . neat."

She wrinkled her nose at him. The gesture made his stomach quiver.

"I would have loved to look forward to that every year." Her voice was wistful. As though she'd had little to look forward to. When she turned those blue eyes on him, he could see empathy. She lowered herself into the chair across from him, her hands atop one another on the table. "Tell me why you said what you said earlier. About being born."

"Don't put me on your couch. I'm not going to spill my guts. I can't complain about my childhood, not compared to what some people endured. I lived in a nice house, had new clothes, got into my fair share of trouble." He couldn't help but glance up at the steep pitch of roof behind him. "Does anyone have a perfect childhood?"

"No," she said on a long breath. "But having clothes and a roof over your head doesn't equal a good childhood. Some of those children are poorer than the ones who live in the slums and get love."

She knew. He could see it in her eyes, hear it in her voice. She had felt the same aches he had, suffered the same loneliness. That's what he saw in her eyes—a kindred soul. He felt the unfamiliar urge to embrace the darkness they shared. He fought it.

Maybe he ought to remind her that she was uncomfortable around him. It didn't take much to get him out of his chair, he thought with disgust. Any excuse to walk close to her.

She watched him approach, and her arms automatically crossed in front of her. Yet she steeled herself, facing him with both wariness and determination in her eyes. "I'm not going to let you intimidate me into leaving," she stated even as she swallowed hard when he crouched into her zone. "If that's what you're trying to do."

"Tell me why it's so important that you stay."

"Because . . ." Her eyes were locked to his, and he realized that she was more beautiful than he'd given her credit for: wide cheekbones, glossy eyebrows, thick, wavy hair that would wind around a man's fingers just so.

"Do I make you nervous?" he asked.

"Yes, especially when you look at me like you're doing now."

He admired her honesty. "And how is that?"

"Like you want to eat me."

He kept his expression perfectly neutral. "Maybe I do."

"See, that's just it. I don't know how to act around you. I don't know if I can trust you."

"You can't trust me." She blinked at his honesty. "You can't analyze me and you can't fix me either."

"You don't know that."

He'd expected her to deny that she wanted to fix him. "I thought you were here to help Brian."

"I . . . I am. But . . ." Her gaze drifted to his mouth, then quickly back to his eyes.

"Rita . . ." Her name sounded right on his tongue, the same way her mouth had felt right moving against his. "I don't need help. I'll tell you what some of my clients tell me. I don't want an upgrade. No new software or hardware. I like my system just the way it is. I've gotten way past whatever my childhood lacked, so stop looking at me with soft, mushy eyes." He didn't like the way her sympathy burrowed into tender parts he didn't want opened.

She pushed up out of the chair. "I'm going to try to catch the parade."

She didn't look back as she walked across the courtyard and into the house. He knew that because he watched her the entire way. Watched the sway of her hips and the way she tried to keep her shoulders straight . . . the slight pause when she opened the door before pushing on.

Why had Brian done this to him, brought this warm, caring woman into his life and made him want to share that warmth? As if she could wave her magic wand and set his life straight.

He shook his head, returning to his chair and his beer. Even if he shared his childhood aches and pains with her, she couldn't fix the fact that he wasn't worthy of holding love in his hands again. Two people had died because of him. His family had almost gone broke because of him. He couldn't hold on to his family, his friend, or to the woman he'd sworn to protect and let die anyway. Wasn't he reminded of that every time he looked in the mirror and saw the scar across his chest?

He tossed down the last of his beer and listened to the remnants of the parade going by on St. Charles. That was what he'd always hated about Mardi Gras. All around him everyone celebrated, making his darkness even blacker in contrast.

Masses of people flowed toward Rita as she made her way to Napoleon Avenue. She arrived at the street to find the crowd dispersing and no sign of the floats. The sounds of cheering and music floated through the air as the end of the parade moved farther away.

She picked up a string of gold beads lying on the side-walk. The two ends dangled, making her feel silly. She let the beads slip from her fingers and walked into the remnants of the crowd.

Shivering now, she turned back to the house, to Christopher. She'd stood up to him, had been maybe a little too honest for her own good. She'd done well considering her startling realization: he was, indeed, part of the reason she couldn't leave yet.

She didn't *want* to help him; she *needed* to help him just as much as she needed to find the truth about Brian. She couldn't explain it, but fixing him had something to do with fixing what was wrong with herself.

Why didn't he deserve redemption? *I was born.* No, it was more than that, darker and deeper than being the child who didn't belong. Despite his dark eyes, despite his warning that he couldn't be trusted, despite all that masculinity that he used to intimidate her with, she couldn't forget that he had taken in five helpless kittens. And he had come back for Brian.

The next morning Christopher let Rita take his car to the hospital, telling her he needed to catch up on his work. A new guard took a break when she got there and told her he'd sit outside the room until she left.

"I remembered the word *Sira,*" she told Brian. "But I don't know what it is. I've looked through your things but can't find anything. You have to help me. All I get are the scenes you showed me, and really, at the most unexpected times."

But that kiss had been unexpected, too. She felt a need to confess her sin, to assure Brian that he was the only one who could guide her past her fears. She held in the words. He wasn't the man she thought she knew. Or perhaps she only knew a small part of him. He'd never shared any of those inspirational messages with her, after all. He'd never spoken of the hotel he loved.

She squeezed his hand. "You've come to mean so much to me, yet I know so little about who you are. I want to understand your childhood, but Christopher is no help there. He's so . . . so . . ." She couldn't find the word she wanted. "I don't know, Brian. But he makes me . . . I. . . ." At the end, she couldn't put into words what he did to her, or how she felt about him. Probably she didn't want to know.

A shuffling sound made her turn to the doorway. Trent was standing there, looking a bit disconcerted at being caught. How long had he been standing there?

When he started to turn away, she said, "Hello, Trent. You can come in."

He jammed his hands into the pockets of his linen pants and ambled in. "I was just stopping by . . . to see how he was."

She looked at Brian's monitors, but the numbers were stable. She turned back to Trent and studied his behavior. He was clearly nervous around her, or nervous about being there. He looked as though he were waiting for the right moment to bolt. She wondered what his feelings were toward Brian, but that was too personal to broach.

"How are things at the hotel? You mentioned how tough it was without Brian around."

"We're managing. We always do."

"Always do?"

He shuffled his feet, the sound that had caught her attention earlier. "He wasn't around on Mardi Gras day last year. I mean, he came in early in the morning, but left in the afternoon."

"He took Mardi Gras off? Isn't that the busiest time of the year?"

"He made sure we were covered."

"Where did he go? It must have been important, to take that day off. Or did he just want to party?" But even as she said it, it didn't make sense. She knew enough about Brian to know he wouldn't be so cavalier about his responsibilities.

Trent shrugged. "He never said either time."

"He did it more than once?"

"Just twice. And probably this year, if . . ." He rubbed his nose and glanced away for a moment. "Actually, it's not all that busy in the evenings, not as much as you'd think. We don't let anyone but guests into the hotel, and most of them are out. Even Tammy escapes for a while to check out the crazies." He gave her a faint smile. "All the crazies come out on Mardi Gras. The rest of the time they hide what's underneath. But it's always there. You know what I mean?"

"No, explain."

He glanced at his watch. "I'd better get going."

She wasn't sure what to make of Trent. He seemed odd in his own right. Brian wasn't much help, giving no indication of being in his body. "Come back, Brian. I need your help. You haven't left nearly enough clues to figure this out."

As she talked to him, she kept the doorway in her peripheral vision. Aris was keeping a low profile. Rita had looked for her coming in, and when she left Brian's room an hour later, she kept an eye out for her. Aside from the green eyes and red hair, though, she recalled few details about the woman. On the way to the car, Rita called Tammy Rieux at the LaPorte to see if she had time to talk.

"About what?"

"Brian. I'm trying to put the puzzle pieces together. I think you can help."

"I don't have . . ." Tammy seemed to reconsider.

"Yeah, sure, we can talk. But not today. I've got two temporary desk clerks starting, three overbooked rooms, and two employees to reprimand. Don't they know there isn't *time* for a booty call during Mardi Gras? Between that and disappearing employees, I've got my hands full. If you want to talk, come tomorrow at noon. We can get a quick bite."

Rita drove back to the Garden District, relishing the shards of sunshine peeking through the clouds. A teal bicycle was parked outside the house. She wondered if she should knock on the door first. She opted for knocking, then entering. The scent of pine cleanser nearly knocked her over with memories of helping her mother clean houses on Saturdays. *Baby girl, hand your mama that bucket, would you? Don't spill it. I know it's heavy, just take your time.*

A woman's Cajun-spiced voice floated from the kitchen, breaking into her thoughts. "Well, baby, it ain't the place to be anymore, let me tell you."

The honey-thick voice belonged to a sleek woman of about twenty-five who wore tight jean shorts and a pink T-shirt knotted in front. Bountiful curls bobbed from the top of her head where they were bound with an elastic. She wore too much makeup for this early in the day, especially for the task she was undertaking: cleaning the stove.

Although Christopher's laptop computer sat open on the table with a screen full of codes, he was obviously more interested in watching the woman lean over the stove and lovingly rub a sponge over the surface. They both looked up when Rita walked into the kitchen.

That's when she saw the woman's eyes. She couldn't help but flinch at the oddity of two yellow smiley faces staring from beneath fake eyelashes.

"Why, *coo-zahn,* you didn't tell me your girlfriend was

here," she said, turning from him to Rita. "Where y'at, baby?"

Rita smiled uncertainly, not sure how to address any of that.

He answered for her. "She ain't my girl, she's a friend of Brian's," and to Rita he said, "*Where y'at* means 'how are you,' 'hello,' whatever. You're supposed to say *awright*. Emmagee is Brian's—what's the politically correct term?"

Emmagee grinned, showing off a thick, lush mouth set in a delicate frame of honey-colored skin. "Hell, you know I ain't politically correct. I'm his housegirl." At Rita's confused expression, she said, "I clean his house twice a week. Everything but his bedroom; he always was a private boy."

"How long have you been doing that?" Rita asked, wondering how she cleaned anything wearing five-inch heels.

"'Bout four years, after his last housegirl died. Poor thing choked on a raw hot dog, don't even want to know what she was doing with the thing down her throat all one piece." Emmagee shuddered dramatically, holding out a hand encased in a pink rubber glove. "Round N'awlins, nothing surprises me anymore, but I don't want to know any details, if you know what I mean. You'll find out why, you stay round long enough."

"How do you know I'm not from around here?" Rita asked.

Emmagee rolled her eyes. "Baby, you got Northeast written all over that face of yours. Never-out-in-the-sun skin, uptight blouse buttoned to your chin, no-nonsense blue pants and the pumps to match. Forget it. And that accent, whoo-ee."

Accent? She didn't have an accent, they did. Rita tried not to look down at her outfit, instead remembering the way it looked before she left her room. Conservative, professional. Her fingers automatically went to her collar, not buttoned to her chin, but close.

"You like my new contacts? Aren't they just the coolest?" Emmagee asked, hardly failing to notice Rita's gawking.

"They're, uh, interesting." They made Rita think of Aris's eyes—phony.

"Got 'em just for Mardi Gras. Makes me stand out in a crowd."

Christopher chuckled. "You never had a problem with that, *chérie*."

What was the deal, him using that term for this woman when he'd used it for her? Emmagee winked at him, then went back to her task, moving the sponge in circular motions while her perfect behind kept perfect time. Rita made a promise right then and there to start using her Exercycle on a regular basis.

She forced herself back on track. "Emmagee, did you notice anything . . . different about Brian's behavior before he fell?"

"Chris asked me that, too. I hardly ever saw the man. Seen Chris here more in the last few weeks than I ever saw Brian. I came in while he was at work. I got the feeling he wanted his nights to himself." She lifted her hand again. "Like I said, I don't ask for details, I just do my job."

Emmagee called him Chris. Somehow it seemed intimate.

"Did you ever see Brian on Mardi Gras night?" she asked Emmagee.

"Mardi Gras night? I'm sure he was at work."

"No, he wasn't." She looked at Christopher. "Trent from the hotel said he hadn't worked on Mardi Gras night for the past two years. As far as he knew, Brian had planned to take it off this year, too."

He said, "That's odd. That's the night he'd be the most needed."

"And as dedicated as he seemed to be to the hotel, it had to be something big." She hoped Tammy would know.

Emmagee nodded toward the refrigerator. "I made groceries if you're hungry."

Made groceries?

He plugged his cell phone into the laptop and connected to the Internet. He sent the file and collected several new e-mails before closing it down. Then he walked over to Rita and held out his hand. When she looked at him in confusion, he said, "My keys."

"Oh. Yeah, here. Is it okay if I use your phone to make a few calls? My cell phone died and I didn't bring the charger. I need to let my three clients know how to reach me in case of an emergency."

"Sure." He backed toward the door. "I'm going to cut for a while. We're gonna have a crawfish ball tonight. Catch you later, Emmagee."

"Sure thing, baby. Oh, sheeehit, hate when that happens." She held up her gloved hand, her long nails poking through the fingertips. The effect was like a cat's paw—a cat with green, purple, and gold nails. "Go through a box of these a week."

"A crawfish ball? Do I want to know?" Rita asked when she heard the front door close. She hoped the disappointment that he had left her behind didn't show in her voice.

"That's what it looks like when there's a whole pot of 'em swimming around in the berling water. They're really not swimming, of course, being dead and all."

It wasn't exactly an appetizing thought. "Where's he going?"

"Maybe to check out the old neighborhood. We was talkin' about the places that used to be hot way back when, how everything's gone to hell." She laughed, a throaty sound. "There was always fights, drugs, too much of everything. But now it's different. Everything's dirtier, older. The fights are meaner, the drugs are given to you when you don't even want any. Guys'll slip something in a girl's drink jus' to get her out of her mind. Can't leave your juice alone for even a second."

Emmagee stared off for a moment. "He seemed a little blue, you know. All the places we used to hang out, gone, crumbled away. When you stop lovin' something, it jus' dies. That's what's happening to places round here. My oldest brother Tommy was the first in our group to desert our city. Now most of 'em are gone. My folks left by default; they died. Can't hardly blame 'em for that."

"I'm sorry about your parents." Rita couldn't imagine Christopher looking blue or driving around town steeped in nostalgia. "Did you know him when he lived here?" She sat down in the chair he had vacated, finding it warm from his body heat.

"He used to hang out with Tommy, go to the blues clubs. I used to tag along, back when they weren't cardin' everyone. Chris would sometimes dance with me. Was before I had these." She gave her small breasts an affectionate squeeze. "I was jus' a skinny kid back then, bit of a tomboy. I knew he was jus' being nice, dancin' with me 'cause no one else would, but . . ." She fanned herself. "He was the thing, you know. I was too young, that's what he always said. But when I was around him, I didn't feel too young, know what I mean? He didn't act like he was too good for anyone. He had it, f'sure, but he didn't flaunt it."

Rita poured herself a cup of coffee and sat back down. He still had it. She wasn't sure what it was, but he had it. "What was he like back then?" He was Chris back then.

Emmagee stopped wiping down the inside of the refrigerator door for a moment. "He was tough and sexy and into trouble, but he had a good heart. Always help out a woman in need, no matter if she was trash or not, know what I mean? I used to think he was lucky, living in the Garden District and all." She shook her head, making her ringlets bounce. "But he never seemed to want to go home. Something happened there, when he was younger."

"Younger? You mean before Brian was supposed to be king?"

"Long before that. A boy died here. I don't know much about it. It wasn't something that came up in conversation, know what I mean? But he always had a shadow in his heart. Wish he'd move back to N'awlins. Ain't been the same round here without him." She dropped her sponge in the bucket of soapy water and picked up the bucket. "But something happened to him after he left here, too, something that took the life from his eyes. Maybe Carnival can heal him. It has a special kind of magic, you know. It can make a sensible person wild and free, and sometimes it can bring back the dead." She shrugged. "I see the dead Elvis every year. Worked for him, maybe it'll work for Chris, too."

Dead Elvis? Rita decided not to ask. "You said that Carnival could work its magic on Christopher. Is . . . there anything I could do? To help?"

Emmagee looked her up and down. "Maybe. Depends on how far into the dark you want to go. It's okay to sacrifice yourself, as long as you know what's in it for you. *Lache pas la patate.*"

"What does that mean?"

She waved her hand. "It's a saying. Means 'Don't forget what's important.' "

"And what's that?"

"It's different for everyone."

Rita thought she knew. Her job. Image. Friendship

with Marty. None of that factored into her situation here. And yet, she couldn't leave. For better or worse, a voice whispered in her head.

After Emmagee packed up her supplies, hung the bucket on her bicycle, and went home, Velda started her nightly ritual of music. Rita walked up to the trees separating the houses at the far right corner and tried to peek through the leaves. Velda also had a courtyard surrounded by trees, with lots of unkempt bushes and a weedy yard. Dark mildew washed down the graying paint of the house where a gutter was broken. The French doors in back were open, letting the music drift out to tantalize her. That was as far as she could see, though. Inside, the house was cave dark. Still she waited, hoping for a glimpse.

Something touched her shoulder, and she turned. A red creature with pincers and antennae looked back from the proximity of her nose, and she screamed.

Christopher laughed, and if she hadn't been so startled, and annoyed at getting caught spying, she might have been dazzled by that magnificent smile of his.

"What *is* that thing?"

"It's a crawfish." He tipped a paper sack that was filled with the things toward her. "Our dinner."

She followed him as he walked back into the kitchen. "How long had you been standing there?"

"Long enough to watch your Peeping Tommette antics." And long enough to have filled a pot with hot water and set it on the stove.

"Hmph. Sounds like we're both peepers." A few minutes later, she watched him dump the bag of critters into spicy boiling water.

She watched the crawfish "swim" around in the water, not feeling much different than they, swirling helplessly around in hot water.

A short while later they were seated at the table, which was covered in newspaper. He demonstrated, picking up a crawfish, snapping off the tail and peeling away the outer skin. "See, easy. And then if you're into eating the brains, you just suck da haids right out of 'em. Or you can scoop it out with the back of your nail if sucking don't appeal."

"Augh." The greenish ooze wasn't at all appealing. She walked outside. That's when she heard the sounds of a parade again. "I'm going to catch this parade. I missed the last one," she told him as she passed through the kitchen to the front door.

She didn't bother to ask if he wanted to come along. He was busy cracking tails. She pulled on her coat as she stepped into the cool evening air, this time going with the flow of people instead of against them. She found a spot three rows deep at the corner of St. Charles and Napoleon and watched the floats go by. People had ladders equipped with baby seats and virtual campgrounds set up, along with boxes for their treasures. Someone grabbed for a pearl necklace that whizzed by her head. Everywhere she looked, people lunged for goodies and called out, "Throw me something, mister!"

The floats were fanciful things, mythical creatures with mysterious masked riders who dangled beads as though they were made of real gold. And they might as well have been, for the way people begged. The float would pass by, and as soon as the next float approached, the begging started again. Occasionally a marching band separated the floats, and everyone got caught up in the music.

Five floats and two marching bands into the parade, she could feel the magic Emmagee mentioned. She decided that she wanted to catch just one necklace. So when the sea creature rolled by, she waved her hands like everyone else. A green necklace went flying overhead, but someone more zealous snagged it out of the air. The woman already had at least twenty necklaces strung around her neck.

The next float was a huge octopus, and once again Rita lifted her hands. One of the masked riders nodded at her and tossed a purple necklace her way. She grabbed for it, caught it, and held it close to her chest until she was sure no one else was going to snatch it away. Then she smiled at the rider who had tossed it to her, as though he'd bestowed real jewels upon her. She slipped it over her head and turned to catch the next float. Being a spectator was usually more comfortable, but oddly enough, being part of the crowd now made her feel special.

Only after the parade had proceeded up the street did she remember that Velda's house fronted St. Charles. She wasn't sure why she was so curious about the old stripper, but she was. Rita weaved her way through the departing crowds to the house she guessed was Velda's, with the pink paint, lace curtains in the windows, and a white picket fence around the front yard. Most of the yards were filled with families who had set up to party, but Velda's house was dark and the yard weedy and empty. It wasn't until she saw movement that she realized someone was standing at the window. She couldn't see a face, only a shadow.

She averted her gaze, pretending to look beyond to Brian's house—and her heart stopped. She could see Christopher standing on the steep part of the roof. What was he doing up there? Planning to jump like he thought his brother had done?

She made herself into a battering ram, jockeying through the crowd, leaving behind a string of apologies. The crowd became an obstacle course, blocking her way, moving in front of her just as she tried to dart around them. "Move, move," she muttered, pushing around shoulders, bumping arms. Cold air stung her nostrils and seared her lungs. The block-long sidewalk stretched to infinity in her desperate eyes, jammed with thousands of people. Nobody moved for her, nobody even noticed her. They were caught up in their triumphs while she was consumed with her fear.

She nearly tripped over a little girl who suddenly decided to reach for a necklace lying on the sidewalk. Rita jumped, dodged, all the while darting glances toward the house. It was obscured now by the houses in between. Cutting across the lawn of the corner house, she tromped on a bush and found herself apologizing to it without even thinking.

It was like a dream, no, a nightmare, running against time, her legs thick and heavy. It was taking too long, people died in the time she was taking, people married, women gave birth. *Too late, too late,* the words chanted in her head between her breaths. He was up there and she was still so far away, yards, miles, too long, too far away.

And then she was at the house, her legs shaky as she ran up the walkway, up the front steps, her hands cold and stiff as they grabbed at the doorknob. The carpet swallowed her steps, the staircase looked a mile high, but she clutched at the railing and pushed herself onward.

Her door was slightly open, a savings of one second, and she tore through her room and fumbled with the lock to the French doors and then shoved them open. She wanted to scream out his name, but she couldn't breathe. All she could do was look over the railing, for a second, and thank God he wasn't lying there the way she imagined Brian had lain.

She was gasping for breath as she reached the end of

the balcony and then swung around to the back where she found a spiral staircase going up. All she could think about was Emmagee's words about the life not being in his eyes anymore. She had to make it in time.

11

Christopher heard a door slam open, then the creak of the spiral staircase. *What the hell?* he thought, as heavy breathing preceded Rita before she leapt onto the deck.

"Don't jump!" she said in one long breath, coming to a stop in front of the railing. He slid down the steep roofline and climbed over the railing in front of her.

At first he thought she was kidding, but he saw the anxiety in her eyes and knew she wasn't. The dim lights up on the deck washed over the curves of her nose and mouth. She looked over the railing before meeting his eyes again. "I didn't . . . wasn't sure . . . whatareyoudoing-uphere?" she said at last, holding the railing to catch her breath.

"I was thinking. What are *you* doing up here?"

"I thought . . . you were going to jump."

He could see the apprehension in her face. She had obviously nearly killed herself to get to him. He wanted to laugh at her assumption, but a lump formed in his throat instead. The laugh became a smile as he reached out and grazed her cheek before catching himself.

How long had it been since someone had been concerned about him? She didn't know him, probably didn't like him. Yet she was afraid for him. He wanted to tell her how much that meant to him, how it made his chest hurt with something he could not define. He turned and looked down into the lit courtyard so she wouldn't see that he wanted to know what she'd been thinking as she'd run to the house, how fast she'd run, every detail.

"Well?" she demanded. She was still concerned about his state of mind, and all he could think of doing was to slip inside that coat of hers and bury his face in her hair. Maybe that would warm him from the inside out.

"I wasn't going to jump. I wouldn't let the world off that easily."

Relief relaxed her face. She fingered a strand of beads. "I saw you from the sidewalk." She smiled faintly. "Guess I overreacted."

"I was trying to put myself in Brian's mind." He'd been wondering why, of all places, he would choose the roof from which to jump. Why that one place?

"From over there?" When he only shrugged in answer, she leaned against the railing next to him. "Whew, I feel dizzy. I've got to start working out on that exercise bike more often."

The sentence invited his appraisal of her body. Not thin and feline like Emmagee's, but soft and curvy and much more interesting. Rita started fingering her beads again, then lifted one of the strands over her head. He could not move as she slipped the gold necklace around his neck.

"What's this for?" He touched the curved beads as he looked at blue eyes filled with something he didn't dare identify.

"Magic." She swallowed hard. "Emmagee said Carnival is magic, and sometimes that magic can heal people."

Why was she doing this to him? He did not like the

way this exchange was going, didn't like the destination his mind was taking him to. "I don't need healing." He lifted off the beads and handed them back to her.

"I know you think the beads and everything are silly; I did too until I watched the parade go by. It is magic, if you believe." She took the gold beads only to put them back over his head. "Let yourself believe, just for a few minutes. Forget those tableaux and your father's krewe and all of that. Pretend this is your first Mardi Gras."

"Rita . . ." He looked away from her, wishing he were still alone sinking into his dark thoughts rather than faced with this beautiful woman offering him magic. "I'm no good at pretend anymore."

"Sure you are. I'll bet if you tried hard, you could pretend you want to kiss me again."

He turned at those words. Didn't she see that he wouldn't have to pretend? No, maybe she didn't. That glitter was gone from her eyes. Her breathing was getting heavier again, as though she were trying to draw strength from a reservoir deep within. Her fingers were working one of the purple beads, betraying her nervousness.

His body clamored to give her that kiss. "What are you doing, Rita?"

"Isn't it obvious? I want you to kiss me."

"Why?" His voice had gone soft. The real question was, why was he bothering to ask? Why didn't he just take her right there, kiss her until her knees went weak, then bring her down to his room? But he couldn't. She had touched those tender spots inside him, and if he made love to her, he'd have to open them even more. Besides, she was Brian's girl, and he wasn't going to take anything away from his brother.

Hurt shadowed her eyes at his hesitance. He hated hurting her, but it was better than opening doors best left closed.

"I want to see if . . . I want to see if I can kiss you without my nose bleeding." She shored up her shoulders, pride edging in. "That's all."

He moved closer, without his shield of intimidation and purpose. He could smell her sweat, faint and sweet and womanly. Sweat she'd expelled for him. His chest felt tighter. He pushed the waves of her hair back from her damp face but did not lean down to meet her mouth. He'd put that question in her eyes, but it was for the best.

"Why does your nose bleed?"

She let out a soft breath, and its warmth caressed his throat. "It's silly."

"You don't think so."

She parted her lips to dispute him, paused. "No, it's not silly to me." He waited, giving her time. Finally she pushed out the words. "I have a great life. I have a nice condo, I'm saving up to buy a little brick house in a neighborhood I pass every day. Nothing fancy or trendy, mind you, but a home of my own. I love my job, helping women overcome debilitating psychological hang-ups. Everything is in order, except for this one tiny problem. My nose starts bleeding whenever I get into an . . . intimate situation with a man. Intimate emotionally. Especially with a man like you."

He traced the edge of her chin with his finger. Soft skin, cool to the touch. "Why a man like me?"

She let out another one of those soft breaths. He wished he were making her do that by kissing her crazy, not by making her weigh how much to tell him.

"A man surrounded by a wall and a moat filled with alligators."

"And why is that, Rita Brooks? Who did you fight alligators and try to scale walls for?"

"My father." She stared hard at a place to the right of him, someplace and no place at all. "I tried everything:

telling jokes, singing and dancing, getting good grades, getting bad grades . . . nothing worked." She looked at him again. "Why am I telling you this? All you had to do was say you didn't want to kiss me and be done with it."

She started to turn away, but he caught her arm and swung her back to face him. "You don't want to kiss me. You want to prove something to yourself."

She opened her mouth to argue, but closed it again. "Maybe that's all it was. Maybe I just wanted to use you." She squared her shoulders, and he found her strength so endearing he wanted to pull her close again. But her words chipped away at that softness, saving him from doing something he'd later regret. Something she would surely regret.

"Oh, I see. Kissing me was a test, to see if you could kiss Brian when he comes out." He hated the idea of that, so he embraced it.

"I won't have trouble kissing Brian."

"How do you know?"

"Brian was gentle, poetic. And we eased into our friendship. I was ready—am ready—to embark on a relationship with him."

Christopher hoped Brian deserved her faith and love. Of course, he hadn't missed the comparison between him and Brian, even if she hadn't meant to do it.

She took a step back. "The beads . . . they were for you. I meant what I said about magic. There's something about you that makes me want to build a bridge over the moat."

He had seen that compassion in her eyes before. Ironically, he'd felt jealous when she'd aimed it at Brian. Now that she was aiming it at him, he hated the way it made him feel—as needy as the boy he'd once been.

He had to erase it, so he pushed himself to say, "I don't have alligators in my moat; I have sea monsters with fangs and talons." He flexed his fingers to demonstrate.

She searched his expression, perhaps looking for a sign of sarcasm or jest. He had trained his face to betray none of the commotion inside him.

She lowered her head, turned and walked toward the spiral staircase. He hated himself for her slumped shoulders and the hurt he'd seen cross her face. It only proved again that he was a bastard. He knew that well enough, but he had to get it across to her so she wouldn't think she could save his soul.

She stopped by the first step and turned back to him. "I answered your question about why my nose bleeds. Now it's your turn. Why did you kiss me?"

The cold words he wanted to use failed him. "Because I wanted to."

He ran his fingers back through his hair as he ducked his head for a second. That kiss was already haunting him like a voodoo spell. When he looked up at her sudden intake of air, she was staring hard at the railing Brian had gone over. Her eyes were wide, as though she were seeing something. But nothing was there. A few moments passed before she blinked and looked at him.

"The images Brian showed me—the significant events of his life—have been replaying through my mind. Like when I saw the sword fight, sometimes they go slow enough for me to see them clearly. Just now I saw what happened in the moments before Brian fell. He followed someone up here. He felt panicky and afraid, but angry, too." She shivered, wrapping her arms around herself. "I'm pretty sure it was a woman; I could see the curves of small breasts beneath her black bodysuit. She was wearing a mask, the same one I saw in Boston." Several expressions crossed her face as she struggled to remember the details of her strange vision. "She was saying something about Xanadu."

"Xanadu hasn't been around for twelve years. It fell apart when my father died. And women weren't allowed in anyway."

She was ignoring him, chewing the tip of her finger in thought now. "Earlier I remembered the word *Sira.* I looked around in Brian's stuff but couldn't find anything about this Sira person, thing, whatever. Was there a rival krewe named Sira? A character in one of your tableaux?"

"Not from our tableaux." He shrugged. "There's no krewe named Sira that I've heard of."

"Let's look at his computer." She was on a roll now, her fear forgotten. She started down the stairs, then stopped and looked up at him. "Come on, we don't have time to dawdle."

On the one hand, Rita was grateful to have something other than her stupid, stupid, stupid request for a kiss to mull over. She tapped the heel of her palm against her forehead over that. And telling him about her nosebleeds. *Oh, and don't forget thinking the man was going to throw himself off the roof, Rita. Brilliant, aren't we? That's why we're a psychologist, so we can accurately read people.*

She leaned down into the cubbyhole beneath Brian's desk and pressed the button on the computer case. Along with the black carpet, he favored a black CPU, black flat-screen monitor, and even a black mouse pad. She paced while she waited for Christopher to come in. He finally did, a skeptical look on his face. "I've already checked his computer."

"Let's check it again. I'll bet you were only looking for e-mails or maybe a suicide note, right?"

"Pretty much."

He sat down in the tall-backed chair and pulled up the file organizer on the computer. What looked like a thousand file folders filled the left side of the screen. He clicked on Search and typed in *Xanadu*. Nothing came up.

He turned to her. "What was this word you 'got' from Brian? *Sira*?"

She found a notepad and wrote it every conceivable way it could be spelled. He typed in each version with no luck.

"Uh-oh," she said, staring at the way she'd just written it. "Why didn't I realize this before? Because I never wrote the word down." She pointed at the spelling of *Sira* and then wrote it backward. "Christopher, it's Aris! The mystery nurse. It's too much of a coincidence to ignore."

He gave her a patronizing look. "Are you sure this isn't all in that pretty head of yours?"

"I—" She clamped her mouth shut for a moment, taken aback by his sort-of compliment. Better to ignore it, she decided. "I am not imagining this. All right, so most of what I have is in my . . . head, but only because Brian put it there. I did see her!" she added at his skeptical look. "So we know that Sira is a person, specifically a woman."

"Yeah, we know that much."

She waved away his sarcasm. "Well, have you searched for the last spelling yet?"

"Not with you distracting me."

She settled back on the desktop again. "Yeah, like I could distract anyone." Her mouth was in overdrive tonight. Her heart jumped at the look on his face, a look that disputed her statement. He shifted his attention to the screen and started punching keys. No results for *Sira*.

"What about deleted files?" Rita asked.

He trailed the mouse across the screen and checked the Recycle Bin and then did a more intricate search. "If someone deleted files, they knew what they were doing."

"Just like she deleted all my e-mails. Why would Brian have erased them? Let's check his in-box again."

Several messages appeared, including some that promised to increase one's penis size and decrease one's mortgage rates. Two e-mails were obviously hotel-related, and he forwarded them to Tammy through the hotel's website address.

"He has two e-mail addresses, one for the hotel and one personal, and they both dump into this in-box or the one at his office, depending on where he checks his mail. I've already looked at his in-box at work; nothing there. The only odd thing I've found is this PC." He tapped the case with his foot. "This is Alienware, makers of serious gaming PCs. People who buy these systems are big-time into playing sophisticated video games. I have friends who'd have orgasms at the thought of owning Alienware. I know people who wear Alienware hats and shirts and hell, if they made boxers, they'd wear them, too. But Brian's not a gamer. I didn't find any gaming software on his PC or online games in his Internet history or Favorites list."

"Maybe he was just thinking about jumping in," she said. "Or considering investing." She mentioned Brian's question about whether she liked video games.

"Could be." He turned the chair to face her. His casual posture belied the seriousness in his eyes. "Look, I'm sorry about . . . the thing upstairs. I just don't want you to get any wrong ideas about me."

She slid off the desk. "It was no big deal. A test, that's all." And then she walked downstairs to watch her regular television lineup and forget about her misguided ideas.

She wished she could totally lose herself in TV-land like she did when she was a kid. Charlie bought a television for her room, and she spent all her free time watching it. *The Brady Bunch* was her favorite: She'd pretend she was Jan. She carried it too far, coming home from school and having conversations with Alice and "her" siblings, relaying the events of her day to her two parents who listened with rapt attention. Charlie had once caught her in one of these dialogues, but he never commented on it. Probably didn't care if his kid was nuts as long as she didn't bother him.

She didn't have make-believe conversations anymore, but she still sank into those imaginary worlds. She once caught herself thinking about what kind of baby gift to give Ross and Rachel on *Friends*. Of course, she'd never actually bought the gift. She wasn't that nuts.

But once she was settled in front of the television in the family room, she couldn't stop thinking about reality. She had opened herself up, faced the rejection she feared, and hadn't died a thousand deaths. Only a few hundred.

And she had not felt the tingle of the nosebleed when she'd asked him to kiss her. Her experiment had worked; well, sort of. She'd probably cheated. After all, she had looked at all that muscle and those dark eyes and imagined him playing with five kittens.

Late that night, Christopher tossed and turned, unable to push dreams from his sleep.

"Dad, can't I be the good prince? I'm always the bad prince. Let me be good just this once. Please?"

Theodore LaPorte looked at his young son with a stiff smile. "The older son always has his pick of roles, and he chooses to play the good prince again. Don't be a baby. Play your part, son."

The firstborn, the boy who did no wrong. His parents held on to the old-line belief that the firstborn was the one who carried the family name and honor and took over the family business. Everything was black and white. If Brian was first, Chris was last. If Brian was good, Chris was bad. More than ever, he needed to at least pretend he was good. More than ever he needed to know his family still loved him.

"Dad, can't you ask Brian to let me be good this time?"

The stiff smile gave way to the bitterness Chris suspected was just beneath the surface. "You deserve the role of the evil boy who kills his friend and destroys two families. That is your role." He walked away, leaving Chris to deal with the guilt and pain by himself.

The year before he'd proven that badness dwelled inside him, not only to his family but to himself.

Christopher rolled over in bed, not sure if he was dreaming or merely being tortured by his memories. Moonlight pooled on the floor, telling him it was too early to get up yet. But when he forced himself back to sleep, he once again saw his father's face. This time it was pale and lifeless.

He stared at the man who had been his father, waiting to feel . . . something. All around him people cried or sniffled or railed at the injustice of the cancer that had taken his life. Christopher couldn't force the sadness he knew he should be expressing. He'd given up acting a long time ago.

"I'm surprised you bothered to come," Brian said, walking up beside him. "The role of dutiful son doesn't suit you."

Christopher turned to his brother, the man with his eyes, but with lighter hair and two less inches of height. Those two inches may as well have been a foot in Brian's eyes.

"Yeah, the role of do-gooder was always your specialty."

Brian's mouth tightened. "If you've come for some kind of inheritance, you came for nothing. You'll have to wait for me to die before you get a cent. You ruined everything, you know."

"I didn't come for anything, not for reconciliation or for money." Christopher kept his gaze on the white lilies near the coffin. Why had he come? Because the man was his father. "As for ruining everything, you give me too much credit."

Although Brian was now twenty-two, he sounded like a whiny little boy. "Dad couldn't bear to see anyone else head his krewe when he got ill. Said I wasn't ready for the responsibility." He laughed, and the sound was as bitter as poison. "He left me the hotel, but not Xanadu. He made sure Xanadu was history before he died. I had one chance to be king, and you ruined it."

"It was an accident. And the krewe was falling apart anyway due to bickering and waning interest."

"You were always the troublemaker. Just ask Billy Franklin."

He stiffened at the mention of the name. "It's time to let go of the past." Too bad he hadn't.

"When are you leaving?" Brian asked.

"When I'm ready." And that could not be soon enough.

As always, Brian had to have the last word. "The prodigal son returns. Too bad no one wants you here."

Christopher sat up in bed, naked in the darkness. Maybe it was being in Brian's old room that had brought the dreams. Or driving through his old haunts and finding them broken-down and dangerous, old friends gone or dead. Or maybe it was the tender spots Rita had touched with her words. No matter, he wasn't chancing having more dreams.

He settled in at the small table that overlooked the darkened courtyard below and turned on his laptop computer. The gold beads Rita had given him were lying on the table in a figure eight. He picked them up, remembering her words about magic. Then he let them drop to the table where they skittered over the edge to the floor. For a while he worked on gathering competitor data for an up-and-coming software company. After a bit, he got restless.

He changed e-mail identities and became the Highwayman.

The faint glow from the laptop computer screen washed over the French doors, but didn't reach the balcony outside. He watched, comfortable that he was invisible in black. Christopher had a stern expression on his face, but once in a while he stared off at nothing and his expression became troubled. Then he rubbed his face and returned to whatever he was doing on the computer.

Sira had wanted to come tonight. She wanted to take over as usual. She thought he wasn't man enough to handle this. Damn her. Sira, as she called herself, thought she ruled the world.

In Xanadu did Sira a stately pleasure-dome decree . . . She had changed Samuel Taylor Coleridge's "Kubla Khan" to fit her needs. She would spout off some part of it whenever it suited her.

He feared her. He feared her power. But mostly, he feared that Rita and Christopher could destroy her.

He walked to the French doors outside the room Rita was sleeping in. The key to those doors was in his hand, and he rubbed the ridges against his gloved fingers. Time to pay a visit. He started to push the key into the lock when a sound stopped him.

The door to Christopher's room opened, and he walked out. He didn't look around suspiciously, so he hadn't heard anything. He leaned against the railing and stared out over the courtyard. And he didn't see the shadow at the end of the balcony slinking farther into the darkness.

If he did . . . the shadow reached down and pulled the letter opener from his belt, fingering the pointed tip. If Christopher dared walk this way, then an evil shadow would come to life . . . and take his.

12

Mornings were Rita's favorite time of day, when she looked forward to filling the hours with purpose and routine. But here in this strange city, in this strange house, she was back in that Jell-O again, trying to swim to a place she wasn't sure existed. The least she could do was dress as though she had purpose, in pleated slacks and white blouse. It was all in the appearance.

She glanced in the mirror over the dresser. A no-nonsense appearance. Blah.

Christopher wasn't up yet, or at least she guessed that he was still behind the closed door in his room. She started a pot of coffee and found a tray of pastries that Emmagee had obviously bought when she'd . . . made groceries. New Orleans was indeed a foreign city.

Restless, she found Christopher's keys, left him a note, and drove to the hospital to talk to Brian. She told him about the weather and the parade she'd watched. But what she was thinking between her chirpy sentences was how afraid she was that Brian wasn't going to come out of this coma. How scared she was that they wouldn't find out the truth or discover who Sira was. Seven days had already passed since she'd arrived and she wasn't any closer to figuring that part out.

"I'm sorry I'm not more interesting." She touched his hand, looking for any kind of response. Nothing. "I'm not even creative enough to make up stuff. But let me tell you about a friend of mine and her napkin phobia. Now, she's interesting."

When Rita returned to the house a while later, Christopher was leaning against the kitchen counter with a mug of coffee in his hand, his hair slightly rumpled from being towel-dried. He wore black jeans with fade lines that accented the tight roundness of his derriere; his gold sweater molded the contours of his chest. His feet were still bare, and she wondered if there wasn't anything on the man that wasn't sexy and then she stopped her thoughts right there.

"Good morning. You slept in late." *And see, he didn't even bother to comb his hair, a sure sign that he doesn't care to impress you.*

"Couldn't sleep last night." That was all he offered. So much for chitchat. "Someone named Anna just called. She was all panicked because she'd just run over what she thought was a child. I told her to call the police."

"No, no, no," Rita said, starting to look up her number in her address book.

"But she said she's not supposed to do that, so she's been driving around in circles for an hour." He lifted his eyebrow, but Rita was already dialing the number and walking around the corner.

She talked Anna out of the panic attack she'd worked herself into and eventually helped her drive to her destination without stopping. Twenty minutes later she hung up and returned to the kitchen where he still lingered with his coffee. "I'll leave you money for phone calls."

"I take it she didn't really run someone over," he said.

Rita shook her head. "She has an obsessive-compulsive disorder that makes her think every time she hits a pothole or a speed bump in the road, she's run over someone. So she circles back looking for them, and then she'll hit another bump and it literally becomes a vicious circle. Plus it puts her into a panic mode. We've been working on exposure therapy, where I ride in the car with her and we purposely run over potholes and bumps. She'd been doing well until her marriage also hit a pothole and that's set her back."

"Do you deal with a lot of that kind of thing?"

"That and phobias and other oddities." Out of respect for her clients, she didn't want to get into too much detail, so she shifted the subject. "You match this house, you know."

"What?"

"The colors you wear." He looked down, then around. She said, "You never really left New Orleans. Think about it: the coffee you order, the accent."

He contemplated as he took a sip of his coffee. "New Orleans is the woman you left behind and never forgot."

Perhaps New Orleans hadn't let him go. He probably felt at home in the city, at least, if not in this house.

"Stop looking at me like that," he said.

She blinked. "Like what?"

"Like you're analyzing me. Didn't we get that straight last night?"

Her face flushed, and she lifted her hair off her heated neck. "It's a habit. Analyzing, that is." Not asking men to kiss her, not putting herself on the line only to get trampled. "We have a lot in common, you know." He gave her a skeptical look. "With our fathers, I mean. We both had fathers we couldn't reach. And now they're gone."

"But my father's indifference stopped hurting me a long time ago."

She winced at the unspoken side of that statement. "At least I found out why he was . . . the way he was." She tried to force a casual smile of bravery. Okay, maybe the indifference did still hurt, but only a little. "When I finally mustered the courage to tell him, I found out he'd died of cancer two days earlier. I never got to make peace with him. Did you?"

"I let him go long before he ever died," he said, and left it at that.

"Did you?" Before he could get defensive, she quickly said, "I worked through a lot of my anger and other hang-ups during my college studies. But I still needed to make peace with him. And I'd figured out what his problem was. I used to think that simply knowing the source of a person's behavior was the key to fixing the problem. I thought that if I explained it to him, he'd see the light. It doesn't always work that way."

He finished off his mug and then poured more for himself. As he started to put the pot back, he stopped and held it up in question. He was getting better at this host thing. His eyes were on her as he poured the coffee, though he knew when to stop pouring. He smelled of deodorant and shaving cream, intrinsically male scents that sent heat pooling inside her.

"What was his problem?" he asked.

"You really want to know?"

His eyes warmed for a moment. "Sure."

Did she really want to tell him? Well, she'd started it, hadn't she? "In layman's terms, Charlie was the victim of a sensual mother. From what I knew, Maura's husband had ignored her, so she lavished all of her affection on her only son. She dressed in sexy clothes, moved like liquid. Once I started studying psychology, I figured out what had happened.

"When a man becomes an adolescent and starts having sexual feelings, if his mother is draping herself all over him, some of those feelings are transferred to her. He gets disgusted at himself for these wrong feelings and shuts them off. Because of that shame, he doesn't date women or get into relationships with them; he feels like a freak. And when Charlie suddenly got custody of his young daughter . . . well, he didn't know how to relate to a woman, even a girl, in a nonsexual way. It was probably the same kind of shame all over again, just the thought of having sexual feelings toward his own daughter. So he kept me at a distance." She decided to turn the tables. "What about you?"

He put the coffeepot back on the burner. "I was a mistake, that's all." He met her eyes. "Did you say you were meeting Tammy today?"

"Yes," she said, feeling cheated. Why did women always give so much more? They talked more, that's why.

He was already walking out of the kitchen. "I'll take you in to the Quarter. So you don't get lost," he added over his shoulder before heading around the corner.

"I wasn't going to get lost," she stated. No point in arguing anyway. He was right—she'd get lost.

Rita headed to the car fifteen minutes later, but stopped when she saw Christopher strolling down the sidewalk. "Aren't we driving in?"

"Nope. Too many people, too many beads dropping from the sky."

She caught up to him. "Beads are going to drop from the sky?" She squinted up at the sun.

He chuckled. "Not literally. People throw them from galleries. Those are balconies to you and me."

"This place is like another country."

"For sure. Balconies are galleries, sidewalks are banquettes." He offered her a pack of bubble gum, but she shook her head. She didn't want to be reminded of kissing him. He popped a purple chunk in his mouth and stuffed the pack in his pocket. Would she ever smell grape again and not think of him?

Along the parade route naked trees were treated to a new look: beads of all colors draped from their branches. Groups of people wandered around, wearing Mardi Gras colors and looking at the houses.

"Come on, let's try to catch the next streetcar." He grabbed for her hand as he broke into a sprint, but let go as soon as they made contact.

Once they were settled on the old wooden seat of the streetcar, a bell clanged twice and they headed toward the Quarter. Sunshine slanted down into her window. She closed her eyes and soaked up its warmth. When she opened them, he was watching her with something that looked like hunger. Instead of looking away, he gave her a soft smile.

Several stops later they disembarked at Canal Street. They crossed a large expanse of road flanked by hotels and shops and continued straight on Royal Street. The buildings were old, but what character they had. Some of them had character of an X-rated kind. Naturally, he had to catch her as she peered into one of the open doorways.

"Just holler if you want to stop," he said with that sly grin.

"I was just . . . there was . . . oh, never mind!" She really had no decent excuse, other than curiosity.

He chuckled. "I'll start calling you my peeping Annie."

That smile of his arrested her as surely as the words he'd just said. *His* peeping Annie, huh? He probably hadn't even noticed it, but those words settled into her belly like a dose of peppermint schnapps.

"One block over is Bourbon Street," he said, pointing to the left as they crossed the street.

People flowed from Bourbon down the side street,

draped with beads and wearing silly hats. She absently placed her hand on her collarbone; she hadn't put on her beads. Almost everyone was wearing at least one necklace and as many as thirty. Without those gaudy beads, she was the one who stood out.

"Mawtha a' Gawd, a condom shop!" She stopped, gawking at the sign over the doorway proudly proclaiming their specialty. "A shop that sells nothing but condoms. Who would have figured?"

"Oh, they probably sell a few other things."

She started to ask what but caught herself. She didn't want to know. Okay, maybe she did a little, but she wasn't about to ask.

He shook his head. "What was that first part you said? Mouther something?"

She thought back over what she'd said. "Mother of God? It's just an expression Kevin White—one of our former mayors—used to say."

The crowds got even thicker as they ventured farther into the Quarter. Several party animals were already nearing the bottoms of their large plastic cups of beer. "Huge-ass Beers," according to a sign one guy was carrying around. She looked over at Christopher, who was oblivious to his surroundings.

"Did you spend a lot of time at the hotel?" She wondered if the place would evoke painful memories.

"I helped out during Mardi Gras and over the summers."

Rita thought about what Emmagee had said. "New Orleans must have changed a lot since you left."

"For sure."

Well, that was deep. But she already knew he wasn't into sharing, and for a moment she envied Emmagee for having known him when he wasn't living in the dark.

When he danced. When he was Chris. Maybe she could have . . .

She stopped herself right there. She had lived with too many maybes and what-ifs. First with her father, and now she seemed to be repeating the pattern with Christopher. He had already told her he didn't need her help, that he had dragons in his moat. That should be more than enough to convince her to steer clear. But every once in a while she glimpsed something other than all that anger and indifference. She saw a man who deserved a woman who would not give up on him.

"Where you headed?" he asked.

"A dangerous place," she said, then realized she'd walked on without him.

He steered them toward the dark green awning covering the LaPorte's entrance. The tall doorman nodded without a smile as he opened the door, but he obviously had no idea Christopher was a LaPorte. Then again, Christopher probably hadn't identified himself as such.

"Have you been here much since you came back?" she asked as they passed beneath an ostentatious chandelier hanging in the lobby.

"A few times."

She wondered if his father had left him any portion of the hotel. Charlie had left her a few thousand dollars, but everything else had gone to his mother. Rita would have traded every dollar for an hour with him before he'd died.

Even though Christopher did not have any ties here, he walked through the office door as though he had authority. Behind the white carved door, a hallway split right and left, and a series of offices lined both sides. Along the walls were framed pictures of nature scenes with inspirational sayings beneath them such as "TEAM: Together Everyone Accomplishes More," and "Persistence prevails when all else fails." It was strange that she'd never seen this side of Brian. It made her feel as though she hadn't known him at all.

"I'll meet you over at Pat O'Brien's when you're done chatting Tammy up," he said, slowing down in front of the last office. "Go up to St. Peter and turn toward Bourbon. Once you walk in, I'll be in the piano bar on the right."

"You're leaving me here?" Although at first she'd intended to go into the Quarter by herself, now she was disappointed he wasn't staying.

"I'm going to check out Brian's office again, look for anything I might have missed the first time, and then I'm outta here. Unless you need me to wait."

And inconvenience him? No way. "I'll be fine."

He smiled. "Don't look so worried, *chérie*. This part of the Quarter's not so bad during the day. Just don't go wandering or making friends on the way."

"Like I would."

Tammy came around the corner of the hallway. Her blond, curly hair was a bit disheveled.

"Hi, Rita. Christopher," she said, acknowledging him more carefully. "Slumming?"

Rita answered for him. "He walked me in to make sure I got here in one piece."

Tammy's eyebrows rose. "Really, now? Better watch it, Christopher. Your chivalry is showing."

He merely gave her a lift of his eyebrow and turned away.

Tammy said, "You said you wanted to talk to me. I've got about fifteen minutes to squeeze in lunch, so let's go."

Tammy secured a table in the crowded courtyard. Most of the patrons here were dressed in fine clothes and jewelry, though a few were decked out in Mardi Gras colors.

"Make it fast, Dave," Tammy said to the waiter, who

eyed Rita curiously. "I've got fourteen minutes." Once they'd ordered, Tammy said in the same no-nonsense voice, "You're obviously still snooping around Brian's life. Have you found anything to prove Christopher pushed him off the roof?"

"He had nothing to do with it."

"But you do still think someone did."

"I think it's more likely than him falling by accident. After all, he spent his whole life in that house. He knew his way around that deck. You obviously cared a great deal about him," Rita ventured. "Don't you want to know what happened?"

"I didn't only care about him. Any fool could see I loved the man. But not Brian. As far as romance goes, I might as well have been the palm in the lobby. All those women he dated, and not one measured up to him."

Or to you, Rita didn't say. "Christopher said Brian hadn't dated anyone in some time. What about business ventures? Had he shown any interest in video games lately?"

Her brows furrowed. "Video games? I can't imagine that. But you know, he could have been into anything for all I know. And the more I think about it, the more I'm sure he *was* into something. I told you he was distracted, but it was more like daydreaming. He had this light in his eyes, too, and sometimes a faint smile." She crumpled her linen napkin. "Doesn't sound like a business venture, does it?"

Rita shook her head. Another dead end. "Did he ever mention the name Sira? Or anything about Xanadu?"

"Nothing about Sira. Xanadu was the name of his father's krewe, but he never talked about that anymore."

When Tammy looked behind Rita, Rita turned to find Dave the waiter with their sandwiches and hot teas. How long had he been standing there listening to them? He placed their food on the table and left.

After taking a bite of her shrimp salad sandwich, Rita asked, "What did Brian do on Mardi Gras night? Trent said he's taken the night off the last two years. Since that's one of your busiest times, it surprised me."

"Trent has a big mouth." She ripped away the curly edge of the lettuce. "Brian's the boss. He can do what he wants. He always made sure everything was covered."

"What did he do, go to a party?"

Her expression stiffened. "He only said he had an engagement."

"Did you notice a nurse who was at the hospital that first day we met? You may have passed her on the way out. She had vivid green eyes, probably contacts, bright red hair, and her name was Aris Smith." She noticed the other woman's eyes, an unusual shade of gray-green. Not contacts.

"No, why?" Tammy answered without giving it any thought at all.

"I wanted to talk to her, but she doesn't seem to work there. Maybe I just got her name wrong."

Rita studied her: smooth complexion, plain features, long Mardi Gras–colored nails, and enough time to have changed clothes, thrown on a wig, and put in contacts before waltzing into Brian's room to bathe him—or specifically to get Rita out of the room. Tammy claimed not to have known him in the past year, but who would have known him better? Throw unrequited love into the mix—

"Trent, I need to talk to you when I'm done here," Tammy said to the right of Rita's shoulder. He was passing through the courtyard. "About you-know-who," she added, indicating a man sweeping bread crumbs from beneath a nearby table. Trent nodded and continued on.

Tammy turned back to Rita. "Have you actually found anything to substantiate your theory that Brian was pushed? Obviously not, since you're here. Otherwise you would have gone to the police, and they'd be here asking me questions. You're still desperately trying to find something. So let me ask *you* a question. Why are you so sure someone tried to kill Brian?"

"Call it a feeling."

"You know, I'd suspect you were some nut with an obsession for Brian, except for one thing. The way you look at Christopher. Unless it's just, what do you call it? Transference? Maybe you're transferring your feelings for Brian onto his brother. Either way, I think you're chasing a story that's not there."

When Dave dropped off the bill, Tammy signed for it before Rita could even get her purse. "I've got to get back to work. The only person who can solve this mystery is Brian himself, and it doesn't look like he's going to be able to tell us anything anytime soon." She pushed back her chair. "I have some of Brian's personal mail I forgot to give Christopher. Can you pass it on to him?" She stood. "I have to give him credit for taking care of Brian's personal affairs. It's more than I thought he'd do."

"You were wrong about Christopher. He's as worthy as Brian is," Rita said as they walked through the lobby.

"Be careful," Tammy threw out as she handed Rita the envelopes a minute later.

"Careful?"

She nodded toward the entrance. "Watch yourself out there. Never know what kind of kooks you'll run into."

"Thanks for the warning. And for lunch."

Rita headed to the restroom. She glanced back to find Tammy and Trent discussing something—her, by the way they looked in her direction. The restroom was as elegant as the hotel's lobby. There was even a chandelier in here, though of a smaller scale. She stepped into a stall and took a few moments to clear her head and prepare to walk the streets of New Orleans alone.

• • •

That bitch knew way too much. He could have walked over and slid his fingers around Rita's throat . . . if there hadn't been fifty other people sitting in the lush courtyard enjoying their lunches.

She knew about Sira, which meant she definitely knew about Xanadu. Brian wasn't supposed to tell her until she was voted in by the High Council, and they hadn't reached a decision yet. Apparently he had. That was reason enough for his execution. And for Rita's.

All he had to do was get her alone. That was beginning to be a challenge with Christopher around. But she was alone now.

He ducked into the men's room and pulled some items from his duffel bag. Exiting the restroom at the same time she did, he made sure to catch her eye but saw no flicker of recognition. Rita walked out of the hotel and into the stream of foot traffic on the sidewalk. She kept glancing back, as though she could feel someone watching, following. *Yes, be afraid of me. I have the power to end your life.*

When she turned to look in his direction, he shifted his gaze to a woman walking toward him. She lifted her chin and snubbed him. A man flicked his cigarette butt dangerously close to his sweater. Dickhead. The guy challenged him, and he saw disdain on his face. *Freak. Queer.* The echoes of adolescent taunts bounced through his brain.

He wasn't big but he was strong. *I could hurt him without your help, Sira. I could do it myself. I'm the boy.* He swung his gaze ahead. *Focus. She's the one you want. She's the threat.*

Didn't these people realize his power? No. He was no one. Sira was his power, his strength. As much as he hated to admit it, without her he was nothing.

He trained his gaze on Rita, who was now turning onto

St. Peter. He scooted closer as she merged with a crowd of bead beggars. He adjusted the hokey purple cap he now wore and moved up behind her. If he could only get a little closer . . .

The afternoon skies had become cloudy again, and Rita pulled her coat around her as she made her way to St. Peter. Trash littered every surface, spilling out of full garbage cans and piling up in the gutters like so much dirty snow. The smell of refuse mixed with aromas from the hot dog vendor nearby.

The hairs on the back of her neck stood on end. She slowed down, looking from side to side. Nothing out of the ordinary. Well, for New Orleans anyway.

So why did she have the eerie feeling that someone was watching her? She surreptitiously glanced behind her and found that the crowds were thickening. Music floated out of restaurants and bars, jazz clashing with a dance beat. As she scoped around, a few people met her eyes. But this feeling wasn't the kind one might have if someone were admiring her. This felt . . . different. Malevolent.

She glanced back again, but no one stood out. Or rather, everyone stood out. A woman in black tights with a purple and green leotard, a man wearing baggy black clothes and a purple fuzzy cap. A tall man wearing a cap covered with yellow, phallic-looking spikes. Oh, brother.

Maybe she was imagining it. Maybe she was just off balance. She breathed out in relief when she saw the sign for St. Peter. Getting closer to Christopher, closer to safety.

The crowd was spilling out from Bourbon Street, with louder groups gathered below iron balconies—galleries—to beg for the beads others dangled from above. She migrated toward the crowd, hoping for safety in numbers. "Do you know where Pat O'Brien's is?" she asked one woman.

"Right down there." Barely distracted by Rita's question, she lifted her shirt to reveal bare pendulous breasts as she danced for someone above. "Throw me somethin', mister!"

A din of shouting and whistles ensued, and as Rita slipped out of the crowd, something hard hit her on the head.

And then the world went black.

13

Christopher sat at a small table near the back of what he called the dungeon. It was dark and cavernous in the piano bar, the only real light coming from the two bronze-clad pianos with their mirror backdrop. Two women were at the helm, taking requests and trading off this song for that.

He wasn't in the mood for songs, but he was in just the right mood to sit in a cave. He'd forgone the famous Hurricane drink for a beer, then another. He didn't like what Rita was doing to him. She was opening up places inside him, old wounds she wanted to heal. He downed another half a beer to the chorus of "When Irish Eyes Are Smiling" and thought of Rita's eyes.

She was also opening up bizarre possibilities. He glanced at the cylinder of paper sitting on the chair next to him. Rita wasn't a crackpot. He'd liked it better when he suspected she was. She'd been telling the truth all along, and he'd been an idiot for not believing, for rationalizing away the obvious.

He couldn't wait to show her what he'd found. He glanced at his watch, but it was too dark to see the time. Where was she?

• • •

"Breathe, lady, breathe."

Rita heard the voice, but her heart was pounding beyond her control. Too many faces hovered over her, and she tried to suck in air. She was sitting on the ground with her back against a flimsy metal column.

"Move back, she's hyperventilating," a man wearing a purple cap said, pushing everyone aside. He was wearing baggy clothing, and the strands of beads around his neck brushed her face as he knelt down beside her. "Are you all right?"

"These beads hit her on the head," the girl who had lifted her shirt said, holding up a strand of large pearls. "I earned 'em, but she deserves 'em." She leaned forward and, with the utmost care, put them over her head.

Rita was sure she was losing her mind. Carnival was supposed to be magic, not manic. Part of the crowd was still begging for beads. What with the fear of being watched racing through her, the shock of getting pelted by a strand of beads was just too much for her nervous system to handle. She could feel her breathing getting calmer.

"She's all right," the man said, helping her to her feet. He smiled, injecting warmth into his hazel eyes. "I've been whopped myself. Hurts like the dickens, doesn't it?"

He had smooth skin and a friendly smile. For some reason, he looked vaguely familiar, but she couldn't pinpoint any particular feature. She brushed the debris off her backside. The crowd had lost interest in her. She obviously wasn't wigged out enough for them. The woman with the breasts was trying to get another pearl necklace. Rita rubbed the bump on her head. Lifting one's shirt was the easy way to get beads compared to getting them pounded into your head.

"You still look a little pale," the man said. "Maybe we

should get you back to your house. Wouldn't want you to pass out on the street, would we?" He gave her a friendly pat on the arm.

"Maybe it would be best to just get back to the house." She did feel a bit woozy, but the walk back to the streetcar looked awfully long. Christopher had the passes they'd need to ride.

"Come on, I'll walk you."

She pulled back. "I should get my friend . . . he's waiting at O'Brien's for me."

He nudged her the other way. "Aw, he's probably having a good time. You don't want to spoil it, do you? Tell you what. Let's get you back to where you're staying, and I'll find this friend and tell him where you are. Promise."

She didn't want to spoil Christopher's fun, didn't want to make him leave just because she wasn't feeling well.

"Believe me," he was saying as he led her away, "you don't want to pass out around here during Carnival. Some real weirdoes come to New Orleans this time of year."

"Excuse me." Rita tugged her arm free. "I appreciate your help, I really do. But I don't want to put you out, and my friend is right there at the piano bar, so I might as well go find him." As she spoke, the urge to get to Christopher intensified. She wasn't going to analyze her feelings or try to talk herself out of them. "Thanks, though."

"Don't you trust me? All I want to do is help you. I don't want to see you get hurt."

"I understand that. I just want to get to my friend."

"You don't trust me, even after I helped get all those people away from you," he said in a hurt voice.

"I do trust you," she heard herself say, though it wasn't necessarily true.

"Then let me help you. I love helping people. You said you trusted me." He'd turned her words against her, giving her a smile that rivaled any cherub. "I'm not trying to pull anything on you, I promise. Okay, you're pretty, and I'd love to get to know you better. But I just want to make sure you're okay. When I got hit on the head, I thought I was fine, but about ten minutes later I started getting sick to my stomach and nearly passed out. You can be in the quiet haven of your room if that happens. I'm only going to walk you to your house, make sure you get in all right."

He had a good point. A lot of them. He looked harmless enough, and there were people around in case he did try something. And she wouldn't be alone out here. "Well . . ."

"Good choice," he said, pulling her arm.

The more steps she took, the uneasier she felt. No particular reason. He seemed nice. He wasn't much bigger than she was. Yet her stomach kept tightening with anxiety. Finally she stopped. "I need to find my friend."

Frustration crossed his face; then his smile took hold again. "You're just not going to let me help you, are you?"

The way he said it made her feel like a real ingrate. "It's not that—"

"After all I did for you, you don't trust me. It's a sad world when a guy can't help a girl out."

"I just want to get to my friend, and I don't understand why you're so . . . willing to go out of your way to help me." And so pushy about it.

"Maybe I'm a nice guy."

Too pushy about it. "I'm sure you are, but I'm going to O'Brien's. If it'll make you feel better, you can walk me to the bar. I'd . . . appreciate that." How had this man gotten her to lie like this?

"Don't do me any favors," he spat out, turning away.

An icky feeling washed over her, and she pushed onward to the bar, not wanting to think about what could have happened if she'd let him walk her home. When she glanced back, he was there, watching her. There wasn't a trace of good Samaritan in his eyes now. How easily she'd been fooled.

She shivered as she made her way down the corridor and into the bar on the right. The place was cave dark. It took a moment for her eyes to adjust, and for her ears to adjust to the sounds of the piano and the raucous voices singing along. A hand slipped over her arm and pulled her around.

"Ahh!" She cut her scream short when she saw Christopher, who jerked at her reaction.

"Sorry. I just . . ." She rubbed the knot forming on her head. "You surprised me, that's all."

"I figured you wouldn't be able to see me in here. I've got a table over there. You look like you could use a Hurricane."

"If it has liquor in it, you're right."

She followed him to a small table toward the back wall as the song changed to "Que Sera, Sera." He ordered another beer and a Hurricane for her. She settled at the table and tried to make out the faces of the people around her. She could barely see Christopher clearly, and he was sitting next to her.

"You didn't warn me these things were so big!" she said when her mammoth pink drink arrived.

He tipped his glass toward hers. "Que sera, sera," he said, and took a long drink. He'd apparently had a few, judging by his languorous movements.

She took a sip of the super-sweet drink as she looked around the bar. In all of the confusion with the beads and hyperventilating, she'd forgotten about the reason behind her panic. She could still feel those eyes watching her. The guy in the purple hat could be anywhere in the murky bar and she'd never see him.

"How'd lunch go?"

"Tammy's in love with Brian."

"She is?"

"I didn't learn much, other than that. Tammy didn't know where he went on Mardi Gras night. She'd never heard of Sira, supposedly. I'm not sure about her."

"Obsessive love can make someone do things that have nothing to do with real love." He looked as though he spoke from experience, and she got another shiver.

"I was trying to remember what Aris Smith looked like. She had very generic looks, nothing distinguishable. Tammy's the same way. Take away the ever-changing hair and change the eye color—" She shrugged.

"You think Tammy is the nurse?"

"Here in New Orleans, nothing is what it seems. What if she found out Brian was involved with someone else—me—and tried to kill him? You know, crime of passion." *And what do you know about passion, Rita?* "If she got on to his PC and saw my e-mails, she could track me down just like you did. And she'd probably erase them."

He regarded her with no small amount of disbelief. "How could that woman push a man Brian's size off a roof?"

"Maybe she took him by surprise. The railing isn't that high." Rita rubbed the knot on her head and winced. All this thinking made her head ache. She took another sip of her drink, noticing that he hadn't touched his beer since his silent toast.

"Nice beads," he said. His smile was laced with mock suspicion. "A woman doesn't get beads like that without showing some flesh."

"Given the choice, I would have preferred the flesh way of getting them." She fingered the beads for a moment, and then looked up at him. "I thought I was being followed on my way here."

He stiffened. "What made you think that?"

"It was a feeling. A strong feeling. I don't go around thinking people are watching me."

"You don't often meet people in comas either, do you?"

Did he believe her? She couldn't tell. "No, I don't."

"Did you see anyone who looked suspicious?"

She laughed at that. "Are you kidding? *Everyone* looked suspicious. But no one in particular. Then some beads hit me on the head, and I lost a few seconds." She left out the hyperventilation part. "And this guy offered to walk me back to the house because I still looked a bit shaken."

Christopher leaned closer. "What guy?"

"I don't know, some guy. He looked safe enough at the time, but I decided to come here instead, since I was so close."

He pushed aside his beer and signaled the waiter to bring the bill. "Good thing you did."

"He got weird when I declined his offer. He had this way of turning my words around, getting me to say things I didn't mean." She wrapped her arms around herself. "Creepy." Her eyes widened. "Wait a minute. I think . . . no, I'm pretty sure. When he first offered to take me back to my house . . . he said *house*. Before I'd mentioned it."

"How sure?"

"Ninety-nine percent. I'll bet that's why I got a feeling not to go with him. My subconscious registered his slipup even when I didn't realize it."

"Don't trust anyone around here." His fingers wrapped around his beer as he studied her in the near-darkness.

"Not even you?"

He took one last swig from his beer. "Not even me." He paid the tab, but before he stood, he said, "I found something in Brian's office. I don't know what it means, but you'll find it interesting."

"Lemme see."

"When we get back to the house. Come on, let's go. When we walk out, I want you to casually look around for the guy. Subtly point him out to me."

Rita rubbed her arms as they emerged into the sunlight. How did the guy fit into all this? Or did he? She glanced around but didn't see him. Instead of getting answers, she was only collecting more questions.

He wanted to make this right. It was his fault for not catching Rita's last e-mail to Brian, but Sira's fault for not taking care of Rita in Boston. He wanted to show Sira he was strong. He followed Rita and Christopher out of O'Brien's and spotted a rolled-up tube of paper in his hand. Uh-oh. He recognized that type of sketch paper. It was the same kind he'd taken from Brian's bedroom. He knew Christopher had gone into Brian's office at the hotel, but he hadn't been worried. He'd checked it out. But had he missed something?

He had trashed the purple cap and turned his coat inside-out so the plaid interior was now on the outside. He'd put on his curly wig and ditched his contacts. Rita had looked right at him when they'd exited O'Brien's but didn't recognize him. He rounded the corner and ran to Exchange Alley, down to Canal and back up to St. Charles, approaching the couple as they reached the streetcar stop.

He boarded the streetcar right behind them, holding on to the strap as the car moved forward. They had to stand too since the car was full. He looked straight ahead, but watched them from the corner of his eye. What were they on to? How much did they know?

He stepped off the streetcar one stop ahead of them and walked casually down the banquette like any other tourist. Up ahead, he saw them get off the streetcar and head down Napoleon. When they disappeared from view, he stepped through the dainty gate of one of the houses and then let himself inside. It was dark, just as he liked it. He stepped out of his clothes, relishing the cool air that brought his flesh alive with goose bumps. He walked into the narrow room on the right. Green eyes stared at him from the darkness. He wasn't alone.

Sira was there, and she wanted control again. She was stronger. It wasn't right. *I'm the boy. I'm the boy,* a childhood voice chanted, but it didn't matter. It never had. *Boys are stronger.* But Sira always won.

"You failed," she said. He didn't mention that she had failed, too. He was afraid to.

It was early, but Sira walked over to the French doors in back and swung them open. Then she turned on the computer and opened the music software. The CD was already in the player. She clicked play and changed into her black cat suit.

" 'I've got the fever.' " She inserted her own words into Peggy Lee's song as she cut through the line of trees that separated the corner of her yard from Brian LaPorte's. " 'And it's going to burn you up.' "

14

"I figured you'd think I was crazy, feeling like someone was following me. Or for any number of other reasons." Rita hung up her coat and the beads and followed him into the kitchen where he started a pot of that coffee he liked so much. That she now liked.

He concentrated on filling the carafe with water from a gallon jug. "I don't think you're crazy." He said it so seriously it caught her off guard. There was something strange in his expression.

"Really?"

"Really." He left it at that, but she knew there was more to it. Maybe it had something to do with what he'd found in Brian's office.

"Velda's playing her music already," she said, nodding toward the house behind them. "It's early."

"Maybe she's entertaining."

"Ew. Don't want to think about that." She held out her hand, and in Emmagee's accent said, "I don't want any details, you know what I mean?"

His smile caught her full in the stomach. *And I'm not doing a thing about it. Remember how you feel about Brian, how he's the only one who can save your messed-*

up self. She didn't feel that way anymore, she realized; didn't feel the fear of losing that opportunity as acutely.

He glanced up at the clock. "Babylon starts at six-thirty."

"Is *Babylon 5* still on out here?"

He laughed. "You watch too much television, you know that? It's a parade."

"Oh." He handed her a mug of coffee after he'd poured it. Then, amazingly, he handed her the creamer. He remembered, and that made her smile. "Do you really think I watch too much TV?"

"Just because you know at any given time of the evening when a show you want to watch is on, just because you can tell me the history on everything we've watched, just because you know the names of all the characters . . . nah, what was I thinking?"

She'd only babbled on about that because she'd been nervous. The night she'd watched television, he'd joined her for a while. "I think you're analyzing me now."

He walked up to her. "Don't like it much, do you?"

"I don't care." Marty would have hooted with laughter if she'd heard that.

"Yeah, right."

For a moment their gazes locked, and then he leaned forward and she held her breath, wanting to see if he was going to kiss her, waiting to see how she'd feel about it. Instead, he reached past her and grabbed the roll of paper he'd taken from the hotel. "Come upstairs."

She released a breath and convinced herself it was a good thing he hadn't kissed her. She pulled the envelopes from her pocket and followed him up the stairs. "Tammy gave me some mail for Brian." The room smelled like Christopher, a mixture of his aftershave and that grape gum he chewed. "Is this your old room?"

"No, it was Brian's childhood room."

"Mm," was all she could say, wondering why he'd chosen to stay here instead of in his old room, which must be . . . the one she was staying in.

He shoved the rumpled sheets off the bed and dropped down onto his stomach. She looked around for someplace to sit besides the bed. Bad idea, that. Real bad. Then why was she staring at that wrinkled place next to him? Spotting the chair at the table, she dragged it over.

He unrolled the paper cylinder. "I found these under his desk mat."

The pastel chalk sketches were well drawn in broad strokes. The first was a man draped in robes, shoulders held high and a crown on his head. Beneath it were the words *King Alta.* Christopher peeled away that picture to reveal a woman in a green cat suit, with a mask, cape, and knee-high boots.

"She looks like Xena, Warrior Princess," Rita said, realizing she was giving away her television addiction again. He pointed to the name written below her picture. "Sira," she said on a breath.

"I thought they were Mardi Gras costumes until I saw the name."

"This is the woman I saw, the one who pushed Brian! She was dressed in a bodysuit and this style of mask. I'm pretty sure it's also the mask I saw in Boston. The police found a black feather in the car that hit mine. If we could find the mask, I bet they could match them up microscopically."

He didn't give her a skeptical look. In fact, he'd had an odd expression on his face since she'd met him at O'Brien's. He held up another picture. This one was a cityscape. No city she'd ever seen before, though. The buildings were dome-shaped and clustered together. The sun setting behind the city gave it a surreal glow. Beneath it was the word *Xanadu.*

"Like the border in his bedroom," she said. She went back to Sira's sketch. "Did Brian draw these?"

He shrugged. "Maybe. When we were kids, he used to write stories, and he drew illustrations for them. He kept them hidden from our parents, even from me." At Rita's questioning look, he added, "I was a nosy kid, what can I say?"

"Wait a minute." She went to Brian's current room and returned with the science fiction magazines. "I think he still wrote stories. I found these in one of his drawers. Guess I'm nosy, too." She opened each magazine to a story that was flagged by a Post-It note. "Each of these stories is written by a Brian Caspian. Maybe it's a pseudonym."

"He got it from Prince Caspian."

"From the *Chronicles of Narnia*?" He looked surprised that she knew, and she shrugged. "I must have read the set at least five times. But why would Brian use *Caspian* for a pseudonym?"

From the dark look on his face it had to be from one of the tableaux.

He set the sketches and the stories' black-and-white illustrations side by side. "They're the same style." He flipped over the magazine covers. "These were published five years ago. Are there any more?"

"This was all I found." She scanned each of the stories. "I don't see any mention of Xanadu or Sira, though, so these still don't answer any questions."

He came to a sitting position and faced her. "You knew the name *Sira* because of what Brian showed you while you were in a coma." It wasn't a question, and yet he didn't sound quite convinced either.

"You believe me?"

He scrubbed his fingers through his hair. "I'd like to say hell, no, but the truth is, you know too much. Brian wouldn't have told anyone about our last swordfight. He'd be too ashamed. You knew what he told me at the funeral, and it's not likely he'd share that with anyone either. Especially someone he wanted to impress." He lifted one of the sketches. "And you knew about Sira."

"Do you believe he was pushed?"

He stared at nothing for a moment, absorbing it all. "As this gets weirder and weirder, I'm not discounting it anymore."

She nodded toward the drawings. "Does this have anything to do with your father's krewe?"

"I don't think so."

She leaned over and grabbed the envelopes. "Maybe something here will help. You never know," she added at his skeptical look.

"All right, pass me the letter opener on the table."

She searched around his laptop and under some papers lying nearby. "I don't see it."

He looked over at the table. "The opener should be there. It's hard to miss. It's gold and has an *X* on the handle. Xanadu gave it to their royalty."

"It's not here."

He looked for himself. "That's strange; it is gone."

"Maybe Emmagee put it away."

He looked beneath the table and then under the bed. "Maybe I took it downstairs." He tossed two envelopes after giving them cursory glances. "Junk mail." He opened the credit card bill. "Mostly recurring monthly charges like his Internet service." As he started to set it aside, he pulled it back. "Wait a minute. He shouldn't have an Internet bill. His account is tied into the hotel's account."

She was left to follow him to Brian's room, where she

found him already turning on the computer. He checked the two e-mail addresses on the account and then checked the files for a different e-mail program.

"He has a gaming computer but no games. He has two Internet providers but only one installed. Something's not right." He went back to the file organizer and pored over every folder. "A-ha. The sneaky bastard's divided his hard drive into two drives. I didn't even notice the second one. Called simply *X*, by the way."

Rita's heart sped at the prospect of finding something concrete at last. But when he clicked the drive, a password prompt appeared. He tried a series of words and then glanced around the desk.

"What are you looking for?" she asked.

"A lot of people use something that's around them for a password, so they don't forget it. It also makes it easy for someone else to guess what it is."

"Oh." She was guilty of doing just that.

She searched the walls for clues. "Have you tried Xanadu?" He nodded. "King? Masquerade?"

He tried those, and then *Caspian, Brian Caspian,* and *Prince Caspian.* "Bingo." More folders appeared. "He's got other software in here, though none look like games. But here's another Internet and e-mail program." He opened the mail program and clicked on account information. The ID was *Alta.*

He pulled a square of gum from the pack in his shirt pocket, as though to fortify himself. She perched on the arm of his chair and watched as he checked Brian's inbox and found one e-mail, a new letter from someone named Vitar.

King Alta:
Please respond right away. I find your absence disturbing in light of Sira's last declaration.

"Sira," Rita whispered.

"*King* Alta?" He shook his head. "Cripes, he was still hung up on being king."

She leaned forward, bracing her palms on the edge of the desk. "This Vitar guy obviously doesn't know Brian's in a coma. We could answer as Alta and see what we find out."

"Exactly what I was thinking."

> Vitar:
> Am here, but have been ill. Please advise status and Sira's declaration.

He signed it "King Alta" and sent it off. When he opened the Internet browser, the Web site selected as the home page wouldn't load. The Web address was a series of nonsensical letters and numbers. He checked the list of recently visited Web pages; they were all connected with the defunct address. The list of Brian's favorite sites didn't include anything other than the default selection.

When Rita turned to look at him, the waves of her hair brushed his ear. A warm, bubbly feeling overtook her and intensified when he looked at her. Her throat went dry and she had trouble swallowing. What was he thinking? What did he see when he looked at her? More than she saw when she looked at her reflection, that much was evident.

She focused on the border Brian had painted—the one that matched the cityscape. She considered that instead of the enigma beside her, feeling her insides caving in and not wanting him to see it on her face. The man didn't want to kiss her, didn't want to let her help heal the pain of his past. She shouldn't want to do either, not with the way her nose was tingling at the mere prospect.

She focused again on the two pieces of tape on the wall with the traces of sketch paper left on the sticky side.

"The sketches you found at the office." She walked back into Christopher's room, but movement stopped her short. The filmy curtains undulated in a cool breeze. The French door was ajar, and the sketches were on the floor between the bed and doors.

The wind must have blown the sketches off the bed. She picked them up and locked the door.

He was leaning against the desk facing the door when she returned. "Just as I suspected," she said, holding the paper up against the tape. "Brian had sketches like these hanging here. Someone took them."

"Maybe Brian tore them down but didn't remove the tape." He nodded toward the clothes piled over chairs and the lump of bedclothes at the foot of the bed. "It's not like he was trying to be neat in here." He tapped the rolled-up sketches on the edge of the desk and then walked out.

"Like you can talk," she said, following him back to his room. "Your room isn't much better."

He tossed the sketches on the table next to his laptop. "I've never had to impress anyone. Who are you trying to impress, making your bed so neat I could bounce a quarter on it?"

"Myself," she said, wondering when he'd seen her bed. "I like my space to be orderly. That's just the way I am."

He hooked his thumbs through the belt loops on his jeans. "Did your father make sure you made your bed every morning?"

Her throat went tight at his words. "My father never came to my room. I kept it neat for myself."

He lowered his head. "Or just in case he looked in and saw how neat his daughter was."

Because she didn't want to be a bother. "Stop it."

"What's the matter?" He moved closer and stood in front of her. "Thought you didn't mind being analyzed."

"Don't throw my words back in my face. I trusted you when I told you about my father."

His voice was soft and low, his eyes smoky. "Didn't I tell you not to trust me?"

"I know about the tableaux, about how you were always the bad guy. It was only pretend. You didn't have to take your role so seriously. You still don't."

His expression gave away nothing, but her words did quiet him for a few moments. At last he said, "Maybe I like the role."

"I think you do. It keeps people at a distance."

"I don't see a lot of distance between us right now."

"You're just trying to intimidate me."

"Is it working?"

It was working, but not the way he wanted. Her heart was rushing heated blood through her veins, but not out of fear of bodily harm. It was for the possibility that he would grant her earlier request. She had been sure she'd only wanted to prove herself, but now. . . . now she wasn't so sure.

"No," she lied.

He grasped her chin and made her betray her earlier word with a slight intake of breath.

"You struck me as someone who could easily be intimidated that first day we met." He was leaning over her, forcing her to look up at him. "Now I don't know what to make of you."

Just as she was ready to back away, those words filled her with a heady power. Rita, tower of strength. Yeah, right. But hey, she'd fooled him; maybe she could fool herself, too. Unfortunately, just the thought of him kissing her, with that gorgeous bed so close, made her knees feel wobbly, and worse, made her nose start to tingle. So much for the tower.

"Who is the Highwayman?" she asked, annoyed that it came out a whisper. That'll make *him* back away, she thought.

He, however, did not back away. He did drop his hand from her chin and shove the tips of his hands in his jean pockets. As he looked away for a moment, she realized she needed to know. Because despite his warning, she did trust him, at least on some level. She needed to know more about the boy mentioned in those newspaper articles and the teenager Emmagee had had a crush on. She wanted to know Chris.

She could see by the dark glitter in his eyes that he wasn't going to let her into that part of him.

"Maybe I'm a masked bandit who roams the information highway in search of victims to pillage."

"Maybe you are, and maybe you're not." A masked bandit wouldn't make sure the kittens that had adopted him were being fed. "Maybe you find out things about women and track them down. Find them at work, and try to intimidate them."

He leaned slightly toward her. "You know I do."

"But with me it was to find the truth about your brother. What else does the Highwayman do?"

"Why do you want to know?"

"Because . . . I just do."

He searched her eyes, waited her out, possibly weighing what to tell her. She would not relent, would not be intimidated. The tower was back. Finally he let out a long breath and looked away.

"Like I told you, I'm a hacker."

"When you need to be."

"Yep."

"What do you hack, exactly?"

"Creeps."

"Explain," she said, following his one-word precedent.

"Does it matter?"

"Yes."

"Can't we leave it at me being a plain-out-evil hacker?"

"As a matter of fact, no, we can't."

He flopped down on the bed, his arms bent and hands beneath his head. "Say that someone was harassing you on the Internet. It happens a lot. Sometimes it's vengeance, like sending e-mail bombs—so much mail that it bombs out your account. Other times, it's sexual harassment. A man you met in a chat room won't leave you alone, finds out where you live, and shows up at your door. The creep might post a message in your name, giving your address and phone number and inviting men with kinky tendencies to drop by."

She shivered as she perched on the corner of the bed. "Is it that easy to find out where people live?"

"Easier than you want to know."

"Like how you found me?"

"Exactly. All I need are a few pieces of information and I can find out almost anything."

He was staring at the ceiling, and she leaned over him to get his attention. "So what does the Highwayman do?"

"I intervene. First I send the harasser a threatening message, telling him to cease and desist. If he's only annoying, I might sign him up for an e-mail list at the Prayer-a-Day site. I might call him if he's menacing. If he—or she, I should add—doesn't get the message, he might find that a large chunk of his bank account is now missing, but he'll never find out it's been wired to the Make-A-Wish Foundation."

"You can actually do that?"

"When I have the right information. That's why it's not the best thing to have your mother's maiden name as your password to authorize bank transactions, especially if you use online banking."

Oops, she did that. She raised an eyebrow. "So you're an Internet vigilante?"

He shrugged. "Sort of."

Now the message she'd seen made sense. He was helping some woman who was being stalked on the Internet. She rather liked the image of a cyber-angel anonymously helping strangers. "But why you?"

His expression shadowed. "Someone has to."

"You could have left it up to someone else. Why you?"

He still stared at the ceiling, his eyes somewhat glazed now as he shut her out. "It doesn't matter why."

"Maybe it does to me." The Highwayman wasn't the whole story. She knew there was something behind it, something that compelled him to help.

He shook his head. "I'm a hacker. Let's leave it at that."

"You would rather have me think of you as a no-good hacker than to know the reason behind it?"

"Yes."

She nodded. "You do like playing the bad boy, don't you?"

My, she wanted to reach this man. The need twisted her insides. "If you were really all bad, you would have taken advantage of me up on the roof. You would have taken my kiss and then more, purely for your own gratification. But you held back, for me and, I suspect, for Brian." The subject of his rejection was still a fresh wound, but she ignored the sting.

He sat up, but as he spoke, he shifted his gaze. "Maybe I didn't want you." The words came out in dull thuds, each one another lance to her wound. Her fragile ego writhed in pain. She had to look away, wondering why she was putting herself on the sacrificial altar for a man who had no problems with his own ego.

He issued a soft curse and looped his hand around the back of her neck. Before she could even gain her senses, he had pulled her close. His mouth devoured hers, filling her senses with the taste of grape. Could the fingers that caressed her throat feel her pounding pulse?

She had been kissed before, but no one made her feel as though she were cresting on a tidal wave. No one made her terrified that she would drown in the surf. No one made her feel as though this were her first kiss, that her awkwardness would show as their tongues slid against each other.

And then she wasn't worried anymore. She gave in to the tightness inside her that threatened to explode. She gave herself to all of the sensations bombarding her: the way he smelled, the texture of his tongue.

He finished the kiss, though he kept touching his mouth to hers as though he couldn't bear to part from her. Then his hand slid up into the hair at the nape of her neck. He lowered his head and pressed his forehead against hers. What didn't he want her to see in his eyes?

Disgust? No, she wouldn't believe that, not with the way his chest was rising and falling in an effort to restrain his desire.

Finally he looked at her, cradling her face in his hands and taking in every feature. His eyes looked like the sky just after a thunderstorm, dark blue and hazy.

"Rita, I want you." Those low, thick words ran through her body like molasses, salving her wounds. His thumb traced her lower lip. "But I shouldn't."

"Because of Brian."

"That's the simplest reason. I can't steal my brother's girl while he's in a coma."

"No, not even the bad prince would do that." Rita wondered what the other reason—or reasons—he shouldn't want her were.

She had to remind herself that she shouldn't want him, either, for reasons other than Brian. She couldn't think straight with his hands on her face. She wanted him to run his thumb over her lower lip again, as though that were as close as he'd allow himself to another kiss. That simple touch was nearly as powerful as the kiss it tried to substitute. Instead, she moved out of his grasp. What was going on here? Why was she so drawn to him? Because of her need to save him, that's what it had to be.

"Christopher, what we have here is double transference. I feel a strong need to help you, and you feel a need to reach out to me—for help."

"I don't want your help, and the only transferring going on here is you transferring your feelings for Brian to me. He was the man who was going to rescue you from your insecurities."

"I had built him up as my rescuer. That was a lot of my attraction, I admit. But I'm not sure I need rescuing anymore. And I'm not sure Brian is the man I thought him to be. I didn't know him at all. I'd convinced myself I did. I care about him, but I'm not in love with him. And now, I don't think I ever could be." There, she'd said what was lurking in her mind. "You may not want my help," she said in a low voice, "but I think you need it."

He slid off the bed and stood by the French doors gazing into the darkness, as though he couldn't trust himself to be there with her any longer.

She had another test for herself, this one having nothing to do with putting her ego on the line and having it stepped on. Quietly she got to her feet. She reached out to his shoulder, hesitated, then pressed her hand into the thick fabric of his shirt. His muscles were concrete-hard. He stiffened even more but didn't move away.

"Christopher, have you ever been loved? I mean, really, truly loved no matter what you did or who you were?"

He waited a long time to answer, so long that she thought he was ignoring her. Finally he said, "No."

"Me, either. I wonder what it would be like to be loved that way. And to love someone that way."

He turned slightly, leaving her to look at his profile. "How would you know if you were doing it right? How would you know that it was even love?"

They were the last two people who should get involved in any context.

She let her hand drop. "Emmagee said something the other day, something in French. I don't remember the words, but the gist was: Don't forget what's important."

"Lache pas la patate."

"Yeah." It sounded even better on his lips, and she felt the same way Gomez Addams did when Morticia spoke French. "What is most important? To you, I mean."

"Justice."

Taking a deep breath, she faced him and put her arms around his waist. The fabric of his shirt was soft and warm against her cheek. She was heartened to feel his hands on her shoulders, even though he'd eyed her dubiously, as though she had a trick up her sleeve. "*Lache pas la patate*. What's most important?"

His fingers tightened on her shoulders. He opened his mouth to say something, but nothing came out. Not the word *justice* the way he'd said before without giving it any thought. That's probably what he'd programmed himself to believe.

She closed her eyes and gave in to the solid strength of him. His arms went more fully around her. She could feel him breathe deeper, but not in the same sexually charged way when he'd kissed her. This was softer breathing, laced with resignation. His arms tightened, and she felt his cheek rest against the top of her head.

It was that moment when she knew what was most

important to her. Not her work. Not her parental guidance campaign. Only to be held like this. To love, and be loved back.

He hadn't answered her, but she let herself believe that maybe, just maybe, he was coming to the same conclusion. If he admitted it out loud, he couldn't take it back. She had to get him to say the word. Not justice.

Love.

"Chris," she said, using the shortened version for the first time. The accessible version. He tightened his hold. She wanted to stay there, but she needed to see his face. She backed away enough to look up at him. There was something raw in his expression. *Say the word, Chris. Say it.*

That's when she saw movement in her peripheral vision. She turned in time to see eyes set in a gold mask surrounded by black feathers.

"Someone's out there! On the balcony," she said in an urgent whisper.

He jerked around to catch the shadow of someone running toward the end of the balcony. "Stay put and lock the door," he ordered and rushed out to give chase. She ran to the doorway, frozen in fear at the thought of someone standing there watching them.

Christopher climbed over the railing and dropped down to the ground. With her heart pounding, she ran to the edge of the balcony and tried to see what was going on. His dark form raced through the courtyard and struggled through the tangle of trees at the corner. Then he disappeared, and his footsteps faded into the distance. Suddenly she felt vulnerable and alone, standing where some masked stranger had stood.

"Oh, my God, the door . . . it was open." She remembered the French door in Christopher's room, the drawings on the floor . . . as though someone was about to abscond with them. She shivered. She'd been in the room just seconds after the stranger had been. Stranger . . . and murderer.

She couldn't tear away from the railing where she watched for Christopher's return. Her fingers gripped the ironwork so tightly the edge bit into her palm.

Was this what it felt like to care about someone? To experience this nerve-shattering fear that they would be hurt, that they might never come back?

"Chris, please be all right."

She listened to the sounds of the night: the rustle of wind in the trees, music, voices, laughter. People having fun while Christopher chased some shadow into the darkness of New Orleans.

Just as the time she ran to save him from his alleged jump, fear settled into her being. This was far worse. Last time the villain would have been Christopher's despair.

This time the villain was an unknown evil. And Christopher was in real danger.

15

Christopher walked back through the trees, limping slightly, but in one piece. He saw Rita at the balcony. Her body sagged when she saw him, relief palpable in her eyes.

He stopped below her and looked up. "I want you to go home."

He hadn't even caught his breath yet when she opened the kitchen door to let him in a minute later. He had the crazy urge to hold her. He held back, mostly because she looked like she was contemplating the same thing.

She opened her mouth to say something, but he beat her to it, emphasizing each word. "I want you to go home."

"Why?" She sounded breathless, too, but it was her bewilderment that stuck to him.

I can't do this again. The pressure in his chest had nothing to do with exertion or the ankle he'd twisted. The feeling that she'd been followed, the guy knowing she was staying in a house, the missing letter opener, this creepy Xanadu thing . . . it added up to something sinister. He could not let her get dragged into it.

He turned on the lights in the courtyard. The shadows from the branches reached like fingers across the floor.

He pushed her back against the refrigerator and blocked her with his body as he watched the backyard. He detected no movement out of the ordinary.

"What is going on?" she whispered, soft and afraid and too damned close to his ear.

He turned to her, planting a hand on either side of her face. He wanted to kiss away the fear. Instead he had to compound it. "I don't know. I lost the guy in the crowd for the parade."

"The guy?"

"Ran like a guy. If it was a woman, she's in damned good shape."

"Aris *was* pretty fit."

"Yeah, but what about the guy who wanted to walk you home? He may be involved in this, too."

"You're right; we can't discount him." She took him in. "Are you all right? You were limping."

"I twisted my ankle when I jumped. I'm fine." Her concern wrapped around him. What was most important? *Justice,* his brain screamed. Justice and keeping her safe. "I'm fine," he repeated, and felt her muscles relax slightly. "You were right. Something is going on here, and it probably has to do with whatever Xanadu is. This Sira has been in the house."

"I know. I didn't think much about it at the time, but when I went to get the sketches from your room, the door to the balcony was open. I thought the wind had opened it."

"No, she's been in the house before tonight." He held up the letter opener with the *X* on it. "Look what she dropped."

"Who has access to this house?"

He shrugged. "Someone at the hotel, maybe. Anyone with a pick kit."

"Emmagee has a key, and she's certainly in good shape."

He shook his head. "I've known her most of my life. I can't see her involved in something like this."

"But you haven't been in touch with her for years."

He hadn't really known her that well. She'd just been the tagalong younger sister of a friend and a bit of a tomboy misfit. "I'm going to get a locksmith over to change the locks tonight."

"Should we call Detective Connard now that we have a little something?"

He couldn't help the bitter laugh that escaped. "The police are no help. Not without proof." He could see another woman begging the police to help her. He pushed the memory away. "All we've got is our story about someone lurking outside the balcony." He looked away, trying to control the anger and feelings of helplessness raging through him. *Not this time.*

"You're right, I suppose. Connard already thinks I'm a kook."

"Go home. I'll keep digging and keep you posted."

She was shaking her head. "I can't just sit and wait a thousand miles away and wonder what's going on. I can't leave."

"Stubborn, narrow-minded—are you plain-out stupid?" He held up the letter opener. "It's not a knife, but she had it for a reason."

Instead of being afraid, she asked, "What if there were fingerprints on it?"

He let out an agitated breath. "She wore gloves. I couldn't see any skin at all. Besides, this isn't a common criminal we're dealing with. We don't even know what we're dealing with or what she wants. Rita, you have to go." His voice had gone hoarse with those last words, and he could see her expression as she detected the desperation.

In a soft voice, she asked, "What are you afraid of?"

"I don't want you to get hurt."

She reached out and touched his raspy cheek. "I'll be all right."

He closed his eyes at her touch. Her hand was cool, yet her skin burned into him and made him want to press up against her and kiss her the way he'd really wanted to up in his room. He wanted to shake her silly and tell her that her promise was useless.

He'd known this woman for mere days, yet she had him so twisted up, so worried, now that her delusions weren't . . . delusions. He removed her hand from his cheek before he did something rash, like he'd done earlier. But he didn't let go. Her hand was small and soft. He squeezed hard.

"Do you know what it's like to have someone stalking you? Do you know what it's like to live in constant fear, knowing he wants to kill you, knowing he's ruined your life without even touching you? But that's not enough for him. No one can help you, not the police or your parents or your friends. And even though you promise to be careful, to stay alive, you know deep down inside that he'll probably get you anyway."

She tugged her hand free. "You're not talking about me, are you?"

He turned away from her. "Just go home."

"No." She stepped in front of him. "This isn't about me at all."

"Oh, yes it is."

"All right, but it's about someone else, too. The reason you put sea monsters in your moat, I'll bet."

He walked away to call the hospital and warn the guard to keep a sharper eye out than usual. Rita hovered nearby, fear shadowing her eyes. Good. She needed to be scared and, more precisely, scared away. He walked into the parlor where the light from the chandelier washed down over the room. He heard the sound of her breathing, felt her warmth as she took hold of his arm. She looked beautiful, ready to fight him, ready to pull out his heart and tackle every tear and hole with needle and thread.

"I'm not even thinking about leaving until you tell me why you're so adamant that I go."

He held his breath for a moment before releasing it. "If you stay, then I'll be responsible for you. I don't want to be responsible for anyone again, but especially not you."

"Why me especially?"

Why did he want to hold her when all she wanted to do was drag answers out of him? "I don't know why. Maybe because I know you, because—"

"I remind you of her?"

"No." Even he did not want to examine why. "It's as plain as chicken broth. My brother was into something, and someone may have tried to kill him because of it. We don't even know what this someone looks like, other than your description of the nurse. This person put Brian in the hospital to get whatever it is she wants." He lowered his voice. "And if you're in the way, you'll be killed."

He let that sink in and hoped to God he'd convinced her to go.

"My motivation for staying isn't as clear as broth," she said at last. "It's as murky as gumbo. I can't leave until I know what happened to Brian and why. He came to me in the gray place, and I believe he asked for my help."

"You've convinced me that he was pushed. Mission accomplished. Time to pack up and go. Bye, have a nice trip."

She looked away, then back at him. "But I'm involved now. With Brian. And with you."

It was happening all over again, that feeling of falling into a dark pit, his hands scrabbling for purchase. Not knowing what awaited him at the bottom. "Let me handle this."

Damned stubborn woman was shaking her head. "I can't leave. I can't. I'm not going to end up like her, whoever she is. You're just going to have to accept that. But you don't have to accept responsibility for me. I don't want you to." She wrapped her arms around herself, but dropped them again. "I've been taking responsibility for my life for a long time, for my risks, fears, and hurts. I'm not letting you take that away now. This is my choice, my decision."

"Damn you, Rita." Not only for staying, but for revealing too much of her soul.

She winced at his words, at the passion in them that surprised even him. He walked away from her, wishing he could walk away from all of this. But he owed Brian and he certainly couldn't leave Rita to handle it alone.

Outside, remnants of the crowd wandered in the streets, loaded down with beads, not a care in the world other than planning for the next parade. And someone out there lurked with other intentions, ones he couldn't fathom. He turned around.

She was still standing by the bottom of the stairs, watching him with those analytical blue eyes. Maybe once he could have stalked toward her and intimidated her into backing down. But something had changed since that first day here in the parlor. She had grown stronger.

He had one last chance to sway her, and it had nothing to do with intimidation. All he had to do was keep the pain from his voice, keep the armor tight around him. He stayed in the shadows, checking outside the window for movement.

"Her name was Sherry. Her ex-boyfriend was stalking her."

He didn't want Rita close while he told the story, but she walked over anyway. She kept a distance of a few feet, leaning against one of the gilt-edged chairs. He didn't—couldn't—look at her now, focusing instead on the lit stairs winding up to the balcony behind her. His gaze strayed to the two swords, increasing the ache in the pit of his stomach. He didn't want to see the apprehension on her face or what he thought was concern in her eyes. He wanted to hate her for making him go this far.

"Damen wouldn't leave her alone. She'd come home and find him sitting in her apartment waiting for her. We were friends, and she came to me for help. The police couldn't do anything until he actually made a move toward her. The restraining order only pissed him off more, and he did everything he could to let her know he'd been within five hundred feet of her.

"I moved her into my apartment and later . . . into my bed. I thought she was safe there. I didn't want to get a gun, or any kind of weapon, not after what had happened with the swords. I was stupid enough to think he'd give up when he couldn't get her alone. We were going to wait him out. I promised to keep her alive." He swallowed, finding a wad of virtual cotton lodged there. "And she promised to be careful, to stay alive."

Rita wrapped her arms around herself. Maybe he was getting to her. Maybe tearing out his guts would be worth it.

He continued. "Damen hated being kept from anything he wanted. I didn't know he had a full set of locksmith tools. While we were at work, he picked his way into the apartment and unlocked a window so that when he was ready, he could simply nudge it open. He picked the room in the back where he could enter undetected. This time he wasn't going to leave a clue. This time he was going to make sure no one kept him from Sherry again.

"She had nightmares. I left a night-light on for her." He took a breath, gathering strength for the demons that would come in the form of memories. The demons that still haunted his nightmares, that lifted their heads and growled every time he saw the scar. "When I heard her scream, I thought she was dreaming again. Until I saw the knife coming at me."

She gasped, covered her mouth.

"I shoved her out of the way and threw myself at him, not knowing he'd already stabbed her. When I saw her blood, and heard her crying, I wanted to kill Damen. She needed my help, but I had to deal with the bastard first." To be unable to hold Sherry as she whimpered in pain and shock nearly did him in. "I rushed him. Wrestled the knife away. I would have killed him, but he got out from under me. He crashed through the window. Only he didn't go all the way through and ended up impaling himself on the glass."

She winced. Then she pushed away from the chair and came closer. "What happened to Sherry?"

He had scarcely been aware that he'd been cut, hadn't noticed the pain searing his chest. He went to Sherry's side, where she lay bleeding all over his bed. He held her, called 911, and commanded her not to die. But he knew by the glassy look in her eyes and all the blood she'd lost that it was too late. He pressed the sheet against the hole in her chest and held her tight until the paramedics got there.

With every long second that passed, he closed himself away, moving further from Rita and the parlor. "She was still alive when help arrived, but the moment they took her from me, she died."

As he'd sat there while the paramedics did what they could to revive her, he knew his father had been right. He could never be the good prince; only the bad prince who was cast to lose every time. He looked away. He could not let her see the pain he knew racked his features.

He didn't know that she had walked close enough to trace a finger from his shoulder down to his chest. "You were stabbed, too, weren't you? That's how you got this scar."

"The knife just grazed me." He should have died that night, and Sherry should have walked away with only a scar.

Her hand flattened over the place where the scar was. "You left that little detail out."

"It *was* a little detail compared to what happened to her."

He had dumped all of that out to scare her into leaving, not to make her look at him as though she wanted to enfold him in her arms like a baby. Just the thought of that made his throat tighten.

"Did you love her?"

He swallowed. "I loved being needed by her."

She cocked her head at an angle, studying him. "That's why you don't want to be responsible for me. You blame yourself for her death."

"Of course I blame myself. I promised to keep her safe."

"That's a mighty big promise. You did the best you could."

"It wasn't good enough. My point in telling you all that was not to elicit your sympathy."

"I know." She placed her other hand on his chest. "It

was to scare me away. Earlier you accused me of getting my feelings about Brian mixed up with you. I think you're getting your feelings for Sherry mixed up with me."

"Go home, Rita."

"I'm not going to let you off that easily by dying," she said, using his earlier phrase. "Or by leaving."

He swore under his breath. She had no idea what she was doing to him. He felt himself spiraling downward, helpless to stop. "Let me get you a gun, then."

"No. I don't know how to use one, and I don't want to. I'm not asking you to make the same promise you made to Sherry."

With a ragged breath, he said, "Yes you are," and walked to the kitchen to call the locksmith.

16

Rita woke the next morning and looked for Christopher, who was sleeping on the floor in front of the bedroom's French doors. He'd taken off his shirt and kicked off the sheets during the night. His short, dark hair was mussed. She knew he hadn't slept much the night before; it was midnight before the locksmith had finished installing dead bolts on all the doors and locks on the windows. Even with that extra assurance, even with Christopher's insistence that they sleep in the same room, and change rooms every night, he had still stayed up long after she had fallen exhausted into Brian's bed.

But her mind hadn't let her fall right to sleep, either. She kept seeing the eerie masked face in the darkness. She kept replaying Christopher's words. He had opened himself up to her, yet he seemed farther away than ever.

Probably because he hated her for making him tell that awful story, especially since it hadn't scared her away.

She got out of bed and told herself she would not pause and look at him. He was lying on his back with one arm slung across his stomach. She looked at the scar in a whole new way, and knew that every time he saw it, he must be reminded of his failed promise.

Well, that resolve lasted long.

He had a beautiful body, at least as much as she could see of it. Skin smooth and taut, stomach flat and hard, and, she noted, nipples tight from the cool air in the room. She found herself wanting to pull up the white blanket to cover him but stopped herself. For one terrible moment, she envied Sherry for having shared a bed with him, and more than that.

After a hot shower, she went downstairs. She smelled coffee and told herself that the jump of her heartbeat was only because of the spicy coffee and not the spicy gumbo that would be in the kitchen.

He was wearing white sweats and looked just as sexy and disheveled as he had the previous morning, with a fair amount of stubble darkening his face. She'd always told herself that having a man around in the mornings would throw off her whole routine. But as she took him in, leaning against the counter with a steaming mug in hand, she wondered if routine was such a good thing after all.

"I could get used to this . . . coffee," she added quickly. She accepted the mug he poured for her.

"It's addicting, isn't it?"

"Oh, yeah." Addicting. "How'd you sleep?"

"I feel hungover."

"You don't have to sleep on the floor." As those words that had come so easily from her mouth sank in, she realized what she was saying.

"Oh, yes I do." He finished his mug and rinsed it out. "I'm going to take a shower, then we'll go to the hospital."

She reached out and touched his arm, making him pause. "Christopher, I'm sorry."

She wasn't sure exactly what she was sorry for, but it included making him tell her about Sherry. He nodded and then continued on. Apology accepted. Maybe. She glanced out the back window and sipped her coffee.

When one of the trees at the corner of the two yards moved, she narrowed her eyes and stared at it. Maybe she'd imagined it. Why would Velda be watching her? She didn't have the allure of a mystery. Except she *had* been a mystery once, when Christopher tracked her down at work. When she remembered the scene, she saw Marty's protective stance and that sent a stab of guilt through her. She owed her friend a call.

"What is going on with you?" Marty asked the second Rita identified herself. "You are worrying me out of my mind."

"I know, I'm a lousy friend. Everything is so . . . complicated. I don't want to get into all the details, but I can't leave yet."

"Why are you doing this?"

"I don't know if I'm staying for me, for Brian or for—"

"You're in love with him. I can hear it in your voice. You are, aren't you?"

"No, of course I am. Not. Am not!"

"Are, too! Don't deny it. I'm a trained professional."

"Okay." Her heart thudded in her chest at the admission.

It took Marty a moment to digest that. "Okay? Just like that?"

"Well, you said—"

"I know, but I figured I'd have to cajole you some more." Another moment passed. "You're in love with him."

"I think so. I've never felt this way before, but I have a bad feeling that's what it is."

"Rita, this is nuts. The man is in a coma."

"I'm not talking about Brian! I'm in love with . . . the other one." She let the words drift off, then turned to make sure he wasn't standing there listening. That was all she needed, like the scene in *Jerry Maguire*.

"That's almost as nuts! The guy gave you a nosebleed without even touching you."

"But he kissed me last night and I didn't get a nosebleed." 'Course, he'd taken her by surprise.

"Kissed you! That guy is bad news."

"Marty, I can't explain this, not even to myself. I'm probably going to end up with my heart in pieces on the floor, but I cannot leave."

"Well, babe, you know I'll be here to pick up the pieces. I'll even bring the Scotch tape."

"You're a good friend."

"Yes, I am, and don't you forget it. Call if you need me. And speaking of that, your mom called me a few days ago. She really wants to make things right with you. She asked me for advice. I told her, 'Heck, Rita doesn't even open up to *me.*' I think it would be good for both of you if you forgave her."

"I know."

"But?"

But she couldn't seem to let go of her anger.

Marty let out an exasperated sigh. "You could at least call her. She's worried about you, about this trip. I haven't told her anything, but that only worries her more."

"I'll think about it. How's Pauline doing with the mirror OCD?"

They discussed the patient that Marty had taken over and her obsessive compulsion to look at every reflection she passed by. Rita was satisfied that Marty was doing a good job with her continued therapy. "Thanks for taking some of my patients. I'm just going to stick with my three until I'm really back in the swing again. I'd better get going. I've got to make a few more calls."

After she hung up, she took a slip of paper out of her purse and dialed the phone.

"Angela?" Rita said when a woman's voice answered.

"Rita? Is that you, girl?" *Baby girl,* the voice echoed from long ago.

She twirled the extra-long phone cord around her fingers. "Yes, it's me. I just . . . I just wanted to say hello."

"Hello? *Hello?* What is going on with you? I've been worried to death!"

Rita turned to the courtyard. "I didn't mean to worry you."

"Rita, you are my daughter." She enunciated those words, as though Rita could forget. "Oh, hell." Silence for a few seconds. Angela's voice sounded thicker when she spoke again. "Let me worry some, will you? I've got a lot of worrying over you to catch up on. Why are you down in New Orleans?"

"Just taking a vacation, that's all. I needed to get away for a while." No need to tell her more than that.

"Then why is your friend worried about you?"

"Marty said she was worried?"

"She didn't have to. I could hear it in her voice. You going to tell me what's going on or are you going to keep punishing me for being a lousy mother?"

Rita couldn't swallow. "I'm not punishing you. Maybe I'm not ready to be your daughter yet. It's not a role I'm familiar with, okay?"

"Oh, hell." Rita heard more pain in those words than she cared to. "Just tell me you're all right. Just tell me that."

"I'm all right. Mama." The word choked in her throat, painful and bittersweet. Rita heard something on the other end of the line, something too close to a sob. "I have to go now."

"Rita . . . you call if you need me, okay?"

Her hand clenched on the phone. She couldn't imagine needing her mom again. "Bye." And for a few minutes, she held on to the phone, even after hearing the click on the other end.

"Get assaulted by the phone gremlin?" Christopher

asked, looking way too good in white pants and a plum-and-white-striped sweater.

After giving him a questioning look, she followed his gaze to the curly phone cord wrapped around her. "Oops. I'm not used to corded phones anymore. I really need to find a charger. And I will repay you for my calls." She untangled herself. "You look less hungover."

"Amazing what a tub full of cold water will do. Ready?"

"Tub? As in bathtub?"

He nodded slowly. "Yes. Those concave porcelain structures designed for holding water."

"I know what they are. I just can't see you . . . taking a bath, that's all." And then she could, legs propped up on the edge, chest slick with suds. And then she really wished she couldn't as heat engulfed her face.

He was probably wondering just what she was thinking then. Could he tell she'd fallen for him? She hoped not; the guy would push her so far away they'd be in different states.

They both stiffened when the phone rang.

"It's only rung a few times since I've been here," he said as he went to answer it. A faint voice asked for Brian. "Brian's in the hospital, but I can help you. I'm his brother, Christopher." She gave up trying to hear what the man on the other end was saying and let her gaze roam down his white jeans as he continued to talk. "Okay, I'll be in to make it right." He hung up. "That's odd. Brian rents a warehouse over in one of the run-down areas of the city. I recognize the address; it's where the krewe used to store their parade floats. For some reason he's been renting it from this real estate office for the last two years. He always pays cash, one lump sum a year, and he's late. I told the guy I'd settle up, but I want a key so I can check it out. Maybe we can find out more about Brian's secret life."

Before she gathered her purse and coat, Christopher's cell phone rang. After talking with someone, he said, "That was Dr. Schaeffer. He wants to see us."

Brian's doctor met Christopher and Rita at the nurse's station. He had a hopeful light in his gray eyes that quelled the anxiety his call had produced. "I'd like to show you something."

The guard left the room to give them privacy as the doctor led them into Brian's room. He directed their attention to his hand. "Brian, if you can hear me, move your hand."

Rita held her breath as they waited. And then, slowly, Brian's hand contracted.

"Brian!" She rushed forward and took his hand in hers. "You're coming back to us!" She turned to Christopher. "I can feel him move."

"Some patients move involuntarily, but he's responded several times in response to a question. It looks like he may be coming out." The doctor nodded for them to join him at the far corner of the room and spoke softly. "As I told Christopher before, once he starts to come out, we don't know how long the process is going to take. It's not like in the movies where the patient suddenly wakes and is his old self. Especially a patient who's been in a coma state for as long as Brian has. It might take months or even years. It's going to be a slow process. I just want you to be prepared for that. He may improve to a certain level and then plateau, perhaps even permanently.

"You're going to need to get some training from the rehabilitative nurses for when Brian goes home. You'll want to hire someone to work with him. I've already contacted a physiatrist to evaluate him. That's a physician who specializes in physical medicine and rehabilitation. Dr. Stonam is an expert in neurologic rehabilitation. He'll be overseeing Brian's rehab program."

Christopher looked over at Brian. "Sounds hopeful."

Dr. Schaeffer's voice went low again. "Yes, but hope is relative where brain injuries are concerned. He'll likely have to relearn the most basic skills, like walking and talking. He may never fully recover, but he can make a lot of progress."

"He's still in there," Rita said. "He just has to learn to communicate with us again."

Christopher asked, "Will he remember what happened the night he fell? Will he remember his life at all?"

"We won't know until he comes out, but most patients have no memory of the event that put them in the coma. I'll keep you posted about any major improvements. The medical staff on this floor will be instructed to give Brian around-the-clock stimulation. In the meantime, I encourage you to stop in as much as possible and talk to him."

"Absolutely," she answered for both of them, relieved that people would be in and out of his room.

Dr. Schaeffer took in Rita's enthusiasm. "The man you knew will be different from the man who comes out of this coma. Don't be surprised if your feelings change. And don't feel guilty. Just be a friend and see what the future brings."

"I will." She'd already grappled with those issues. He *was* different from the man she'd met online. Her feelings had changed. She'd definitely felt guilt. But no matter what, she would be a friend.

After Dr. Schaeffer left, Rita knew Christopher was thinking about all those months ahead, and his role in the process, as he stared at the man on the bed. "Are you going to stay?" she asked softly.

"He's my brother."

He looked like a man who had no choice in the matter. No matter what he said, no matter what anyone had ever told him he was, he was a man of honor. He just didn't like it.

She reached out and took Brian's hand. "Brian, Christopher and I are here. Can you hear me?" The movement was almost imperceptible. "He can." Their eyes met, but Christopher dropped his gaze to her and Brian's linked hands. "Brian, we're going to figure this all out. We know about your alter ego, Alta. We even understand why. You know, the whole king thing. But we still don't know what Xanadu is yet. We're going to the warehouse after we leave here. I hope it will help us solve this puzzle you've given us." She glanced up at Christopher, who stood there looking a little lost. "Do you want to say anything to him? I can leave if you'd like."

He kept his gaze on Brian. "I don't know what to say."

She reached over and took Christopher's hand, linking all three of them together. "You're here. That says a lot." She turned to Brian. "Brian, when you come out of this coma, you and Christopher need to have a long talk. I think it's time you got to know each other." She smiled at Christopher. "He squeezed my hand! He agrees."

Movement near the open doorway caught her eye, and she disengaged her hand to check it out. She was hoping to catch Aris out there, but all she did was startle both the security guard and a janitor.

"Sorry, I just thought . . . never mind."

The man shrugged his slight shoulders and returned to his mopping.

"Something wrong?" the guard asked.

"What's up?" Christopher said from behind her.

"Just checking."

When she returned to Brian's side, she didn't get any

response. "He's gone back to the gray place." She tried coaxing him back with no luck.

He kept his gaze on Brian, or more specifically, on all the tubes keeping him alive. "Did you have someone trying to bring you back from the gray place? When you were in a coma, I mean."

"Marty, the one who came to my rescue in the lobby. She's a good friend. And my mother surprised me and came up from Jersey. She's trying to be my mom after all these years."

"The one you're not ready to be a daughter to yet."

She blinked. "You heard my conversation?"

He merely lifted one shoulder. Of course, she could hardly reprimand him for eavesdropping.

"It's a start. Calling her, I mean. I have to get used to the idea of having a mother. It's strange."

"At least you have the chance to make it right."

"Yeah, I do, don't I?" She wanted to tell him he had the chance, too, but decided not to lecture him. "If you knew my life, you'd understand why I went into counseling. I wish I could make all parents take a course and get a license. Can't leave the hospital without one, and it has to be renewed every three years. Then there wouldn't be people like us dealing with the crap our parents dumped on us. I even did my thesis on it." She ducked her head. "Sorry, I get on my soapbox sometimes. It's a personal issue for me."

He regarded her with a speculative smile. "I can see that."

"Don't you get angry when these women on the Internet come to you because no one else will help them?"

"Sure. But I don't get involved personally."

She thought of Sherry. "No, I don't suppose you can."

He met her gaze, and she felt a frisson of understanding pass between them. It didn't surprise her that he was the first to turn away. He turned to Brian, staring at the man beneath the tubes. She wanted to touch Christopher, to lend her unspoken support. But she pressed her hand against her thigh and walked to the window.

He stood there for a few minutes, and each one of them felt like an eternity. Finally, he turned around. "Let's go check out the warehouse."

He watched Christopher and Rita head down the hall to the elevators as he pushed the mop across the floor for what was probably the hundredth time. He'd better move on before someone noticed he'd been outside Brian's room too long. Then they might notice that his identification badge didn't even apply to this hospital or that his overalls didn't fit.

They'd hired a security guard to protect their precious Brian. The skinny guard was probably keeping an eye out for a green-eyed nurse named Aris. She'd never return again. But someone else would. Brian couldn't come back from his coma. He had betrayed Sira, rejected her, and had tried to cheat her out of her rightful place. He was a traitor and would be treated as such.

Rejected! He felt an ache in his chest and bent over the mop handle. Now he would take care of things.

"You all right there, buddy?" the guard asked as he walked back into Brian's room.

He only nodded and pushed onward. He couldn't let himself think of those pages Brian had written or especially the way they'd brought tears to Sira's eyes. It was all before Rita had stolen him away, he reminded himself. Too late for regrets.

Rita and Christopher already knew too much. He couldn't hear everything they said, but he'd heard *Xanadu* and *Alta*. They'd even found the warehouse, damn them. It was too late to change the location for the

Gathering. No, it had to go on as scheduled. That meant he had to get rid of them.

He wasn't sure how. Brian had been easy to push from the roof. It was all a matter of timing and surprise. Christopher would be another matter. He would figure out a way to deal with him, some way to weaken his defenses. Perhaps by getting rid of Rita first.

She was going to be easy to dispense with. All he needed was the right opportunity.

17

After squaring things at the real estate office, Christopher and Rita made two stops on the way to the warehouse. One to a gun shop to get Rita a can of pepper spray and another to a cell phone store to get her a charger. She fingered the holster and watched the scenery go by as they drove through town.

"What's your house in Atlanta like?" she asked.

"It's beautiful, but it needs a lot of work." He thought of the oak floors that needed to be scraped of ugly red paint, of the walls he'd only half torn down, and of the bedroom that consisted of an antique dresser and mattress on the floor. Two stories of history, of wood and glass, and the little touches that all the people who'd lived there before had added. Some of them were hideous, like the green paint on the marble fireplace. Some were nice, like the pedestal sink. With the history surrounding him, the laughter and tears, the fights, the routines of other lives, sometimes he felt very alone in that house. "I've owned it for about a year. It'll take me ten years before I'm done fixing it up." Or longer. Somehow it was more comfortable the way it was.

"I'll bet it's nice, even with the work to be done."

"Yeah, it is nice. It's got a great front porch. My favorite place in the house." He wished he were there right now, far away from New Orleans and Rita.

"Is that where the kittens live?"

What was it with her and the kittens? "Underneath it." He'd put some towels under the porch for them.

"Aw, I'll bet they're so cute."

She had the warmest smile he'd ever seen, as though she were imagining him and those kittens, seeing him as this gentle, caring guy. Her light blue eyes crinkled at the corners. He turned up the music. He wanted to tell her he kicked them for fun. He'd tried to send them away at first, but for some reason they had no fear of him. He glanced over at Rita. Like someone else he knew.

He launched into a story about a friend's coon dog and how it had followed them to school and then howled until they got out. Nice benign stuff. No more soul baring. And what was that business with him asking if someone had been there during her coma? He'd done well at keeping distance between them and out popped that question.

He already knew more about her than he wanted to, yet there seemed to be some deep part of him that wanted to know more. Well, forget about that. No more questions about her life, no more kissing her. It was bad enough sharing a room with her, and then that little comment of hers about not having to sleep on the floor . . .

"What's wrong?" she asked.

He realized he was frowning. "You can tell it's getting closer to Mardi Gras. All this traffic."

She gave a bewildered glance forward, where traffic was light. He couldn't tell her that she was driving him crazy, that he was only human, and if she kept tempting him it was bound to get ugly.

And she'd called him Chris.

He pulled to a stop in front of a corrugated metal warehouse. It hadn't changed much since he'd last seen it, except that the paint had faded to a powdery gray. He got out of the car, wondering if the floats were still in there. That was the only part of the krewe he had enjoyed, working on the floats and riding in the parade.

Generations of spiders had set up house in the crevices of the large door, undisturbed for what looked like years. He unlocked the regular door and stepped inside, expecting to find dusty floats or maybe boxes and old furniture jammed inside. It was as black as the darkest shadows of his nightmares. He felt around for the switch and turned on the lights.

"Wow, look at this place," she said, taking it all in. "What is it?"

"Nothing to do with the krewe, that's for sure."

The ceiling was forty feet high, and in some places a network of grids served as extra storage in the upper space. It had been wide open before Brian redecorated.

"It looks like a kid's dream fort," he said in a low voice, studying the elaborate structure.

"It reminds me of that cityscape he drew," she said. "This must be Xanadu."

Huge, shimmering sheets of fabric made hallways and rooms, complete with windows and doorways. All of the interior walls were covered in the fabric. Brian had removed the yellowed fluorescent panels and installed studio lights. Shades of teal, pink, and gray colored everything. Mixed with a slightly musty odor was the tang of incense.

She started to wander over to one of the corridors on the right. "All this fabric must have cost a fortune."

He walked up behind her as she peered behind one of the doors. "Stay close to me. We don't know if anyone's in here."

She turned with a start. "I hadn't thought about that," she whispered.

She was wearing a long blue sweater over cream leggings, and over that a long black coat. Not thin and bony like some of the women he'd shared a bed with, Rita was just curvy enough. She slid out of her coat and caught him watching her. He took the coat from her and slung it over his shoulder, then nodded toward the main corridor. He walked behind her, close enough to smell her apple-scented shampoo on her thick, wavy hair—close enough to make sure no one leapt out to grab her.

He peeled back a fabric door. "It's a miniature house."

"It has a bed, a table, even a couch."

They peered into another room, then another. Each one had the essentials, though they were all decorated differently. Some had personal items, like dishes or a vase or colored silk pillows on the beds. The largest room was at the end. Its entrance was fancier than the rest, with the fabric making an arch above the doorway.

The bed was draped with shimmering gold fabric. Hanging from a coat rack in one corner was a costume like the one Brian had sketched on Alta. The robe matched the gold material on the bed and the interior was lined with black velvet. Panels of metallic teal and deep pink adorned a black leotard; the built-in shoulder pads would put a football uniform to shame.

"The king's suite," he said. "What the hell was he into?"

"Maybe this will help." She walked over to a desk of sorts and picked up a ball of scrunched papers. She flattened it as best she could. "This looks like Brian's handwriting." She sat on the edge of the bed. "It looks like a speech he was writing. 'Welcome, citizens of Xanadu.' Is that what you call people who are involved in a krewe? Citizens?"

He shook his head. "This isn't a krewe. The balls they hold might be elaborate, but they're not quite . . . this elaborate. No respectable krewe would hold their ball in this area of town anyway, and not in a warehouse."

She returned to the papers. "He's welcoming them to something called the Gathering. He's gone to a lot of trouble finding just the right words." She held up a page covered in corrections, then turned to another page. "Maybe even sweat and tears." She pointed to a place where the words smeared together. "Ah, here's something. 'I would like to present to you the queen of Xanadu . . . Sira.' "

He scrubbed his fingers through his hair. "Kings, queens. This seems to be some variation on a krewe, then. Maybe he re-created Xanadu so he could finally be king. In regular krewes, the leader is called the captain. The king is an honorary position and changes every year. Brian grew up with the mentality that being king was it, the only thing. I think he took it too far."

They had to find out how far. It was creepy, digging into his brother's life like this, finding his secret life.

She walked over to him, bringing that sweet scent with her. "Do you think this is why Brian withdrew from life? Because he was too busy doing . . . whatever this is?"

"Maybe." He nodded for her to follow and continued around the corner to another large room. There were lots of pillows that were probably used as chairs, and at the end of the room was a throne. In another room they found a long table where they obviously ate. He saw no signs of anyone living there or of recent occupancy.

"Let's go."

He helped her into her coat, and then out to the normal world. He opened her car door for her. It wasn't until she thanked him that he realized he'd been doing these small, gentlemanly things for her. He didn't even know he had it in him. He wondered what else he had hiding inside.

• • •

It took Rita forever to get to sleep that night. She kept running everything through her mind: Xanadu, Sira, Christopher, the surreal warehouse . . . Christopher.

The fact that she was lying in that magnificent bed he'd slept in so recently wasn't helping. The fact that he was lying at the foot of the bed in that dark room *really* wasn't helping. He'd offered to change the sheets, but she'd said she was too tired to care.

Only now, crushing a pillow to her chest, could she admit that she wanted to sleep on the same sheets. It had been way too long since she'd slept in a man's bed amid the faint scent of deodorant, a smidgen of aftershave, and his scent on the pillow, and it had never been the scent of a man she cared about.

The lights were on in the courtyard, and the wind moving through the trees sent shadows dancing across the room. They were keeping her awake, too, even though the lights were on for their safety.

The sounds of a physical struggle sent her upright in bed searching for the perpetrator.

"No . . . no . . ."

Christopher's words pulled her to the foot of the bed where she expected to find him fighting with some masked creature. Adrenaline pumped through her, mixed with a healthy dose of fear.

He was only fighting shadows.

"Rita!"

That word, along with his sudden jerk upward sent her sprawling back on the bed. She could see him rubbing his face, hear him breathing heavily as he came awake.

"Are you all right?" she asked, sliding down the side of the bed to kneel next to him.

"A dream. It was only a dream." He seemed to be assuring himself, not her.

"More like a nightmare, I'd say."

His bare shoulders gleamed in the dim light, and she placed her hand on his damp skin. He dropped his hands and let out a long breath. His eyes were wide and haunted as he stared straight ahead.

"Sorry I woke you," he said in a hoarse voice.

"I wasn't asleep." He turned to her at that, perhaps picking up the huskiness in her voice. "Was it Damen?"

After a moment, he nodded. "I get them every once in a while. I think I'm waking up, seeing him standing over me with the knife."

"But you called out my name."

"When I looked over to see if Sherry was all right . . . it was you. Lying there with blood all over . . ."

She gave his shoulder a squeeze, and he seemed to just then realize her hand was resting there. "But I'm okay. See?"

"Go back to sleep." It was an order.

"Why?"

His knees were drawn up, and he rested his forehead against them. "I need some time. I always have to think it through."

He had closed her out, and that little girl inside her cried at that. That girl wanted to crawl up in bed and hide under the covers. If she were smart, she'd do just that. But she couldn't. This was the moment, the turning point. She could turn away and save herself. Or she could stay and try to save him.

She placed her hand on his back, rubbing up and down. "It wasn't your fault." She felt him stiffen. "I know what you're doing. You're going over the scene again, just like you have a thousand times, trying to find that one thing you could have done differently. No one could have kept him away."

"Rita, stop. Stop analyzing me."

"I'm not talking to you as a counselor. I'm talking to you as a . . . friend." Her strokes were getting longer, going lower before going up into the nape of his neck to brush against the ends of his hair. She knelt so close beside him that her breasts brushed against his arm, separated only by the thin cotton of her pajama top. "She did not die because of you."

He lifted his head and met her gaze. "Rita, stop." It sounded more like a plea than an order this time.

Her fingers slid up into his soft hair. "It wasn't your fault."

"No."

"Stop blaming yourself. You're not the bad guy."

He shook his head. "Rita, stop it. Stop."

She drew him closer, aching to pull him against her and make it better. "You called for me. Let me help you."

He stared to the right, and his voice was thick when he said, "I just wanted to do something right. Just once."

Her heart filled for him. "You did everything you could."

"Don't defend me. You don't even know me. You know nothing about me." His words were harsh, but he hadn't pushed her away.

"I know enough about you. You try so damned hard to hide it, but I see the good prince inside."

She expected more argument. She did not expect him to lean forward and capture her mouth with his, to force her lips to part so he could make the connection more intimate. Her body, so close to the edge already, responded instantly. She felt it come alive from the top of her head right down to the bottom of her curled toes. His hands swept up into her tangle of hair, sending chills scurrying down her neck. She was pinned against the side of the bed, crushed between his chest and the iron footboard.

The tingling started slowly, only a tickle. She could leave, and he would understand. She could stop these crazy gyrations in her stomach right now. Her body stiffened.

"Isn't it time to run now?" he asked between kisses.

Her mouth fell slack. He *wanted* her to run away. Not because he didn't want her, that much she could tell. She wasn't going to let him scare her away. She closed her eyes as he nibbled on her lower lip. Her body was melting, her nose tingling, and her anger was getting red hot.

"You'd like that, wouldn't you?" she said on an elongated breath as his tongue traced down the side of her neck.

"Be the smartest thing you could do, *chérie*."

That soft-spoken, foreign endearment mixed in her blood and added fuel to the flames roaring inside her. She squeezed her eyes shut and forced the tingling back. She wanted this. He was starting to unbutton the front of her pajama top. She took wavering breaths as another, and then another button freed her breasts.

"M-maybe I'm . . . not . . . that smart."

He positioned himself over her, pinning her with his legs, and peeled her shirt back. For a moment, he held her wrists against the bed's foot rail and hovered over her.

"Are you sure you wanna play with fire, *chérie*? You gonna get burned." His voice had taken on that thick, Louisiana accent again and washed over her like warm molasses.

She could see the gleam in his eyes, even in the dim light. "I've stayed away from the fire too long. Maybe I'm cold. Maybe I want to get burned."

His legs tightened against hers. "You'd better be real sure. No maybes."

This was her last chance to save her sanity. "I'm sure."

"What about Brian?"

"I can't be disloyal to a man I never really knew. I owe him only my friendship."

He walked over to the dresser and grabbed his wallet. She heard the crinkle of plastic, but before she could give much thought to it, he had returned. He pulled her up to stand in front of him, though she wasn't sure her legs would hold her. She placed her hands against his bare chest. Her shirt hung loosely over her shoulders. He cupped her chin, and then slowly dragged his hand down her throat, over her collarbone, and lower yet. His fingers brushed the inner curves of her breasts.

"You're beautiful," he said on a soft whisper.

"Don't." She shook her head. "Don't say anything you don't mean."

He slid his finger down her stomach and tugged at the waistband of her pajama bottoms, pulling her up against him. "I never say anything I don't mean." He looked at the shoulders he was baring as he pushed her shirt back. It fell to the floor with hardly a sound. Then he tugged down her bottoms in one move, and she stepped out of them.

With enviable unselfconsciousness, he untied the string of his sweatpants and let them drop to his ankles. She couldn't help but stare as he stepped out of them. The shifting lights played over his body and highlighted the contours of his chest and the whiteness of his hips.

He took her hands and slid them around his waist, pulling her close and branding her with another kiss that left her breathless. Branding her with other parts of his body, too, long and hard and pressing into her stomach. His hands traveled over her and hungrily explored every curve. Did he see her as beautiful? The way he touched her and looked at her sure made her feel beautiful.

He lowered her to the pile of blankets he'd been sleeping on. They were warm from his body heat. She let her hands explore him, at first tentatively and then with growing sureness. He felt as gorgeous as he looked.

She ran her fingers through his hair and made him groan as she circled his ears with her fingertips. Then she lost her mind as his mouth closed over her breast, as his tongue teased and made her back arch. She could hardly catch her breath, and then he sent her flying again when his fingers explored farther down, sliding into her feminine folds of skin. Pleasure shuddered through her as her body tightened.

For the first time, she didn't have to think about what she should do or the way she should act. She let go and let her body react the way it wanted to. She loved the sounds he made, a soft groan here, a sigh there. Sounds of pleasure were coming from her, too. When he kissed across her stomach, she didn't worry about the softness he would feel there. She could only concentrate on his acceptance of her body. And then she could not concentrate on anything but the way her body filled and filled and finally exploded. She heard his soft laughter and the echo of her frantic gasps for air.

When she caught her breath, she reached down and traced the rounded edges of his penis, her finger sliding over the slick essence of him. When she had gone as far as he would let her, he rolled onto his back in one swift movement and took her with him. She straddled him, taking in the taper of his chest to his slim waist, and continued to stroke down the length of him until he shoved a small, square packet at her.

After maneuvering the slippery sheath over him, she let her body swallow him, feeling a tickle in the pit of her stomach. He took her hands and placed them on his chest. And from there, some other part of her took over. She gave herself up to the rhythm, not thinking about anything but the way her insides felt with each thrust, building the fire until it overpowered her.

She wanted to feel him, skin against skin, sweat to sweat, wanted to sink into his body, drown in his blood, breathe his breaths. She wanted it all, sunlight, darkness, the joy and sorrow, every emotion and sensation. She wanted to be a vixen, an innocent, and his mother, to take him into her arms and soothe away all his hurts. She wanted to be his little girl, to crawl into his arms and hide there forever.

She was burning up, damp with perspiration. When she felt him release, that bonfire burst and sent heat shooting into every vein in her body. She said his name, once and then two more times to make sure he had no doubts: she was making love to him—not a substitute for Brian.

As her body went slack, he pulled her down to lie on top of him. She rose and fell in the same rhythm as his breathing, her cheek pressed against his skin, his hand pressing down on the small of her back. From her position, she couldn't see his face. Maybe she didn't want to, didn't want to see that this had meant nothing to him. She had tasted real intimacy for the first time. Not just physical or emotional, but a tangle of both. She didn't want him to see that written all over her face, either. She had fully opened herself to him, and her nose hadn't bled. She had finally overcome that problem, but at what cost?

She thought that he might have fallen asleep. One of the things she had learned about men was that after sex, their bodies produced a chemical that made them sleepy. And in a twisted biological irony, women's bodies produced a chemical that made them fully awake afterward. As if PMS weren't enough. She leaned up on her arms and found him staring at the ceiling.

His gaze shifted to her and she saw something she

never thought she'd see in his eyes: tenderness. He reached out and touched her cheek. "You all right?"

She nodded, though *all right* was hardly the word she would have used. "You?"

He smiled. "F'sure."

She leaned against her hand. "You did everything you could to scare me off."

"Mmhm."

Well, at least he wasn't a liar. "Now what?"

She felt his hand stiffen. Shadows swallowed the tenderness, making her wonder if she'd imagined it.

"This doesn't change anything."

"Sure it does. It changes everything. Don't move away from me now. Something happened between us. Let's just sit on it for a while."

But he did pull away, leaving her feeling empty inside. He got to his feet. "We acted on our hormones, that's all. Now it's out of our systems."

She started to feel vulnerable and naked, but she fought it. "So this was only. . . ."

"Sex."

She hated that word, hated it so much she grabbed up her clothes and walked to the bathroom. But she had felt something from him, too. Had it only been Mardi Gras magic? He told her he never said anything he didn't mean. The only hope she harbored was that he didn't like the way he was. She'd heard the lie in his voice despite his impassive expression.

That was a lot to pin her hopes on. It was a lot to stake her heart on. She wasn't sure if she was up to it.

Christopher used the bathroom in Brian's bedroom to wash up and get back into his sweats. He took his time returning to his room. Like a smoker, he reached for his pack of gum and popped a piece in his mouth.

Rita was still in the bathroom, so he opened the French doors and walked out onto the gallery. Balcony, he reminded himself. He wasn't part of this place anymore.

No, but this place is still part of you. He wrapped his fingers over the railing and breathed in the cool air, let it wash over his damp skin. He could hear the sounds of a party in the distance. Then he heard her open the bathroom door. He hoped she hated him. It would make things easier. But he hadn't been entirely truthful with her.

It had been sex, plain out. But the way he'd *felt*, that had been different. He'd seen the uncertainty in her eyes turn to strength. He'd wanted her to back down, but he'd also just wanted her.

The worst part was when he'd climaxed, and then felt her tighten around him as her body stiffened with her climax. For that moment, he wanted to hold on to her, to give her everything he had, more than he had.

For that one moment, his eyes had watered.

Thankfully she hadn't looked at him right away. He didn't know what his face had shown, but he sure hadn't wanted her to see that. He'd never had anything like that assail him after sex, or ever. When he should have been relishing pleasant aftershocks, his throat had gotten thick and his eyes had teared up. What was wrong with him? Was he so messed up that he couldn't even enjoy sex anymore? All he felt was this mysterious ache. He didn't want to kid her or himself. It would never work. Like everyone else in his life, she'd slip through his fingers.

"You see the irony in all this, don't you?" She walked up beside him, and all he could think of was that she must be cold, just wearing those white cotton pajamas. "You grew up thinking you were the bad boy, the troublemaker who could never be the good prince. Yet you're the one helping victims of harassment on the Internet. Brian was always the golden boy, and yet he's been living this secret life."

"Don't try to make me into the good prince. I'm used to being the bad seed. Life has proven it at every opportunity."

"Like when that boy died here."

He tried not to give away his surprise at that statement but knew he failed. "Don't tell me Brian showed you that." He couldn't have. He hadn't been there.

Rita shook her head. "Emmagee mentioned that a boy had died here, but she didn't know anything about it."

Maybe if he told her, she'd see that everyone he cared about died. "I was a rebel. I guess I figured that since everything in our family was always black or white, that I had to be black. Brian was a goody two-shoes, so I acted up. The rule was neither of us could go up to the roof deck unless an adult was present. Not only did I go up without an adult, I convinced my best bud, Billy Franklin, to go with me. And not only did we go up to the deck, we climbed over the railing and onto the roof."

"Where you were that night when I thought you were about to jump."

"Yeah. I wasn't only thinking about Brian; I was thinking about Billy, too." He could see it as though it had just happened. He looked up to the right, where the steep roof was. "He was also a rebel and had no problem breaking the rules with me. We climbed to the top and felt superior for a while. We decided we'd better get down before we got caught. Billy lost his footing. One second we were laughing, literally on top of the world. The next, he screamed. I tried to reach him." His hand clenched at the memory of trying to grab Billy's hand as it scrabbled on the shingles. Their fingers brushed, but Christopher couldn't get a grip. Billy kept screaming as he slid down the roof, and Christopher screamed as he nearly fell trying to grab him.

"I couldn't get a hold on him. He fell backward and cracked his head on a stone table. He died at the hospital that night. A month later, we found out that Billy's family was suing us. My parents were woefully underinsured. Things got shaky for a long time. And my parents hated me. I was too broken up about Billy to care much about anything else." He turned to her, and when he saw compassion in her eyes he almost didn't want to go on. But he made himself. "Don't you get it yet? I don't want to be the good guy. I just want to be left alone."

Without another word, she wrapped her arms around herself and walked back into the bedroom. He felt cold. Not just on the outside, but all the way through. Still he waited, giving her time to settle into bed. Only when he was sure she was asleep did he return to his bed on the floor and try to gain the false peace that was sleep.

The phone rang in the middle of the night. Christopher fumbled around in the dark until he found the handset. Rita turned on the light. She didn't like the puzzled expression on his face.

"He's what? *Monkeys?* We'll be right down. Keep an eye on Brian. Thanks for the call."

"What was that about monkeys?"

He hung up, shaking his head as he grabbed his sweatshirt. "That was one of the nurses. The security guard, Dumas, is freaking out, thinks there are monkeys everywhere."

"Monkeys?" She was gathering her clothes, too.

"Yeah. Let's find out what's going on."

18

Neither Rita nor Christopher spoke as they drove. It was still dark, only three in the morning when they reached the hospital. She knew he was worried; he hadn't turned on that infernal rock and roll.

"What's going on with Brian?" he asked the first medical person they saw on Brian's floor, a young man in scrubs. "Where's the guard?"

"They have him subdued."

"Subdued? What the hell happened?"

"The guy went nuts, screaming, knocking into things. Took three guards, two doctors, and a nurse to pin him down." His expression changed. "You're Brian LaPorte's brother, aren't you?"

"Yes, why?"

"It happened while everyone was preoccupied with the security guard."

"What happened?"

Christopher looked past the guy's somber expression toward Brian's room. He rushed forward, Rita behind him.

"Where's Dr. Schaeffer?" he asked a male nurse who was in the room.

"He's not on duty tonight."

That's when Rita realized it: the monitors weren't on.

The respirator wasn't pumping air into Brian's lungs. The nurse was pulling a sheet over his head. They didn't do that to people who were alive, that would suffocate them, they did it when someone died, and Brian could not be dead. Her chest was already aching, her eyes hot and tingling.

Christopher pulled back the sheet to reveal Brian without the tubes that had kept him alive. He looked pale and gaunt, yet strangely peaceful.

"Mr. LaPorte, I'm so sorry."

They both turned to Sasha, who had just walked into the room.

"What happened?" he asked.

"His heart stopped. We tried to bring him back, but it was too late."

"His heart stopped? Just like that?"

Sasha looked at Brian. "His whole body has been under a great deal of stress. His heart couldn't handle it anymore."

Christopher looked shell-shocked as he gazed at Brian. "Could someone have done this to him?"

"You mean on purpose? But why?"

"Never mind the why. Could it be murder?"

"We can test his blood for toxins. If you want an autopsy, I can help you arrange it. It'll cost you about two thousand dollars."

"I don't care what it costs."

Sasha was studying Christopher, who was oblivious to her curiosity. "All right. Let's wait for the blood tests to come back first, then we'll proceed from there."

"What happened with Dumas?" Rita asked.

"They think he brought some of the Mardi Gras celebration in here. It appears to be drug-related, acid from the looks of it. Never know what you'll see this time of year. He seemed fine when he came out and got a drink of water. A short while later he was screaming about killer monkeys. I'm sure he'll be fired and prosecuted."

"Do you know if anyone talked to him prior to the monkey episode?" Rita asked. "Did anyone have contact with him?"

"I'm afraid I was in the middle of something else and didn't notice." Sasha stood there looking as though she felt awkward. Finally she said, "I'll leave you alone with him."

"Maybe it *was* death by natural causes," Christopher said. "Maybe Sasha was right about the strain on his heart."

He wanted to believe that, but she wasn't about to let him. "This was murder, don't you doubt it. And it was Sira. Somehow she got in here and drugged the guard to cause a distraction. Even you can't deny the coincidence of his going nuts at the same time Brian died. What if Sasha is part of this?"

She could tell by his expression that he couldn't deny the coincidence. He didn't comment on Sasha, just stared at the man who had been his brother in name only.

"Do you want a minute alone with him?" she asked.

"What good will it do now?"

"They say that the soul lingers after a person dies. I don't know if I believe it, but . . . I'd like to." She walked over to the bed, but looked up instead. "Brian, I know you're not in there anymore. And you're not in the gray place, either. I hope you're on the way to heaven. I hope someday I'll see you there. But don't worry; we're going to find out who did this. We're going to keep fighting for you."

Her eyes welled with tears, and she wiped them away. He had touched her life. She looked back at Christopher, who stood there like a statue. Brian had changed her life, too, by bringing her here. He had pulled her from her safe little world to this strange place, and into the lives of two brothers. And here, she had found a strength inside her she hadn't known. "I'm glad I met you, Brian. Thank you for making my life better. Goodbye," she whispered before walking out of the room for the last time.

The pink house on St. Charles looked dull and washed out in the muddy moonlight, a reminder that everything bright had a dark side. He stepped into the doorway and closed it behind him. He'd stuffed the janitor's uniform in his tote bag before leaving the hospital. He set the coffee cup on the mantel.

As a considerate hospital worker, he'd been glad to bring that nice old guy a cup of java—laced with some of the best stuff he could get his hands on. On his way out of the room, he'd taken the cup and planted the suggestion to watch out for killer monkeys, describing them in detail. Once the acid took hold, the guard had created enough fuss for him to inject potassium chloride into Brian's IV and slip out unnoticed.

The fireplace was warm and toasty now, a healthy flame that devoured the clothing, the cup of coffee, the brown curly wig, and the plastic part of the hypodermic needle. He'd called up an old friend who worked at a hospital pharmacy, and pretending he was doing research for a novel, asked what would cause a man's heart to stop but would be virtually impossible to prove as a murder weapon. Since potassium chloride could be present when the blood hemolyzed, no one would suspect a thing. His friend had virtually walked him through the process.

He walked into the room where Sira waited for him. "I took care of Brian," he told her.

"Yes, I know. I know everything you do."

"You're not pleased," he said. "You wanted to do it."

"I thought you didn't like killing people. You were too squeamish."

"Let me be the man once in a while. Let me do the dirty work."

Her upper lip twisted in a sneer. "You're not a man. You're just a wannabe. I'm in control here."

Sometimes he hated her. She had given him strength these past two years, but she could just as easily take it away.

"I saved your life," she said. "Never forget that. 'From this chasm, with ceaseless turmoil seething, as if this earth in fast thick pants were breathing . . .' "

She *had* saved him from the ceaseless turmoil, when his isolation and loneliness had gotten to be too much to live with. When death seemed the only escape.

Death . . . it was her weapon. Now it had become his, too. He didn't have to like killing. But he would do it again if he had to.

Christopher felt as empty and numb as he had when he'd made arrangements for Sherry's burial. Her parents had been in too much shock to be of help. He had owed them that much, and though they never blamed him outright, he had failed them, too.

The *ifs* haunted him now. If he'd believed Rita sooner, if he'd looked harder. Watching Rita wipe away her tears and hearing Tammy sobbing on the phone reminded him that he had the feelings of a doorknob. All he could dredge up was this incessant guilt, just as he had with Sherry.

After making the necessary calls, he sat at Brian's desk and logged back into his hidden Internet account. His jaw was working hard on the piece of gum he'd popped in earlier, and he wondered if it would disintegrate if he chewed it long enough.

He felt Rita walk into the room before she made a sound. He couldn't pinpoint what it was, but something in the air changed when she came in.

Without turning to her, he said, "The funeral is scheduled for Wednesday, the day after Mardi Gras. After everyone has cleansed their souls of their sins and promised to give them up for Lent."

She came up behind him. "What are you doing?"

"Checking his e-mail."

She pulled one of the chairs beside his and sat down. Vitar had answered.

> King Alta:
> Have attached Sira's declaration. Am relieved you are still here. I wish to discuss Sira. I believe she is dangerous, that she is taking Xanadu too seriously. Forgive my references to the real world, but I have traced her to New Orleans. She has hidden her identity quite well, though, so I have no more information. Will keep working on it. I advise you to be careful, since you are probably there preparing for the Gathering. There is more, but I must speak with you in person. I will not be online again until we meet at the Gathering. You must reassert your authority in Xanadu and attend as our king, Your Majesty.

"She lives here," Rita said. "Which still includes Tammy, Sasha, and Emmagee."

"Or it might not be anyone in Brian's world. Sira's just as likely to be someone on the fringes . . . in the shadows."

He clicked on the attached file. A document that looked like a scroll opened. It proclaimed that Alta had become ill and rescinded his position as king of Xanadu. Sira would now reign. Xanadu's Web site had been moved, and the new "doorway" address was listed. All passwords would remain the same.

He looked over at Rita. "So we pay a visit to Xanadu."

"Definitely. But we'll need a passport . . . er, the password."

They found the Web page, a patterned gold screen with no visible place to enter the site.

"This can't be right," she said. "There's nothing here."

"There's probably a hidden door somewhere. It's a trick I've seen before."

He moved the cursor all around. Way up in the right corner, part of the background disappeared and became the log-on. He typed in *Alta* and, after trying several words, *Prince Caspian* melted away the background to reveal a purple screen. New age music poured from the speakers. A man appeared on the screen, dressed in what looked like the costume they'd found in the warehouse.

"It's Brian," Rita said. "Or at least I'm pretty sure it's supposed to look like him."

Christopher clicked on the gold *X* just below Brian's image. It came to life, opening its arms to them. His mouth moved along with his words.

> Welcome to Xanadu. I am King Alta, creator of this amazing and diverse place. If you are a current participant, pull on your cloak and enter by clicking the golden *X* again. If you are new, you have been invited by a participant and must read the following to acquaint yourself with our world.
>
> I wished to find a special place where prejudice, hatred, crime, and disease did not exist. Where emotions are celebrated. Where the meek can inherit the earth. Every player sheds a flaw or weakness when they join. Each player is sworn to secrecy, must abide by the code of Xanadu, and must stay in their persona at all times. Anyone who breaks the rules, introduces an outsider without permission, or acts out of character will be banished from Xanadu forever.
>
> Of course, Xanadu has its hazards as well. It

> wouldn't be exciting otherwise. You may choose from many places in which to travel, all filled with fascinating creatures and people, beauty, and danger. You will be challenged, tempted, and given many choices, all depending on how the other players act.
>
> As a new player, you will first meet the Tailor, who will help design your persona. You have many choices from which to choose, many creatures or types and races of people. These are only outlines. From there, use your imagination to make your persona whatever you want to be. Read the backstory and get acquainted with the residents of Xanadu. I encourage you to click on the link to "Kubla Khan," Samuel Taylor Coleridge's poem that inspired my vision of Xanadu. Then your sponsor will introduce you into the current story, which you will contribute to.

"Wow." She sat back and absorbed the implications.

"Like the stories Brian wrote for those magazines. Since he couldn't be the king of the krewe of Xanadu, he must have created his own version." Fatigue washed through him, and he slumped back in the chair. "He was king, all right. The king of nothing."

Sadder yet, he wondered if he weren't much different. Brian had been living in his role of the good prince, just like when they were kids. And Christopher still lived in his role of the bad prince. Both he and Brian ruled worlds they thought were real: Xanadu and that lonely place where Christopher lived with virtual iron gates to keep out anyone who cared to come close enough. Not many did. He rubbed his hands down his face, then sat up and placed his hand over the mouse.

A detailed map filled the screen. Xanadu was the civilized part of a land called HeavenX, all overseen by Alta. A few small communities dotted a vast landscape of wilderness that included the Plains of Evil, Mountains of Change, and Lake Illusion. The city of Xanadu had a tight, neat layout.

"It looks like the warehouse," Rita said.

"You're right. There's the king's castle, the dining room, the gathering room. Way in the back is Sira's house."

"He asked me if I liked video games."

"Maybe he wanted to test the waters, see if you'd be interested in playing." He looked at her. "Would you have?"

She considered it. "Some of it would have appealed to me, like shedding your identity and hang-ups and becoming someone else. I feel more comfortable doing that by reading a book, though."

They found a chart of the current citizens. When they clicked on Citar, his animated character, draped in blue robes, introduced himself as the prince of thieves and shared what weakness he had shed. Appropriately enough, it was being too honest. A troll named Cragmar had shed his vanity. Sira's flaw had been her complicity where others were concerned. She did not want to fit society's parameters. Brian's flaw had been his need for approval.

"That poetic way he speaks," Rita said, a trace of wistfulness in her voice. "That's the Brian I became infatuated with. Which means I was actually infatuated with Alta. I still can't believe he's gone. I keep thinking he's at the hospital and I'll get to see him soon."

He didn't want to think about it, so he continued and found the area that Alta participated in the most. They could scroll through the story over the last several months, watching the action or reading the text messages between the players.

"Sira and Alta were on here the most, though he seems to have tapered off about a month before his fall," Rita said.

"When did you and he start your thing?"

"It wasn't a *thing*. We started e-mailing . . . well, about that same time."

"Apparently he was infatuated with you, too." He clicked on the next archive. "Alta and Sira seemed to be having some kind of power struggle. Here she wants to preside over the banishment ceremony."

They referred back to a page of codes, finding that the ceremony entailed a character be put into a cage until the hearing. King Alta had the final word on whether someone would be banished or merely warned. He had denied Sira's request. Just like their father, loath to part with any of his power.

"There are some parallels between this place and some krewes. You have to be invited in by another member, and the captain has the final say on who is let in and who isn't," he said, remembering how much Brian had looked forward to being invited into Xanadu after Mardi Gras that last year. "They don't put people in cages, though. That would be illegal, not to mention creepy as hell. Krewes can banish members. They have codes and rituals, and they have gatherings, which are all linked to Mardi Gras."

She wrapped her fingers over the arm of his chair as she leaned forward. As they read on, they found that Sira and Alta had become lovers several months ago, going off into private "rooms."

"Another thing some people do," he explained as he used the *Prince Caspian* password to get into Alta's room, "is use the same password for everything. At least change one thing about it, just to keep a hacker off track."

"I'll remember that." She met his eyes for a moment

and let him know in some unspoken language that she no longer considered him a hacker. But he was sure she considered him a bastard.

The private rooms used text messaging rather than graphics. Three entries in, he looked over at her. She had a tint to her cheeks as she read. "But he did have a *thing* with Sira. This is like phone sex, only written out. Maybe we shouldn't read any more."

"Don't tell me it's getting you hot," he said.

"It isn't!" The tint deepened to a becoming pink. "It's just . . . private. Very private." She leaned closer to the screen. "Oh, my. Is that physically possible?" She shook her head. "And don't give me that snarky grin of yours. Your face is flushed, too."

"Snarky?" He wasn't commenting on the flush.

"Yeah, like a shark's smile, mixed with a smirk. That's my definition, anyway." She nodded toward the screen. "Can we leave this room now?"

"All right, so it's apparent that they were hot and heavy. No wonder he didn't have a social life. He had more right here than he could handle. It tapers off around the time he met you. Here he's trying to let her down easy."

"I'll bet she never knew he was going to make her queen. She hinted about it a lot, though."

"Obviously he changed his mind before he mentioned it to anyone." He went back to the main story and they continued reading. "Brian did intend to invite you in. You were being considered by the high council about a week before he was pushed off the roof," he said when they got to the end.

"I can see why Sira wanted me dead, at least from her warped point of view. I was her competition. And from what I can tell, she hates to be left out of anything. Or left behind." She crossed her arms. "Whoever this Sira is, I'll bet she's been an outcast her whole life. Xanadu is probably the only place she's ever really fit in. To her, this isn't just an imaginary world; this *is* her world."

He kept clicking on the various links. "It looks like this Gathering that everyone's talking about is when they all come here, dress in their costumes, and act out their particular fantasies. And interestingly enough, it's held on Mardi Gras day."

"Interesting because of the krewe parallel?"

"And because it's the one day a lot of people dress up in costumes. Men dress like women, women dress like men, there are clowns, cowboys, nuns, you name it, it's out there. Anyone going to the Gathering would fit right in. In fact, I wouldn't be surprised if a lot of these people live in New Orleans . . . the city of masquerade."

"That's why Brian couldn't work on Mardi Gras night." She touched his arm. "Look, Sira is already changing the codes. If someone doesn't participate at least once a week, they'll be banished."

"Find a notepad, and we'll take notes on the key players, particularly those who were banished. Maybe someone who's not involved anymore can shed some light on this."

When they were done, he wrote down the Web site information. "I want to try to track the IP address and find out where this is being hosted. A site of this scope requires a gaming server, something that starts in the tens of thousands of dollars and goes way up from there. My guess is that Brian kept it at a server farm."

"A server farm?"

"It's a company that sets up a collection of computer servers to host large Web sites. They've got the power, fast connections, and backups to run a site like this."

He went back to his room and returned with Brian's credit card bill. "Last month's bill has a charge from APK Systems. It could be a server farm." He located the company's phone number and confirmed that Brian had had an account. And interestingly enough, a month and a half ago, he had called to move the site. Just *after* his fall.

"Did you verify that it was Brian?" Chris asked the accounts manager.

"That's our policy. The guy who handled our accounts has left, but it looks like he followed procedure. Brian provided the credit card number and last four digits of his social security number." Both of which could be obtained by anyone with access to this house.

"Do you know where the site was moved to?"

"We usually ask that, where and why, especially with a large site like that one. We match prices to keep big accounts. But there's no notation."

Christopher hung up and relayed the conversation to Rita. "I should be able to figure out where the site is now, but I doubt it'll do much good if it's at another farm. They're not going to tell us who owns the account, but it's still worth trying."

He turned back to the monitor and clicked on the icon to submit a proclamation.

> Citizens of Xanadu:
> Alta, your king, is back. I thank Sira for keeping things on track, but I am now able to resume my duties as your leader. The Gathering will commence as planned, and I look forward to meeting with my faithful followers.

"You're planning on going as Alta?" she asked.

"Sure am."

"She'll know it's you."

"Exactly. It'll rile her up. As much as I plain-out hate this whole role-playing thing, posing as Brian is the only way to flush her out."

"Then I'm going, too."

"Hell you are. You can go to the funeral, but you're not going to the Gathering."

She crossed her arms over her chest, ready for the fight. "I am part of this. You would have never even found out about this if it weren't for me."

He rubbed his forehead. "Rita, I won't let you put yourself in danger."

She waved her hand at him. "Everyone makes his or her own choices in life. Brian chose to create this strange Internet world. Your girlfriend chose not to leave town, but to trust a man who had all the best intentions and not the right training. Your friend, Billy, chose to climb onto the roof with you. And I am choosing to stay here and take part in the Gathering. There is nothing you can do to stop me, so you see, you can claim no responsibility for me."

With that, she leaned forward and added a few more lines to his message.

> I would also like to introduce a new resident to Xanadu: Atir. The flaw she is discarding is that she will no longer care what people think of her. She will not have to maintain an image of the perfect, got-it-together person. I beg your forgiveness for using my authority to forgo the High Council's decision, but timing is imperative. I am making Atir my queen and presenting her to you at the Gathering.

"There. That ought to get her blood boiling."

"You're not—sending that," he added when she clicked on the submit button.

"See, you couldn't do a thing about it. Besides, I'm a psychologist. I can read people. And I know what Sira looks like, so you need me. Two is better than one. You have no choice. 'Nuff said?"

"Rita. . . ."

"Don't yell at your queen," she said with a tilt of her head and a gracious smile. "Oh, my, I'll have to get a costume."

"That's where you're out of luck. You won't find a costume anywhere this close to Mardi Gras. And you can't show up at the Gathering wearing worldly clothing."

She had a gleam of determination in her blue eyes. "Then I'll make one. I got an A in my high school sewing class. I'm sure I can find a fabric shop around here. When can we go?"

He wanted to throw her over his knee and spank that . . . that snarky little grin off her face. "Rita, you're a fool."

Her smile did fade at that. "I know. But there's nothing I can do about it."

Oh, great, she'd shot an arrow right into his chest, and that sad quirk of her mouth twisted it. He exhaled a breath. "We'll go after I get back from some errands."

"Can't I go with you?"

"No. I'll wait until Emmagee gets here so you're not alone."

"Yes, king."

He opened his mouth to say something but closed it again. His queen. Those words had a strange effect on his stomach, somehow getting mixed up with the pain in his chest. Before he realized what he was doing, he slid his finger beneath her chin.

"You're the queen of nothing."

"Nothing can be turned to something. With a little magic. Or with a little hope."

He wanted to kiss her so damned bad it hurt. She knew it, too, when his gaze dropped to her mouth. She moistened her lips, never taking her eyes from his.

His whole body was rigid with the fight, and finally his good sense won out. "Nothing is nothing. Don't ever forget that."

Later in the day, Emmagee came by to do her twice-weekly cleaning. Christopher had left Rita in her company while he went out to deal with the hospital, attorney, and the funeral home. The smell of pine scent sent a rush of those Saturday-cleaning memories again. The sound of Emmagee sloshing a sponge in the bucket brought a new memory: squeals of laughter, suds flying between mom and daughter, sliding over the tile floor, first Rita falling on her butt, then Angela. And Angela hugging her. *Aw, baby girl, I know it's work helping your mama out like this, but I enjoy our Saturdays together.*

Why had she buried that memory? She felt something moving closer to her consciousness. Another memory? But Emmagee interrupted her thoughts.

"I cannot believe he's gone. That good-lookin' guy locked away in a vault. It's so sad, so sad." She tossed her sponge in the bucket and shook her head, making her curls bob to and fro. She still wore the funky contacts. "So, I guess you and Chris are gonna be heading home, huh?"

Eager to get rid of us? "We have some things we need to take care of." Best not to give too much information, just in case. She didn't want to think Emmagee was Sira. Still, she couldn't afford to be off guard. "You said you didn't know Brian well."

"Not really. I knew who he was, growing up. He wasn't in my social group, know what I mean?"

"Did you like him?"

"Didn't have to. I kep' his place clean and cashed his checks."

She didn't seem to harbor any ill will toward him. Or possessiveness.

"What did you mean when you said Brian was locked in a vault?" Rita was sipping coffee and nibbling on a beignet. She leaned against the counter while Emmagee scrubbed away.

"We don't bury our dead in the ground like most places. Can't. We're so close to sea level that the bodies come floating right back to the surface."

Rita choked on powdered sugar. "Oh, yuck."

"I bet it was, walking to the cemetery to say hello to your loved one and having him laying there all rotted saying hello back. The fences are to keep the dead in, not to keep the livin' out." She shivered dramatically. "If you know what I mean. Speaking of cemeteries, you gotta go to Marie Laveau's tomb before you leave. She's the famous Voodoo Queen. Her spirit'll grant you a favor if you go to her tomb, turn around three times, knock three times on the slab, and mark a cross with a piece of brick."

Rita waited for Emmagee to laugh at her own joke, but she merely went to work on the front of the refrigerator. "You're not kidding?"

"No, ma'am. I asked for a favor, to never grow old." She gestured down her body. "Ain't seeing a dimple or wrinkle yet."

"And you're what, twenty-five? It sounds silly."

"Nothing's silly in New Orleans, baby. You should give it a try. Maybe you can combine it with that Carnival magic I told you about."

Rita shook her head. "That kind of thing goes against my Christianity. Besides, magic isn't going to help Christopher. He doesn't want to be helped."

Emmagee smacked her lips. "Well, honey, sleepin' with him ain't gonna help matters any."

"I didn't—" At Emmagee's knowing nod, Rita caught herself. "How did you know?"

"A woman's got a glow about her when she's been thoroughly loved. You certainly didn't have that look last time I was here. You had that uptight it's-been-a-while look."

No, she'd had the it's-been-forever look. Rita sighed. "You're right; it didn't help."

"Don't give up on him yet. Maybe his brother's death will help knock some sense into him. You know, the whole mortality thing." She pulled out a long-handled squeegee from the utility room. "I hate doing windows, that's f'sure. Be outside if you need me."

Rita picked another beignet off the tray and wandered out to the parlor. She searched through the family pictures again. She and Christopher had something in common: they'd grown up in a home that appeared normal and substantial on the surface, but belied a neglect deep within. She looked at the swords and felt a spike of sadness for two brothers who'd lost out on each other's love and closeness.

The doorbell rang. She looked out one of the side panels first, finding Henri standing on the doorstep with a handful of dark roses. His longish silver hair floated on the breeze beneath his cap.

"Hi, Henri. Listen, I don't know what kind of deal you had with Brian, but he's . . . well, passed away. I'm sure Christopher will pay you whatever you're owed. He may have you continue on, I don't know."

Henri didn't remove his dark sunglasses as he held out a gloved hand. "I heard he passed on, and I wanted to offer my condolences. It's a sad thing when one that young goes beyond. I brought these for you."

She stared at buds black as death. "Thank you, Henri. I've never seen anything like these. They sure are . . . dramatic. I'll put them in a nice va— Ouch!" When he'd shoved the bouquet at her, a thorn pricked her finger. She sucked on the tiny pinprick.

"Sorry 'bout the thorn. Thought I'd gotten all of those. Well, have a nice day."

He tipped his cap and walked down the steps. She looked at the bouquet. That was the only thorn on any of the stems.

A few minutes later, Emmagee walked back into the kitchen.

Rita was putting the flowers in the vase she'd found beneath the kitchen cabinet. "Strange traditions you have here: black roses for a condolence bouquet. Henri brought them just now."

"That's no New Orleans tradition I ever heard of. Who's Henri?"

"The gardener. Don't you know him?"

"Nope." Emmagee dumped out dirty water from the bucket.

"People are so nice here, at least some of them. Even Christopher has his moments." Rita started to pick up her coffee, but felt her stomach turn at the aroma. She set it down and took a seat at the table.

"It's getting to you, ain't it? New Orleans, I mean," Emmagee said.

"It does have a magic all its own."

Emmagee slanted her a wise look. "Does it have anything to do with Christopher?"

"No, of course not. He doesn't even like it here." Her voice sounded airy and thin as gauze.

"Ah, I think it calls to him. He says he orders the coffee from a shop here, won't even drink regular coffee. He jus' has some bad memories. He needs some better ones. Hey, what's wrong? Your head's a-tilting."

Rita held on to the edge of the table. "I just feel a little dizzy, that's all."

"Baby, you can't be getting morning sickness already!"

Rita forced a laugh. "I'm sure that's not it. I was in a car accident a few weeks ago. Sometimes I still get dizzy." She pushed herself to her feet, then had the strangest sensation she was floating. She checked, just to be sure. "Think I'll go upstairs . . . lie down."

"Sure thing. Need some help on those stairs?"

"I'm fine, thanks. I'll be careful." If she did get sick, she wanted to be alone. That old inconvenience thing was hard to break out of.

She navigated the stairs by clutching the banister. As soon as she reached the landing, though, she started to feel better. Maybe it was something Emmagee was using to clean with. She glanced down to find Emmagee watching her.

"I'm fine," she told her. The girl shrugged and went back into the kitchen. Rita sucked in a deep breath to clear her mind and then looked over at Brian's bedroom door. "I wonder if anyone's responded." Her words sounded slurred.

When she walked inside, it seemed the room was deeper and that the computer was blocks away. She took another breath and started the journey, using furniture to guide her. She dropped into the chair and stared at the screen. Even it looked farther away. She reached out and touched the flat, cool surface.

It took three tries before her hand connected with the mouse. Her throat tightened. Was this some kind of delayed reaction from the accident?

After navigating the passageways, she reached Xanadu's continuing story line. There was a new entry, a graphic picture of Sira holding an apple. Rita blinked, trying to make the letters beneath Sira stay together.

> Sira wanted to know who this stranger was, this Atir. She didn't like this sudden intruder and was

> suspicious about Alta's intentions. After all, he had been her lover for more than eight months, and she had been part of Xanadu since the beginning. If anyone deserved to be queen, she did. Atir would get a visitor who would give the intruder a poison apple. Rita couldn't hide from a woman scorned.

Rita blinked several times, staring at the correct spelling of her name. A typo? No, Sira was playing the game, too. She knew exactly who Atir was.

The room tilted, and she felt herself shrinking. Worse, she couldn't feel the chair anymore. The odd floating sensation had returned. All at once, her bones turned to rubber, and she slumped to the floor. She tried to call out to Emmagee, but her mouth wouldn't obey her command. *What's happening to me?*

A poison apple. The words drifted through her mind. No one had given her an apple. Only . . . roses. She hadn't eaten them, for gosh sakes. No, no, not eaten. Just put them in a vase. Henri wasn't Sira. He was an old man.

With no wrinkles on his face.

Rita's vision undulated like a moving fun house mirror. She kept trying to open her eyes wider, tried to move the hand lying in front of her. It wouldn't move. A drop of blood oozed out of a hole in her forefinger. Seemed to have a luminescent quality. Like pearls. Like blood-red pearls.

The rose had pricked her.

What had he put on the thorn?

She tried hard to get up. It took a long, long time to even move a little. Legs were feeling rubbery. Had to get . . . where? Who to trust? She heard a humming noise downstairs, like a thousand bees. Bees were coming to sting her. *Get out! Hide!* She couldn't move. Maybe they wouldn't see her. If she didn't move. The black carpet looked like oozing mud, and she was sinking into it.

Then she saw a shadow moving just beyond her vision. What was happening? She tried to lift her head. Everything looked tiny and far away, like looking through the wrong side of a telescope. Whenever she could turn her head, everything flowed in a colorful stream.

"Chris," she said in a slurred voice.

"No, baby, it's not Chris," a disembodied voice hissed. "Sira wants a word with you."

19

Christopher knew he'd hurt Rita by not including her on his errands. He needed some time alone to sort through everything.

He maneuvered through French Quarter traffic and people, Metallica's booming bass pounding into his head. Walking into the LaPorte this time seemed strange. It wasn't Brian's hotel anymore, wasn't his father's hotel. For the first time, he appreciated the building's charm and beauty, with its ornate railing and fancy detailing around the windows. Inside, it was too stuffy for his tastes, too formal. The employees nodded at him, obviously at a loss as to what to say. He knew the feeling.

He walked back to the offices to find Tammy, but she wasn't there. He wanted to see her reaction to Brian's death. When he looked in Brian's office, he found Millie, Tammy's assistant, sitting at the computer.

"Where's Tammy?" he asked without preamble, making her start. He walked to the desk and watched to see if she'd switch screens or close down whatever she was working on.

She didn't try to hide whatever she was doing. "Home. She dragged herself in and looked like hell. Trent took her home a little while ago. He said he'd be back in a bit.

They're both taking it pretty hard. We all are." Millie's eyes were red-rimmed, too.

"Yeah." As he headed back out through the lobby, his gaze trailed over the colorful flower arrangements in the vases—and stopped on the last one. Black roses. As black as his mood, black as death.

All these years he'd lived his life answering only to himself, having only himself to take responsibility for. Now he had Brian's funeral to arrange, Rita to take care of, and the hotel to deal with. All of it weighed down on him forty minutes later, pushing him into the plush seat at the funeral home as he waited for Mr. Royce to return with the paperwork.

The music was probably standard funeral home fare, soft and light, with an upbeat touch to soothe the tortured souls ready to bid loved ones goodbye. And open their checkbooks. He snapped his grape gum and sank lower in his chair. Brian's death left him empty. Not sad or angry, but the same emptiness he'd felt his whole life. A long time ago something had been shut off inside him. He didn't know how to turn it on again, or if it could be turned on.

Before, he'd relished that emptiness. It had kept him together, especially through the mindless days after Sherry's death. Now he caught himself searching for a nugget of emotion, something to prove to himself that he was human. Rita had done that to him. She made him want to feel, made him want . . . more.

"Sorry to keep you waiting, Mr. LaPorte," the man said, returning to the paneled office. "If you'll just look these papers over and sign here. We take care of everything else so you can grieve in peace."

Great funeral slogans.

He ran his fingers down his face and focused on the

words in front of him. A simple ceremony, interment in the family crypt, some people would cry, some would wonder why he wasn't crying or wonder why he'd come back at all.

No one wants you here. Had Brian regretted those words?

He signed the papers and tried to shake off the thoughts. He finished his business with Mr. Royce, then walked out into the dingy, cool day. He got into his car but didn't start it yet. What would he leave behind? Some cats, an old house, and a successful business, with no one around to take any of it. Like Brian. He'd never thought beyond his life. He leaned forward until his forehead pressed against the steering wheel.

The king of nothing.

He picked up the car phone. After a few rings, Emmagee answered.

"Hey, it's Christopher. Rita around?"

"She is, but she wasn't feeling too good. She went upstairs to lay down."

"She okay?"

"Said she got dizzy sometimes since her accident. I'm sure she's all snuggled into bed. Want me to get her?"

For a moment, he did. He wanted to ask her if she'd like to talk to Dumas with him. "No, don't bother her. How much longer you got?"

"Oh, a couple of ten minutes. I'm going to sweep up in the courtyard when I'm done with the floors. I won't vacuum upstairs, so's I don't wake her."

"I'd appreciate it if you could hang around until I get back, all right? See you in a bit."

Next he called information and got Dumas's address. As he drove toward the Quarter, mindful of the parade routes, he had the urge to turn back to the house. He chided himself and kept going. The last thing Rita needed was to have him wake her up if she wasn't feeling well. And the last thing he needed was to need Rita.

Dumas lived in the East End of the Quarter, and not in the greatest of areas. Christopher approached the three-story apartment complex with the rusted galleries surprised at the pity he felt. Not for the man's living condition, but for the mess he'd been thrown into.

Dumas's expression went from down in the dumps to downright regretful when he saw Christopher at his door. "You're probably here to fire me. Well, you're too late. The agency's already done it. I didn't do no drugs. I told the police, the agency, and I'm telling you, too."

"I know. Can we talk?"

Dumas absorbed Christopher's exonerations and then stepped back to let him inside.

"Tell me what happened."

"You really want to hear it? 'Cause no one else bothered to hear my side of things."

Christopher sat on a faded armchair. "I'm listening."

Dumas lowered himself onto the couch and took a cup of coffee in trembling hands. "Everything was going along jus' fine, you know, like always. I was talking to Brian about my wife who died last year, bless her soul. This maintenance guy came in with two cups of coffee, said he figured I could use a cup. Thought that was mighty nice of him, nobody's thoughtful like that nowadays. I drank part of it, wasn't real hot."

A guy. "What'd he look like?"

Dumas squinted his bloodshot eyes. "Average. Brown hair, brown eyes, maybe. Nice-looking, but nothing special."

"Small guy?"

"Yeah, I s'pose so. He wasn't no Rock, that's for sure."

"But definitely a man? Not a woman dressed up like a man?"

"Well, 'course not. He was a guy."

It sounded like the guy who'd been lingering outside Brian's room when the doctor had told them he might be coming out of the coma. If a man was also involved. . . . Christopher thought about the man who'd tried to force his help on Rita in the Quarter. He'd known about her staying in a house whereas most tourists stayed in hotels. He got a sick feeling in his stomach. So there were two of them, then. A man and a woman.

"He started talking 'bout these monkeys," Dumas continued, "describing their yellow eyes, sharp teeth, and black hair, how he thought he'd seen some in the hospital. Now that doesn't make sense thinking back on it, but at the time, he had me looking for the things under Brian's bed. Then I got dizzy. Everything in the room got weird, wavy kind of. I could see all these squares and triangles floating around. I done pot as a youngster, but this was different. This was wild.

"I told the guy, who was all wavy too, that I wasn't feeling right. He pointed and said there was one of the killer monkeys right there in the corner. I looked at Brian and he had killer monkeys all over him. They were in the air, on the floor, everywhere. He said to go out and get help. I freaked out. Never did like monkeys, man. Swear, if my hair wasn't already white, it would be now. The police figured I'd dropped angel dust, locked me up for the night. I never done anything like that." He scrubbed his hand through his hair. "How am I going to get another job with that on my record? I didn't do nothing, honest." He looked at Christopher, as if gauging whether he believed the story.

"You think the guy slipped acid in your coffee?"

"Was the only thing I could think of. But why would he do that?"

Christopher stood, jamming his hands in his front pockets. "We'll get this all straightened out. We'll get the charges dropped and your job back. Give me a few days."

Dumas's eyes widened in hope before dimming again. "Brian died, didn't he? While I was"—he made crazy motions with his arms—"freakin' out."

"Yeah, he died. But it wasn't your fault."

He left before Dumas could do more than thank Christopher for believing him. When he got back to the house, he was going to find out who belonged to the Sira ID. He had one more stop to make, though. But as he pulled away from the curb, it was Rita who haunted his thoughts.

20

Fear became a living thing inside Rita. She imagined it as a snake, writhing inside her, making her stomach churn. She had to be hearing things. No one seemed to be in the room, at least as much as she could see. Everything was still so small. There was another sound, a humming that went on for a second, then stopped, then started again. She could *see* the humming, a vibrating silver streak floating through the air.

"Whazz happening?" she said, or at least that's what she tried to say. Her words sounded all garbled. Her lips felt numb. "Whadd jugive me?"

She had the sensation of floating out of her body, as if she were watching, and the room wasn't really the room at all. Maybe it was another gray place.

No, not gray. Salmon. The salmon walls were undulating, like a school of fish. The color kept getting brighter and dimmer, brighter and dimmer. And it was making noise. She could *hear* the color, like a tiny instrument wailing, making the texture throb. She saw it, heard it, but none of it seemed real. She stared at it, felt as though she were moving to the beat. But it wasn't there. There, but not there.

"Poishon," Rita said.

"Not poison; too traceable. Only a dose of ketamine, baby. Just enough to make you pliable. You're going to do exactly what I tell you."

Hands squeezed her shoulders, pulling her toward the wiggling squares of light. The French door, she thought. Then someone crouched over her. A monster! Rita pushed the monster away and stumbled to where she thought the door out of the room was. Hands grasped her arms and jerked her back. She tried to fight, tried everything within her power, but her body would not cooperate. Her blood had turned to Jell-O, her limbs to rubber. Was she melting?

"Rita, are you listening to me?" a voice hissed from the monster face. She couldn't see eyes in the face of gold and black, only ghastly black holes. She had seen that face before. Her mind could not get around the thought, though. Where?

Fingers pressed into her cheeks. Her flesh felt like clay. Fingermarks would stay in her face forever.

"Rita!"

She nodded in response.

"Good. We don't have much time." Words floated at her, those silver waves again. "Listen to me, you little witch. I don't know who you think you are, but you are not the queen of Xanadu. You will never be the queen. I am the only ruler, not Alta, not Christopher LaPorte, and certainly not you."

Sira. That's who this was. Rita tried to say something, but her words got lost before she could even attempt to open her mouth. She had lost control of her body, and this horrible *thing* was hovering over her. All she knew was she had to escape. Call for help. *Run! Fight, dammit!* Her body would not cooperate.

"I will not let you contaminate our world," the thing said, tugging Rita toward the small squares that had converged to form one big square. Over that triangles and circles danced. Rita let herself drop to the floor. If she couldn't fight, she wouldn't go, either. The floor felt wavy, shifting and moving beneath her.

"I want you to stand, Rita. Come on, stand."

Her body now chose to cooperate, but only under Sira's commands. *How could this be happening?*

"Very good." She helped Rita walk out onto the balcony. Not walk; float. If Sira hadn't been holding on to Rita's arm, she would have floated away. Dizziness assailed her, closing in the edges of her vision. More nausea. Not morning sickness. Rita wanted to laugh at that. She thought she made a noise. Not a laugh. A sob.

Sira kept walking her toward the far end of the balcony. It was miles away; Rita didn't know if she had the strength to make it. When she looked at the railing to her right, she shoved away from it. It was melting, puddling on the deck, slithering toward her like snakes.

Strange sounds converged around her, and then became the music she'd become so familiar with. Velda! Maybe she could help. Rita mustered all her strength and opened her mouth to scream. No sound. No feeling, either. Had Sira cut out her tongue? The snake of fear became even bigger. No more intestines inside her, only snakes. *Run*, she told herself. *Get away!* She couldn't move. Couldn't even feel her body.

"You're going to take a fall, head first. Go on, up the stairs. Go, Rita."

The words swirled around her like a carousel, colorful and loud. And out of tune. She shrank back from the melting staircase and bumped into the monster behind her. She pushed it away, but her hands were limp.

"Go up the stairs," it said.

"Donn wan to."

Why couldn't she fight back? Sira pushed her up the

stairs from behind, and Rita sprawled to the deck at the top. Pain! She felt pain in her knees. She managed to shake her head as the dripping railing loomed closer. Crying. Tears, burning her face. More tracks in the clay. Maybe her tongue was clay, too.

Sira's arms clamped around Rita's waist. Guiding her closer. Pretty courtyard down below. Concrete squares. Octagons, triangles. The moss in the cracks became green snakes. The trees groaned, shuddered, then cracked apart.

"I won't let you spoil the Gathering. You first, then your boyfriend."

"Rita!"

She closed her eyes at the sound of Christopher's voice. Her imagination, like everything else.

"Dive, Rita. Go, now!"

Sira's voice after all. Rita doubled over the railing, her arms in front of her. Dive. Swan dive. Cold metal beneath her stomach.

"Dive!"

The voice moved away. Rita didn't want to dive. Diving was a bad thing. But her body wanted to listen to that evil voice. She had no will to resist. She leaned farther over, until the ground was no longer beneath her feet.

The wind beneath her wings. She could fly. She stretched out her arms. Dive, dive, swan dive.

"Rita, stop!"

Christopher's voice again from a long way away. Harsh, deep red waves pulsing at her. She swayed. She'd made him mad again. Or was Sira playing with her mind? She tilted forward, feeling momentum taking over. Arms wrapped around her waist. A sob tore from her throat. Sira was going to throw her over. She wanted to do it herself. She felt herself being dragged back, pulled against a hard body.

"God, Rita, what are you doing?"

Her head lolled back against Christopher's shoulder. Christopher? His face looked distorted. The railing grew farther away, but she couldn't trust her vision. Or the sense that filled her brain with Christopher's aftershave. Or the feel of his arms around her.

She felt herself being tilted, felt weightless and floating again.

"What happened to her?" Another female voice. Breathless. Floating through the other senses. "She said she didn't feel well, but I never thought . . ."

Everything went dark. Sun was gone! No, just a crack of light. She struggled to see more, to open her eyes. Salmon walls dancing around her again. Christopher's face above her, making the nasty snake inside her go away.

"What did she eat? Did she drink anything?" His voice sounded garbled with a faint echo. Red lights pulsed to each word.

"Jus' some coffee and a beignet, and I know they were fine, 'cause I had 'em, too."

Too many voices. Rita couldn't keep up with them, but the mention of coffee turned her stomach. She heard a groan and thought it came from her.

"Was anyone in here?"

"No one but me."

"*Could* someone have been in here?"

"I suppose. I was outside doing the windows, and then vacuuming downstairs. I didn't see anyone in the house, but I wasn't looking. What's going on?"

Rita was glad she wasn't expected to answer any questions. She wasn't even sure she still had a tongue. She tried to move her mouth, but it felt big and fuzzy. She tried to grab their words, to make sense of them. Happy faces bounced in front of her. Bright yellow, happy, happy, happy.

"Damn it, I should have come back. You didn't see anything suspicious?"

"No. Nothing. Christopher, what is going on?"

Rita tried talking again. It took three tries. "Rose." It came out all slurred, but at least it was a word.

"Who's Rose?" Emmagee asked.

"I'm taking her to the hospital," he said.

"No," Rita managed, trying to grasp his arm. She didn't want to leave this familiar place, or his arms. No moving, no car. His hands cradled her face, and she tried to make her vision clear.

"Rita, can you tell me what happened? Come on, baby. If you don't, I'm taking you to the hospital. You're scaring me."

His words filled her with warmth and strength. "Sira." She took a deep breath and felt as though her chest were expanding twentyfold. What was happening to her senses? Everything seemed more potent, louder, brighter.

He was shaking her head. "Rita, come back. Sira what? What did she do? Was she here?"

"Who's Sira?" Emmagee asked. "I feel so bad. I should have come up with her."

Rita tried to sort through the questions. There was something important she needed to tell him. Sira! No, she'd already said that. What had happened to her! That's what she had to tell him. What was the word Sira had used? "K-ket . . . keta . . . mmm . . ."

"She's saying *ketamine*, I think. Is that what you're trying to say, Rita? I know that stuff," Emmagee said. "It's been going round lately, along with ruffies. It's a drug that vets use to sedate large animals. Guys have been lacing women's drinks with it, in bars usually. The woman starts to get sick, the guy escorts her out, and that's the last thing she remembers. Then the guy does whatever he wants to with her. The paper's been warning women to watch their drinks at all times, and not to do snort. Scary stuff. No, don't worry, it won't hurt her. It's sort of like PCP or angel dust. It distorts the senses and breaks down your will to resist. You can get someone to do whatever you want."

Dread filled Christopher's chest at those words. "What do I do?"

"There was something . . ." She snapped her fingers. "Cranberry juice! The article said it draws the drug out of your system. I remember thinking I was going to start drinking Cape Cods from now on. I'll run out and get some."

"My keys are still down in the car, or maybe on the sidewalk. I pulled up and saw her on the roof and ran. I don't even know what I did with them."

"I'll find them. Be right back."

He looked down at Rita and tried to swallow past the huge lump in his throat. His heart was still hammering. Her eyes were open, but they were unfocused and dilated. Her body was limp and her mouth slack. Saliva glistened on her lower lip. But she was all right.

"Come on, baby, stay with me." God, what she'd done to him. "You're all right, you hear me?" He brushed her thick hair from her forehead, letting his fingers remain against her skin. "If I could take it for you, I would. I wish I'd come back. I'm sorry." He squeezed her tighter against him, and for the first time in a long time, he prayed.

He heard the front door open and close a few minutes later, then a sound in the kitchen. His body stiffened. If Sira had come back to finish her dirty work, he would kill her. He had his plan of attack ready when he heard footfalls on the steps.

"The roses!" Emmagee said, bursting into the room with a glass and bottle of cranberry juice. She filled a glass and handed it to him. While he lifted Rita's head and helped her to drink, Emmagee said, "I didn't even think about it when she said *rose*. She probably meant the roses Henri brought by."

"What are you talking about?" he said, his attention on Rita who was taking little sips.

"Some gardener guy came by and gave Rita some roses, condolences for Brian's death. Black roses. She knew him, so I didn't think anything about it. But I don't know how that would have gotten ketamine in her system."

Rita nodded the slightest bit. "Henri?" he asked, and she nodded again. He had to have given it to her somehow. How was an old gardener involved in this? The janitor was young. Unless Henri was young, too, and in disguise. He tried to remember what he looked like. Unfortunately nothing specific came to mind. He was becoming convinced the two men were the same. He turned to Emmagee. "Did you say black roses?"

"Yeah. Rita thought they were some New Orleans mourning tradition."

Black roses, like in the lobby. Black like death. But what did roses have to do with ketamine? "Go down and see where she put them. Don't touch them."

When she returned a few minutes later, she said, "I didn't see them, only the empty vase." She looked down at Rita. "When are you going to tell me what's going on?"

He kept his eyes on Rita. "Come on, baby, keep drinking. This'll make you feel better." She responded to his coaxing. "Brian was into a role-playing game on the Internet. I think it got him killed."

"Killed? I thought he jumped."

He wasn't going to get Emmagee involved, but he didn't want her ignorant of the danger, either. "I can't get into all the details. I'm not even sure of all the details. But someone pushed him from the roof."

"This is getting weird."

"You don't know the half of it. I want you to stay away from here. I appreciate what you've been doing, but I don't want you hurt. Take my car and go home."

Emmagee's expression went from curious to somber. "This is serious, isn't it?"

"Yeah. I can't walk you down, so you'd better get going. Before it gets dark."

She scooted off the bed but paused to look at her. "Take good care of her. That girl feels a lot for you."

His arms involuntarily tightened around Rita. "Go on, and honk the horn twice once you're inside the car and the doors are locked. Call me when you get home so I know you're okay."

"All right."

She backed out of the room, and he heard her footsteps as she ran down the stairs. A second later, he heard two beeps and the sound of his car heading out. He focused on Rita again, giving her more juice. He glanced at the French doors, closed but not locked. How had Sira gotten in? Too many questions. And he wasn't sure Rita would remember enough to help.

Without letting go of her, he maneuvered to the phone on the nightstand and called the emergency room. A nurse answered after the twentieth ring, yelling over noise and obvious chaos. "You can bring her in, but it's going to be a while before anyone can see her," she said after listening to his story. "But there isn't much we can do unless she's been physically assaulted."

He looked her over. "No." That's not what this was about. "Can she overdose on this stuff?"

"Doubtful. Just keep an eye on her."

"What can I do in the meantime?" He didn't want to take her down to any chaotic place to wait for hours anyway.

"Get her to drink as much cranberry juice as possible. Make sure someone stays with her at all times. Keep her in a safe place. Within an hour the effects should start to wear off."

He was sure that Sira had only intended to use enough to get Rita to jump from the roof. He scooted back against the headboard and cradled her. He couldn't think of a safer place to keep her. "Come back to me, baby," he whispered, stroking her hair. There was an ache in his chest as he watched her look around at imaginary scenery. "You're going to be all right." He closed his eyes for a moment and rested his forehead against hers. For the first time he admitted he was afraid. And even worse, he had no idea how to deal with this faceless evil.

21

It was another hour before Rita tried to talk again. She'd drunk most of the juice, and her eyes were focusing better. He'd been trying to keep her calm by talking about the kittens, some of his trickier information-retrieval jobs, his house, anything. Her mouth started working, though no sound came out at first. He tilted her chin up a bit so he could read her eyes better. She reached up for his face, though her hand was six inches too far to the left. He took it in his.

"Rita, you okay?"

She blinked, nodded. "I think so," she said in a light, airy voice.

He smiled and felt his chest filling with something like helium. She looked small and frail, like a lost little girl. He squeezed her against him. "You're going to be all right." She was, but he wasn't.

"No," she said, looking very serious. "I'm going to be sick."

"All right, come on."

She shook her head again. "No, not you. Emmagee."

Despite her unsteady voice, he couldn't help but smile. "She's gone. It's just you and me." He scooted off the bed and pulled her up with him.

"No," she whined as they neared the bathroom.

"You must be feeling better if you're embarrassed. Come on, tiger, do what you have to do. I'll keep the lights dim."

She squeezed her eyes shut, but in the end let him lead her into the bathroom. He felt every heave of her body as his arms were wrapped around her waist. Then he washed her face, let her rinse her mouth out with Scope, and turned around to let her go to the bathroom. When she was finished, he locked the French doors and helped her back to bed. Looking utterly humiliated, she tried to fight him again when he tugged her pants down.

"I've already seen you naked, *chérie*. Besides, you're going right under the covers. That's my girl." His instincts had told him to get back to the house, but he'd ignored them. He'd let himself care about her against his good sense, and she'd almost died.

No, not his girl. He didn't deserve her. Hadn't he proven that again today?

But tonight . . . for a few more hours, she could be his. He wasn't letting her out of his sight. He sat on top of the covers once she was tucked underneath with her back against a pile of pillows. He smoothed her damp hair from her face.

"You don't know how beautiful you are," he said, wondering how his mouth had gotten so loose. She rolled her eyes, but he ran his thumb across her lower lip and said, "No doubt about it."

"I'm not . . . even beautiful . . . when I haven't been drugged and got sick."

He remembered thinking that, too. Somewhere along the way she'd become beautiful. But he wasn't used to giving compliments, so he just tried to let her know with a pointed look instead of words.

"No one ever took care of me like this before." Her voice was still thready. "It must have been awful."

"It wasn't," he said, when he was really wondering why no one had ever taken care of her.

He leaned back against the headboard and pulled her close. She sighed softly and said in a slurred voice, "I'm not giving up on you, Chris. You try to make me believe you have no feelings, but after the way you held me, I don't believe that anymore. I'm in love with you, and I don't care if you didn't save your girlfriend, or if that boy died, or whatever other human things you did." She settled against him and closed her eyes. "I just wanted you to know."

And then she fell asleep.

Christopher thought he was imagining the sounds of laughter and music in the distance, until he remembered that the parades started early on Sunday. He rolled onto his back and looked over at Rita, who was also waking up. She blinked as though she were surprised to see him. Her brown waves were in disarray, her cheeks flushed with sleep.

"I had the weirdest dream last night . . ."

"It wasn't a dream," he said. "Wish it had been."

"I was trying to pretend it was." Her voice was still hoarse. She squeezed the pillow beneath her cheek.

"How are you feeling?"

"I'm not sure there's a word to describe it."

He hadn't wanted to upset her last night, but now he risked asking, "Do you remember anything about what happened?"

She took a shaky breath. "Not really. I can remember being scared. I knew something terrible was happening, but everything was distorted. And I had no control over my own body, that was the worst part. I could only do what she asked me to. The rest comes in flashes. What happened?"

"Sira gave you a dose of ketamine. It's a drug used to sedate big animals. It does some pretty nasty stuff, including breaking down your will to resist and distorting reality."

"Ketamine. Emmagee mentioned a drug that was going around. A date-rape drug."

"She said that Henri had brought by some roses. Do you remember if he gave you something to drink?"

"No, nothing to drink or eat. Just the roses. Wait, I remember. There was a thorn and it pricked my finger." She showed him the tiny puncture mark on her finger. "The weirdness started after that. It had to be on the thorn. It put the drug right into my bloodstream. Where are the roses?"

"Gone. He must have come in and taken them."

"But . . . Henri is a man. Sira is a woman."

"I'm beginning to believe both a man and woman are involved, working together. Maybe they're both in the game. Maybe they're lovers. It was a janitor who gave Dumas the acid in a cup of coffee. Henri gave you ketamine. They've got to be the same person. I want you to think about this. The guy who knew you were staying in a house and Henri: could they be the same man?"

She squeezed her eyes shut and pictured the two men. "Maybe. Yeah, I think they could. Henri isn't old, I realized that last night. He has no wrinkles." Her eyes popped open. "You said a janitor gave Dumas the acid?"

"Yeah, why?"

"Remember the day Dr. Schaeffer told us that Brian was coming out of the coma and I saw movement in the hall? The security guard was out there and so was a janitor mopping the floor. He heard about Brian . . . and came back to kill him."

He kneaded the bridge of his nose. "So we have two murderers."

"I keep thinking of Trent and Tammy. They have a close relationship, and yet Tammy seemed in love with Brian. For that matter, Trent could be, too. Maybe they're into some weird stuff, even weirder than Xanadu. It should be easy to find out where Tammy was."

"Supposedly she was so broken up about Brian she went home. Interestingly enough, Trent took her."

"Ah-hah." She seemed to consider that, but there was something else on her mind. "Was Sira . . . trying to kill me?"

"She wanted you to dive off the roof." She shuddered, and he mentally kicked himself for being so blunt.

"Thank you for . . . well, for everything. You saved my life."

He shook his head. "I—"

She reached out and placed her finger over his mouth. "Just accept it. Sorry, but you can't be the bad guy all the time." With a soft smile, she pushed herself off the bed and made her shaky way to the bathroom. She was only wearing a shirt and panties.

"Need help?"

She stopped at the door. "Absolutely not. Besides spilling my guts to you—in more ways than one—that is one part of last night I wish I didn't remember. I'm going to take a shower. A long one." And then she disappeared inside.

That was something else he couldn't shake from last night. Her words of love. He wanted to shove them away, but they kept coming back to haunt him. Sherry had said she loved him, but he had never been sure she'd meant it.

She needed him, and maybe she'd been in love with him. But Rita . . . her words sounded different. They made him feel different; warm and soft, confused and angry. He hoped it had just been the drug or fatigue. He hoped it hadn't.

He went to his room to get dressed, bringing the portable phone back to the bathroom door with him so he could call Emmagee and arrange to get his car back. He leaned against the grooves of the door and listened. As long as the sound of the water changed as it hit her body, Rita was all right. It meant she was moving. He wasn't taking any chances with her, not anymore. Sira and her cohort wouldn't fail next time.

Even though Rita hadn't been physically violated, she found herself scrubbing hard beneath the hot water. That someone had total control over her was more frightening as she thought about it. The balm on her soul was hearing Christopher's voice as he talked on the phone. It rumbled through the door and beneath the sound of the water. She couldn't hear his words, but that didn't matter. Just that he was there comforted her. Made her feel loved . . . cherished. When she opened the door thirty minutes later, he was sitting on the edge of her bed facing the door.

"You all right?" he asked, coming to his feet.

She couldn't help her smile. "Yeah, I'm okay. Thanks for watching over me."

"I'll let you get dressed."

She dried her hair, put on a sweater and blue jeans, and readied herself to go downstairs.

When she walked into the kitchen, Emmagee came toward her with arms outstretched. "You poor baby! My goodness, we were scared. Chris says you're feeling better."

Rita accepted the hug. "I'm okay. I think it's all sinking in now, what could have happened. I've got a headache and if I move too fast, I still get dizzy. But otherwise, I'm okay."

Emmagee's eyes weren't smiley faces this morning; they were coffee brown. "I won't be coming round here no more. He says it might be dangerous, what with all that's been going on." She nodded to where Christopher was sitting at the table. "Not that he'll tell me much. I guess you'll all be going back home soon, anyway, now that Brian's . . . well, you know."

Rita already knew what he'd say.

"Rita's going home as soon as I can talk her pretty head into it," he said, complimenting her and sending her away in the same sentence. Typical Christopher. "I have to figure out what I'm going to do with this place, and with the hotel."

Emmagee's eyes lit up. "You thinking you might stay?"

He glanced out at the courtyard. "*Stay* is a big word. *Hang around for a while* might be a better choice."

Emmagee gave Rita's shoulder a squeeze, then headed out. "Be careful, you two."

Rita fixed her coffee and took a seat at the table. She nibbled on a pastry to test her stomach. Not too bad.

"I put in a call to Connard," Christopher said. "He's on a murder case right now, but I left a message that we need to talk to him urgently. I could have talked it over with his partner, but he didn't seem to know much about Brian's case. I'd rather stick with Connard."

She nodded. "It's easier to convince one person of something than two." She took another bite of her pastry. "Can I borrow your car?"

He narrowed his eyes. "Why?"

"I need to find material for a costume."

"Like hell."

She stood at his firm words. "I'm going to the Gathering. I won't let that crazy woman stop me. If we talk to this Vitar person, maybe we can figure out who Sira really is before she makes her appearance."

"I know you're going, though I'll tell you again I think you're a fool for not packing up and getting the hell out of here. But you're not going anywhere from now on without me. Until we find Sira and her partner, we're stuck with each other."

"Oh, stop. I'll start feeling special." That earned her a wry smile. "Well, then, I'll look up some fabric stores in the Yellow Pages and we'll be on our way."

Rita found two stores open on Sunday, and they headed out.

Christopher locked the front door behind them, but he looked at the key as though it were useless. Against Sira, it seemed to be. "When we get back, we're going to pack up and go to the hotel. I don't want you staying here anymore."

She noticed that he had only thought of her, not himself. If Sira wanted Rita dead, she most likely wanted Christopher out of the way, too. She followed him to the car. "What if we can't get a room?" she asked.

"We'll sleep in a broom closet if we have to."

Sleeping in a broom closet with him would be an interesting proposition indeed. But if Trent and Tammy were involved, staying at the LaPorte would put them right into their enemies' hands.

22

When they returned to the house two hours later, Christopher shadowed Rita's every move as she packed her belongings. Her eyes widened as another piece fit into place. "Christopher?"

"Yeah."

"You need to read the last entry in Xanadu. It's probably still on the computer. Sira posted a response to your post about me being queen. All right, to *my* post. She said something like I would never be queen, and that she'd give me a poison apple. It was a threat, one she tried to carry out."

"And you want to play this game to the end?"

She closed her suitcase. "Aren't you?"

"So?"

"So? If she can get to me, she can get to you. Besides, we can work the room better, keep an eye out for each other. We'll find Vitar, and he'll point her out to us. I'll blast her with my pepper spray." She pulled at the holster clipped to her coat. "And we'll haul her off to the police."

He shook his head as he followed her to Brian's room. "You have it all figured out, don't you?"

"Of course. That's my gig, having it all together."

"Remember, her accomplice will probably be there, too."

"All the more reason for me to be with you. Two against two evens it up."

He opened his mouth to argue, perhaps, but instead said, "Hopefully Vitar will have more to go on—like her name. First I need to size up Sira and assess the situation. I may confront her about killing Brian in front of everyone. The truth is, I'm not sure what's going to happen. I'm going to play it by ear, which is why it would be better if you weren't there."

"That's why it's better if I am there. Go on, read the post."

He gave her an exasperated look as he cleared the screen saver and read Sira's post. He swore under his breath.

"The drug was kicking in when I was reading this," she said.

When he looked over at her, she saw fear in his eyes. He'd almost lost her, that's what he was thinking. And it scared him. Her heart tumbled for a moment, until she reminded herself that he would never acknowledge those feelings. But she would always remember the way he'd held her and talked to her.

He closed down the computer. "Let's get out of here."

She had found an old sewing machine and box, and she packed that along with the rest of her things. They piled it all in the back of his Eclipse and headed out. He took the long way around, backtracking and keeping an eye on the rearview mirror. She wondered if he'd done this kind of thing with Sherry. He looked experienced at it, and grimly resigned.

The crowds were gearing up for Bacchus. There were a lot more people choking the streets. The parking lot at the LaPorte was full, so he had to go around the block to find a fenced-in pay-to-park lot. He had already found out that, short of evicting a guest, there wasn't a room available anywhere at the LaPorte. Fortunately, they didn't have to stay in a broom closet. They had Brian's office. Christopher had already arranged for a locksmith to change the lock on his office door.

Even the traffic within the LaPorte's prestigious lobby had increased. People now had to show passes to enter the hotel. The doorman nodded at Christopher and Rita, and she felt proud that he was being recognized as someone important.

Christopher said, "A man from Orleans Locksmith is going to be coming to see me. Please send him to Brian's office."

"Yes, Mr. LaPorte."

"Mr. LaPorte," Christopher repeated when they walked inside. "No way will I get used to that." He stopped at one of the sculpted white vases, a grim look on his face.

"Oh, my." She felt her heart go as black as the roses in the vase. "These are just like the roses Henri gave me. Does this confirm that it's someone in the hotel?"

He gave that some thought. "These were here last night, before we required passes. I'd think someone would notice if a person who wasn't an employee was messing with the flower arrangements, but as busy as it is, who knows?"

"Wow, some office," she said a couple of minutes later, taking in the rich wood paneling, built-in bookcases, and huge desk. More of those inspirational posters adorned the walls. A window opened to the courtyard area, where a few people drank cold drinks in the cool weather. Like Rita, Brian displayed evidence that his life was normal, together: a framed certificate of gratitude from a civic organization, a picture of Brian and an important-looking man. In one corner of the office was a cot, neatly made up with a pillow and blanket.

"Just one bed?" she asked.

"Tammy said she'd try to get us two, but apparently she couldn't. You'll take the cot."

She would have thanked him if it hadn't sounded so much like an order.

Tammy walked in a few minutes later. "That's all I could do." Her voice was as flat as her expression.

"We're happy to get this," he said.

Tammy looked at Rita. "How terrible that someone tried to break into the house while you were there."

"It was a bit upsetting." Rita studied Tammy's face for any trace of malice. Christopher had told her that a burglar had broken in the night before, and that Rita was too unnerved to stay there any longer.

Tammy looked too tired and pale to be malicious. Even her shiny beads didn't liven her any. Rita didn't discount that it could be an act.

"Tammy, what's the deal with the black roses in the lobby?" he asked.

She looked perplexed. "Black roses? Are you sure they're not purple? The florist was supposed to get purple, gold, and green roses." She turned to the door. "They probably got the color wrong, and I sure don't have time to deal with it now. Let me know if you need anything. I've got to get back to the front desk."

"What are we going to do about a bathroom and shower?" Rita asked after Tammy left.

"There are employee restrooms at the other end of the hall. There's a shower in each one. But I don't want you going in unless I've checked it out."

"Yes, boss."

"Don't get smart with me." He plugged in his laptop. "After the locksmith gets here, we'll grab dinner in the restaurant and then we'll stay in for the evening. I've got more checking to do on both Sira's identity and the banished citizens of Xanadu. I haven't had any luck tracking down the Web site location."

By the time the locksmith had done his thing, she was famished. Christopher's clout did get them a table in the packed restaurant, and they shared a quiet dinner before returning to the office. She started working on her costume while he plunged into his search on the Internet.

She had pieced together a black tank top and yoga pants and fashioned a belt so it looked like a bodysuit. Then she designed some simple adornments to dress it up. She was so immersed in her project she was surprised to discover two hours had passed. Christopher was asleep in the chair, his feet propped up on the desk. He looked uncomfortable with his head turned to one side. At that moment he opened first one eye, then the other.

"What?" he asked in a voice that matched the dreaminess in his eyes and the dishevelment of his hair.

She couldn't help smiling. "Nothing." She walked to the window. "Did I wake you?"

"No, I just sensed your observation."

Despite the late hour and the chill, several people sat at tables in the softly lit courtyard. "I'd love to have a courtyard like this. Plants that are green all year long, a wrought-iron table to enjoy my morning coffee at. Or a late-night drink." She stretched and turned back to him . . . catching him with an appreciative expression.

He got out of the chair. "New Orleans has already infected you, hasn't it?"

"Maybe a little. What about you?"

He walked up beside her and looked out at the courtyard. "I've come to realize you never really leave New Orleans once you've lived here." He turned and met her gaze. "It's like the woman who once snagged your heart; she never lets go."

"You're going to stay, aren't you?"

He looked at her with denial on his face. That's why it surprised her when he answered, "Yeah. I'm going to move my business here and oversee the management of the hotel. That and the house are all I have left of my heritage." He lifted an eyebrow and sent her heart fluttering. "Think I'm crazy?"

She laid aside the pieces of teal tulle. "Do you care what I think?"

"I asked."

"Yeah, I think you're crazy. But that's not my professional opinion."

He gave a half-laugh and moved away from the window.

"I think it's the right thing to do—right for you." When she turned back to him, though, no trace of that smile was visible.

"I tried to ferret out Sira's real Internet account ID, but she knows what she's doing. She has it blocked under layers of phony addresses and dead ends, just like the Web site. Even my computer-geek friend couldn't figure it out. And I tried the address of every person who's been banished from Xanadu. Not a one still has an Internet account. I'm going to do some snooping and find out where they are."

A knock on the door startled both of them. He opened the door just enough to see out. She could barely see a man with a tray. He was peering into the room, but Christopher blocked his view of Rita.

"Tammy saw the light beneath your door," he said. "Thought you might like some coffee."

"Oh. Thanks." Christopher took the large tray, then started to look in his pocket for a tip.

"No tip, man. Have a good one."

Christopher shut the door and set the tray on the desk. "Coffee?"

"No, I'm ready to turn in."

She settled onto the cot and watched him fit back into the chair. She thought about asking if he wanted to share the cot, but he'd already closed his eyes . . . and closed her out.

Typical Christopher.

Now he knew where they were staying. He'd wanted to put something in the coffee he'd delivered, but he wasn't sure he could have gone back in and retrieved the evidence without being seen. Removing evidence was critical; Sira had taught him that.

He wondered if Christopher and Rita had noticed the black roses in the lobby. Sira had been so damned close to getting her out of the way. If she'd had a few more minutes, Rita would have flown right off that deck. The woman *was* blessed, that was for sure. But every blessing had its expiration date. Every silver lining had its cloud.

Unless he could get them apart for a while, there wasn't much of a chance of eliminating them before Fat Tuesday. Which meant they were going to show up at the Gathering.

He smiled. Fine, let them come to the party. Let them play their little game. When they were through, Sira would be the winner. And they would be dead.

Lundi Gras day dawned sunny and cool. Closed up in Brian's office, Christopher and Rita worked on their respective projects during the morning. The only interruptions were lunch and two calls; one from a client and one from the medical examiner's office, which he put on speaker phone. They found high potassium levels in

Brian's blood, but the man explained how that could occur naturally.

"Any signs of foul play?" Christopher had asked.

"I can run a tox screen. That'll take a few days, though."

"See if you can get it through faster."

Faster probably wouldn't be fast enough. She shivered. Tomorrow.

She called and left another message for Connard. "Why isn't he calling us back?" she said in frustration.

"Because he probably has a 'real' case to pursue. A bona fide murder with clues and everything."

She wrinkled her nose at him but knew he was right. Darn him. "I'm going to the break room and get a soda."

He didn't say a thing, just walked to the door and opened it for her. The break room was a mess, indicative of harried employees and a few stolen moments of peace and quiet. He stood patiently by the door while she chose her selection and popped the top. Cold Coke prickled down her throat as she looked at the notices and pictures on the bulletin board. Curled pictures of what was obviously their Christmas party were pinned in the upper corner. Brian was handing out silver-wrapped gifts to the employees in one. In another, several people danced in the courtyard where the party was held. She caught herself smiling at the gaiety, moments of happiness that so easily slipped through one's fingers. And Brian, laughing at something, his secrets held deep within. She could see the shadow of those secrets in his eyes, just as Tammy had said. The party was a necessary task. He wanted to be elsewhere.

Her gaze shifted to someone standing behind Brian, and she felt a catch in her throat. Just as when she'd seen Christopher who looked like Brian, this man in the background looked like someone she knew, too. He was turning away from the camera, though he hadn't turned fast enough. She could see enough of him to know exactly who he was. She pulled the picture down and studied it.

"What's that?" he asked, walking closer.

She showed it to him. "Christopher, he works here."

He shrugged. "Yeah, that's the guy who brought us coffee last night."

"No, you don't understand. This is the man who foisted his assistance on me when I was going to meet you at O'Brien's. And maybe I'm imagining it, but he could be Henri, too. And the janitor. You asked if I thought they could be the same person. I definitely think they could. This is the male part of the team."

Christopher took the picture. "Let's find Tammy."

"That's Edward Sharp," Tammy said a few minutes later. "Why?"

"I need his employee file."

"You're the boss. He doesn't work here anymore, though. I fired him the other day."

"The disappearing employee you mentioned," Rita said, putting it together.

"What I don't need as we head into Mardi Gras." Tammy led them into an office and headed to the files. "He wasn't here when I needed him, but I caught him hanging around when he wasn't on the schedule. Even after I fired him."

"Last night," Christopher said.

Tammy nodded. "He was always skulking around. I escorted him off the property and alerted the security staff to keep an eye out for him."

His face paled. "You didn't send us coffee last night, did you?"

"No." She pulled out a file. "Here it is. I caught him in here once, too. He said he wanted to see his file."

"To take it," Rita said. "Could he have put something in our coffee?"

"Maybe. Damn, I threw out the cups, dumped the coffee down the drain." He took the file from Tammy, who asked, "What's going on? What do you mean, 'put something in your coffee'?"

"Never mind. Keep a sharp eye out for him. He's more dangerous than you think. If anyone sees him, have security detain him and find me."

"Us," Rita added.

The sun was slanting through the sky as they headed to the car a few minutes later armed with Edward Sharp's application. Christopher was looking at it as they walked.

"His address is in the Garden District. Wait a minute. If this address is really his, no wonder he and Sira had easy access to the house."

They were even more surprised when they found the pink house, shadowed by the draping trees on the west side of the property where the driveway was completely in shade.

"Velda's house," they both said simultaneously.

"Could that old woman actually be involved in all this?"

He parked the car on a side street. "My guess is she doesn't live here anymore. Edward and his friend may even be squatting here."

"What should we do now?" she asked.

"Let's see if anyone's home."

No one answered his quick rap on the warped wood door. Rita peered through a crack in the curtains in the front window but saw nothing in the dim house. When he found the door locked, he walked around to the back, pausing to make sure she was following him. She kept an eye on the windows, looking for movement. Where was Edward now? Where was Sira?

When she turned back to Christopher, he was standing

by the French door he'd opened. "Be quiet," he said. "And stay close."

She followed him into the dim house. It smelled of old wood, mothballs long faded, and perfume. There was no furniture, only large pillows on the living room floor. A computer sat on an old nightstand in the kitchen. Speakers were wired from the computer to the living room, where Sira played music each night for their benefit. Teasing them, laughing at her cleverness. Christopher turned on the computer, but it halted at a password prompt. He looked around, probably hoping for a clue. When nothing he tried worked, he turned it off.

Everything was old and sad, even the thick air inside the house. She and Christopher never let down their guard, checking two empty rooms, and even looking behind the doors. They both jerked at the sound of the heat coming on. It felt like the warm, fetid air of an aging monster breathing down her neck.

The bedroom contained a sagging king-sized bed and a nightstand that matched the one in the kitchen. Two faded pictures depicted the days of burlesque, probably Velda's. Maybe the music was hers, too, left behind when she either moved or passed on.

Nothing in the room itself indicated that anyone lived there permanently. If they were squatting, though, why was the electricity on? In the bathroom there were toiletries for both a man and a woman. The bathroom cabinet was crammed with wigs and the kind of makeup a stage actor might use. The closet seemed to hold all of the secrets. It was jammed with boxes and clothing. Christopher paused to listen before stepping inside and turning on the overhead bulb. The chain creaked as it swung from the movement.

Men's clothing hung on the left, crammed into the small space. Rita pointed to a janitor's uniform and the sloppy jeans Henri had worn that first day she'd seen him. Leather gloves had been tossed in the far corner. On the right was a full complement of women's clothing. The black cat suit hung there, legs flaccid. Toward the back an outfit was wrapped in plastic.

He indicated that she wait there and stepped out of the closet to make sure no one had returned. She reached up on tiptoe and pulled down a shiny black box. Inside was the mask she'd seen so many times, including in the car that had run her off the road and in Brian's final moments. She was so struck by it that Christopher's reappearance startled her. The black feathers could be matched to the one found in the car, she bet. She pulled one free from the bottom row and wrapped it in a piece torn from the plastic. She showed the mask to him before replacing it.

He pulled down a metal box and opened it. Ashes filled much of it. Human remains? He grimaced and replaced it, then pulled down another box filled with ashes. They had better luck with a larger box pushed to the back of the shelf. It contained pictures ripped from magazines, curiously all masculine men. Some had been crumpled into a ball and then smoothed out again.

Beneath the pictures was a yellowed photo album. Pictures of a family, mother and father, two sons, and a much younger daughter. Rita could see so much in these pictures, just as she saw Christopher's distance in his childhood photos. The girl was miserable, though the rest of her family seemed happy enough. She never smiled, was never interacted with or embraced in any of the pictures. In candid shots, she was sometimes looking at one of her older brothers with resentment. She looked at her parents that way, too, especially as she grew older.

Rita studied the two brothers, looking for Edward's face. It wasn't there. Both men were stocky and tall with chiseled features like the men in the torn magazine pages.

Was the girl Sira? She peeled away a picture of the girl making mud pies and looked at the back. The words had been violently marked through.

As she started to show it to Christopher, she saw that he had a birth certificate for Edward Sharp, born in 1971. Rita peeled back a picture of the two brothers and looked at the names on the back. Neither was Edward, which meant the girl was likely Sira. It also meant they weren't brother and sister and that they both probably lived here. One of the pictures had to have Sira's real name on the back, hopefully not scratched off.

Before she could look further, the sound of a car pulling into the driveway sent her heart into action. They shoved everything back into the box and returned it to the top shelf. A car door slammed shut. They raced down the hallway as keys jingled at the front door.

Rita led the way to the French doors at the back of the house, Christopher right behind her. She glanced back long enough to see the front doorknob turn. He closed the door behind them just as the front door opened and pulled Rita around the side of the house. They dashed through the line of trees into the next-door neighbor's yard and then circled back to the street. They crossed the street and took the long way back to the car. She saw the black Buick in the driveway, nearly hidden by the trees. The front door of the house was open, and just inside she saw a man.

She could *feel* his eyes on her, eyes full of hatred. He was there, watching them. Hating them for finding his lair. She could feel his hatred even as they got into the car and drove away. The way Christopher was looking in the rearview mirror, he must have felt it, too.

"Let's go to Connard," she said. "We may not have proof, but we have a name. Maybe he's squatting, as you say. That would give Connard reason to question him. If he could get a look at that computer, he'd realize this is all tied together. A feather off that mask could prove one of them was in Boston."

"We'll tell him everything, even about the Gathering. If we can convince him that something is going on, maybe he'll give us some help."

She lifted up the picture of the girl, now damp from where she'd grasped it as they'd run. "Maybe he can figure out what was written here."

He pulled around to Brian's house. "I want to get a couple of things. You stay here and call Connard, tell him we're coming in and we'll wait until he can see us."

"We have to convince him this is real. The best thing for everyone is to get these two into custody before the Gathering."

They had been in his house. In his things. He stood in the closet where his box had been thrown back on the shelf. How had they found him? It didn't matter. He had to get out of here. His fists clenched at the invasion of his privacy. First into Xanadu, then the warehouse, and now his house. Fury washed through him. He would kill them. Oh, yes, and he would enjoy it.

He threw his clothing into the trunk of his car, not caring about anything but the costume wrapped in plastic and the mask. Sira would need those tomorrow. Within minutes he'd dismantled the components of his computer and placed them in the back seat. He wiped every surface clean of prints. If the police got involved, they could find out who had a lease on this place. But they wouldn't find him. He would locate another place to stash the car, but he would return here. They would be back, he was sure of it. And he would be waiting.

23

Detective Alex Connard looked at the notes he'd taken when Rita Brooks and Christopher LaPorte had come in to talk to him. Rita he could write off as being a little unbalanced, but Christopher was a different story. He hadn't recently sustained an injury to his head, and he was a successful businessman back in Atlanta. He didn't look like the kind of guy to be swayed by a woman, even one he obviously cared about.

Detective John Porter stopped by his desk. "You heading out? We got a long day tomorrow."

He considered telling Porter about the strange case of Brian LaPorte, but nixed it. "Yeah, see you in the morning."

He was ready to go home and pack in some sleep. But he couldn't quite dismiss this. If the mask was in the house, he could verify whether a feather from it matched the one found in the car that hit Rita. Even though she had given him a feather from the mask, he had to take it from the mask itself. No way could he get a search warrant, though, based on what they'd told him. There wasn't enough. But there was enough to pique his interest. He pulled Brian's file again.

It read much as it had before, but this time he wasn't

looking at it as an attempted suicide. The injuries from impact were in line with the fall. What did strike him as odd were the four small marks on his collarbone. Fingermarks? And the cufflink. Why remove one link and not the other?

He studied the back of the girl's picture. Whatever was beneath the marks would probably reveal Sira's real name. If she existed, he reminded himself. He did a background check on Edward and found something curious. He had legally changed his name several years back. Using his Social Security number, he pulled up his previous name.

"I'll be damned."

He took the picture down to a colleague in Forensics who verified what he suspected.

"I'll be damned," he said again. Christopher and Rita were on the right track—and the wrong track.

He looked at the address in the Garden District. He'd stop by on his way home just to check things out. If the guy was illegally in residence, he'd have reason to check further. Some of the old homes were undergoing renovation, and he'd had problems before with homeless people holing up in a house waiting to be torn down.

He bid everyone a good night and headed out.

From Brian LaPorte's living room, Edward watched the back corner of his previous home. The new locks here had only been a temporary setback. Now he sat in the warmth and peered through the broken branches that allowed him a view of his driveway.

It wasn't long before his patience was rewarded. Headlights slashed across the trees before the car came to a halt.

"Let me handle this," he said. "I'm the boy. You get tomorrow. Tonight is mine."

Sira protested, but he ignored her as he stole through

the back yard. The West African exorcism dagger was warm in his hand, warm from where he'd been holding it all this time. He'd seen the name on the brass plate up in Brian's room and knew he had to have it. It fit. He was the exorciser.

He didn't recognize the car in the driveway, but once he got inside, he did recognize the man knocking on the door. It was the detective who had investigated poor Rita's near-fatal accident in the hospital parking lot. So Rita and Christopher had apparently convinced him that something might be awry. All allies must be banished.

Twilight colored the sky deep blue. Edward toyed with the idea of answering the knock at the door, but his lease was packed away with his other papers. He knew where the detective would go once he came inside. The man was already walking around to the back of the house. Edward threw the breaker and slinked into the darkest shadows.

A flashlight's beam slashed through the house. The man once again identified himself and called out to anyone who might be inside. He tried the door and found it unlocked. And he stepped inside.

Edward heard the useless flick of light switches and then soft footsteps. It wasn't long before the detective was venturing down the hallway, still calling out his identity. He only took a few moments with the empty rooms. He took a little longer checking out the old mattress and nightstand. The beam of light trailed along the floor, creeping toward the closet. The door was half-closed, so that the detective had to push it open before he could look inside.

Sweat trickled down Edward's armpits, and his mouth felt as though he'd licked the dusty floor. He couldn't moisten his mouth enough to swallow, and the dry, gulping sound seemed explosively loud.

I should have done this. Look at you, sweating like a pig. Nervous sissy.

Sira's voice taunted him, and he blinked furiously when sweat dripped into his eyes. He should have let her do this. She was good at it. Cool, calm. His muscles ached from clutching the knife in front of him. She wouldn't be sweating now.

I'm the boy. I can do this. I'm the boy.

He blinked again, grimacing at the sting of sweat and tears and the truth. He *was* a sissy. His body didn't make enough testosterone to grow more than a few hairs on his chin. Even with the supplemental shots, when he could get them, he wasn't man enough.

His eyes snapped open at the creak of the door. A hand on the wood, the beginning of the sweep of light that would reveal him cowering in the corner.

He lunged forward, feeling the knife sink into flesh, and he kept pushing harder and harder. A gun went off, startling him so much he let go of the knife's handle. He hadn't seen a gun. Why hadn't he thought about a gun? He waited for pain but felt nothing. He hadn't been hit.

The detective slumped to the floor, making guttural noises in the dark. The flashlight had skittered to the far corner, lighting only that part of the closet. The gun made a louder *thunk.*

Finish it! Sira's voice commanded.

"I don't want to see," he whispered, his voice high and near tears.

Sissy boy! Finish it!

The man was struggling, his breath raspy. Maybe the knife had slashed his lung. How long would it take him to die? No, he had to make sure it was done. Sira would never let him live it down. She would never let him do anything again.

He didn't want to hear those taunts again, never, ever again. He looked down at the man who was trying to reach his gun. Edward grasped the knife handle and pulled it out. Blood was everywhere. This was why Sira did the killing. She liked blood. Liked death.

"I'm a boy! I'm a boy! I'm a boy!"

With every sentence, he stabbed again and again, until he collapsed on the floor crying.

Get up, pansy boy.

He got up before she moved on to the nastier names. He had to clean this up, had to get rid of the body. All of the anger drained from him now that it was over. What had he done? He'd killed a cop. He'd fry for that.

He walked to the adjoining bathroom, Sira screaming at him to clean up the mess and get the hell out of there. He didn't see her looking back at him from the mirror this time. He saw Edward. Edward who had taken care of the intruder on his own. But he could feel her trying to take over. His mouth twitched; the muscles at his temple throbbed. His vision blurred. He squeezed his eyes shut and pushed her back inside him.

"Not this time. I'm the boy," he whispered. "I'm the boy."

He returned to the closet. Instead of looking at the detective, he lifted his gaze to the two boxes he'd left on the upper shelf. He had been determined to leave them behind. Now they watched him, judged him.

Clean this room! his mother's voice echoed. *Girls are neat and clean. You're a slob.*

He looked at all the blood on the floor. Blood on his shoes, his clothes. He'd have to burn them in the fireplace before he left. He'd have to leave naked.

Clean up this mess! You're an embarrassment to the whole family.

He looked at the boxes again. "Ya didn't raise me to be a slob, did ya, Mama? Ya raised me to be a la-dy, didn't ya?" He sneered at the box. "You and Daddy only forgot that one detail, 'bout me being born with a pecker."

Susan Sharp had been the third child in an average, middle-class family. Her mother, Pauline, ran a seamstress business from the house, sewing for uppity New Orleans women like Iris LaPorte. Bob was an auto mechanic with a short temper and little patience.

From an early age, Susan got the impression that her genitals were not to be discussed. Whenever she touched the ridges of scar tissue there, her mother slapped her hand away.

There were the doctor's visits when the place between her legs was poked and prodded, and then she was sent out of the room so the doctor could discuss her own privates with her parents. There were the pills she had to take, pills that were never adequately explained. She had vague, nightmarish memories of her mother putting something up inside her that would press against her vaginal walls with excruciating pain.

From her earliest memories, Susan hated dresses and frills and dolls; she wanted to dig around in the dirt with Matchbox cars and wrestle with the neighbor boys. When she started going to school, the other girls teased her, and even the boys called her a girl-boy. The boys were surprised that she was as strong as they were when she punched them. Several times she was reprimanded by teachers who told her she should start acting like a girl. She contemplated what girls were like: frilly, giggly, whiny, delicate. Acting like a girl was too much work.

When she got older, she asked why the doctors studied her down there. "Don't show anyone your privates," her mother said in answer. "Yours are a little different."

How different? she wanted to know. And why? But the subject was taboo, as though she harbored a terrible secret between her legs.

She found out how different when she, another girl, and a boy played doctor one day in the fort in Susan's back yard. First the two girls "treated" the boy, poking and prodding his penis and testicles. Carla, the other girl, giggled incessantly. Susan didn't giggle. She looked at the boy's penis and felt a strange ache inside. She touched the squishy flesh and watched in wonder as it grew firm. Like magic. Somehow, she felt she should have one of those.

Carla was next. The boy touched her fleshy folds of skin and pried out the pink nub. Susan could only stare. She was pretty sure she didn't look like that. Carla's skin was smooth, pretty. Her folds of skin fit together perfectly.

"Your turn," Carla said as she pulled on her clothes.

Susan shook her head.

"You looked at us," the boy said. "Now we get to look at you."

She started to turn away, to run, but they grabbed her. She was afraid to scream out, because if someone rescued her, she'd have to admit what they were doing. It was wrong, and that had made it so interesting.

It wasn't interesting anymore.

The boy pinned her down while Carla pulled down her pants and underwear.

"Oh, my gosh," Carla said as she pried Susan's legs apart. "Something happened to your privates."

"Lemme see, lemme see!" the boy said, lying across Susan so he could see and still pin her down.

Her stomach twisted and turned, but she stopped fighting. It only hurt more, though nothing could hurt as much as the horror on their faces.

"Your pee pee's all ugly, like Frankenstein!"

Susan started crying. She'd gone against her mother's wishes, and now everyone knew she was a freak. Now *she* knew she was a freak. But hadn't she suspected it all along?

• • •

Susan was drunk the first time she had sex. It was only *because* she was drunk; she swore she'd never show anyone her privates again. She had never been attracted to men, but had squelched her occasional attraction to women. That had only added to her constant shame about her sexuality and the confusion that reigned inside her.

She'd been at a party, so ecstatic at having been included. She had few friends during high school, hampered by her lack of self-esteem and feelings of being abnormal. She had drunk too much beer and was stunned at the attention of a football player. She didn't desire him. But she desired to be normal, to experience the things she heard girls whispering about in bathrooms. That desire, combined with the alcohol, was why she let him lead her to the bathroom. She'd insisted on turning off the lights, leaving only a night-light's glow.

The boy roughly fondled her small breasts before pulling her pants down and doing the same to her genitalia. When he pulled out his penis, she touched it. Exquisite rippled flesh, hard, with a velvety tip that made him gasp when she ran her fingers over it. It was the first time she felt sexual desire deep in the pit of her stomach. Only she wanted what he had, what he was feeling. She wanted his penis for herself.

He flipped on the lights and thrust her legs apart. She saw revulsion pass over his expression, but he aimed his penis and thrust it into her. Only it got stuck.

"Why aren't you wet?" he accused, ramming harder.

She didn't know. All she knew was this hurt, and she was convinced the girls had been lying about how wonderful it was. He searched the medicine cabinet and found castor oil. He poured it on himself and pushed into her. It hurt and it felt so damned wrong, shame washed over her.

"You're on the pill, aren't you?" he huffed in her ear as he thrust.

She nodded. She was on pills, had been since she was eleven. They were to fix some problem that couldn't be explained to her. Her mother had told her she'd never get pregnant.

She couldn't feel it when he came, but she knew because he grunted and stopped moving. Before he'd even caught his breath, he pulled out of her as though her vagina had bitten him. He glanced between her legs, but she pulled a towel from the rack and covered herself with it.

"What's wrong with you? You don't feel right."

Heat flooded her face. She didn't answer, only bowed her head.

He stretched his flaccid flesh as though he were checking to see if she'd done something to him. Then he grabbed her towel and wiped himself off. She pressed her legs together. He flung the towel back at her and walked out of the room.

"You lose! *It* doesn't have a penis," she heard him say to someone. "She has a hole . . . and I made use of it."

She covered her ears to the rest of it, railing at herself for giving in to a temptation not of the flesh, but of wanting to fit in. She wanted to kill herself. It wasn't the first time, but she'd never felt it so strongly. She even checked the cabinet for pills, but she didn't think taking ten Tylenol would do it.

She crawled into the tub, ignoring the impatient knocking on the door she'd relocked. She ached, but the physical pain was nothing compared to how she felt inside. Every wave of laughter she heard was the football player telling a new group how deformed she was. She was so sure of it she stayed in the bathroom for two hours.

That night she wanted to kill herself. Later, she wanted to kill the jocks. Susan was sixteen.

• • •

The next week, she gathered enough courage to ask her mother what was wrong with her. Pauline wouldn't even look her in the eye. "You're just different. Leave it at that."

She never imagined what the truth would be when she searched through her parents' closet a few weeks later. She found the box with her family's financial documents, a will, expired passports, and her and her brothers' birth certificates. She sat cross-legged on the closet floor going through it all. Buried at the bottom was another yellowed birth certificate. It read Edward James Sharp, born January 15, 1971, at 4:57 A.M., same as she. A lump formed in her throat. Was he a twin, long deceased? She compared it to her certificate. They were on different paper stock, signed by different people. Both read "single birth." Not a twin.

The realization hit her. She'd been born Edward Sharp. The word *male* seemed to glow in the dim light. Her stomach turned. At first it didn't make sense at all, and then it made perfect sense. She'd always felt like a boy, had always wanted a penis, and had had feelings for girls. She grabbed a mirror from her parents' bureau and, for the first time, looked at her genitalia. They were a mass of twisted flesh. She remembered what Carla had looked like, the way the folds of her skin fit so neatly, the nub of flesh between. Not so hers.

Now she knew why she was so deformed. *They had made her into a girl.* "Oh, God, oh, God, oh, God. Why? How?"

As soon as her parents returned from their weekend trip, she shoved the birth certificate in their faces. "Why am I a girl when I was born a boy?"

Her mother's cheeks went red, and she snatched the paper from Susan's hand. "You went snooping in our things?"

The anger pummeled her from within, that they would hone in on that when she had been so betrayed. Her father left the room, apparently unable to address any of it. He was ashamed of her, of whatever had happened to make her a freak. Her mother was ashamed, too, and she tried to turn away. Susan wouldn't let her. She pushed her against a wall and demanded the truth. And finally it came out.

Edward's birth was not an altogether happy event in the Sharp household. They had wanted a girl, had in fact tried for a third child with the sole intention of having a girl. They had chosen the name Susan and envisioned a plump-faced little girl who would play with dolls and wear frilly dresses. And indeed, Pauline even carried low and wide like a girl.

Edward was a letdown. "We loved you, of course. You were a beautiful baby, so happy. We were disappointed, yes, but we buried it."

Until the accident.

And then the Sharps got what they wanted.

When it was time for Edward to be circumcised, his father was between jobs and they had no insurance. They'd taken him to a family friend who still practiced medicine despite the fact that he'd lost his license five years earlier for leaving his wedding ring in someone's body—on purpose. He worked out of the back of his house, treating criminals with bullet and knife wounds, performing abortions and an occasional sex-change operation. He agreed to help out the Sharps in their time of need.

He sliced off Edward's penis nearly down to the base.

"We didn't know he'd been drinking, I swear. He seemed perfectly normal."

Dr. Bale was remorseful and begged the Sharps not to sue or report him. He saved people's lives, and he would save this mistake, too. He had become familiar with the plight of transsexuals, people who felt as though they were born with the wrong sex organs and those born with ambiguous sex organs. Through his studies, he discovered that half of them committed suicide because they couldn't overcome the disparity in their sexual and physical selves and the humiliation and ridicule that accompanied it. He had also studied an eminent surgeon who had done sex reassignment surgeries in other cases and believed that babies were sexually undifferentiated and learned their sexual nature from conditioning.

"There was no way for anyone to construct a penis, so he made you into a girl. He said it would work."

It was stunning news, too large to absorb completely. Still, anger flowed through Susan's veins. "If this was a mistake, then why are you ashamed of me?"

Guilt colored Pauline's expression. "Because it went so wrong. We failed you. And we didn't know how to make that right."

"I know how you can make it right," Susan said in a low voice. "Make me a boy."

"We can't do that now. Everyone knows you as a girl. What will they think? They'll think we're horrible parents, and . . . and . . . they'll make fun of you."

That's when she knew she hated them. All Pauline cared about was what people would think of *them.* Hadn't her mother ever once heard her when she said classmates teased her for being so masculine? No, she hadn't heard because she hadn't wanted to.

"I will be a boy," she said and went upstairs.

Later, at dinner, her parents tried to set her straight on what she should do with her life. They would not tolerate her changing sex midstream, not while she lived under their roof. They would help her in whatever way they could to make being a girl easier.

That's when she realized it: her parents blamed her for

not accepting her reassignment. It should be simple. That's what the research had shown. They thought she should fix her attitude.

There was no way to fix any of it.

Well, there was a way of helping it. She dreamed of it every night, strangling them, shooting them, stabbing them in their eyes and mouths and their genitalia.

Further complicating matters was the fact that her body was still producing male hormones despite the female hormones she took. Her walk changed, and her voice started cracking. Her parents became angrier at her "rebelliousness." They forced her to take the pills and were sure she was throwing them back up again when she continued to exhibit male traits.

To escape her misery at home, she sank into the murky world of transsexuals, where for the first time she found others who were living in bodies of the wrong sex. She took drugs that numbed the ever-present shame and conflict within her body. During one of those drug-hazed sessions, she confessed her situation. And suddenly she was not one of them anymore. She had, after all, lived their fantasy, men who longed to be women, changed against their will. They wanted to see her genitalia, to study it and long for it as their own. When she wouldn't show them, they rejected her.

Her stay with the transsexual community did give her one thing: access to T-shooters—testosterone shots. She went off estrogen and became Edward. The first wispy beard hairs on his chin were the final straw. His parents asked him to move out. They banished him. He was almost eighteen.

And so he drifted, finding temporary solace with different transgender groups but never really fitting in. He most related to the intersexed, formerly known as hermaphrodites. They had often been surgically mutilated at birth, too, when doctors excised under-developed penises and testicles and made them into girls. Unfortunately, he knew no one like that, not personally. He was alone in the deepest, biggest way. Even with the testosterone, Edward never felt fully at home in his body. The hormones had left his breasts as female appendages. His resentment of his parents grew to monstrous proportions after he asked them for money to have them removed, and they refused.

That's when he met a drag queen who confided how much he made a night. It was Edward's only recourse, the only legitimate way he could make that kind of money. He was only entry-level at the computer software company he worked at.

For the first time, he enjoyed being a woman, dressed in frills and black lace, holding the crowd at rapt attention. Touché made a name for herself. She was accepted, admired, even loved. Edward enjoyed being someone else, so much so that by the time he'd earned enough money for the breast removal, he decided to keep the breasts and the estrogen pills. He'd already become a shape-shifter of sorts, living as a man during the day and a woman at night. He had no close friends in his life to whom he'd have to explain the change, no family to be shamed. Touché wanted to take over, but he pushed her away when he got dressed and went to work at the software company each morning.

He was lucky he'd found himself by the time petty jealousies made him lose his job at the club. By then, he had other pursuits to occupy his evenings. Like killing his parents.

He pulled down the box as he dropped down to the wooden floor of the closet next to the detective's body. "Oops, sorry, Mama. Did I hurt you?" He opened the box and sifted through the ashes with his fingers. "It didn't hurt much, did it? Drowning's supposed to be peaceful.

Didn't Daddy always tell you not to go swimming alone? It's a shame you got all tired out in the pool." He lifted his hand and blew his mama into the air. Then he licked the dust from his fingers.

"It was your fault, Mama. You wanted me to be a girl. You created Sira in a way. She introduced herself to me as Touché, but then she became even stronger. She took control, reaped justice. She was the person I wanted to be, a woman with no question as to her sexual identity. It was Sira who pushed you under. You said you were sorry then. Yeah, well, I was sorry, too. Sorry you never loved me."

He took the other box down from the closet shelf. "Should've been more careful taking a shower with the razor plugged in so close by, Daddy. Sira didn't even give you a chance to say you were sorry. It was enough to see your face as she dangled the razor over the water you were standing in, enough to hear your strangled sound of horror."

And it had been a bonus that his parents had left him a nice chunk of money. Guilt money, probably, but he'd taken it.

Sira paid a visit to the old doc, too. Fire was the only way to cleanse that man's soul. It had taken a while to reap that revenge, but it had worked perfectly. One small device, timed to light a small kitchen fire in the middle of the night. That pan of cooking oil right there, not even an accelerant to tip off the police. Amazing what you could learn, hanging around the lowlifes on the streets. The lowlifes were the only ones who were so screwed up they couldn't look down on him.

He was nobody, and he was everybody.

His life finally changed for the better when he found Xanadu, the one place where he could have sexual urges and live out fantasies that only existed in his mind. He'd found it in the early days of its creation, before Brian had closed the gates and restricted access. He was learning the ins and outs of the Internet when a search for a New Orleans slang word had pulled it up by accident. He'd been tempted enough to investigate. And join. He'd started out as Fallo, an all-male macho sort. Touché became Sira, his female personality, the strong, dominant woman with curvy hips and a round bottom and buttloads of sex appeal. Sira had taken over, just as she did in real life.

Eventually, Sira had become obsessed with Alta, gravitating to the leader. In June, they began a relationship, Sira's first. His first relationship ever. During their intimate online encounters, Sira played "Fever" over and over. Everything about Alta was scintillating: his power, the way he "talked," and especially the artwork he'd posted that captured all of that muscular, male power. No one was supposed to know who the players really were. That's what made the fantasy so real, though Sira had long ago violated that rule. But only when absolutely necessary.

She was tantalized by the certainty that he lived in New Orleans. First the references to the French Quarter and the peculiarities of New Orleans language and food . . . and the fact that their annual Gathering was always held there. Like Xanadu, New Orleans was a world of masquerade, a place for people who wanted to be someone else.

She had valiantly fought the temptation to find out who he was.

For five months, everything was perfect. Sira reveled in being wanted, being loved, and mostly, being accepted. Their relationship eventually escalated to erotic realms filled with pleasure and tenderness. Sira began to dream of being the queen of Xanadu. The power of the position and the pairing with Alta erased the unhappiness and rage of years past. The only thing that shadowed Sira's bliss was how to handle the physical aspects of the Gathering. How could Sira avoid having sex with Alta?

And then in late November, things changed. Alta started to back away. He didn't visit Xanadu as often, and when he did, he didn't stay as long. He didn't come when Sira was likely to be there, and if she was, he avoided her. Sira could think of only one reason for his distance: another woman. She didn't think it was a resident of Xanadu; she would have picked up on any interest. Which meant the interloper was someone in the other world.

Before she could even consider what to do about that, Alta made a startling announcement: he wanted to bring in a new resident. A woman. Though he was the king, he too had to ask permission. The residents, eager for dissension, urged him on.

Sira could not let that happen. She would find out who Alta was, and then who this woman was who had usurped Sira's place in his life. Finding Alta wouldn't be too hard.

But to find out Alta was Brian LaPorte . . . huge disappointment, that. Wealthy, a member of society. It made the rejection sting even more. She started casing his house, and then gained access by pretending to be a city official testing water quality. The extra key had been on a ring near the telephone in the kitchen.

It was on her forays to his place that she found the house behind his for rent. It was a relic that was going to be knocked down and renovated the following year. The new owners wanted a short-term lease to make the payments in the meantime. Pure serendipity.

Edward had surprised Sira by quitting the software company and getting a job at the hotel. Sira wasn't pleased. She wanted to handle this on her own. It was all Sira, her will, her plan. She had invaded Alta's home—

no, not Alta. Brian LaPorte. She had felt a certain amount of power, lying on his bed, going through his things. She had gotten onto his computer to find evidence of the usurper. Even though the string of e-mails from Rita Brooks was to the mortal Brian, Sira still felt the sting of betrayal. This was the woman he intended to bring into Xanadu.

While her anger had simmered, while she continued to read their e-mails that were so different from her relationship with him, Brian walked in and caught her. And he wanted her to leave. He'd rejected her . . . and then he'd threatened to banish her.

The thought was paralyzing. Banned from the one place she belonged. Sira would die and he would be left with powerless Edward. Never, never, never!

It had all happened so fast, Sira hadn't had time to realize what she'd done. She stared down at the courtyard where Alta lay, expecting him to get up and accuse her of pushing him on purpose. He'd taken a nasty fall last year from the Mountains of Change and survived.

But he wasn't moving. She considered calling on Rakir, who could raise the dead. That would mean crossing the Plains of Evil and staying the night in Utopia to fortify herself for the journey to the Summit of Truth. Utopia was a world populated by thieves, liars, and performers of Magik, but she was sure she could survive a night there. The climb to the Summit was supposed to be strenuous, nearly impossible, but she would manage it.

Once she reached the Summit, that's where she would encounter trouble, she realized. One must have pure motives for approaching Rakir. He would know that she had caused Alta's fall. He would punish her by not helping.

She couldn't undo the damage. But she could erase the evidence. She'd copied all of Rita Brooks's e-mails and then deleted them. She'd stolen the phone bills with

Rita's number on them. She took his sketches. Anything of Xanadu was removed. She rubbed a towel over the doorknobs and keyboard. And then she fled.

After tracking Rita's e-mails, she'd discovered that the woman resided in Boston. It wasn't too difficult to find where she lived. Sira had insisted on banishing Rita, even though she wasn't officially part of Xanadu. If she learned of Alta's death, she might tell the police about Xanadu. No, Rita must be banished . . . for good. Sira had gone to Boston on that rainy, cold night, and run Rita off the road. The car had been totaled, and Sira had been sure Rita wouldn't survive the accident. She had returned to Alta's side to see if he'd come out of his coma. To make sure he didn't. She'd moved the site to a safe place, where she ruled Xanadu.

It was supposed to end there, but things had gotten so complicated.

Edward stripped away his clothing, turned off the light, and settled into a fetal position on the cold wood floor. The blood was cold now, too. He smeared it on his skin, his cheeks. He inhaled the coppery smell of it, licked it off his fingers. Even Sira was quiet. She was probably too disgusted to harangue him. He was disgusted, too. He would pay his penance here in this room. He would breathe death and feel the cold prick of his sins on his flesh.

Three more people had to be banished for the good of the world. Then Xanadu would be safe. And there would be no more regrets.

24

"Do you think Connard will check into it?" Rita asked once they were back in Brian's office. "He didn't seem as skeptical as before."

"He was hard to read. Hopefully we'll hear from him soon. Otherwise, we're on our own."

A knock sounded on the door, and a young man brought in a cart with their dinner and a FedEx delivery. They set the dishes on the desk but Rita's attention was on the box. "What is that?"

He opened it and pulled out a set of handcuffs and a small tape recorder. "I had a friend mail these from my house. I got the cuffs when I was with Sherry. I had planned to cuff the bastard the next time he went near my apartment, to prove he'd been there. That's what the police needed: proof." She saw that dark shadow cross his face as he ran his thumb over the shiny metal surface. "The recorder I've had for years. I'm going to tape anything critical."

After dinner, Rita returned to stitching gold edging on her outfit. She jabbed her finger and a drop of blood popped to the surface. As she stuck it in her mouth, a memory popped to the surface of her mind.

Come here, baby girl, let me kiss it and make it better.

Angela had made it better. Rita had forgotten so much where her mother was concerned. She'd forgotten the tender moments.

Angela had failed her as a mother. She'd made bad judgments and had been unable to handle responsibility and pressure. Now Rita was failing as a daughter. Angela had apologized and was reaching out. Why wasn't she able to reach back? Because she was still holding on to her anger. And because . . . the other reason eluded her. When she shifted her gaze, she saw that Christopher was looking at her.

She used his earlier response. "What?"

He leaned back in the chair and ran his thumb along his jawline. "You should know something before you think about putting on that outfit tomorrow."

"What's that?"

"I've found seven of the ten people who were banished from Xanadu."

"And?"

"They're dead. I've been tracking them down, finding their accounts closed, then contacting the service provider, then looking up newspaper articles. A lawyer in Newark, a housewife in Albuquerque, a plumber in Washington, DC, and a college student at the University of Miami. Sira's been a busy girl. The ones I found all died by either accident or suicide. Just like Brian."

"Should we call Connard about that? Do you think he believed us at all?"

"He wasn't sure what to believe. Every bit of evidence will help." He called and left a message for him. Then he turned to her. "I want you to think about this. Sira has tried to kill you three times. She murdered Brian. And she may have murdered seven others."

"She's willing to do whatever it takes to preserve Xanadu."

"Including kill you. That's what I want you to think about."

She started to wrap her arms around herself but halted. She was afraid, yes. But he'd taught her that she could overcome her fear. "That just gives me more reason to put this outfit on. I can't walk away from this, not now. And I'm not leaving you to handle it by yourself." She returned to her sewing, turning away so he couldn't see that she hadn't exorcised the fear completely. He didn't have a choice about her attending . . . and neither did she.

Christopher turned off the computer at eleven and rubbed his face. "I logged onto Xanadu. A few of the players left private messages for Alta. They're excited about meeting his new queen."

Rita had hung up her costume, changed into her pajamas, and was now snuggled into her small bed. "I'm ready to meet them, too." He looked at her for a moment, and she saw warring emotions cross his face. She said, "I'm not going to die because you care about me. It's superstitious to think that because someone is in your life, they'll die."

He looked as though he were going to say something in response but stood instead. "I'll be back in a minute." He locked the door behind him, and his footsteps faded down the hallway.

She let out the breath she'd been holding and listened to the hoots and hollers of people having a grand time in the streets of New Orleans. He returned a short time later, damp from a shower, dressed in his sweatpants with his sweatshirt flung over his shoulder. He flicked off the overhead light, leaving them in the soft glow from the lamp on the desk. The curtains were closed. As he headed toward the chair, she stopped him by saying his name.

"There's room here for both of us."

He eyed the small cot, barely big enough. She wasn't being chivalrous. She hoped he could see that, and that he wouldn't make her come out and ask. She let him war with himself and didn't give him an out. He was going to have to turn her down or give in. Instead of shuttering her expression, she let him see her need to be held.

He lost his internal battle and walked to the cot. "Are you afraid? You can still back out. I won't think any less of you."

She *was* afraid of tomorrow. Of facing their enemy, of pretending to be a queen, and of losing Christopher. She reached out, and he slid his hand into hers. "I could say the same to you."

Neither would back down. Not now and not tomorrow.

Rita wasn't sure what had awakened her, but her eyes opened, and she lay very still listening. She had no idea what time it was. It wasn't light out yet. Shadows crossed the room, accompanied by murmurs as a small group of people walked past the window. Her heart was pounding a steady beat of fear as she thought how few hours were between then and the Gathering.

She had shifted during the night and was now on her back. Christopher was on his side, one leg over her lower body and one arm over her stomach. The pounding in her heart increased, but not out of fear anymore. It was now desire that made her breathing heavy. She synchronized her breathing so that when he exhaled, she inhaled. As she breathed him in, the other reason clicked into place. She set it aside to consider it later.

Something else was clear, too. She wanted this every night, wanted him close like this. She was ready to let a man into her life. This man. Wanting him had nothing to do with Brian or transference. It had everything to do with finding the man who gave her the motivation to open herself to love, and figuring out why she'd been plagued with nosebleeds.

In the deep, dark hours of the morning, she could no longer fool herself. She wasn't just in love with him. She loved him.

His question had echoed in her mind. How could you know if you loved someone if you had never loved before? Now she could answer him. You just knew. Blind trust.

It exhilarated her. It scared her. Mostly, it hurt. He was too valiant to bring her into his darkness.

She reached out to him, sliding her hand along the arm slung over her. She trailed her fingers across his shoulder and down his side. He awakened instantly, and his hand slid up into her hair. In the dim light from the courtyard, she couldn't read his expression, could only see the shadows of his face. He ran his thumb over her mouth in the way that went right down to her soul. She kissed his thumb, then nibbled on the pad.

She heard a quick inhale. "Rita, I don't know how to love you the way you need." He slid his hand up against her cheek. "But I want to love you the only way I know how." He leaned over and kissed her. Not a tender kiss, but a hungry one that told her how long he'd held back. He offered her nothing more than this night, this kind of love. And she took what he offered, without consulting her common sense. She opened her mouth to his, fully engaging him, showing him how long she had restrained herself, too. She could show him what being loved felt like.

She turned to her side and let everything she felt for him rise unheeded from the depths of her soul. Men understood actions, and that's what she would give him. She cradled his face with her hand as he paused mid-kiss and looked at her.

I'll take what you have to offer me, she told him with her eyes, with her hands. *And I'll give back more than you've ever been given.* She ran her fingertips over the curves of his face and feathered his eyelashes. She trailed the edges of his mouth and traced the ridges of his ears.

She thought he'd stopped breathing. He'd taken one deep breath when she'd started touching him and hadn't yet exhaled. She sat up and took his hands so that he would sit up, too. They faced each other on the tiny bed, both on their knees. He leaned forward to kiss her, but she ducked and kissed his chin instead. She continued her exploration of his face with her mouth. As tenderly as a mother would kiss her newborn, she planted tiny kisses over his skin.

"Rita, what are you doing?" he asked in a thick voice as he exhaled at last.

She ran her thumb across his lips in the same tender way she loved. "Making love to you the only way I know how." She leaned forward and kissed him, a soft, gentle kiss that could not heat their blood and lead to mere sex. Her mouth moved down to his chin before he could try to deepen it.

He tilted his head back, and she heard his breathing go deeper. She felt his surrender. She moved to the place just beneath his ear, soft skin that made him growl low in his throat. She wanted to take him not to that place of heated passion, but a place she knew he had never been. She kissed down the length of that scar that haunted him. She knew that he had never been loved for who he was inside.

His hands tangled in her hair as she moved lower. For a moment she got caught up in the way his fingertips moved over her scalp and the tingles that shivered down her spine. But this was not about her, not now. She moved behind him and kissed down the indent of his spine. His muscles flexed beneath her tongue as she trailed it across his shoulder blades. When the level of sensuality rose too high, she lightened it by trailing sweet, chaste kisses across his back. When she had covered every inch, she unbuttoned her pajama top and slid her arms around him. She pressed her cheek against his back and squeezed him tight, as though she could meld right into him and chase away all the darkness inside.

"Rita, I can't . . . give this back."

"Shhh."

He didn't know how to be treasured. And though she didn't know, either, she knew that's what she was doing: treasuring him. He took her hands and pressed first one palm and then the other against his mouth. She could feel the tremble of his lips. Was it from restrained passion? With a deep intake of breath, he turned around and gave her the longest kiss she'd ever experienced. He was driving now, she realized, and let him take the wheel. And before she surrendered to his kind of love, she wished she knew: was her tenderness too much for him? Or not enough?

When Rita awoke the next morning amid the tangle of blanket and sheets, Christopher was gone. Sunlight streamed through the cream curtains and pooled beneath the window. She wrapped the blanket around her and walked over to the warm puddle of light. A couple huddled at the table in the far corner, sipping coffee and laughing.

She heard the door lock click and turned to see Christopher. He stopped, as though he'd come across a force field. His expression was shuttered, but for that one second, she'd seen something glimmer in his dark blue eyes. He blinked, swallowed, then pushed himself to move forward and close the door behind him.

She wrapped the blanket tighter around her. "What's wrong?"

Beneath the long coat he carried, he revealed the sword she had seen at Brian's house, keeping his eyes on that as he laid it across the desk. "It's just . . . when I . . ." He looked up at her. "You're so beautiful standing there in the light." He concentrated on the sword again.

"Th-thank you." She had never heard a more sincere compliment in her life. He didn't want to make a big deal out of it; she wouldn't, either. She walked over to the desk and looked at the shiny blade and the ornate handle. "My, what a big sword you have." She batted her eyelashes at him when he met her gaze and was rewarded by that snarky grin of his.

"All the better to penetrate you with, my dear." He held the sword with both hands and moved it in circles. "I thought a king should have a sword to protect his queen with."

She swallowed hard, knowing how he felt about weapons, about that sword in particular. But her throat had gone dry at the words *his queen*. "Where's my sword?"

Though she was kidding, he surprised her by reaching beneath the coat and presenting her with the Silent Shadow. "For extra protection. You'd better get dressed before I get careless with my sword."

She couldn't believe she didn't feel self-conscious standing there naked but for the blanket. "Is that supposed to be a threat?"

He moved the chair from behind the desk and took the stance of a true swordsman. "I don't want to be distracted. I've got to remember how to use this again."

"Mm," she answered, before adding, "I think you

know how to use it just fine." She cleared her throat. "When did you get that? It's from the house, isn't it?"

"I got it last night when we stopped. I was hoping I wouldn't need it, that Connard would have found something. I spoke to his partner just now. He doesn't know where Connard is. He didn't know anything about our situation and had the patience of a dog looking at a bone."

Rita let out a sigh. "So he obviously didn't buy anything we told him."

She watched him parry and thrust for several minutes—or at least she thought that's what it was. The grace of his body and the warrior fierceness in his eyes impressed her. He had learned hatred in the tableaux. Now he would use it for good.

She could spend all morning watching him, and she wished she had all morning to do so. "Well, think I'll go change . . . when you can break away from the battle."

His mouth quirked in a smile. "Nothing is more villainous than a full bladder."

He checked out the bathroom and then returned to Brian's office alone. He stared at the blade and remembered all the other times he had held this sword. He'd left his behind; odd that Brian had chosen to display them considering their meaning. Maybe he'd just remembered the times he'd won.

As much as he tried to focus on the cold, hard steel, images of the night before crept into his consciousness. He shivered at the memory of her touches and started to feel lost again. In the guard position, he made an advance by placing his right foot forward along the line of attack. He lunged and thrust the sword forward, then retreated quickly to avoid his opponent's riposte. He lunged again, but took too long. His opponent was able to parry, and Christopher retreated to the guard position.

If anything happened to her today . . . he lunged artlessly forward and impaled his opponent. No matter that she gave him no choice. If she were hurt, he would never forgive himself.

Sira wandered the fabric hallways of Xanadu, her heart thumping as though it were buried in mud. The wrinkled script was clutched in her hand, the paper wet from her damp palms. Bitterness filled her throat. Once Alta had loved her, had wanted her for his queen. Then Rita had interfered. Everything was falling apart. Alta was gone. And now Edward had gone mad, lying there with that man's body, smearing blood on himself. She'd had no control over him that night. Only when he was ready did he throw his clothes, shoes, and his parents' ashes into the fire. Only then did he walk silently to Brian's house.

"No regrets, no regrets," she chanted and dropped the script on the floor. "Focus on Xanadu."

Interlopers had breached Xanadu's security and would be making their appearance at the Gathering today. Worst of all, Sira could not make her own appearance. Not at first, anyway.

She climbed the metal stairs in the back. If she could at least restore the sanctity of Xanadu, then she could regain the happiness she'd once had. She could even find love again.

It had fallen to her time and again to sacrifice. To preserve. Three more people would be sacrificed. Now the physical manifestation of Xanadu itself would be sacrificed. She set a device in the corner and started the timer. Fire would cleanse this physical world of Xanadu. She had a whole year to re-create it somewhere else. It, like she, would rise out of the ashes.

She'd told Alta time and again that having the Gathering in the same place every year wasn't wise. What if those who were banished decided to cause trouble? Some of the participants were a bit unbalanced. Some had made threats when they'd been banished. But Alta was attached to this old place. So Sira had made sure the banished did not return. Ever.

She placed the last device in the back of the gathering room, where the black cage sat. Her fingers slid down the cold bars and she smiled. Christopher LaPorte had one more tableau to perform. Once again, he would be cast as the bad prince, condemned to death as the crowd applauded. And Sira would finally get the glory for all she'd done.

"And 'mid this tumult Sira heard from far, ancestral voices prophesying war!" Like Coleridge's Xanadu, this one was magical and sacred. She would keep it safe forever.

25

Rita wasn't sure when it all started to feel surreal, but while doing some last-minute stitching on her costume and watching Christopher fence with an imaginary foe, she began to feel as though she'd slipped into another dimension.

Worse, time was flying. A tunnel of pressure built inside her. She and Christopher had stayed in the office most of the day, though she was occasionally drawn to the window to watch the crowd in the courtyard. She thought she would feel conspicuous in her costume . . . until she saw the sperm people. Seven of them, holding up papier-mâché sperms on poles, all following a large egg.

"Let's go over the key players again," he said, pulling out the notes they'd taken.

When they'd quizzed each other on who matched what feature, she looked at the clock. He was also looking at it. One-thirty. Their gazes met, and she hoped he couldn't see her anxiety.

"It's almost time," he said. "Are you sure . . . ?"

"Yes," she answered before giving herself a chance to think about it. "I'd better get changed."

He walked her down the hall and checked the employees' restroom before she entered. The offices were relatively quiet. Most of the employees were probably out in the public areas. She pulled on the black "body suit" adorned with tulle and satin. The draping over her shoulders was enhanced by pads, giving her a larger-than-life look. She'd made a belt, and the curled strips of gold fabric trailed down to her ankles. Swaths of fabric wrapped snugly around her waist. For the first time she didn't see a drab woman when she looked at her full-length reflection.

That's because Christopher called you beautiful.

"Mm," she said to her reflection.

She put the finishing touches on her makeup and hair and then draped one last piece of teal tulle over her head as a scarf. Not bad.

As she looked at her reflection, she saw something in her features she'd never seen before: her mother. Angela was more angular and worn by life, but Rita could see her in her eyes and cheekbones. She pulled the cell phone from her bag. Angela answered on the second ring.

"Hi, Mama."

After a moment of silence, Angela said, "Rita? Is that you?"

"Yeah, it's me, Mama."

It felt good to say the word, and by Angela's intake of breath, it felt good to her, too. "Are you all right?" she asked after a moment.

"I'm okay. I just . . . needed to hear your voice."

Rita heard a choking sound. "You . . . you did?"

"I've been doing a lot of thinking. I'm ready to be a daughter again. I'm sorry for being so harsh."

"It wasn't you," Angela rushed to say. "It's all my fault, I made so many mist—"

"Mama, we both did. Let's let all that go, okay? Let's start fresh."

"Oh . . . baby girl, you got a deal." The emotion in Angela's voice choked up Rita, especially the old endearment. Angela hadn't forgotten.

"I'll be done here in a day or so. And then . . ." Rita took a deep breath, fortifying herself for reaching out. "Then I have a feeling I'll need some mothering."

"It won't be an inconvenience. I don't want you to even think that, no matter what you ever need."

Rita rubbed a tear from her eye, smudging her makeup. "Ditto." She sniffed. "I've got to go. I'll talk to you soon."

After disconnecting, she dabbed at her eyes and touched up the makeup. She padded back to the office, anxious to see Christopher's reaction. He wasn't there. She felt under the cot for her shoes, realizing with dismay that they were hardly suitable for the costume. Atir wouldn't wear sensible pumps. Maybe they could stop along the way and find short black boots.

He opened the door after a quick knock. He started to say something but stopped, his mouth slightly open. She was so entranced by the appreciation in his eyes she didn't notice what he was wearing at first.

He wore the Alta outfit they'd found at the warehouse, but she couldn't imagine Brian—bless his soul—looking as magnificent as Christopher did. He didn't need shoulder pads to enhance his shoulders, that was for sure. The shiny "armor" fit his dark looks, and the body suit melted over his muscular frame.

"Wow," she finally managed.

"Wow, yourself," he returned, coming closer.

"When did you get that?"

His expression turned grim. "The day I was running errands, handling Brian's funeral arrangements." When Sira had slipped her the ketamine.

She wanted to chase away the blame she saw on his

face and did a fancy curtsy in front of him. "Your Majesty." She was rewarded by a grin.

"Maybe I could get into this."

"Don't push your luck." She glanced down at herself. "If anybody at home saw me like this . . ."

"Remember, you're supposed to be letting go of your need to put on that image."

"Come to think of it, I'd love for the people at work to see me like this. They'd never believe it." She crossed her arms. "And don't forget, you're supposed to be celebrating your emotions."

"What?"

"Alta's hang-up was holding back his emotions, something I'm sure you can't relate to." She lifted an eyebrow as he realized what she was talking about. "Let's see some tears, Your Majesty."

He laughed. "This is all an act. Don't forget that."

She tilted her head. "Sometimes it's hard to tell the act from the real thing."

He looked away for a moment but surprised her by dropping down in front of her. "Please, Atir, don't break my heart by questioning my intentions." He feigned a devastatingly hurt look that had her again reminding herself this was an act. "Please sit, my love. I have something for you."

She was in serious danger of falling for this act. When she sat down, he gently took one foot and slid on a gold pump.

"Is it a good fit, my queen? You know how I love to please you."

She shivered, remembering how he had pleased her last night when she'd finally let him take control. Then she realized he was talking about the shoe sparkling on her right foot. "Where did you get this, my lord?" She wiggled her toes—a little tight. "It's a perfect fit."

"My mother was, after all, queen of Carnival."

She remembered seeing these shoes at Brian's house. "You didn't tell me you had these."

"I was hoping you'd back out." He gently put on the other shoe and ran his finger down her calf. He stopped himself and reached beneath the coat on the desk for a gem-covered necklace. Only he set it on top of the scarf on her head. It left a rhinestone to dangle at her forehead.

She let him pull her to her feet and looked at her reflection in a mirrored picture on the wall. "It's beautiful," she said.

"You're beautiful." He touched her chin again. "I am proud to have you at my side. But I would never recover if anything should happen to you. My heart would crumble into pieces, and my blood would cease to flow. Do you understand, Atir, how much you mean to me?"

She felt her eyes water as she nodded, then mentally kicked herself again for getting drawn in. He was looking right into her eyes instead of looking away as he did when he said something he meant. Let him think she was acting, too.

She placed her hand against his cheek. "I shall place my heart in your hands for safekeeping. I know that you shall take good care of it. I shall forever treasure your words, spoken from your own heart."

He leaned down and captured her mouth with his, a gentle kiss reminiscent of last night. Gentle though it was, it still stirred her body. His hands possessively settled on her waist.

"Chris, I realized something last night. Before—" She gestured between them. "The anger I felt toward my mother and father, the nosebleeds I got whenever I was in an intimate situation with a man, it was all a way to stay comfortable. Letting that go meant I had to take a chance by restarting a relationship with my mom. Overcoming my nosebleeds meant having to open myself to hurt and rejection. It meant stepping out of my safe zone. Believing you're inherently bad, that those in your life will end up hurt, keeps you in your comfort zone, too." She put her finger over his mouth. "Don't say anything, just think about it. It took some time to settle in."

He acknowledged her request with a nod and turned to pull his coat from the desk. It was long and black, and fit well with the costume. When he slipped it on and situated the sword inside, she was reminded of the *Highlander*. She was living the fantasy of one of the episodes, where the immortal Duncan MacLeod protects his lady love, knowing that someday he will have to go on without her as she ages and he does not. She sure missed that show.

She blinked and brought herself back to reality. Or this alternate reality, as it were. She would not need her television shows anymore, at least not in the addictive way she had. They would pale in comparison to what she had experienced here.

He tucked the handcuffs and the recorder into the pockets of his coat. "I want you to keep your cell phone with you."

She patted the fabric at her waist. "It's already clipped to my waistband. I'll put the pepper spray on the other side." He handed her the canister, and she clipped it on. "The knife I'll wear on my ankle." She used a knit headband to secure it.

He held out his hand, and she slid her fingers between his. "Are you ready, my queen?"

"Yes, my lord."

He helped her into her coat. "From here on, we are only Atir and Alta. There's no turning back."

She shook her head. "There was no turning back the day I arrived . . . in Xanadu," she added.

The lobby was crowded, the bar off to the side jammed with people. For a moment, she felt odd. There were only a few people dressed in costume, and when a man let out a low whistle, she felt distinctly out of place. Then she remembered that Atir didn't care what people thought. She didn't have to be the consummate professional, did not have to live up to anyone's expectations. She smiled at the man, hitched her shoulders and walked out beside Christopher. Outside, it was madness. The people crowding both the sidewalks and street were in all manner of costumes.

She once again felt right in place. Well, in an out-of-this-world way. He walked just behind her, and whenever she paused to stare, he ended up bumping into her. She wasn't so distracted that she didn't enjoy that hard body, though.

"This place is . . . wild," she whispered, gawking at a midget wearing a thong and a sheer pink cape.

"You ain't seen nothing yet. You're not the only queen in this part of town today."

Three transvestites swayed with more sensuality than Rita had, and she'd been born a woman! A group of four people had set up a band on a corner, and the woman wore a cardboard box over her torso. For any passing male, including Christopher, she opened the doors on the box and gave him a peek. Not that he needed it. In the block they'd traversed, Rita had seen four women baring their breasts for beads.

Even in their fantasy garb, she and Christopher barely rated more than a glance. No wonder strange people migrated here. You could be anything you wanted.

They turned a corner and headed north. He tucked her arm beneath his, all the while keeping an eye out for suspicious characters. She supposed she couldn't blame him for occasionally becoming distracted by an outrageous costume or a spectacular chest.

A man up ahead was wearing chaps. As they neared him, he turned sideways. His butt was as bare as a baby's bottom.

"Er, excuse me, sir, but you seem to have forgotten something," she pretended to say to him as they passed. She reveled in Christopher's laughter.

"I forgot how crazy it is," he said.

For a few minutes, she could forget what waited ahead and let herself be distracted by the wildlife. "Look, it's Neptune," she whispered, nodding toward a man wearing a shell over his "jewels" and a fishing net draped over his shoulders. And not a stitch more. He had to be in his fifties, and the sunny air was not much warmer than that. She met Christopher's gaze and they shared another laugh. Was that laughter part of his role, too? Despite the fact that he had been acting earlier, she knew he had the capacity to feel. Making him realize it was a whole other matter.

A young, good-looking man wearing one of those chap-bare-butt things eyed Neptune's butt and said, "Oh, I gotta grab that."

Christopher leaned closer. "Don't be surprised if your own little tushie gets grabbed."

When she realized he wasn't kidding, she moved in front of him again.

"Always thinking of yourself," he muttered goodheartedly. "I'm in more danger of getting grabbed than you are."

She looked back at him. "Better your tushie than mine, your majesty."

He gently pinched her cheek, and her heart swelled. How could a man be so wrong and so right at once?

Three men dressed as nuns and carrying cups of beer went running by as Rita and Christopher neared the parking lot. Within a few minutes, they were out of the harmless zaniness and on their way to Xanadu. This area of town was empty compared to what they'd just left. Their mood darkened as they pulled up to the warehouse. They had arrived early, and so far no one else appeared to be present. He parked off to the side of the building.

"I'm going to leave the car unlocked with the key under the mat, just in case. If anything happens, run out here and get help."

"All right," she said, hoping it wouldn't come to that. She knew what he was doing; he wanted her out of the warehouse at the first sign of trouble.

"It's cold in here," she said when they walked inside. "I don't suppose there's any heat."

"I doubt it. But I imagine it's going to heat up real fast in here."

He walked up behind her, put his arms around her, and pulled her close for a few minutes. The hum of fear going through her veins disappeared, and she closed her eyes and sank into him.

"Better?" he asked, breaking the spell. "Don't want my queen to be cold."

She rolled her eyes, finding it so hard to convince herself he was only acting. Or was he? "Mm, thanks."

"The only player we can trust is Vitar, but cautiously. I tracked him down to an address in Texas."

"White face, vertical brown stripe," she recited.

He lifted her chin, and she hoped for another stage kiss. "Atir, I want you to be very careful. Stay close to me."

"Yes, your majesty." She could see that he did care about her, and that he was worried. "A kiss for good luck?"

He leaned down to grant her request, but before their lips met, the door creaked behind them.

"Alta, it is good to see you again. I've been waiting to talk to you."

The game was on.

26

A man dressed in shimmering blue robes approached Christopher and clasped his hands. "It is good to see that you are all right, your majesty. We have been worried for you."

"Citar." The prince of thieves. Christopher thanked him and introduced Rita. The man seemed to accept him as Alta.

A couple wandered into the warehouse dressed in deep shades of pink, a couple of matching jewels. "Astar and Cosmo," Rita whispered. They greeted both Citar and Alta.

Soon thirty or more people had trickled into the room. It reminded him of the tableaux, all of the colorful costumes and animation. Once again he was trying to steal away the crown from the golden prince. No, worse, pretending he *was* the golden prince.

He put his hand on the sword beneath his coat, reassuring himself that it was still there. Rita was at his side, being greeted and welcomed by curious citizens. He had decided to make the announcement about Atir the way Brian had planned: at the commencement ceremony that evening. That was all they knew about the rituals of the Gathering from that short script Brian had left. He slipped his arm around Rita's waist and held her close as more people arrived and surrounded them. If he lost her . . . he didn't want to think about that. *You have to think about it. Her life is in your hands.* Everything crowded in at once, what he'd felt when he'd held her the night Sira had slipped her the ketamine, what she'd done to him last night, even his words to her that morning haunted him. Who was Christopher LaPorte?

He wasn't sure he knew anymore. The hard man who pushed away love and warmth, sure he would destroy it? A man holding on to superstitious beliefs to protect not others but himself? Or the man who had made love with Rita last night, who had felt that protective shell splinter apart?

"Christopher?" she whispered, watching his inner struggle.

He didn't know how to put any of it into words, especially not now. She knew his darkest shadows, had seen the coldest, hardest part of his soul. Yet she stood there now with compassion in her eyes. And love.

"Your majesty, the city looks stunning again," said a lady who looked like one of the characters from *Cats*.

"We are so glad you're back. Xanadu wouldn't be the same without your leadership."

Both he and Rita asked if anyone had seen Vitar, but no one had. No one had seen Sira yet, either.

"Oh, but I am sure she will be here. You know how she likes to make an entrance, your majesty," one man in a vibrant orange cape said.

"She's not going to miss this," a short person in a troll costume said. Cragmar surveyed Rita. "It's going to be a most interesting Gathering."

Christopher glanced up at the clock he'd spotted earlier. It was made out of papier-mâché and fit the decor of Xanadu. The Gathering would officially start in forty minutes. With every person they met, he had to endure their adulation. Brian had apparently taken his role as king very seriously.

"All that adoration. Can you handle it?" Rita asked when they had a moment to themselves.

He opened his mouth, but stopped his words when he realized he was going to say the adoration he needed could only come from her. Was he getting into this role a little too much? "I think so," he answered to both questions.

He understood how easy it was to lose yourself in a role. That's why he'd accidentally stabbed Brian so long ago, living up to the role of the bad prince. Back in Brian's office, he'd slipped right into the role of being Rita's king. As each word had come from his mouth, it had opened something inside him.

A gong sounded through the warehouse. It was time.

He ran his thumb over her lips, wishing it were his mouth instead. "If you feel anything weird, let me know. We have to be prepared that Sira will try ketamine again."

"You be careful, too. You may be king, but you're human."

"Too human, *chérie*."

He didn't know how many people were crowded into that large room with the strange chairs, but he figured at least forty. Rita was nudged away from him as more and more people pressed close to ask him a question or to merely say how glad they were that he was feeling better. He kept an eye on her, though, as he danced around the questions. She was asking questions of her own, undoubtedly as to Vitar's and Sira's whereabouts. Only two other people knew he wasn't really Alta. He was searching people's expressions for suspicion and hostility.

Someone turned on music, a strange concoction of flute and sitar that fit the mood perfectly.

"Where is Vitar?" he finally managed to ask the group of people around him.

One man searched the room. "I saw him earlier."

"What does he look like? I've forgotten," a woman said.

"He usually wears a vertical stripe down his face and layers of robes. And he has an *A* tattooed on his finger."

"He really should cover it," another man said. "It's an intrusion. And Dracon wears a watch. A Timex. You must address these matters, your majesty."

As his citizens launched into other issues that threatened the fragile fantasy of Xanadu, Christopher couldn't help but feel empty.

How much was real?

The question haunted him. Here he was in this make-believe world, pretending to be someone he wasn't, looking for two killers. He looked at the people surrounding him, listened to their passionate ideas and plans. This was real to them. And to Sira, it was life-or-death.

Someone was pushing his or her way toward him from the back of the room. A man, he surmised, by the potbelly and hairy arms. He tensed, noting that the man wasn't going anywhere near Rita. A glittery green horizontal stripe crossed the man's golden face. Dracon then; he saw the Timex. He obviously had a serious issue of his own to discuss.

"Alta, your majesty," he greeted without warmth. "I have heard the most disturbing rumor. Sira says you are shutting Xanadu down."

Rita wasn't going to play hero. She had tangled with Sira once before and didn't much like the outcome. Her goal was to find the woman and alert Christopher. He would draw her in and cuff her. Rita wished Connard had called them back. Hopefully he would come at their call for assistance, even if he only half-believed them. She touched the cell phone at her side.

From across the room, she met Christopher's gaze. The man was absolutely gorgeous, standing inches above those who crowded. around him. But she'd glimpsed something else in his eyes that had her heart beating faster. Something had changed, and she didn't dare hope he had come to care about her as deeply as she cared about him. Maybe she was being taken in by this act of his. He had probably been good at taking on the role of the bad prince. Perhaps he was just as good at taking on the role of the caring king. And caring man.

Masquerade.

She pushed away those thoughts and focused on the people around her. They observed her with curiosity, and some even greeted her. Not many new members were let into Xanadu, and that made her an oddity.

"I am looking for Vitar," she told one woman wearing elaborate snow leopard makeup. Casca, she guessed.

"I haven't seen him yet." She surveyed Rita. "Shouldn't you be searching for the Tailor? He is the first person you should meet."

"Yeah, sure." Rita shook her head at the nonsense these people subscribed to. Rules, rituals, anonymity . . . creepy.

The rising sound of conversation caught her attention. Those around Christopher were urgently questioning him. One man was raising his voice in disbelief.

Before she could head his way to find out what was going on, a man whispered, "Atir," from behind the fabric wall. She tried to trace the voice. "Over here." She saw a face peeking out from between the folds. He looked around furtively. "I am Vitar. I must talk with you."

He wore a hood over his hair and had a wide, brown

stripe going down his face. His lips were hidden in makeup, as were his eyebrows and eyelashes. His brown eyes blended into the stripe, too. She tried to remember the gardener/janitor's features, but they were too generic. Vitar was taller, however.

"I've sent a message to Alta," he said. "I told one of the others to instruct him to join us in the meeting room where the high council makes their decisions."

She looked over at Christopher, who was being pulled deeper into conversation with the small crowd. She wouldn't be able to drag him away now, judging by the intensity of their voices. He glanced her way for a second but was drawn away again. And then Vitar pulled her between the folds. As she grabbed for the pepper spray, he put a finger over his lips. "I don't want Sira to see us."

She relaxed, though her fingers still clutched the holster. "Have you seen her?"

"Oh, she is here. She's wearing her usual outfit, a brilliant green body suit covered in rhinestones and feathers."

"And the black and gold feathered mask?"

"Yes. But she's clever." He looked around again. "She could be anywhere."

"Let me get Christopher."

"Not with everyone standing around him like that. Sira will know what you're doing, and she'll follow you both right to me. I'm in grave danger. I promise you that Pearla is going to tell him to meet us and that you are with me. She'll pull him away from the crowd. We'll be safe to talk there."

Rita followed, but her heart was creeping up into her throat. She didn't want to be this far from Christopher. She looked at Vitar again. He did look genuinely worried, glancing around, skirting a corner when footsteps sounded in the hallway. They kept weaving through the folds of fabric, walking farther from the Gathering room. Her feet were killing her in the ill-fitting shoes.

They ducked into a room in the far corner of the warehouse, where a long table and chairs attested to the business attended to here. He led her to two chairs and sat down. He hadn't let go of her hand. She remembered the *A* tattoo and looked at his fingers. Which hand was it on? She saw no tattoo on the right one. When she glanced at his left hand, she saw the letter and relaxed a little.

"Alta should be here any moment," he said, looking not at the doorway but at her. "The real Alta is dead, isn't he?"

At first Rita's instinct was to state that Christopher was the real Alta. But Vitar was their ally and he should know the truth. She nodded.

"Sira killed him, didn't she?"

"Yes, but we don't know how exactly." Rita kicked off her shoes.

"She is a clever one."

"She's killed several people, all for Xanadu. You're right to feel in danger."

His expression grew somber. He still hadn't let go of her hand. "You may think she has gone to extremes, but you do see how important it is to keep Xanadu safe, don't you? Do you see how these people love it here?"

"But it's all make-believe."

His grip tightened. "Are you familiar with Samuel Taylor Coleridge's poem, 'Kubla Khan'? *His* Xanadu was make-believe. My Xanadu is better than he ever imagined. It is as real to us as the outside world is to you. But there is no evil here, no disease, no hatred. In Xanadu, we are perfect. We can look the way we want, get rid of all our inhibitions and self-doubts . . ." He stared deeply into her eyes, though his held not a trace of soul. She had seen those eyes before. Not Emmagee's. Not Tammy's. "This is our refuge. No one teases us, calls us names, or makes us feel like freaks. I'm accepted here."

With every word, she felt the dread flowing through her veins getting heavier and heavier. She tried to push the fear from her expression. *Stay calm. You don't know if this is Edward.* She had trouble swallowing the lump that had formed in her throat. "You don't look like a freak to me." She glanced down at his feet beneath the robes. His boots had platforms that made him look taller.

His smile gave her the chills. "You haven't seen all of me."

She forged ahead. "Playing dress-up is good. There's nothing wrong with that. The real world isn't such a bad place, though. I've often felt like an outsider myself." She remembered seeing that much in Sira's posts. "I have hang-ups, too. I'm trying to resolve them and find my place in the world. Maybe I can help you." She tried to casually loosen herself from his grip but to no avail.

He laughed bitterly. "You don't know what being an outsider is like. You have no idea."

"Tell me, then. Maybe no one has ever listened to you before. Maybe no one has ever heard your pain. I'll listen."

The harshness of his expression softened for a moment. "Maybe if Edward were here, he'd hear you out."

Her voice was a whisper when she said, "You're not Edward? Then you're . . ."

His voice changed. "That's right, baby. I'm Sira. Your worst nightmare."

Rita tried not to panic. It didn't make sense. He'd sounded like a man before. Moved like a man. "Where's Edward?"

Sira clenched her other fist and shoved it at her solar plexus. "He's in here. He wanted to come out and play, but I wouldn't let him. He's gone a little mad, you see. It happened after killing that detective of yours."

"Connard," Rita said, her voice still a strained whisper. No, not Connard. The crushing sensation in her chest increased, and she started to shake. She tried to get to her pepper spray with her free hand.

"Sad, isn't it, how he believed you and then ended up dead because of it?"

She needed to understand. That was the only way she could try to stay alive. "Edward and you are . . . you're one person?"

"Much as it pains me sometimes, yes, we are. But he's going to go away for a while. He was bad."

"Because he murdered Connard?" She hoped Sira was only bluffing.

"No, because he didn't listen to me. He sat in the closet and played in the man's blood. He forgot who's in control."

Rita shivered then. Split personalities was beyond her area of expertise. "Sira, I can help you. If you'll talk to me." She couldn't help darting a glance at the door.

"He's not coming, baby. I have a couple of my loyal citizens keeping him busy with accusations about his closing down Xanadu. It put them in a panic." Her eyes hardened, and Rita could see the fake brown contacts. "I won't let you destroy us."

When Rita lunged for her spray, Sira was quicker. She pulled out the wavy knife Rita had seen in Brian's collection and held it to Rita's throat before she could form a scream. She jerked Rita to her feet, keeping the blade close enough to her skin to sting. Her arms were pinned behind her.

Rita couldn't give up. "What happened to you? Were you molested as a child? Did you create Sira as a way to escape whatever horrors were happening in your life?"

Sira's voice lowered. "My horror was a missing penis and a big, fat lie." She pushed Rita ahead of her, not through the doorway but around a curtain in the back of the room. "Now stop talking. Make any more noise, and I'll cut your voice box out."

Rita's pulse was hammering in her throat. A missing penis? What did he—she mean? She didn't ask. Even swallowing made the blade bite into her. Her arms ached from the pressure on them and their awkward positioning.

"None of this would have happened if you'd just died in Boston. Or at least kept your nose out of New Orleans. But no, you had to find out more and more." Her tone was becoming bitter. "It wasn't enough that you had to steal Alta away from me. Then you came here and tried to destroy my world."

At the rear of the warehouse, they came upon some metal stairs that were hidden by fabric. A sign that read Do Not Enter had been taken down.

They made their way up to a catwalk that led to empty storage space. Rita could see down below in some places, though Brian had tried to cover up as much as possible. The metal grate had been painted green, though it was rusted through in some areas. She was relieved to see they were heading back toward the gathering room and the sound of conversation. She would go along pliantly for now. When they were over the room, she'd twist around and make enough noise to get Christopher's attention.

As soon as she saw people through a crack in the fabric, she shoved backward. The knife cut into her, a searing pain that stole away the breath she needed to scream. Sira slapped her so hard everything went black for a moment. Bells clanged inside her brain. She felt herself sliding down, then arms around her, guiding her to the floor. When the world cleared Sira was sitting on top of her, looking down with a feral spark in her eyes. She was crushing her chest, and Rita could barely breathe, much less scream.

She heard a ripping sound, and before she could even react, thick tape covered her mouth. Sira cut the duct tape and ripped off another length. She got up and grabbed Rita's wrists. Rita was too busy sucking in air through her nose to fight the tape Sira wound around her wrists.

"There, my darling Atir." Sira tapped Rita's nose. Rita flinched, terrified that she would pinch her nostrils shut. Sira leaned close, so close Rita could smell her sweat. "I have a special plan for Christopher. Would you like to hear it?" Rita's eyes widened at the thought that he would be hurt. "I've planted three devices inside this building. They're going to start a fire in thirty minutes. I will expose Christopher as an imposter, and he will be banished to the covered cage in back of the gathering room. Everyone will think it's part of the script.

"Once he is locked away, the fires will begin. Sira will save everyone . . . well, almost everyone. The place will go up in a blaze, and I will tell them to leave so no one gets questioned. They'll find your bodies, of course. But no one will know what you were up to. Such strangeness goes on this time of year. Now that I'm in charge, Xanadu will be forever safe." She tweaked Rita's nose, cutting off her air supply for four seconds.

Helpless! And in pain! No escape now. Anger and fear engulfed her, but it was useless.

Sira slid her finger across Rita's collarbone and looked at the blood. "Just a surface cut. Won't even leave a scar." She chuckled softly. "I must go now. Don't worry, baby. You'll be able to watch everything."

She rolled her over and dragged her across the floor. Rita's cheek was pressed into the grating, and her arms were crushed beneath her weight. Through a parting in the fabric ceiling of the gathering room, she could see the front of the room and several people talking. Off to the side, she saw the shape of a large, draped cage.

As she absorbed that eerie picture, Sira taped Rita's ankles together and secured her in place by taping her to the railing on either side.

She laughed softly. "You will go down in Xanadu history as the shortest-lived queen. Negative one hour's reign. Goodbye, Atir, foolish woman."

And then she was gone. Rita heard the footsteps grow softer, and then all she could hear were muffled sounds from below. She tried to move, to make any kind of noise at all, but she couldn't budge. She could only lift her head somewhat, and even banging her forehead down on the rusty grate produced barely enough sound to make the pain worth it. Through the crack, she could see Christopher searching for her, a frantic expression on his face.

It was over before it had even begun.

"See, he uses names of the world."

The crowd agreed with shouts and whistles, fully involved in the tableau. The noise, along with his dread, made a buzzing sound in his head. Rita was gone. The thought nearly paralyzed him, that Sira had hidden her somewhere. That maybe . . . maybe she was—

Something hit him in the back of the head. He didn't have time to even look to see what it was. He struggled to keep his balance, but the pain ricocheted through his body and made him falter. It was all they needed. Two men grabbed him, and a third took the sword. He struggled to free himself, but two men were stronger than a dazed one. The third man searched his garb and found the tape recorder and handcuffs. The crowd gasped as he held up the items.

"She's a murderer," Christopher insisted, nodding toward Sira. "There's a dead man in the back. Vitar."

Sira only laughed as she guilelessly met the eyes of the people in the room. "He tells such lies, anything to free himself. We must find out what Gerard has done to his brother, who probably fought to his death to keep Xanadu safe. But now Gerard is among us, with his evil apprentice, and he must be stopped." Sira had all the dramatics of an actress: blazing eyes, animated voice, and wild gestures. His sword in her hand, she walked over and pulled back a drape with a flourish. He saw a black *A* on her finger before he realized what she'd uncovered: a cage.

"We will hold a banishment ceremony, the first one we can witness in person. We cannot free Gerard until the end of the Gathering. He will only try to destroy everything we have so carefully built here."

The crowd roared in agreement as four men dragged Christopher toward the cage. If they locked him up, he'd never find Rita. These people thought this was part of the game. They would ignore him if he tried to bring them back to reality. They didn't want to hear about reality, or murder.

So he would have to play along, too. The men had pushed him right up to the cage door, but he wrapped his fingers around the bars and turned to the crowd.

"All right, I am not Alta," he said in a booming voice. The crowd gasped and whispered among themselves. "But I am not his evil brother, either." For the first time, those words rang true. He took a deep breath and continued. "I am his good brother . . . Prince Caspian." It was the first name that popped into his head. "My brother has been murdered, and that murderer is among us." Another gasp. "My brother Alta and I parted ways long ago, and I blame myself for that parting. But now I will never be able to make amends, because evil has taken him from me forever."

"Don't listen to him," Sira yelled. "Lock him away! Gag him!"

The crowd listened to the exchange like avid tennis spectators, eating up the drama.

Christopher felt the dread that held his chest loosen as he let out feelings locked away for too long. "Someone here is killing every citizen who was ever banished from Xanadu. If you are banished, you should fear for your life, because Sira will not let you live. She has taken her role as protector too far. You are safe only until you anger her."

He took a step farther from the cage, and Sira made her way through the confused crowd toward him. "He's lying!" She brandished the sword.

He pushed on, too aware that time was running out for Rita, wherever she was. "Vitar is dead. Look at Sira's left hand. She wears the same *A* that Vitar has. She killed him and then posed as him to lure away my queen. Sira has done something to her. I need your help if we are to keep Sira from destroying Xanadu and, worse, destroying human life. I need your help to find the woman . . . the woman I love. Help me look for her, and then we can sort out the rest."

"Is this true?" Citar asked.

"Of course not." Sira pushed away Citar's attempt at grabbing her hand. When he became more aggressive, she held him at bay with the sword. "He is a liar! He brought this to kill us all. Listen to me, I am now your leader."

"If I am lying, then why . . ." Christopher's throat closed up, and he swallowed. "Why am I pleading with you to help me find Rita? Atir. She needs your help." He wouldn't think about it being too late. "Hold both of us, if you must, but I want all of you to search every inch of this place for her."

Rita felt the tears slide down her cheeks at Christopher's words. She could hear the emotion in his voice. It was real.

And it's too late.

Those words whispered through her mind, but she refused to believe them. She struggled to loosen the tape binding her hands together. Her hands had grown cold from lack of circulation. She had been working on moistening the tape over her mouth, using her saliva and tongue on the foul-tasting adhesive to loosen its hold. If only she could reach her knife.

The crowd below was a tangle of confusion, with Sira fighting to get closer to Christopher and everyone else trying to make sense of it all.

"I am your leader!" Sira screamed out. "You must listen to me! Alta was going to abandon Xanadu. I have sacrificed everything for this place, for you people. Put him in the cage!"

Sira was moving closer to Christopher. Rita tried to scream and warn him, but the tape was still too tight to let out any air. Her ineffectualness frustrated her. She writhed and jerked around in a desperate attempt to do something—anything. She leaned on the phone at her hip and heard beeping as buttons pressed. She had activated 911 as the redial number, but even if she could dial it, she couldn't call out for help.

What about the pepper spray? Not that it had done her any good when she needed it.

A whooshing sound behind her made her lift her head as much as she could. She couldn't see the flame, but she could smell the smoke. One of the devices had gone off.

She looked down on the crowd. She couldn't imagine that there was an accessible fire exit. Between the folds of the fabric and confusion, it would be mass panic.

Using her numb fingers, she worked the canister free and shifted it until the nozzle was pressed against one of the holes on the grate. If only she could aim the spray at Sira. But she was too high to nail anyone in particular. Everyone would be affected by it.

Everyone.

Yes! The sudden assault would send the crowd running. Hopefully they'd get out before they even knew that flames were licking away at their world. Hopefully Christopher would leave with them.

She hesitated. Sending everyone away would leave her little chance of being rescued. But her life wasn't worth saving at the expense of forty others. Closing her eyes and saying a silent prayer, she pressed the nozzle as hard as she could.

Christopher watched Sira inch closer as she tried to incite the crowd against him. They were obviously confused as to what was real and what wasn't, and what role they were supposed to be playing.

He no longer had trouble with that. He knew what was

real, at least inside him. And he knew that he had to get away and find Rita. If Sira injected him with ketamine, his chances would be over. She would push him into the cage and have the opportunity to convince the crowd of her intentions.

Suddenly his eyes stung. Everyone around him started calling out in pain, coughing and rubbing reddened eyes. What was happening? What had Sira done? But Sira was as shocked as everyone else, and just as affected. The sword hit the concrete floor with a loud clang. While she covered her eyes and clawed at her throat, he pushed through the crowd and shoved her into the cage. The door clanged shut, and he heard the lock click. He grabbed up the sword in case Sira's accomplice was nearby.

"No!" she yelled. "Someone get me out of here! There isn't a key!"

Her panic touched no one as Christopher pushed the crowd toward the door. "Get outside! Now!" Through burning, watery eyes he tried to find the source of the chemical. He squeezed the tears from his eyes and saw a glistening mist floating down, caught by the teal lights in the corner of the room. *Pepper spray.* She was upstairs.

"Rita!"

"Get me out of here," Sira screamed in a gurgling voice, curling up into a ball beneath the assault of the spray.

And then he smelled the smoke. His throat burned, but not from the spray. The thought of losing Rita was almost debilitating. He pushed on, racing through the fabric hallways looking for the stairs he remembered from years back.

Smoke billowed from the back room where Vitar's body lay. The music cut off. Walls of fabric caught flame. He knew there wasn't much time. Flames would eat the fabric like a ravenous monster.

His face was burning from the spray, but the crushing sensation in his chest kept him going. He found the back stairs leading up to the old storage area and lunged up them two at a time. He heard the powdery sound of rusty metal giving way, but not in time. His leg crashed through the grate. Shards of broken metal cut into his calf. Pain screamed up his muscles. The sword slid across the grate and dropped over the edge of the platform.

He didn't have time to carefully extricate his leg from the ragged hole. He jerked it free, driving the pain deeper inside him. No time for pain, either. He ignored the wetness of his blood as it soaked his sock. Didn't even look at the damage. All he cared about was finding Rita.

When he saw her lying there, he nearly sagged. She was struggling to free herself from duct-tape bindings, stretching the strips taut with her writhing movements. She'd already pulled herself free from the railing, but her arms were still bound tight.

"Rita, I'm here. Hold on, baby." He knelt beside her and tugged on the thick tape across her mouth.

"Use the knife on my right ankle," she said.

He pulled out the knife and cut the tape. In seconds she was free, and he pulled her up.

"Why aren't you outside?" she said in a strained voice.

"Because you're inside." He ripped the tape at her wrists. "Can you walk?"

"Yes, I'm all right. Oh, Christopher, your leg!"

"It's fine. Let's get out of here."

The fire had already consumed the area where he had come up. He tried to remember if there was another set of stairs. Smoke obliterated the top portion of the warehouse and sucked the oxygen out of the air.

"That way!" she said, pointing in the other direction. "I saw a balcony that I think leads to the front area."

When they reached the far side, the railing was already

too hot to touch. Sira's screams filled the air. He was supposed to be in that cage, and Rita was supposed to have watched him die while she succumbed to smoke. He steeled himself against the sounds of Sira's agony. Didn't she have a key?

"We have to jump. It's our only chance."

They both climbed over the railing and hung on to the floor of the upper level. They let go simultaneously and tumbled to the floor. He favored his injured leg but quickly braced himself. His cell phone cracked as it hit the concrete.

"This isn't where I thought it was. I think we go that way," she said, searching for something familiar in the smoke.

They navigated through the rest of the fabric walls. Just ahead of them, one burst into flame. They went through another doorway. Just another room. "Over here!" she shouted, pushing through into the dining hall. The main hall was to the right. The wall of curtains behind them roared to life in a blaze. They ran to the large doorway, then down the corridor.

The open area in front of the door looked miles away. Fresh air and sunlight and worried faces hovered just outside. He glanced at her to make sure she was holding up all right. She was doing great. He was worried that his injury was slowing her down. His legs felt rubbery from pain, but he pushed on. When they emerged from the warehouse, the crowd broke into applause.

"This is the best Gathering yet!" one man said.

"Alta put so much into it this time."

"Everyone, move back!" He led Rita away from the warehouse, as far as his legs would take him. The pain was white-hot now. His chest hurt from exertion. He dropped to the ground, and she knelt down beside him. "Are you all right?" she asked between harsh coughs.

"Fine," he said in a strained voice. "Call for help. I lost my cell phone when we jumped."

She reached for hers. "Mine's gone, too." She looked at the crowd of people. "You, whatever your name is," she said, waving one man over. "Do you have a cell phone?"

"It's in my car."

"Go get it. Call 911."

He tilted his head. "Seriously?"

"Yes, you idiot!" Christopher yelled.

The man scurried away, and the rest of the crowd inched farther back from the building. Reality was dawning on their streaky faces and in their bloodshot eyes.

"Your leg." She sat back to examine his stripped calf. She tore off her scarf and wrapped it tightly around his leg to stanch the bleeding.

"They're just scratches," he said through gritted teeth. He felt the blood drain from his face. He took a deep breath that triggered a coughing fit. "Your throat's cut." He reached out, grazing the skin around the cut.

"I'm all right. It stings, but I don't think it's deep." She ran her finger across his cheek. "Did you get burned?" she asked. "Your face is all red."

"From the pepper spray. That was brilliant."

"You were supposed to get out of there, not risk your life by finding me."

She had soot stains on her face, her hair was mussed, but she'd never looked so beautiful. He pushed the hair from her face. "And leave you behind? Not a chance. You're not getting out of this that easily." His throat tightened. "I thought I'd lost you, Rita. I never want to feel that way again." He moved his thumb gently over her ragged lips.

One man stepped forward. "We know you're not Alta, and we know you're not the evil Gerard either. If Alta is no longer with us, we want you to become our next king." The crowd behind him nodded in agreement.

In the distance, sirens sounded. The warehouse creaked and groaned under the assault of heat and flame. He looked at the building and relived those last harrowing minutes.

"What about it?" the man asked again. "Will you be our king?"

"I gotta tell you, I've lived in this mythical land of yours too long already. Alone in the dark too long." He kissed Rita on the forehead. "And I've been the king of nothing for too long. I can't accept your offer. I'm going to make Rita my queen—my wife—and I'm going to live in the light."

The crowd was riveted to his words, and he wasn't sure they knew what was real or not. "It's time for you all to live in the light, too. Shed your roles and let Xanadu go. Brian—Alta invented this world, and he died because of it. Sira murdered people because of it. No matter how wonderful and pure you want Xanadu to be, there's always a chance that someone will take it too seriously."

They didn't applaud this time, but nodded thoughtfully. The sirens grew louder, and soon fire trucks and police cars swarmed the area. He started to get to his feet, and Rita got up to help him.

"Well said, your majesty," she said, quietly enough so that only he could hear.

"Call me Chris. That'll do just fine."

"Okay, Chris. My answer is yes."

He took his attention from the frenzy of activity to the woman standing at his side. "Mm?"

"I think, somewhere in all that, you asked me to be your wife. I said yes."